THE PORTRAIT GIRL

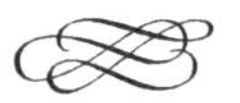

NICOLE SWENGLEY

BREAKTHROUGH BOOKS

Published in Great Britain in 2024 by Breakthrough Books.

www.breakthroughbookcollective.com

Paperback ISBN: 978-1-7393793-8-4

Ebook ISBN: 978-1-7393793-9-1

Cover design and interior typesetting by Ivy Ngeow.

Front cover image: Keith Corrigan/Alamy Stock Photo. Oil painting by Arthur Hughes, 1864 (Private Collection)

PRAISE FOR THE PORTRAIT GIRL

"An ingenious plot, masses of fabulous detail, a compelling mystery and, at its heart, a vindication for the rights of the female artist. Brava." Elizabeth Buchan, author of *Bonjour Sophie*.

"A splendid, mysterious tale about Victorian art in which people are not quite what they seem." Adam Hart-Davis, presenter of BBC TV's *What the Victorians Did for Us*.

"A fascinating, modern mystery with a distinctly Victorian flavour," Nigel West, historian, author of numerous titles on intelligence topics, voted "The Experts' Expert" by *The Observer*.

"*The Portrait Girl* is a real treat for lovers of historical and time-slip fiction. I thoroughly enjoyed reading this clever, complex and engaging novel. The mystery at the heart of the book is certain to draw readers in and the meticulously researched sections about art, miniatures and jewellery are an absolute joy." Louise Douglas, author of *The Sea House*.

"A dark, brooding and atmospheric mystery." Emily Bell, author of *This Year's for Me and You*.

"Rich with historical detail and Victorian flair brought to a modern-day setting, this is a cleverly told story of one woman's quest to learn more about the mysterious figure in a portrait miniature she inherits and getting far more than she bargained for. Fans of Kate Morton's *The Clockmaker's Daughter* will enjoy this layered mystery with fantastic art history elements deftly woven into it." Kristen Perrin, author of *How To Solve Your Own Murder.*

"An enchanting story laced with mystery and tension. I loved it." NJ Barker, author of *The Honesty Index*.

"The writing is beautifully detailed without being overbearing. The richly textured descriptions breathe life into an emotional story with great characters. My interest was held throughout and I looked forward to each reading session. Five stars." Emily Pankhurst, book blogger.

"A wonderful mystery with a brilliant Victorian historical twist. Definitely a book I would recommend and one that I think will appeal to mystery and historical fans alike." The Strawberry Post book blogger.

PROLOGUE

January 1880

Trapped.

A quiver rippled down the rope of the girl's spine as her thought took hold.

'Please keep still,' said the bespectacled woman sitting at a table between them. 'I can't capture the likeness if you keep moving around.'

The girl flexed her shoulders then composed herself, fixing her eyes on the studio clock. At noon she was due to have lunch with her betrothed. It was an encounter she was dreading. Like a fly in a spider's web, she was caught in this situation as inexorably as her face would be trapped by the portrait being painted.

'I've almost finished,' said the artist. 'I just need to add some rose madder to the forehead and make the edge of your frock a little crisper.' She sat upright for a moment, studying her subject intently through the circular eyepieces of her spectacles. Her high-necked, plain brown dress gave the whisper of a rustle as she bent over her work again.

The girl glanced up at the hands of the wall clock. This third sitting was becoming an intolerable burden. Was it only four months ago that she first set foot in this small studio in south-west London? She could clearly recall how a strong smell of turpentine had served to heighten her sense of anticipation. How proud she'd been to sit for a professional artist. How illustrious it had made her feel.

Once the miniature portrait was finished and sent to the jeweller for encasing, her parents were planning to present it to her fiancé at a special dinner-party to celebrate the engagement. It would be a very grand occasion with all their best silver and porcelain, numerous guests and speeches from her father and her betrothed. After the formal announcement, of course, they could start planning the wedding in earnest.

Her stomach gave an unpleasant lurch, and she took a slow, deep breath to quell the queasiness.

How everything had changed within a few short months. Even at the second sitting she remembered entertaining rosy thoughts about the future. Her betrothed, so handsome and clever, would take care of her for the rest of her life. They would live at the Yorkshire estate he'd inherited from his father. She'd be kind to the staff and tenant farmers, and they would adore her in return. Everyone in her family approved of the match, especially as her fiancé's financial position was so strong. Soon he would be standing in the general election as the Liberal candidate for Yorkshire South Riding. How thrilling the possibility of becoming a Member of Parliament's wife had seemed. And yet now....

Now she was about to throw it all away – a secure future

as a wife and mother, her status in society, the wealth and comforts she would enjoy.

She could feel her heart racing unnaturally fast and took another deep breath, attempting to calm her jiggling nerves.

Keep still.

Twisting her clammy hands together more tightly, she resisted the urge to brush away a drop of sweat as it rolled off her forehead and tracked down her cheek.

It was a very uncertain fate to choose. Worse, she might even be putting herself in danger. Her fiancé had a fiery temper at the best of times. Was it possible his anger would explode into physical violence? Would there be some sort of backlash against her family? Her mind reeled at the possible consequences of the action she was set on taking.

As she shifted uneasily in her seat the bubble of sweat reached her neck and continued its downward path.

'There!' said the artist, laying down her brush. 'My work is done. I think you will be pleased. It's a very good likeness indeed.'

'May I look?' the girl asked eagerly.

'Yes, but please don't touch,' replied the artist. 'The paint will take a while to dry.'

Stiff from holding herself in one position, the girl rose awkwardly and smoothed the bodice of her ivory-coloured silk gown then patted her hair to ensure the red silk flowers were still in place. Then she walked round the table and stood behind the artist. Peering over the woman's shoulder, she stared down at the miniature painting and, like Narcissus in the ancient myth, saw her own reflection gazing back at her.

The artist had captured her appearance well. The thick, exuberant hair, pinned neatly back from her face, looked identical to the burnished gold mane of which she was so proud. Greeny-blue eyes sparkled alluringly. The skin glowed warmly and looked enticingly soft. Ignoring the artist's warning, she extended her forefinger to stroke its peachy bloom. In a trice, the artist grabbed her hand and inadvertently knocked one of the brushes lying next to the portrait. As it rolled off the table and fell to the floor, a flick of white pigment landed on the painting. A miniscule splash just below the collarbone.

'Oh no! That was my fault. I'm sorry – can you paint over that mark?'

Fury darkened the artist's face as she twisted round in her chair and glared at the girl. 'You foolish minx,' she hissed. 'I asked you not to touch and now look what you've done.'

'Paint over that mark,' the girl repeated haughtily. 'Surely you can hide it?'

The artist was sullenly silent for few moments as her gaze returned to her work. 'No, I won't do that,' she said in a resentful voice. 'It will remain as evidence of your wilful behaviour. I don't expect it will be the only stain on your character.'

The girl's mouth opened and closed without reply. No one spoke to her like that. Not her mother or father. Nor her brother. Even her betrothed's frequent outbursts were directed at his staff, not her.

Anger surged within her like an uncontrollable tidal wave. She was about to give the woman a sharp rebuke when a piercing sound like chalk scraping across a school-room blackboard rang in her ears. A deadly foreboding shot through her body as viscerally as a drench of freezing rain.

She stepped back from the artist, frightened by the dreadful panic gripping her. It was as if she could feel the bright, beckoning future she'd once envisaged slipping from her grasp and shattering like a looking glass crashing on a marble floor. Yet, in that searing moment, the face she saw reflected in its jagged shards was not her own.

Trembling and nauseous, her gaze returned to the miniature. The mark was tiny – invisible to all but the most exacting eye – yet she knew it would scar the work forever. It would be a sore reminder of her impulsive nature and reckless behaviour. Even if no one else ever spotted it, the girl in the portrait would always remember why the shaming blemish was there.

CHAPTER 1

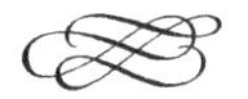

March, this year

'Damn it! Just leave me alone!' raged Freya.

The insistent rap had startled her out of a wistful reverie. She'd been staring at her mother's neglected garden, numb with misery, and the noise was jarring, impertinent even.

The sight of Mrs Taylor standing full square on the doorstep in a thick, plaid overcoat made her spirits sink. A grey mist cloaked the distant fields and the air felt moist. It seemed more like autumn than spring.

'I'm just going to the shops, dear, can I get you anything?' Mrs Taylor asked.

'That's very kind but I've got everything I need,' replied Freya, telling herself to sound friendly. No doubt her mother's talkative neighbour was hoping for a cup of tea and a chat.

Mrs Taylor looked crestfallen then rallied. 'It was a lovely service, wasn't it? And the church was packed. Your mother had lots of friends in the village, you know.'

'Yes, she loved living here,' said Freya.

'And the flowers were beautiful,' said Mrs Taylor. 'Did you choose them?'

'They were all her favourites.' Freya forced a smile, wishing the woman would go.

'Well, I mustn't keep you,' said Mrs Taylor, making no effort to move. 'I expect you've got a lot to do. You'll be selling up, I suppose?'

'I'm not sure right now,' replied Freya, placing a hand on the doorjamb as if barring entry. 'I need to sort out my mother's things first. That'll take a while.'

'Well, we've got some good charity shops in the village,' said Mrs Taylor. Lowering her voice, she whispered in a conspiratorial voice, 'Make sure you lock up when you go out, dear. They've had a couple of break-ins over on the estate.' Then, more brightly, 'Don't forget – I'm only next door if you need anything.'

How could I forget, thought Freya unkindly as she watched Mrs Taylor scurry up the path like a foraging hedgehog. She closed the door with relief and went into the kitchen. Her mother's neighbour meant well but Mrs Taylor was a gossip and all Freya wanted was to be left alone.

Was it only yesterday she was handing round plates of sandwiches to a crowd of strangers after the cremation service? Pouring out wine and juice, she had forced herself to act graciously and hold a fixed smile when all she wanted was to run upstairs, throw herself on her mother's bed and bawl her eyes out. Waking exhausted this morning after a broken night, she was still reeling from the strain.

The number of tasks ahead seemed daunting. Freya felt her

resolve slipping away as she went upstairs to carry on clearing out the bedroom. None of it felt right. Her mother loved this cottage and now her only child was packing it up, bit by bit, and disposing of everything. Then a stranger would move in, and any hint of her mother's presence would be gone forever. It felt cruel and unreal. Just as unreal as the cremation service yesterday. Tears filled her eyes as she entered her mother's bedroom.

Telling herself to get a grip, Freya flung open the wardrobe doors and began removing dresses, jackets and coats from their hangers and bundling them into green recycling bags. Trying not to think about the last time she saw her mother wearing the clothes, she carried on relentlessly until the rails were clear.

Next, she tackled the dressing table drawers. Would the charity shops take underwear? They would surely take socks and tights — those were in the bottom drawer — and right at the back she'd find her mother's jewellery box. Freya smiled as she remembered teasing her mother that potential burglars would be more interested in pinching her resplendent sock collection than her rings.

Oh Ma, I miss you so much, she thought. After Dad died, it was always just you and me. No wonder we remained so close.

Giving a forlorn sigh, Freya sank down on the rose-patterned bed-throw with the jewellery box on her knees. Caressing the worn, leather surface, she released the catch with no expectation of finding anything of significance. She knew her mother had inherited a brooch and two rings from her own mother, wearing them occasionally for sentimental reasons but insisting that none had any great value. Other than those pieces Freya couldn't recall her mother wearing any jewellery except her wedding and engagement rings.

Even though she was expecting to see it, Freya was startled

by the bold, blue starburst brooch winking at her. The jewel cradled within its spiky, gold arms was the deep, ocean-blue of a sapphire although Freya, from her professional knowledge as a jewellery designer, immediately recognised it as a paste imitation. In a dusty-pink, suede cleft sat three rings, one of which was her mother's diamond engagement ring. She must have put it there before she went into hospital.

The other two rings were also familiar: her grandmother's garnet engagement ring and a square-cut emerald ring. Freya held up each in turn to catch the light and marvelled at their clarity, cut and depth of colour. Had these rings, which so intrigued her in childhood, set her on her chosen career path? Well, that was now on hold if not completely over. Focusing on work after her mother's first stroke proved impossible. On the few occasions she attempted a new design it seemed as if her creativity had evaporated into thin air. By the time Freya moved into the cottage to help her mother she had abandoned any pretence at keeping up with orders from retailers. Nor could her studio assistant cope. Oliver tried his best to keep the store buyers at bay but faced with delays and endless excuses, they began to cancel orders one by one.

Freya winced at the memory of Oliver screaming down the phone at her while hearing her mother call from her bedroom upstairs.

Everything had quickly gone from bad to worse. With little income to offset a ballooning overdraft, the bank called in the loan used from the outset to finance the company's growth and pay her assistant. The studio Freya had been so proud to set up and run with her boyfriend-cum-business partner went into voluntary liquidation. The outstanding debts were settled by Oliver's father. Freya shuddered. It had been a humiliation and a defeat for everyone involved. And she was to blame for it all.

Freya sighed and replaced the rings, side by side, in the suede holder. Then she picked up a string of imitation pearls lying curled on a black, velvet pad next to the brooch. Girls in pearls, she thought idly, dangling them between her fingers. Something glittered as the black pad shifted fractionally. Pushing it aside, Freya blinked with astonishment as the face of a young girl stared up at her.

A flash of sunshine momentarily bathed the image in gold, as if it was a religious icon. As the flare abruptly faded, Freya felt a prickle of tension between her shoulder-blades and a shimmer of unease.

'Who are *you*?' she exclaimed, dropping the pearl necklace back in the box and gingerly picking up the oval portrait between forefinger and thumb.

The painting was covered with glass and set inside a gilt-edged case attached to a long, gold chain. She laid it gently in the palm of her left hand, draping the chain between her fingers. Turning the case over, she inspected the reverse which seemed to be lined with silk. Peering at the edge of the portrait, Freya looked for an artist's signature. None was visible. Her jeweller's magnifying loop was back in London. If she had it here she could study the portrait in far more detail.

The striking face gazed up at her defiantly. It looked strong, Freya decided, rather than beautiful. Thick, red-gold tresses, pulled back behind her head, emphasised high cheek-bones and a sharp chin. A generous mouth balanced a broad, intelligent forehead and her skin-tone was warm and dewy. She was young, possibly 17 or 18, and clearly excited to be on the cusp of adulthood. Searing, greeny-blue eyes shone with a penetrating directness that appealed to Freya. Yet she found something about the force of the girl's gaze a little disturbing. It seemed as if this arresting young woman was deliberately challenging the viewer, aware she had the power to exert her will over them.

'Who *are* you?" Freya murmured again, wondering if the girl was a distant relative. Perhaps she was the grandmother she had never known. Or maybe the portrait had been painted even earlier than that.

She slipped off the bed and walked over to her mother's dressing table. Pulling the mirror forward to an angle where it caught the light, Freya compared her reflection with the miniature portrait in her hand.

Her own face was definitely more oval, and the line of her jaw appeared softer. The cheekbones were not as prominent nor the chin as sharp as the girl in the portrait. Her own eyes were grey-blue and her hair, although thick and shoulder-length, was chestnut-brown. Freya flicked her eyes between the mirror and the miniature repeatedly and felt a crushing disappointment that she couldn't see a greater resemblance. The portrait had promised a link to her mother – a whisper from the past – but there was no family likeness she could discern.

Standing there, gazing at the portrait, Freya realised her mother had never said anything about it and yet she had often mentioned the brooch and rings. So how had this remarkable little miniature painting ended up in her jewellery box? Had she even remembered it was there? Realising she was alone with her thoughts and could never ask her mother these questions brought tears to Freya's eyes. Turning back to the bed, she replaced the portrait miniature carefully inside the jewellery box and closed the lid.

Later that evening, pouring herself some whisky from a half-empty bottle in the kitchen cupboard, Freya wished she had a brother or sister to help her. Clearing out her mother's cottage was a daunting task. She was making progress, but the work felt lonely and laborious. Would Oliver have given her a hand if they were still together? She doubted it. Only under duress and even then, he probably would have moaned a lot.

The thought of having to cope with everything on her own – estate agents, solicitors, paperwork – was overwhelming. She could see no respite from the endless chain of decisions to be made about her mother's belongings, her books, her furniture and eventually the cottage itself. So why, with so much else to think about, did she find her thoughts returning again and again to the portrait miniature? What was it about that striking young woman that seemed to have such a hold on her?

On impulse, she picked up her mobile phone from the kitchen table and punched in a number. 'Brooke? It's Freya.'

'How's tricks?' The tone was sympathetic yet brisk.

'Grim, thanks. And you – all fine and dandy?' The relief of slipping back into easy banter with her old college friend made Freya smile.

'Oh, it's the usual colourful chaos here,' replied Brooke drily. 'When are you coming back to London?'

'Hopefully on Monday. I've got someone coming to do a valuation for probate tomorrow then I'll carry on clearing out Ma's things and head back to London after that.'

'Bet that will be a shock to the system,' said Brooke.

'It'll feel very strange to get back to my flat after being here so long,' said Freya. 'Thank goodness I was able to sub-let it while living with Ma.'

'What are your plans after that?'

'There's stuff to sort out on my mother's estate and I've got to think about selling her cottage.'

'Do you have to do that?' asked Brooke. 'Couldn't you keep it and rent it out?'

'Maybe,' sighed Freya. 'I'm in dire straits financially

though. I've earned nothing for the last six months and my overdraft's giving me nightmares. It might be best just to sell up.'

'I thought Oliver's father dealt with all that.'

'Only the company debts – not my personal ones.' Freya doused this unpleasant thought with a swig of whisky. 'Look, I didn't call to talk about my finances. I need your advice. While I was sorting through my mother's things I came across something extraordinary.'

'Oh yes?' said Brooke, curiosity sharpening her voice.

'It's a little painting – a portrait miniature – of a striking young woman,' said Freya.

'That sounds right up my boulevard,' said Brooke.

'Why?' Freya asked warily.

'Two appealing adjectives and one very fine noun.'

Frowning in bewilderment, Freya remained silent.

Brooke sighed audibly. 'Striking. Young. Woman. Keep up now.'

'Oh, yes I see,' said Freya lamely, remembering her friend's preferences a little too late. 'I found it in my mother's jewellery box. I have no idea who she is or where it came from. I'm sure my mother never mentioned it and I don't know if she's some distant relative or nothing to do with our family.'

'How intriguing. What does she look like?'

'I would say she looks interesting rather than beautiful,' said Freya, picturing the girl's face while speaking. 'She's got piercing, greeny-blue eyes and thick fair hair with some red flowers arranged in it.'

'Ah! What sort of flowers?' asked Brooke.

'I don't know,' replied Freya vaguely. 'Is that important, do you think?'

'Could be. Go on. What is she wearing?' persisted Brooke.

'An ivory-coloured dress with a lacy neckline.'

'What sort of period?'

'It looks Victorian, but I'd like to get some professional advice,' said Freya. 'Where could I take it?' If anyone could point her in the right direction it would be Brooke. After their foundation year at art school, she'd enrolled on an arts consultancy course and now worked for one of London's leading contemporary design galleries.

'You could try Boyd & Hart in Albemarle Street,' her friend replied. 'It's a commercial gallery dealing in historical portraits as well as some contemporary work and I think they also sell miniatures if I remember correctly. They'd give you an opinion – and tell you what it's worth if you're thinking of selling it.'

'No, I wouldn't do that,' said Freya quickly. 'Not until I know who she is – but perhaps they can throw some light on that. It's very strange, you know. I just can't stop thinking about her.'

'Bad as that?' teased Brooke.

'Oh, do shut up,' said Freya. 'Okay, I admit I'm getting a bit obsessed, but this little portrait is the only bright thing right now. Everything else I've got to deal with is so tedious and depressing.'

'Then she's your gal,' replied Brooke in a matter-of-fact voice.

Freya smiled. She'd grown used to this sort of comment from her friend over the years. Switching off her phone, she felt a surge of gratitude as her spirits rose for the first time in many months.

Discussing the miniature fuelled a compulsion to take another look and she ran upstairs to retrieve the jewellery box.

Sitting at the kitchen table, Freya held the portrait up to

eye-level. As the unflinching, greeny-blue stare met her gaze she felt a tingling sensation at the nape of her neck. The fierce intensity in the young girl's eyes and the resolute thrust of her chin struck her again as singular. She was certainly no shrinking violet.

Freya took the black velvet pad out of the box, put it on the table and placed the portrait on top like a crown on a regal cushion. Again, she searched for an artist's signature and found none. Nor were there any tell-tale signs such as a landscape or buildings in the background that might offer a clue as to where it was painted. Just the girl. Whoever she was.

Was it valuable? Boyd & Hart would know. What she'd told Brooke about not selling it until she knew the sitter's identity was true though. In any case, flogging it to a commercial gallery or putting it up for auction felt too venal. It would be better to find a private buyer – someone who would treasure it. Now who could she ask about that?

Frowning, she tried to recall a conversation with one of her early clients. Hadn't Rowena Vere sold a Victorian sculpture – a family heirloom – to a London collector? A private buyer with a taste for all things Victorian? She'd call her and find out who it was. After all, if she was offered a decent price, it might resolve her financial problems and prove too tempting to resist.

Freya was about to pop the miniature back in the jewellery box when a pale, yellowy streak at the top of the pad caught her eye. She laid the portrait on the table, picked up the pad and examined it. What she'd failed to notice previously was a slit along the top edge. It wasn't so much a pad as a slip-case – possibly intended to protect the miniature. And the yellowy thing poking from one corner was a snippet of paper. Gently, she slid her forefinger inside and very carefully extracted a scrap folded to the size of a postage stamp.

With a thumping heart, she spread out the flimsy sheet. Peering at the faint, copper-plate script she could just make out three words in faded, rusty ink:

Friday without fail.

It must be a lovers' tryst, she thought. But where – and with whom?

CHAPTER 2

Leaving a spare key to the cottage with Mrs Taylor in case of an emergency, Freya drove back to London with a car packed with bedlinen, towels, a clock, a lamp, two boxes of bills, photographs and paperwork, another box of glasses and the few pieces of china she wanted to keep. The remainder she left behind to sort out later.

A local auctioneer had visited the cottage to conduct a valuation for probate purposes before she left. Even though he turned out to be a charming and sympathetic man, she hated the experience. Watching a stranger pore over her mother's possessions had been thoroughly dispiriting. At least he would sell the furniture once the solicitors had dealt with probate. Her next step was to ask the estate agent who came to value the property to put it on the market.

Freya was glad the jewellery box lay hidden under an upturned flowerpot in the garden during the auctioneer's visit. No paper-trail relating to her grandmother's brooch and rings existed as her mother had told her years ago that none of her possessions was insured. Nor, she assumed, was there any record of the portrait miniature. Even so, these were all family pieces and there was no way she was going to show them to a stranger even if this behaviour contravened her statutory obligations.

It took numerous trips back to the car to carry everything through the building's communal hallway and up to her first floor flat. Feeling exhausted, she made a mug of tea, unzipped her overnight bag and extracted the jewellery box. She planned to hide it under a bookcase but first she wanted to inspect the miniature with her jeweller's magnifying loop.

Freya flicked on a task lamp in the living room and bent over the portrait until the girl's face was less than an inch from her own. The brushstrokes were remarkably fine and the colours seemed unusually subtle. It must surely be the work of a specialist portrait miniature painter. Turning it over, she inspected the back of the case. Despite being at least a century old, the silk behind the glass looked almost new.

She peered at the portrait again. What was that? A miniscule speck by the girl's collarbone. Straightening up, she breathed on the loop and rubbed it gently with a tissue before peering more closely at this area of the painting. Yes, just below the ivory sheen of the collarbone, there was definitely a tiny, white mark.

How strange, she thought. Why didn't the artist remove it or paint over it? Surely, he would have noticed.

A gust of wind rattled the window and Freya felt a chill on her neck as she gazed at the blemish. She bent over the miniature for a few minutes more then picked it up and returned to her bedroom to replace it in the jewellery box and shove it under the bookcase.

Shrugging on her parka, Freya locked the door of her flat and left the building. Glancing across the road, she saw a queue forming outside the local church. It wouldn't be a religious service in such high demand, she thought. The draw would be the soup kitchen run by volunteers and the warm hub on offer. Despite her jacket, she shivered. No matter how precarious she felt financially, at least she wasn't standing in a cool wind waiting for a hand-out mug of soup. Yet.

Pensively, she walked along the street and turned left into a cobbled mews where she rented a storage lock-up in what had once been a stable. Having not visited it for months she could barely remember what it contained. Would there be space for all the stuff brought back from the cottage? She turned the key and stepped inside.

Then it all came jangling back to her like one of her frequent nightmares. Oliver had insisted on taking pretty much everything belonging to their company when it went into voluntary liquidation, saying he needed to go through it all forensically and sell what he could. Freya had been in no position to argue. Leaving Mrs Taylor to look after her mother, she'd spent a very unhappy day in London helping Oliver clear out their spacious studio in Brixton and this lock-up. It had all been done at breakneck speed so she could head back to the cottage in the evening, and she barely noticed what they tossed into boxes and loaded into Oliver's van. She'd driven back to the cottage in torrential rain and had a very sour memory of that day.

Freya bit her lip. We failed, she thought miserably, scuffing her boot disconsolately along the threshold. But then she straightened shoulders. Perhaps they only failed because they never had a backer and started the company without any proper funding. Her *Freya* jewellery line wasn't the problem. Designs like that delicate necklace with the trio of gemstones had been very successful. So successful, she thought bitterly, that Oliver had taken one of her sketches to a celebrity jeweller in Mayfair and sold the design without her permission after their company folded.

Her mood darkened as she recalled Brooke phoning her at the cottage to say she'd seen a silver filigree cuff advertised in the *Financial Times's 'How to Spend It'* magazine that bore such close resemblance to an early Freya design that she wondered if it had anything to do with her. Had Brooke not spotted it she would never have known how treacherous Oliver could be. What a scumbag, she thought.

Reflecting on her past designs brought the portrait miniature to mind. Freya narrowed her eyes as she pictured the young woman's challenging gaze. It felt as if she was being taunted in some strange way.

Hit in the stomach by a flash of resolve as visceral as a shot of whisky, Freya took a deep breath – then another. She would start again. The lock-up was a poky space compared with their lovely studio, but it was big enough for a workbench and most of her hand-tools were still packed away here. She could make a few pieces to test the water with some old clients without taking too much of a financial risk. If she took things one step at a time, she was sure she could make it work.

THE GALLERY interior felt dazzlingly white as Freya pushed open the heavy glass door on Albemarle Street that afternoon. Facing her was a monolithic block of white marble which she assumed was the reception desk. A blonde head jerked up above its glistening surface and – alerted by Freya's boots clacking on the pale, parquet floor – stared unsmilingly as she approached.

'Would it be possible to show one of your experts something I inherited recently, please?' asked Freya.

The blonde raised her eyebrows by a millimetre or two. 'What is it?' she enquired, coolly studying Freya's wind-blown hair.

'A miniature portrait,' replied Freya. 'I'd like to find out who painted it.'

'Are you thinking of selling?' The receptionist sounded sulky, almost resentful. Her pale blue eyes flicked down to the blood-coloured nails on her left hand. She spread her fingers wide, flapped them up and down, then drew them together.

'Possibly,' replied Freya tersely, wishing to avoid further interrogation.

The blonde nodded and murmured into a mobile phone. Freya thought she'd say no one was available Then she was told: 'Liz Russell will see you in 10 minutes. Wait over there please.' She waved her blood-red nails in the direction of a white marble bench.

Freya followed her instruction and sat on the hard, cold bench feeling uncomfortably out of place in this frosty ice-palace. The gallery, according to her internet search, was a specialist in portrait miniatures and yet she could see no evidence of this in the reception area. A huge seascape adorned one wall. Freya studied its chilly depiction of icy spray and foaming white caps. It wasn't something she'd welcome in her own home.

Surreptitiously checking her watch, she waited impatiently as 10 minutes ticked past then 15, then 20, during which time the blonde completely ignored her. Growing increasingly restless, Freya was on the point of leaving when a tall woman wearing black trousers and a crisp, white shirt appeared from the snowy hinterland beyond the reception desk.

'I'm so sorry to keep you waiting,' she said, sounding harassed. 'I've been cataloguing a collection of silhouettes we've just acquired.' She ran a hand over a glossy bob of burnished-copper hair. 'Let's go upstairs to my office.'

Following Liz Russell's pert posterior as she climbed the white-painted staircase, Freya wondered if the silhouette-owner had also inherited his artworks. Perhaps Boyd & Hart was continually besieged by heirs who either lacked the space to accommodate paintings or hated their forebears' taste in art. Liz Russell had certainly shown no sign of surprise at being contacted out of the blue. Nor had the receptionist. Perhaps it was a regular occurrence.

Liz Russell's sunny office could not have been a more complete contrast to the icy snow-scape below. Primrose-coloured walls were lined with shelves crammed with box-files and thick art books. A wide, wooden desk in front of a tall sash-window was covered in papers pinned down by a variety of quaint objects including a ceramic tortoise. As Liz sat down, golden motes of dust danced in a stream of bright, spring sunshine pouring in over her shoulders.

'Well, do please show me what you've got,' she said, clasping her hands together as she leaned forward. Freya took the miniature out of her handbag and unwrapped the tissue paper protecting it. An unexpected tingle of excitement prickled her stomach as she placed the portrait on the desk and looked across at Liz Russell to gauge her reaction.

'Oh, it's enchanting,' Liz exclaimed, picking it up and examining it in the sunlight. 'Victorian, of course. Mid- to late-century judging by the hairstyle. Yes, around 1860 to 1880 I'd say.'

She pulled open a desk drawer, took out a magnifying loop and held the portrait close to her eye. 'Oh, that's a shame. There's a tiny chip on the edge of the ivory. That always knocks the value back a bit. But the watercolours have barely faded despite its age and – look, how charming – the lower lip is painted slightly darker than the top lip. That was a trick some artists used to make the mouth appear fuller than it really was.'

Liz glanced up from the miniature, her blue eyes shining with enthusiasm. 'What do you know about this portrait? Is she an ancestor?'

'I don't know who she is,' replied Freya. 'I was hoping you could tell me that.'

Liz regarded the miniature again. 'She's very beautiful, isn't she? Not in a demure, Victorian way though. Her features are too strong and there's a glint of something – well, untamed, in her eyes. Not a conventional beauty. More of a high-class bohemian perhaps.'

Freya stared at her wide-eyed. How exciting, she thought. Perhaps I'm descended from a model whose liaison with a wild Pre-Raphaelite artist caused a society scandal. Maybe that love-note is evidence of their passionate affair.

'Have you noticed what she's wearing?' asked Liz, studying the portrait intently.

'Yes, it looks like a wedding dress,' replied Freya.

'It was quite common for young Victorian women to have their portrait painted wearing their wedding dresses,' said Liz. 'It was a kind of pre-nuptial gift for their fiancé. A bit like the precursor of an official engagement photograph. Yes, look, there's even some lace entwined with the red flowers in her hair.'

'And she's got a single diamond on a gold chain around her neck,' said Freya. 'Perhaps that was an engagement present.'

'More than likely,' agreed Liz. 'There's no artist signature on the front and the reverse is backed in silk so that doesn't tell us anything either. It might be signed on the portrait's reverse, but we'd have to break the case open to find out.'

'No!' exclaimed Freya more loudly than intended. 'Sorry,'

she apologised. 'I don't want to do that. I only found it a few days ago while I was clearing up my mother's belongings after she died. It doesn't seem right to destroy the case without knowing more about the portrait.'

Liz looked at her keenly. 'Are you planning to sell?'

'It depends—'

'On the price?' interrupted Liz. 'Our valuations team can assess that but unless it was painted by a leading portrait miniature artist like George Engleheart or John Smart – and they were working too early to have painted yours – then I'm afraid it's unlikely to be worth more than a few thousand pounds. However, there are always collectors who are prepared to pay over the odds for something they really want.'

'Well, I wouldn't want to part with it until I know who she is,' said Freya.

'I don't think I can help with that,' said Liz. 'Without any family history or paperwork, it will be almost impossible to track down the sitter's name.'

'The odd thing is I can't remember my mother ever telling me anything about it,' said Freya, feeling her throat tighten at the memory of her mother.

'I can probably find out who painted it,' said Liz. 'Give me a few days. I'll do some research and call you.'

Freya's heart gave a tiny jerk. Could she be a step closer to discovering the portrait's identity? If the young woman turned out to be a distant relation perhaps it would explain this gnawing compulsion to learn more about her. There was some connection between them. She was sure of that.

Tuning back into the conversation, she heard Liz Russell saying '...and you might visit the V&A which holds the national collection of portrait miniatures. There are some Victorian miniatures on display as well as historically early work although the museum doesn't have what's thought to be the earliest surviving English miniature – a portrait of Princess Mary painted around 1525 by Lucas Horenbout. You'll have to go to the National Portrait Gallery for that.'

APPROACHING THE WIDE, shallow steps at the V&A's entrance on Cromwell Road a few days later, Freya paused in the chilly spring sunshine to admire the decorative stonework around the grand portico arch. The building's façade was a work of art in its own right. Sculptures filled a sequence of stone wall-niches – one figure held a palette; another, a book. Gazing upwards, she could read the names of British artists and craftsmen carved in stone below the pedestals on which they stood – John Constable, J.M.W. Turner, William Morris and others.

Angling her head, Freya slowly deciphered an inscription around the arch that she'd never stopped to read on previous visits – "The excellence of every art must consist in the complete accomplishment of its purpose." Well, I'm on a mission here, she thought wryly. Let's hope I can achieve complete accomplishment.

She had come here to meet the collector recommended by her client, Rowena Vere. The choice of the V&A's portrait miniature gallery as their meeting-place had been sparked by her conversation with Liz Russell and having consulted the internet, she knew she'd have no difficulty in recognising him.

After supplying his name and phone number Rowena had hinted that Ralph Merrick was somewhat eccentric, saying how passionately he revelled in all things Victorian – art, books, buildings, even clothes. The credentials on his website about his work as an art historian and lecturer had impressed Freya greatly. Far from being grand and learned, however, he'd sounded approachable and friendly on the phone and his immediate interest in the portrait made her eager to see him.

Although reluctant to sell the miniature, Freya's latest bank statement had alarmed her. There was no harm in initiating a conversation about a possible deal. Besides, he might throw some light on the portrait sitter's identity.

A sweeping stone staircase brought her to level 3, and she made her way towards the jewellery gallery where she'd often sought inspiration for her own work. Slipping through crowds of visitors she felt dazzled, as always, by glimpses of glinting neckpieces and sparkling bracelets displayed in tall glass cases lining the walls.

This brightly lit gallery led directly into Room 90a, the home of the national collection of portrait miniatures. The atmosphere here was a complete contrast. The small, temperature-controlled space felt distinctly chilly. It was also extremely dark. Freya stood inside the entrance, blinking as her eyes adjusted to the gloom. No doubt the dim lighting prevented the paintings from fading but she could barely see where the miniatures were displayed.

After a few moments she could make out the rectangular shapes of a dozen glass cases perching on tall wooden frames. No one else appeared to be in the room The darkness was punctured by a small, vivid screen in the far corner and Freya made her way towards it.

A video ran silently for a few minutes then looped back to re-run its story about the mixing of pigments and historical techniques employed in painting miniatures. Freya watched, fascinated, as a portrait of Queen Elizabeth I emerged from a few lines brushed onto flayed animal skin, taking shape and colour as the hands of an unseen artist worked and re-worked the image until the queen appeared in all her finery.

Standing there, scanning the video's sub-titles for the third time, Freya became aware of a movement behind her. Glancing over her shoulder, she caught her breath as a dark form loomed over her from the shadows.

The figure was considerably taller than Freya. A black overcoat outlined formidably broad shoulders and a barrel chest. Light spilling from the video illuminated a strong, confident face with a crop of curly, black hair and a full beard. This powerful presence, seemingly conjured from nowhere, felt intimidating, almost threatening, in the gloom. Freya involuntarily stepped aside and immediately collided with the sharp corner of a glass case. In a flash the man's arm was round her waist pulling her so close that she could feel his breath on her face.

'Are you alright?' he asked in a low voice. 'Not hurt, I hope?'

Freya wrenched sideways, breaking away from his grasp. 'Yes, I'm fine,' she replied shakily. 'Fine.'

'Damned dark in here. Like a tomb.' He gave a soft chuckle. 'You must be Freya Wetherby I presume?'

'Yes, that's right,' replied Freya, rubbing her sore ribcage.

'Let me introduce myself properly – Ralph Merrick, art historian, collector and connoisseur of the Victorian age.'

He gave a small bow. It was a gesture that belonged to an earlier era, Freya noted, although not entirely out of place given their surroundings. Taking his extended hand, she felt her own crushed by his grasp and was a little intimidated. He seemed so much more imposing than the photograph on his website had indicated.

'What an excellent place to meet,' he said with a gloss of approval warming his deep, mellifluous voice. 'It's a fine collection – have you looked around?'

'Not yet,' replied Freya, noting a strong smell of cologne on his skin - possibly mandarin she thought.

'Come and admire the Virgin Queen in all her glory,' he suggested in a convivial tone.

Freya followed him to a display-case in the centre of the room. As they moved closer, the interior lit up brightly to reveal several portraits of Elizabeth I displayed in a double row like a proud array of medals.

'Nicholas Hilliard – he was the great portrait miniaturist of the day – always made her look about 18 even in old age,' said her companion. 'What a sycophant. Look, there he is. Self-portrait.'

Freya peered closely at the small oval painting, her face just inches from the glass case. The artist in the miniature stared out at a point beyond her right shoulder. He looked clever, confident and at ease with himself. A label beneath the miniature indicated it was painted in 1577.

'Hilliard described his art as "a thing apart which excelleth all other painting,"' said Ralph in a reflective manner. 'And Elizabeth wasn't slow on the uptake. She recognised the propaganda power of miniatures alright and used them to her advantage.'

'Really?' Despite their disconcerting initial encounter Freya found herself drawn into the conversation with this scholarly man.

'Yes, her courtiers wore her portrait as a sign of loyalty,' said Ralph. 'Not something we're inclined to do these days except perhaps by buying souvenir mugs and biscuit tins.'

'Hilliard was one of her favourites, then?'

'He flattered her.' Ralph gave a gruff chuckle as he stroked his beard. 'He paid court by inventing a technique to make her jewels look even more fantastic than they probably were.'

'How did he do that?' asked Freya, intrigued by the mention of jewellery.

'By painting the vellum with real silver and gold,' replied

Ralph. 'Pearls, for example, were painted using a tiny blob of lead-white pigment with silver highlights. Diamonds were created by applying a base of burnished silver to form a reflective surface. For rubies and emeralds, he used a hot needle to place a tiny blob of coloured resin on burnished silver to give the effect of a three-dimensional jewel.'

'Goodness,' said Freya. 'I suppose that makes the portraits even more valuable?'

'Of course. As do the materials used to make their cases. Come and look at this.' Ralph strode towards the gallery entrance where a locket dangled from a thread inside a tall glass case. Spot-lit by a tiny, bright light, an elaborate pattern of swirls and fronds in blue, white and gold gleamed and glistened on the miniature's case.

'Wow!' exclaimed Freya. 'That's really beautiful.'

'Artists began encasing their portraits within lockets when they realised exposure to light fades the paints – this one dates from about 1635,' explained Ralph. 'Now I know you said your own miniature isn't as old as that but I'm sure it's a splendid little masterpiece. Shall we venture out to the courtyard café and take a look?'

Freya was aware of Ralph's hand in the small of her back as he steered her through the crowded jewellery gallery towards the staircase. Flattered by his attention, she dismissed an instinctive nudge of wariness and attributed the gesture to avuncular protectiveness.

It was something she'd always felt was missing. The loss of her father during childhood had left a vulnerability that relationships with men of her own age never seemed to resolve. Anyway, he was clearly highly knowledgeable about art history – a subject close to her heart – and it would be interesting to get to know him better. She found herself calculating his age – possibly mid-forties – and wondered whether he was married. His website had given no clues in this respect. Against her better judgment, she was finding the magnetic pull of his powerful, physical presence hard to ignore.

'I'm sure you're aware the discipline of painting miniatures grew out of the medieval practice of illuminating manuscript books,' he said as they walked through the sculpture court towards the courtyard entrance. 'I've always thought it rather wonderful that the declining demand for manuscript illustration caused by printed book production resulted in the flourishing of miniature painting.'

Weak sunshine dappled the pink brick and pale stone façades of buildings surrounding the quadrangle, although a frisky breeze ruffled the surface of the oval pond at its centre. A group of tables occupied one side of the rectangular space and Ralph courteously pulled out a chair for Freya.

'Will you have tea or coffee?' he asked.

'Tea please,' replied Freya. 'Earl Grey if they have it.'

'A girl after my own heart,' he said jovially, moving towards an outdoor servery.

He returned with a tray containing a teapot, mugs, a dish of lemon slices and a plate of shortbread fingers. After transferring everything to the table he sat down heavily, exhaling hard. Freya could feel his eyes boring into her as she pretended to admire the exterior of the buildings around the courtyard.

'It's a magnificent place, isn't it?' he remarked. 'One of my favourite London haunts – almost my second home, in fact. Here and the museum's archives. .'

'I've never visited the archives,' said Freya wistfully. 'Are they open to the public?'

'Not usually,' replied Ralph. 'But I've been a volunteer for years and I can tell you the work on display here in the museum is just the tip of the iceberg. There's a vast trove of treasures in the archives. Miles of historic documents and artefacts in their thousands. You can stumble across some remarkable things like the interesting *lettre venimeuse* I found recently. Fascinating little gems.' He gave an enigmatic half-smile. 'Well, shall we look at yours now?'

Freya unzipped her handbag and brought out the miniature in its tissue paper wrapping. Placing it carefully between the plate of shortbread fingers and the dish of lemon slices, she sat back in her chair and sipped her tea while glancing surreptitiously at the compelling presence sitting opposite. Beards generally held little appeal for her. This wasn't the usual apology of a wispy goatee, however. It was a magnificently thick, black, curly beard which gave its owner a distinguished aura that was impossible to ignore.

Ralph stared at the package for a moment then, without picking it up, gently peeled back the tissue paper until the portrait revealed itself.

Freya heard a sharp intake of breath and glanced at his face. It registered a mix of emotions that changed as swiftly as an English sky in spring. Shock, surprise, endearment and sadness swept across it in quick succession.

Ralph drew a large, white, cotton handkerchief from his jacket pocket and wiped his hands fastidiously before picking up the miniature. It sat in the cupped palm of his capacious left hand like a gleaming jewel. Pulling a magnifying loop from his jacket's inside breast pocket with his other hand, he examined the miniature attentively.

'She's beautiful, don't you think?' he asked in a reverent tone.

'In an unconventional way,' replied Freya.

'Artistic, of course,' added Ralph. 'And strong-willed.'

Freya said nothing and took another sip of tea. How would he know that? Was he fantasising?

Ralph returned the loop to his pocket while still holding the miniature in his left hand. 'What is she to you?' he asked quietly. 'A family relation?'

'Perhaps,' replied Freya. 'I think it may have belonged to my grandmother, Olive Williams, but I need to look into it.'

Ralph dark eyes glittered. Then he carefully set the miniature down in its tissue-paper nest and kept his gaze fixed on the portrait.

'How much?' he suddenly asked without looking at Freya.

Freya felt caught off-guard. 'Oh, I haven't made up my mind yet,' she said, playing for time.

Ralph looked at her and grinned. Sharp white teeth gave him a wolfish appearance momentarily. 'Everything has its price,' he said in a tone as soft and smooth as cream.

A wave of irritation crossed Freya's face. Feeling under pressure, she said: 'I'm waiting for a valuation and then I'll decide.'

'Please do – it will be going to a good home,' said Ralph. 'I have a wonderful display cabinet in my study where it would hang beautifully. You could come and visit her whenever you want.'

Freya looked at him and then at the miniature, remaining silent.

'Think about it,' said Ralph in a silky voice. 'You can name your own price. I understand you may need a little time to consider what that might be. But at least let me take a quick photograph, won't you?' As he pulled a shiny, silver phone from his pocket, Freya caught a glimpse of an expensive vintage watch on his wrist.

'He's trying to show me how rich he is,' she thought sourly, unimpressed. She felt trapped though. It would seem churlish to refuse such a simple request.

'How will you use the photograph?' she asked. 'I don't want any pictures published online or in a newspaper or magazine.'

He looked startled. 'Just for my own pleasure. Good grief, I would never have photographs of anything valuable published in the press. Collectors don't advertise their cherished treasures to thieves.'

Freya relaxed slightly. 'Okay,' she agreed. 'Just one shot then.'

Ralph fiddled around, positioning the miniature so the sunlight caught the side of the case but not the glass. Then he clicked the phone, breathing heavily as he reviewed the picture on the screen.

'Perfect,' he said, snapping the phone off and replacing it in his pocket. 'She's absolutely perfect.'

Freya quickly wrapped the tissue paper around the miniature, put it back in her handbag and zipped it up. Something about Ralph taking the photograph made her feel uncomfortable and she suddenly had no wish to sit there any longer than politeness dictated.

'Now what can I do to express my thanks? Ah...I know.' From an inside top pocket Ralph pulled out a pen, scribbled a few lines on a business card and pushed it across to her.

As Freya picked up the card her animosity faded. He had taken a keen interest in her miniature – she was grateful for that – and it was flattering that he wanted to stay in contact. She peered at the printed inscription. The flowery, Italic type seemed at odds with Ralph Merrick's bulk and appearance. She noted an address in Chelsea then took in the words scrawled in a loose, Gothic script at the top of the card: 9pm Saturday.

'I hope you'll be able to join us,' said Ralph gravely. 'It's nothing special. Just one of my regular monthly salons.'

'Oh!' Freya dropped the card on the table in surprise. He

really did want to see her again and introduce her to his circle of friends. How astonishing.

'There's a theme – a dress code – which everyone usually finds quite amusing,' he added with a chuckle. 'If you come, you must be dressed as a Victorian.'

Freya's instinctive hesitation was momentary. It was a long time since she'd been to any parties and this sounded like fun. 'I'm not sure what I'm doing on Saturday,' she said, unwilling, as a matter of pride, to sound too eager to accept his unexpected invitation. 'I'll need to check my diary.'

'You do that, my dear.' Ralph stroked his beard between finger and thumb while giving her a long, thoughtful look. Then, tweaking an immaculate white cuff, he checked his watch. 'I must go,' he said, rising to his feet. 'Think about what I said. And I'll look forward to seeing you on Saturday.'

Freya remained seated as he moved off towards the courtyard door. The sun had dipped behind the buildings and the table was now in shadow. It felt chilly and she found her hand trembling as she picked up Ralph's business card. Apart from pressing her to sell the miniature he had behaved very courteously. And yet she felt uneasy. Perhaps she shouldn't have let him take a photograph of the portrait.

The thought nagged as she made her way out of the museum and waited at a bus-stop. Even as the bus lumbered slowly through the busy streets towards her home territory, she still felt unsettled. She had the distinct impression he knew more about the girl in her portrait than he'd let on. Should she accept his invitation to a party? It would be one way of finding out whether he knew more than he had said.

To distract herself Freya got off the bus at a small row of shops several stops before the one nearest her home. She walked past a hairdresser and a newsagent outside which sat a hunched figure half-wrapped in a sleeping bag. A hand-scrawled placard in his lap read: hungry and homeless. She was about to walk past when he raised his head in a listless manner and she realised how young he was. Ducking back into the newsagent, she bought a Kit-Kat and tossed it onto the grimy folds of his sleeping bag. It was a very small gesture, she thought, but better than giving money which would most likely be spent on drugs. It was shocking how many rough sleepers there were on London's streets these days. Almost Dickensian in some areas.

Then she went into a hardware store and bought a spare bulb for the task-light in her lock-up and a pack of batteries. Next to that was a shop selling vintage clothes and, as she passed, a dress in the window caught her eye. It had an ivory bodice with a white lacy trim and long, taffeta silk skirt. It made her think of the dress in her portrait miniature. On impulse, she went into the shop and asked if she could try it on.

A woman with dyed mauve hair eyed her closely. 'Looks like your size,' she said in a friendly manner. 'Give me a minute and I'll get it off the mannequin.'

'Is it Victorian?' asked Freya as she watched her unpin the dress.

'Nah, Seventies,' she replied. 'There was a big trend for Victoriana back then. High collars and fussy cuffs and great big sleeves.'

'But this neckline is quite low,' Freya pointed out.

'Yeah,' replied the shop assistant distractedly, slipping the dress onto a clothes-hanger and taking it into a makeshift changing-room.

Ten minutes later Freya drew back the curtain and emerged transformed.

'Oh, that looks lovely - it fits you really well,' exclaimed the shop assistant. 'Could've been made just for you.' She giggled. 'For your wedding-day.'

'Really? You think it was a wedding dress?' asked Freya, wriggling as she adjusted the bodice around her breasts.

The woman pouted, hedging her bets against the loss of a sale. 'Not exactly a bridal dress but you could wear it for a wedding if you wanted,' she replied. 'I mean, you can wear what you like for any occasion these days, can't you?'

Freya turned back to the mirror and admired her reflection, turning first to the right then to the left. Well, here was an outfit she could wear to a Victorian themed party, she thought. Reaching up to push her hair behind her head, she reflected that all she needed was a sprig of red flowers and a swathe of white lace in her hair and she'd be ready for a pre-nuptial painting.

Dropping her hands to smooth the taffeta silk over her hips, Freya was gripped by a mad idea. Oh, what fun! She would accept Ralph's invitation and go to the party dressed as the Victorian girl in her portrait miniature.

CHAPTER 3

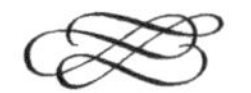

Freya hitched up her dress a little as she climbed a short flight of stone steps then paused in front of an arched, wooden door pocked with iron studs. Tilting her head back, she gazed up at the imposing façade – gleaming, white stucco to the second floor, pale London stock to the next storey, a crisp row of ornamental dentils below a plain parapet and above that the outline of a small tower rising into the night sky. It was the grandest house she had ever visited.

Shivering slightly, despite wearing a black, wool cape dug out from the depths of her wardrobe, she rang the bell. Her mouth felt dry. Smoothing back her hair, she practised a smile, but the door opened more quickly than anticipated and she found herself unwittingly grinning at the slight figure of a maid dressed in an old-fashioned, long-sleeved, black dress with starched, white cuffs.

'Good evening,' said the maid, surveying her with curiosity.

'Oh, good evening,' replied Freya. 'I've come for—'

She was cut off mid-flow. 'Please come in – there's a chilly wind tonight.' The maid closed the door behind Freya. 'May I take your coat?'

'Oh, yes – thank you,' replied Freya, untying her cape.

Folding it over one arm, the maid gave Freya a cool look. 'And your phone please. It's a house rule at our salons.'

Freya hesitated before reluctantly extracting the phone from her evening bag and handing it over. Then the maid spoke again. 'The gentlemen are in the study. Wait here please.' She vanished through a side door then reappeared without the cape and consulted a digital device on the hall table.

'What's your name?'

'Freya Wetherby.'

'This way please.'

Freya followed the monochrome figure along a thickly carpeted passage. It opened into a large octagonal space lit from high above. Tipping her head back, Freya gazed up at a soaring atrium cutting through three levels of the building's interior and culminating in an octagonal structure. This must be the quaint tower she'd seen rising from the roof while approaching the house. How cleverly its stained glass was illuminated by a concealed light-source even though it was completely dark outside. A starburst of ochre, gold and burnt sienna.

Lowering her eyes to take in her immediate surroundings, Freya gazed around at four arched doors set equidistant within the octagonal space. Lining the yellow walls between each door were tall glass vitrines filled with all kinds of objects – ornaments, boxes, vases, figurines. Three of the wooden doors were shut. From the fourth came a buzz of male voices, the chink of glasses and laughter.

Freya felt a fizz of nerves. Then she heard the maid making an announcement at the open doorway.

'Miss Emily Meadowcroft.'

'No, my name is—'. Freya broke off, realising it was too late to make the correction as every eye in the room was already fixed on her. The crowd became a blur of black and grey, swivelling heads, whiskered cheeks and undisguised stares as she moved forward. Gliding through the throng, a curious sense of well-being flooded through her, quashing her nerves. It was as if something inside her was waking up from a deep sleep.

Beyond the haze of figures, she glimpsed wood-panelled walls, tall bookcases and paintings with ornate, gilded frames. Cigar and cigarette fumes mingled with the piney fragrance of logs burning in a grate somewhere in the distance.

At the centre of the space was an octagonal, marble table bearing a gilded statue of a cherub. As she approached, she saw Ralph Merrick wearing a plum-coloured, velvet smoking jacket – a beacon of savoir-faire, beaming genially over the heads of many guests and clearly enjoying being the centre of attention. Striding towards her, he held out his arms in greeting. A powerful waft of mandarin enveloped Freya as he took her hand and pressed it to his mouth.

'My dear you look sensational,' he murmured. 'Your – erhm – ancestor would be very proud.'

Freya blinked with surprise. Did he really think the girl in her portrait miniature was her forebear? Could he detect a resemblance she'd failed to spot herself? Puzzled by his remark but flattered at his tacit acknowledgement of her efforts to emulate the portrait, Freya murmured: 'You're too kind.'

Ralph released her hand but kept his dark eyes fixed on her face. 'What a charming little necklace you're wearing,' he remarked. 'Enchanting.'

Freya fingered the delicate chain with its trio of gemstones. It was her favourite piece from the original *Freya* line. Unknown to Oliver, she'd kept it for sentimental reasons when the company went into liquidation. 'It's one of my own designs,' she said, feeling proud of her abilities and gratified that he – an art historian and collector – should admire it.

'My dear, how clever – you're clearly very talented,' said Ralph affably. 'Let me get you some champagne.' He strode away towards a maid carrying a tray of drinks where he hovered for a moment with his back to Freya then he returned to her side, handing her an oversized flute with an elegantly long stem. Freya raised the glass to her lips and drank greedily, enjoying the champagne's heady effervescence and her host's attentiveness.

'I'm so glad you were able to join us tonight,' said Ralph, his deep voice wrapping her in a warm embrace. 'I've been looking forward to introducing you to some of my other artistic friends.' He turned to a man on his left who was studying the cherub with a pained expression. 'Ned, I'd like you to meet Emily Meadowcroft.'

Turning back to Freya he said in a silky tone, 'Emily, please allow me to introduce Edward Burne-Jones.'

Freya's smile contracted. Why was Ralph calling her Emily Meadowcroft? That was just the maid's mistake in mixing her up with someone else. Was it just superficial politeness because he couldn't actually remember her name? And now – now he was introducing her to a man whose resemblance to the famous Victorian artist was shockingly uncanny. For a moment, the noisy, busy room seemed to spin on its axis then she blinked the giddiness away.

'How do you do?' she managed to stutter.

Stroking his pointed beard with long, slender fingers, the man regarded her with interest. 'Very well, thank you,' he replied with a flash of his fierce, dark eyes.

Freya gazed at the man's gaunt face, taking in his intelligent, domed forehead and hollow cheeks. The severe centre-parting in his hair emphasised his haggard appearance. He wore a long, dark, loose jacket over a black waistcoat, white shirt and narrow, grey trousers. He could, she thought, have stepped straight out of an archive photograph of Victorian artists. Her head swam with confusion. It was extraordinary, this likeness. Could he be a descendant of Edward Burne-Jones and went by the same name?

Clapping a hand on Burne-Jones' shoulder, Ralph spoke jovially to his friend. 'You've still got Gabriel's jewel of a painting in your living room, have you? I did admire it so much when I visited you last Christmas. Such depth of colour.'

'My little *Guinevere*? Oh, I would never part with that,' replied Burne-Jones. 'It reminds me of my early days in London watching him at work in his studio at Chatham Place. I'd like to find a companion piece if one ever comes up in the sale rooms.'

Ralph gave a mock grimace. 'All too rare, I'm afraid, but I'll let you know if I hear of anything,' he said in a courteous manner.

As their host moved off to talk to other guests, Burne-Jones spoke to Freya again. 'Tell me, have you known Ralph a long time?'

'Not very long,' she replied cautiously.

'Would this be your first visit to his house?' asked Burne-Jones gently.

'Yes, indeed,' replied Freya.

'You have a treat ahead of you,' he said, offering his arm to Freya. 'Allow me to show you a small contribution of my own.' Guiding her through the crush towards the rear of the room, he halted in front of a vast fireplace piled with smouldering logs.

Freya had never seen anything like it. Blue pillars on either side of the huge grate rose from a thick, mottled-pink, marble base stretching a third of the way across the wall. Vibrant tiles, elaborately decorated with zodiac signs, flanked each side of the grate. Running horizontally below the marble mantlepiece was a further row of tiles depicting heraldic beasts while a frieze of gilded, repoussé flowers twirled in parallel above them. Painted on the wall, as if standing on the mantlepiece itself, were lively medieval figures engaged in various pursuits from archery to hawking and hunting with dogs.

'Ralph kindly asked me to design the tiles,' said Freya's companion solemnly. 'It was not at all an easy task, but I think they met with his satisfaction.'

'You're too modest – they're wonderful,' said Freya. 'I love the colours – they're so rich, so glowing – and the animals look really alive as if they're about to jump out at us. Did you paint the frieze of figures on the wall as well?'

'That too,' replied Burne-Jones.

'What an inspired idea to paint medieval scenes – they're perfect for this setting,' said Freya. 'The whole fireplace looks as if King Henry could have spit-roasted a hog in it.'

'Thank you, you're very kind,' replied Burne-Jones. 'The medieval era is one to which I'm particularly drawn – brave knights and beautiful ladies, hawking-parties, feasts and all the pageantry of that golden age. It offers an artist a richer, more imaginative alternative to today's drab landscape of bureaucracy and banality from which I, at least, feel increasingly alienated.'

'You've certainly brought the past alive with these paintings,' said Freya warmly. So intoxicating was the impression of conversing with the famous artist that she barely questioned the illusion nor whether this party-guest had really wielded the brush that created these imaginative scenes.

Burne-Jones's eyes gleamed with amusement. 'I live inside

the pictures and look out at a world less real than they,' he said, smiling wryly.

'I find it intriguing to think of people like this as our ancestors,' remarked Freya, pausing to weigh past and present. 'Do you not feel any connection at all between those times and our own?' she asked. 'I like to think there is a thread that binds us down the ages.'

Burne-Jones gazed at her with haunted eyes while considering his response. 'In so much as the past bears the seeds of the future then perhaps that is the case,' he replied in a measured tone.

'What can we learn from medieval times?' asked Freya with genuine curiosity.

Again, Burne-Jones took a little time before giving a formal, almost academic answer. 'A lucid depiction of the historical past encourages us, I hope, to look with fresh eyes at the way our actions – both past and present – can shape our future,' he replied.

'But it needs an exceptional artist to breathe life into a medieval metaphor – to bring the dead back to life, so to speak,' said Freya heatedly, surprising herself with the force of her response.

'It certainly seems important to avoid creating a past that appears only obsolete and archaic to modern eyes,' said Burne-Jones, frowning as he spoke. 'That's why I sometimes include a recognisable portrait of a friend in a historic or mythic setting. It helps to dissolve the distance between a far-off age and our own.'

'I do admire good portraiture,' remarked Freya, thinking of her miniature. 'It must be so difficult to capture a true likeness.'

Burne-Jones looked at her intently. 'A physical likeness is easy to paint,' he replied. 'It's the inner life that takes time to convey.' Leaning closer to Freya's ear, he added, 'That's why I try to avoid society portraiture. I find painting my family and friends far more rewarding.'

'Will I recognise them in your recent work?' asked Freya.

'See who you can find in *The Golden Stairs*,' replied Burne-Jones, smiling mischievously.

'Oh, please give me a few clues,' replied Freya.

Burne-Jones gave her an arch look. 'You might find Gladstone's daughter, Mary, perhaps, and my daughter, Margaret.'

'Anyone else?' asked Freya in an encouraging voice.

'Laura Lyttelton, Frances Graham....' Burne-Jones broke off, chewing the tip of his long forefinger distractedly. 'And you? Do you paint and draw?'

'I design jewellery,' replied Freya, happy to fit so effortlessly within this artistic circle.

Burne-Jones's eyes gleamed. 'Then you must meet Topsy's daughter – my friend William Morris's daughter, May. I believe they are due to join us this evening. She has developed quite an interest in jewellery-making although stitching is really her tour de force. Her embroideries are exquisite.'

Freya blinked, feeling giddily disorientated. A Burne-Jones lookalike was one thing, but she was expecting Ralph's other guests would be – well, hard-nosed collectors like himself, or art dealers. Would May Morris be another Victorian deadringer? She swallowed as the paintings on the far wall tipped and then righted themselves. Still feeling dazed, she shook her head and the dark specks dancing in front of her eyes disappeared.

'Champagne, miss?' A maid held out a silver tray and Freya placed her empty glass on it and seized another sparkling crystal flute. Burne-Jones took one too, staring at Freya as if he could see straight through her.

He cleared his throat. 'Please don't think me disrespectful,

Miss Meadowcroft, but I wonder if you would do me the honour of sitting for me? I have a commission for which I require several strong, female profiles – young women with soulful, expressive features. I've already mentioned this to Topsy and May has kindly agreed to be one of my sitters.' He coughed, then added, 'It would please me greatly if you might consider my request.'

Before Freya had time to reply she found Ralph at her side. 'Now Ned – you can't monopolise Emily all evening,' he said in a sonorous voice crackling with petulance. 'There are others here who are keen to make her acquaintance.'

He crooked his arm and Freya reluctantly placed her hand on it. The soft, expensive velvet of his smoking jacket felt like a caress. She glanced at Burne-Jones. A look of resignation flickered across his face as he turned from them, disappointed.

'The trouble with Ned is that he becomes obsessional about things,' Ralph murmured as he steered Freya towards the centre of the room. 'I can't tell you how long he took to complete my commission. Absolutely fanatical. Wouldn't show me anything until he was totally satisfied with it.'

Freya was on the point of asking whether Ralph's friend really had created the fireplace tiles and medieval-style paintings or whether he was just enjoying the fun of impersonating a Victorian artist, but the words never left her mouth. The champagne had gone straight to her head. It was hard to think clearly and much less effort to let everything wash over her for now.

Ralph nodded and smiled at a dapper young man with a neatly trimmed moustache and beard who was fiddling with the pocket watch on his waistcoat chain as they approached. 'Good evening, GBS. Nice review in *The Times* last week. Queues all down the Strand for the opening night of *The*

Pirates of Penzance, I hear. I don't imagine you'll have much to say about it though, eh?'

Ralph pulled Freya closer as he propelled her forward. 'George Bernard Shaw,' he murmured in her ear. 'Takes himself a bit too seriously. That's why I tease him.'

'We should have dinner again soon, GBS,' he continued in the same cordial manner. 'If I can tear you away from your writing, of course. Now tell me, do you still have that fine Morris tapestry hanging in your house? It was so beautifully embroidered. Quite enchanting.'

Guiding Freya around a group of men in tailcoats, Ralph raised an arm to hail a newcomer helping himself to a glass of champagne. 'Ha! Back from your travels then, Louis?'

'Aye,' replied the man, glancing at Freya with bright, enquiring eyes. 'And married too. Now Fanny and I are searching for a place in the south to call home this summer. We like the look of Westbourne, but canna find a good house there.'

'Before we discuss that any further let me introduce you to Miss Emily Meadowcroft,' said Ralph. 'Emily, this is Robert Louis Stevenson. I'm sure you've read his wonderful stories in *Cornhill Magazine*.'

Gently raising Freya's hand in thin, attenuated fingers, Stevenson brushed it with the ghost of a kiss. She felt the tickle of his droopy moustache and long, floppy hair as a lock escaped from behind his ear and fell forward across his cheek.

'Delighted to meet you,' said Freya, taking in his appearance with interest. A wide, black cravat tied loosely at his neck softened the sharply cut, braided lapels on his dark-red, velvet jacket. He wore a thick, black sash around his slender waist with khaki trousers tucked into shiny, black ankle boots. Although extremely thin – possibly even ill, she thought –

there was an engaging vitality to his presence that she found highly appealing.

'Will you be you staying long in London?' asked Ralph.

'Och no, passing through,' replied Stevenson. 'We're meeting a publisher who—', he broke off coughing then dabbed his mouth with a white handkerchief. 'Excuse my vile body,' he said. 'I'm a mere complication of cough and bones since my illness in America.'

'Aha – busy writing another book about your travels?' asked Ralph, ignoring the coughing.

'Aye, with luck,' replied Stevenson. 'I've been advised to winter in Davos. Fanny and I will stay there until April with her son, Lloyd. Then who knows? My thoughts are turning to the South Seas and the islands in those warmer climes. Better than the Land of Counterpane for sure.'

Freya smiled at his expressive language. There was, she thought, a touch of the elfin about this delightful man. She could imagine him as a cheeky water-sprite or mischievous imp in some parallel existence.

Ralph turned to Freya. 'If you have not yet read *Travels with a Donkey in the Cevennes* you must, if only for the sake of the poor beast of burden, Modestine,' he said in a lofty manner.

'I shall make a point of reading everything Mr Stevenson writes,' said Freya animatedly.

Ralph glanced at her, frowning. With a light tap on Stevenson's shoulder, he placed a hand under Freya's elbow, steering her away from Stevenson and any further conversation about his literary intentions.

'Ralph, why do you keep calling me Emily Meadowcroft?' asked Freya, looking up at her host's face. 'Who is she?'

It was as if he hadn't heard her question amid the surrounding din of conversation. 'I'd like to show you something,' he said, guiding her towards a bookcase at the side of the room where the crush of guests was thinner. Running a finger along a row of slim volumes on a lower shelf, he pulled one out and Freya recognised the livery of an international auction house on its cover.

Ralph flicked through the glossy pages until he found what he wanted and pointed to a colour photograph. 'Isn't this an exquisite piece?' he said lightly. 'Such extremely high quality. Victorian, of course.'

Freya looked closely at the glittering necklace. He was right. It was a spectacular design. The gold chain had links not unlike her own but was fastened with an elaborate, heart-shaped clasp while its array of gemstones was breath-taking. Four glowing rubies in oval settings were interspersed with slim, pointed leaves made from beaten gold. A massive, intricately cut diamond winked from a leaf-shaped setting at the front. The dramatic contrast between the blood-red rubies and gleaming yellow gold gave it an enigmatic, almost mystical character.

She scanned the catalogue description which suggested the piece was inspired by funerary ornaments excavated from ancient tombs. It was thought to be designed by John Lockwood Kipling for his wife, Alice, the sister of Georgiana Burne-Jones and mother of the writer Rudyard Kipling. Spotting the price estimate – £450,000 to £550,000 – her eyebrows shot up. The next thing she heard was Ralph's deep voice close to her ear.

'A very close friend of mine is celebrating her seventieth birthday shortly and I intend to give her a significant piece of jewellery. My dear, given the talent displayed on your website, I'm wondering if you would make a copy of this for me?'

Freya stared at him, astonished. 'Really– are you serious?' she asked, wide-eyed.

Ralph nodded, unsmiling. 'Oh yes, absolutely serious,' he

replied in a low, persuasive voice. 'And the fee I would pay for this commission is serious too.' He paused for a moment then said very quietly, 'Shall we say £20,000?'

The colour drained from Freya's face as her mind went into overdrive. A sum that big would pay off her personal overdraft, cover her rent for months and allow her to invest in the materials she needed to re-start her business. It was too tempting an offer to refuse.

'Well?' Ralph enquired invitingly as the trace of a smile played at the corners of his lips. 'What do you think?'

'I'll do it,' replied Freya decisively. 'How long do I have?'

Ralph's dark eyes glinted. 'I'm planning to hold another salon at the end of the month. Could you bring it with you?'

Two weeks. It was a tight deadline, but she would work around the clock if necessary.

'Yes, that will be fine,' said Freya with more confidence than she felt. Taking a deep breath, she forced herself to crush her doubts. He clearly thought she had the expertise to carry this off. Now all she needed to do was convince herself.

Instinctively, her business acumen kicked in. 'Would you confirm the commission in writing, please? You'll have to pay the stone dealer directly and I'll let you have the prices once I know how much the stones and the gold will cost. I'll need to keep this photograph as a reference, of course.'

'By all means,' replied Ralph smoothly, his eyes scanning the guests behind her as he spoke.

Feeling elated, Freya carefully tore out the page, folded it up and tucked it into her satin evening bag. She closed the catalogue and handed it back to Ralph, noticing a sale date from the previous year on its cover. He slipped it into place on the bookshelf then turned and took Freya's arm, steering her back into the noisy throng.

As they moved deeper into the room, passing animated

groups of guests, it seemed to Freya as if their brief conversation about the necklace commission had been a transitory illusion – some kind of dreamlike glimpse into an unknown future – and now they were returning to reality. The present moment felt bewitchingly honeyed and she was happy to lose herself in Ralph's milieu.

It was overly warm in the study. Freya caught the sweet scent of sweat on her host's skin, despite the mandarin oil, when they paused alongside a trio of women.

'Ah-ha, my favourite septuagenarian,' Ralph said coyly to a tall, slender, grey-haired woman.

'My birthday is a little way off,' she protested, smiling. 'I trust the invitation is still on your mantlepiece?'

Ralph gave a half-bow. 'I wouldn't miss your party for the world, Eleanor,' he said ingratiatingly. 'And I hope it will be one that is recorded for posterity in your yet-to-be-completed memoir.'

Eleanor laughed then turned away as another woman started talking to her. Feeling pressure on her forearm, Freya glanced up at Ralph's face as he murmured into her ear, 'She's a remarkably canny collector of important jewellery and the future recipient of my very special gift.'

Hearing this, Freya studied Eleanor's attire more closely. She was elegantly dressed in a russet-coloured silk gown with a high, frilled collar around which hung a heavy rope of jet beads. Several rings with large, bright stones adorned her slim fingers. Freya instinctively knew the commissioned necklace would be appreciated and prized. She felt a rush of warmth towards Ralph and was on the point of thanking him when she heard his next remark.

'She wishes she were fifty years younger, of course, and looked less like a horse,' he murmured.

Freya gave a little gasp. It seemed such a cruel thing to say, especially about a friend; but before she could reply the maid appeared at the door, ushering in a tall, dark-haired, young man. In the buzz of voices around them Freya failed to catch the maid's announcement. 'Who is that?' she asked Ralph.

Ignoring her question, Ralph removed his hand from Freya's arm and strode forward to greet the newcomer. Freya followed for a moment then halted, hovering a few steps away as she watched the men shake hands. Ralph's head bent closer as he said something to the newcomer. She couldn't hear his remark although the reply came loudly enough through a pause in the surrounding chatter. 'Lawrence, you say?'

Ralph gave a quick nod and patted the man on his shoulder as he continued speaking. Freya strained to hearing what they were saying as short bursts of conversation punctured the general hubbub like static on a vintage radio – 'among papers in the archive…', 'for his diploma show…', 'letter to the principal…', 'moral conscience perhaps…', 'utter betrayal…', 'take it where you like next time…'.

Then Ralph turned and smiled at Freya, beckoning her to join them. 'Emily my dear, here's your brother Lawrence – late as usual,' he said.

Freya moved slowly towards them as if in a dream. What did he mean? She had no brothers or sisters. Was this man another Victorian impersonator? Could this be what Ralph's salon was all about – some sort of giant game of charades? If so, then she would play along. It might seem churlish to do otherwise and inadvisable given the generosity of his extraordinary jewellery commission.

Lawrence looked youthful and lively. Unlike many of the men in the room he was clean-shaven and wore his hair long, curling over the top of his yellow silk cravat. His crimson waistcoat was finely embroidered with gold thread while a cutaway jacket matched the French grey of his narrow trousers. Freya warmed to him, feeling he had taken as much trouble over his appearance as she had with hers.

He moved towards her and took both her hands. His grasp felt dry and warm. 'Emily,' he said in a low, pleasant voice. 'You're looking perfectly splendid tonight.'

'The same could be said for you, except if I did, it would go straight to your head,' replied Freya, her flirtatious tone catching her by surprise. Her voice sounded strange to her ears, as if coming from another person.

'Don't tease me,' said Lawrence. 'You know mother says that's unfeminine.'

'Then she must endure my masculine ways – at least until I come of age,' replied Freya. Her own voice and yet not her own.

'And then you can do and say whatever you please,' said Lawrence with a touch of sarcasm.

'I shall always do that – you'll see.' A quiver of excitement ran down Freya's spine. It was a very long time since she had felt so strong, so powerful. A maid passed by, and she placed her empty flute on the tray and seized another. Lawrence also took a glass and raised it to his lips, smiling at Freya.

Ralph had moved away during this exchange, although Freya saw him looking at them over the shoulder of another guest. She felt glad he wasn't party to their private conversation.

'Who's here tonight?' asked Lawrence, glancing around the crowded room.

'Robert Louis Stevenson, George Bernard Shaw – or GBS as Ralph calls him – and Edward Burne-Jones,' replied Freya. 'He's standing over there by the fireplace.I was rather flattered – he wants me to sit for him,' she added grandly.

Lawrence chuckled. 'Of course he does. There's no need to worry though – that Zambaco affair is past history. He's very much a family man these days. He and his wife, Georgie, spend a lot of time with the Morrises and their daughters.'

'They're coming tonight as well,' said Freya, feeling pleased to have some information to offer.

Lawrence looked thoughtful. 'Oh good, I want to talk to May about her time at the National Art Training School. I'm finding the design course harder than I expected.' He narrowed his eyes. 'Look – there's Jack. I didn't know he knew Ralph.'

'Who is Jack?' asked Freya, trying to follow the direction of his gaze and failing. There were far more men in the room than women and it was difficult to see which one he had spotted.

'He's on my course,' replied Lawrence. 'Never does any work, though. Come with me and I'll introduce you.'

Lawrence proffered his arm. Freya happily slipped her hand through its crook, noticing embroidery on his shirt-cuff as his jacket-sleeve rucked up. A bit of a dandy, she thought with amusement. How were they described in Victorian days? A boulevardier – was that it? A flaneur?

Lawrence appeared to know several guests, nodding, smiling and exchanging a few words as they made their way through the crush. At one point he murmured in Freya's ear: 'Look to your left.'

Freya saw a middle-aged woman wearing a forest-green silk dress with long, ruched sleeves talking to an elderly, grey-haired man with side-whiskers. Her hair, pulled back severely from her face, accentuated a long nose and worn features. She was peering up at the man from under droopy eyelids, yet the tilt of her sharp chin made Freya think she could be assertively strong-willed. The pair were deep in conversation and ignored the maid who passed by with a tray of drinks as if she was a ghost.

'Who are they?' Freya whispered.

'Christina Rossetti – you know, the one who wrote the poem "Goblin Market" – and I think she's talking to John Ruskin. Let's not get involved. It's a bit too highbrow for me.'

Lawrence steered Freya around a group of fat, red-faced men chatting loudly about the general election. As they passed, Freya heard the phrase 'Midlothian campaign' mentioned twice, which seemed to provoke one man into a fury.

'Jack?' Lawrence tapped the shoulder of a fair-haired young man wearing a long, loose blue shirt that looked like an artist's smock. His face broke into a crooked smile as he spun round. Before he could speak Lawrence quickly muttered something in his ear.

The grin grew broader. 'Lawrence – well, well,' he said knowingly.

'Let me introduce my sister, Emily,' said Lawrence solemnly as he untwined Freya's arm and cupped one hand under her elbow, propelling her forward. 'Emily, this is Jack Hunter, artist manqué and occasional designer.'

'Ah, the belle of the ball,' said Jack, bowing slightly. 'Delighted to make your acquaintance.' Taking Freya's hand, he raised it to his lips while his mischievous cat's eyes swept over her face.

Freya was aware of her pupils dilating involuntarily and felt a sinking sensation in her stomach. He was, she thought helplessly, the most attractive man she had ever met.

CHAPTER 4

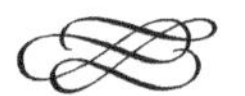

'I see you dressed for the occasion,' teased Lawrence, raising an eyebrow in mock outrage at his friend's attire.

Jack let slip Freya's hand and glanced down at his smock as if surprised to find it there. 'I couldn't forgo the chance of meeting your lovely sister, so I rushed here straight from my studio,' he said disarmingly. 'Besides, it looks as though Ralph's laid on the arty types thick as pie tonight. I don't feel out of place.'

'I wasn't aware you knew him,' said Lawrence, glancing over at Ralph, who was chatting with a group of men in black tailcoats in front of the fireplace.

'Everyone who's anyone knows Ralph,' replied Jack gnomically. He turned to Freya. 'You haven't attended one of Ralph's salons before, have you? Your brother has clearly been hiding you in a box.' He glanced at his friend. 'You're a wicked man, Lawrence.'

Lawrence grinned. 'Not half as wicked as you. Tell Emily about that prank in the junior common room.'

'I need refuelling first,' replied Jack, looking around for a drink. Spotting a maid near the cherub statue, he strolled over and plucked a glass from her tray. On returning he squeezed between Lawrence and Freya, forcing his friend to step aside. As he downed a long draught of champagne his sea-green eyes flashed teasingly from one to the other then he addressed Freya directly. All the while the corners of his impish eyes crinkled with amusement.

'It was a dark and stormy night,' he intoned in a low, theatrical voice, 'and the students at the National Art Training School in South Kensington rose up and started a rebellion. It was a worthy cause – a call-to-arms against the dim and dusty dungeon their professors call the junior common room. For too long they endured this unsavoury pit without a murmur. Now they decided to take matters into their own hands. Conscious of their status as designers-in-waiting, they set about transforming the room into a magical, dream-like space straight out of a medieval bestiary.'

Pausing to drink more wine, Jack's eyes flicked lazily around the room then returned to Freya's as he continued his story.

'These intrepid students took up their brushes and palettes to begin their creative mission, painting the walls with here a lion and there a bear. And then they painted and painted until every inch was covered with animals – leopards, tigers, deer, elephants, zebra, even a unicorn. All night they painted. It was a heroic performance.'

Freya – who hadn't taken her eyes off Jack's face while he was speaking – was aware of Lawrence shaking with silent laughter on her other side.

Jack's voice grew more emphatic as he piled on the theatrics. 'This glorious work was greatly enhanced by the faces of the creatures which bore an uncanny resemblance to some of the professors at the school of art. It could so easily have been a triumph of skill and artistry, but the Fates intervened, and tragedy struck.'

Here he lowered his voice and adopted an anguished tone. 'Sadly, these highly creative and well-intentioned students were all designers – not artists. They had never studied the art of painting frescoes and failed to use the correct materials. Before the paint had even dried the wonderful wall-paintings they created just disappeared. Into thin air. When other students ventured into the room the following day all they found was an unholy mess of peeling paint and bleeding colours that bore no resemblance to the vision of beauty and imagination that spurred the scheme.'

'Oh!' Freya began laughing as she pictured the scene.

'Worse still,' Jack continued in a tone of mock despair, 'the president of the JCR not only insisted that the perpetrators cleaned and scrubbed all the walls, but fined and gated them for the rest of term.' He drained his glass, adding casually, 'not that we minded too much about that.'

'You were fools even to attempt it,' said Lawrence, still chuckling. 'Brave fools, though. That place needs a shake-up.'

'What we should have done, of course, was to have it photographed before it all disappeared,' said Jack plaintively. 'Frankly, that's the future as far as I can see.'

'What? Photography displacing painting? I don't see that happening,' said Lawrence.

Jack turned to Freya with a sly grin. 'What is your opinion, Miss Meadowcroft?' he asked coyly, cocking his head to one side.

Freya considered her response for a moment then said earnestly: 'Photography will have its own place in the artistic pantheon, but I don't think it will ever displace painting.' Again, she experienced the strange sensation that her reply was spoken by another person. Pantheon? It wasn't a word she generally used in conversation.

Undaunted, she carried on. 'There's something fundamental about the physical activity of painting – the way a thought, an idea flows from the head or heart to the hand, and on to board or canvas or paper. Photography is different – the subject is already there in front of the photographer.'

Jack tutted dismissively. 'So is a still life. The artist merely expresses what is right in front of his eyes.'

Freya frowned, determined to stick to her point. 'All the emotion – the interpretation – belongs to the artist though,' she said firmly. 'That isn't the case with photography. You must admit that.'

A look of irritation flashed across Jack's face then disappeared as it creased into a crooked smile. 'Perhaps – but I still think photography will put a lot of artists out of business. Who, I wonder, will want their portrait painted when a photographer can perfectly reproduce an exact likeness?'

'People who want a flattering result?' suggested Lawrence with a cynical grin.

'Or a charming keepsake that can be passed down the generations without fading or decaying,' added Freya, thinking of her own portrait miniature.

'It sounds as if you've signed your soul away to the Aesthetes,' said Jack, twisting the conversation onto new ground.

'I see no reason why beauty should not be valued for its own sake,' replied Freya.

Jack's eyes glittered insolently. 'You favour a sensual response?'

Freya felt the colour rush to her face and remained silent.

'Do you prefer sensuality to an uplifting moral, or a fine story told in paint?' Jack persisted.

'Oh, do stop teasing,' said Lawrence roughly. 'Can't you see you're embarrassing her?'

'Oh – am I?' replied Jack, affecting innocence. He seized Freya's hand and put it to his lips. 'Please forgive me. I intended no such thing.' Raising his head from her hand, he looked deep into Freya's eyes. 'Let me make amends by showing you some objects whose beauty really can be valued for its own sake. Come with me.'

He hooked an arm through Freya's and before she could reply she found herself tugged through the crowd. Glancing over her shoulder at Lawrence, she felt reassured to see him smiling back at her. They're good friends – not rivals, she thought.

Jack paused at the doorway, placed their empty glasses on a tray and picked up two more flutes of champagne before leaving the study. Then they moved into the octagonal hall where Jack stopped in front of one of the vitrines. Pointing to a small stained-glass panel propped on a lower shelf, he said, 'Here's a thing of beauty.'

Freya stepped forward to examine the piece more closely. The panel was shaped like a cloud and divided by a wavy lead-line into two sections. The upper part was a clear bright blue – the crisp blue of an English summer sky – while the lower half was a deep shade of sea-green. A country scene of fields and trees, etched lightly in black, filled the top section. Below it lay a faint outline of a prone figure lying head-down on folded arms. It was hard to say if it was a woman or a man.

'She's dreaming,' Freya murmured, acutely aware of Jack's presence at her side. She straightened up, looked at him directly and thought she glimpsed sadness in his face. He moved away from the vitrine towards the door next to it, pausing with his hand on the handle to look back at her.

'Are you sure we can go in there?' asked Freya with an uncertain little smile.

Jack ignored her query and opened the door. It creaked a little and he closed it behind them as soon as Freya was inside. She found herself in a small sitting room with walnut panelling. Above the dado rail the walls were lavishly painted with figures from mythology – Venus and Adonis, Zeus and Apollo. Lustrous golden stars studded the midnight-blue ceiling, and the floor was tiled in a colourful, radial pattern of zodiac signs. Freya felt dazed as her eyes darted from one corner to another, her head swimming from the champagne.

Either side of the tiled fireplace stood tall vitrines. Jack moved towards the left-hand case and Freya followed as if magnetised. A collection of delicate porcelain, gilded and elaborately painted with botanical motifs, filled the glass shelves. 'Oh, look at this tiny teapot – how enchanting,' she exclaimed.

'You wouldn't think a man as big as Ralph would find pleasure in such dainty objects, would you?' said Jack sardonically, moving past her to the other display-case.

This vitrine was entirely devoted to silver animals. Some objects, like the penguin-shaped cocktail shaker, were functional. Others seemed purely decorative – tiny spiders, leaping gazelles, furry-looking bears. A silver monkey hung from the top shelf by its arm. A hand-mirror with a serpent-like handle, positioned on its side, reflected Freya's flushed face as she bent to inspect it.

'Oh!' she cried, spotting a ladybird whose tiny wings were hammered into a perfect representation of the insect. 'I could never make anything as charming as this.'

She straightened up, stepped back and bumped into Jack who was standing directly behind her. Wrapping his arms around her waist, he bent his head, placing it against her cheek. She could feel the thud of his pulse beating in his throat. As he gently kissed her neck, she leaned her head back further and gazed at the ceiling where the painted stars seemed to shift and collide.

Jack was first to hear the door creak. He sprang away from Freya and was already standing alongside the vitrine as their host entered the room.

'Admiring my collections, eh?' said Ralph with an edge to his voice. 'You'll miss out on supper. It's in the dining room.'

'Jack was just showing me your beautiful collection of porcelain and silver,' said Freya with the quick response of an intruder caught in a beam of torchlight. 'I've never seen such exquisite work.'

Ralph's tone mellowed. 'My dear, these are mere trinkets. My important collections are upstairs. I will personally show them to you, if you wish, but not tonight. My esteemed guests take priority this evening.'

Taking the hint, Jack moved towards the doorway. Ralph stood aside to let him pass but grabbed Freya's arm as she followed. He kicked the door shut with his shiny black shoe, still holding Freya's arm. As his grip tightened, a shard of fear jabbed her stomach.

'Now don't get any fancy ideas about Jack,' he murmured into her ear, so close that she felt his breath stir her hair. 'He paints well but he's lazy and lacks the discipline to become a serious artist or designer.'

'I wasn't—'

Ralph brushed aside her protestation. 'Your brother's the one to watch. He's very dedicated, very talented – and so, I sense, are you.' An idea seemed to pop into his head, and he loosened his grip on Freya's arm. 'Perhaps you could both help Jack. Pull him back on the straight and narrow, as it were. You know he's likely to be expelled from the art school for skipping classes and failing to complete his projects?'

'Oh, no!' exclaimed Freya. The words came out before she realised what she was saying. She took a gulp of air, wondering why she felt shocked. Surely this story about Jack was just part of the evening's curious charade. Yet on some strange level she felt personally involved. Flailing around mentally, trying to separate the play-acting from reality, felt like pulling filings from a magnet. Her brain was clogged and foggy. It must be all that champagne.

'You should talk to Lawrence. See if you can come up with a plan to help him. After all, he's your brother's closest friend.'

Ralph placed a hand firmly under Freya's elbow and pushed her out of the room. The octagonal space ahead was now teeming with guests as they surged out of the study, through the hall and down a short corridor to the dining room.

Freya glided along in a daze. The grand, double doors were wide-open when they reached the dining room and she felt dazzled by the interior's exuberant decoration. Pompeiian red walls, contrasting with moss green paintwork above the gilded dado rails, were lit by crystal sconces. Red velvet curtains concealed tall windows along one side of the room while monumental blue-and-white porcelain urns, luxuriant with ferns, stood each side of the drapes.

A cage of stuffed birds with bright plumage enlivened one corner of the room; another was occupied by a vitrine displaying pastel-coloured birds' eggs.

In the centre of this opulent space stood a massive, oval table above which hung a vast chandelier with elaborately branching arms and thousands of crystal drops. Its glittering light danced and glimmered across the bronzed ceiling, giving Freya the impression of standing inside a lustrous jewellery box. Laid out on the table was a great spread of dishes arrayed on huge, silver platters from which guests were liberally serving themselves.

'Service *à la française*,' said Ralph, propelling Freya forwards. 'Do help yourself. I must return to the study and make sure everyone knows supper awaits them.'

Freya squeezed through the throng and reached the table. Ralph had certainly provided an impressive spread for his guests and paid meticulous attention to its presentation. In front of each dish was a small card bearing its name in Gothic script. French pigeon pie. Chicken fricassee with rice. Roast pork with stuffing. Curried fish. She dodged around a line of guests to the far end of the table and found the puddings. Fancy cake. Lemon posset. Vanilla ice-cream. Meringues with mottoes. She looked at the latter twice, thinking she had read the card incorrectly.

A maid handed her a plate and she served herself a meringue and a piece of cake. Wondering where to eat, she made her way out of the dining room and down the passage to the octagonal hall. Here she discovered that all the doors were now wide open. In each room she could see guests, some sitting, some standing to eat their supper. Maids were circulating with trays of claret and Freya grabbed a glass as she returned to the study, hoping to find Lawrence there.

He was leaning against a bookcase, forking up fricassee and chatting to a woman in a greyish-blue velvet dress whose long sleeves were fringed by white lace cuffs. Freya noticed the material was exceptionally good quality and the style – loosely tied at the waist – gave her considerably more freedom of movement than some of the stiff gowns, skirts puffed out by petticoats, on show that night.

Thick, light-brown hair, drawn softly away from her face, tumbled loosely behind her shoulders. It framed strong features and direct, blue eyes that conveyed confidence and intelligence. She seemed, Freya thought, very much her own woman.

'Ah, Emily,' said Lawrence, waving his fork in the air. 'Let me introduce you to May Morris. May – this is my sister, Emily.'

With a plate in one hand and a glass in the other, Freya was unable to shake hands and bobbed unintentionally. Feeling awkward, she nodded at Lawrence and smiled guardedly at May wondering whether, in reality, the grey-blue velvet cloaked an art dealer or learned academic and how she could find out.

'Good evening, Emily,' said May, eyeing Freya's dress. 'That's a beautiful gown you're wearing. The lace-work is very fine indeed.'

'Thank you,' replied Freya. She glanced at Lawrence who, finishing his fricassee, deposited the plate on the lip of the bookcase next to him.

'Shall I hold your glass while you enjoy your meringue?' he suggested in a kind voice. 'Are you not eating a main course?'

'I'm not very hungry,' replied Freya, gratefully handing Lawrence her glass of claret and regaining a sense of composure.

'What a pleasure to meet you,' said May. 'Lawrence and I were talking about the merits of attending the National Art Training School. Are you thinking of enrolling too?'

'I was considering the possibility, but my brother is finding the work rather daunting,' replied Freya, recalling what Lawrence had said earlier in the evening. 'Have you taken the same course as Lawrence?'

'I specialised in embroidery, although we studied many other aspects of design and were constantly drawing, drawing, drawing,' replied May. 'The part I enjoyed the most was studying medieval embroidery – opus anglicanum, or English work, as it's called. I'm hoping I may be of some help to my father who runs the embroidery department of his business from our home.'

'Your mother and aunt are excellent stitchers too,' said Lawrence.

'Does the business only employ family members?' asked Freya, seeking to test May's authenticity. She could remember reading somewhere that Morris had run his company like a cottage industry and wanted to judge the plausibility of her response.

'No, my father also employs out-workers, but all the pieces are hand-stitched with the work supervised by my mother and aunt Bessie,' replied May.

'Your mother – Jane?' asked Freya, still hoping to catch her out.

May glared at her apparent stupidity. 'Yes, we are all completely committed to hand craftwork – no machines are used in any part of the process.'

Her reply sounded perfectly credible to Freya's ears. It was her own response that astounded her. 'It is in the combination of designing and hand-making, I believe, that one can derive the greatest satisfaction,' she said, bewildered at how such a remark could tumble so readily from her mouth.

May's eyes burned as if lit by a fire. 'Exactly so,' she agreed vehemently. 'To create an original design from your own ideas then execute it meticulously to perfection – that's beyond riches.'

Jolted by her passionate response, Freya suddenly remembered Ralph's admonition concerning Jack. She turned to Lawrence. 'Ralph thinks we could help Jack,' she said, more abruptly than intended.

Lawrence looked at her with an expression of cool amusement. 'To work harder towards the examinations?' He shrugged. 'I'm not sure anything we could say would have any effect. Jack is a law unto himself.'

As if he had heard his name mentioned, Jack extracted himself from a knot of guests and strolled towards them holding a glass of claret in each hand. 'Ralph seems to have equipped us with his smallest glasses tonight so I'm doubling up,' he said thickly.

The remark was misjudged. His voice sounded slurred to Freya, and she felt the colour rise in her cheeks. Lawrence raised an eyebrow and turned to May. 'Excuse this ruffian. Please let me guide you to fresh fields and pastures new.'

He gave Freya's glass back to her then offered May his arm. She didn't take it but walked in step with Lawrence as he moved away.

Jack cocked his head and looked at Freya. 'Something I said? Or is Miss fire-and-ice-cool Morris just a hell of a lot more interesting than a college failure?'

'No, Jack, it's just—'

'Just what?' he challenged, his sea-green cat's eyes turning stormy.

Freya returned his stare without faltering although her stomach gave a lurch. Even when he was acting like a fool, he was still impossibly handsome.

Holding Jack's gaze seemed to break a spell. 'You haven't eaten your meringue,' he remarked in a friendlier manner. 'Don't you want to break it open and read your motto?'

'You break it for me,' said Freya, taking a sip of claret.

Jack picked up the meringue and snapped it in half. Sugary pieces broke off and crumbled across the plate revealing a small strip of paper inside. He picked it up, read it, then shrugged and put it back on the plate.

'What does it say?' asked Freya.

'Just nonsense.'

'Tell me.'

Jack picked up the strip reluctantly and read in a flat voice: '*Cherchez la femme.*'

'What?' Freya looked as startled as she felt.

'Like I said, it's nonsense,' said Jack dismissively. 'Ralph loves teasing his guests. Don't think any more about it.' He paused and glanced towards the door. 'Look, I've had enough of this party. I think I might slip away if you don't mind. Believe it or not, I've got a project to hand in this week that I haven't even started work on yet. I need to get going.'

'Oh,' said Freya limply, wondering how she could detain him then discarding the idea as it was clear he was in no mood to stay.

Jack gave a charming, crooked smile as he made a half-bow. 'I will see you at Ralph's next salon, I hope. He holds them regularly, you know.'

Freya stood watching his back as he dodged awkwardly through the crowd. On reaching the doorway he turned briefly and blew her a kiss. Then his blue smock vanished from view.

Without Jack, the party seemed to lose its lustre. Making her way back to the octagonal hall, Freya saw Ralph chatting with some men in black tailcoats. More penguins, she thought cynically. Catching sight of her, he broke away from the circle and moved towards her.

'I've come to say goodbye and thank you for a wonderful party,' said Freya politely.

'My dear, I'm so glad you were able to come,' he replied, giving her hand a crushing squeeze. 'I very much hope you will join us for the next salon and bring the – er – item we discussed. As you can see, your presence is highly prized.'

Freya took a deep breath. 'I'd like to do that,' she replied, thinking of Jack.

Their exchange was cut short by one of the men in tail-coats tapping Ralph vigorously on the shoulder. 'Excuse me,' he said, briefly kissing Freya's hand then letting it fall as he turned back to his circle of friends.

Hoping to find a cloakroom, Freya walked along the passage to the hall where the maid had taken her cape on arrival. Seeing a small group of women standing near a closed door, she decided not to wait with them and doubled back into the octagonal space. Keeping close to the wall she evaded Ralph who remained enmeshed in the penguin circle and swiftly mounted some wooden stairs adjacent to the corridor leading to the dining room.

The walnut staircase curved upwards, levelling out at a minstrel's gallery running around the octagonal atrium at first-floor level. All the doors around this space were shut. Freya could see no obvious sign of a bathroom and carried on climbing the stairs to the next level. The layout here echoed the floor below and, again, all the doors were shut. This was the top floor. Surely, she would find bedrooms and bathrooms behind the closed doors.

Turning the knob of the first door on her right, Freya glanced inside. It was a small bedroom, beautifully furnished in pinks and greens, but not what she wanted. She tried the next door. Drawn by the rosy glow of shaded oil lamps, she stepped inside the room. On the far side she could make out a dressing room and, next to that, another door. She crossed the space in front of an enormous double bed, opened the door and stepped into a white, marble bathroom smelling strongly of mandarin oil. She realised these must be Ralph's quarters.

Sitting on the lavatory, Freya gazed at an oval, egg-pod bathtub the size of a small plunge-pool. Scared of being caught here, she hurriedly dipped her hands under the basin tap and softly closed the door as she left the bathroom.

Tiptoeing across the thick, creamy carpet, she glanced at the huge bed with its golden velvet cover and elaborately worked, metal headboard. The rosy lamplight picked out cherubs and angels in the headboard's tableau and glinted on the gilded frame of a painting hanging above it on the wall. She paused for a moment. Unable to see it properly she moved nearer, inching along the side of the bed to get a better view.

The painting showed a young girl with thick, golden tresses, high cheekbones and a sharp chin. Greeny-blue eyes stared out directly from the painting, challenging the viewer. Freya recognised her instantly.

With a cold knot coiling in her stomach, she seized an oil lamp and held it close to the foot of the frame. It bore no title. Yet it was, without doubt, the same girl as the one in her portrait miniature. Tilting the lamp to the lower right-hand side of the picture, she stood on tiptoes looking for the artist's signature. A shiver ran between her shoulder-blades as she made out the scrawling letters.

Jack Hunter.

What the hell was this doing in Ralph Merrick's bedroom?

Shocked and now even more terrified of being caught trespassing, Freya rammed the lamp down on the bedside table and hurried back the way she had come. Reaching the top of the stairs at first-floor level, she paused to breathe deeply and wait for her pounding heart to subside before descending.

Standing there, clasping the stitched-leather handrail, Freya felt baffled and dazed. It was like a fairground hall of mirrors. Posing as the alluring girl in her portrait miniature, she had been introduced as someone she had never heard of to handsome Jack Hunter at a mock-Victorian party and now she had stumbled on a real painting of the girl signed by the real Jack. How was that possible?

With clammy beads of sweat trickling down her back, it

wasn't until she was out in the cool night air, wrapping her cape closely around her body and stumbling towards the night bus-stop, phone in hand, that the distorted reflections of the mirrors settled into register. Even so, it took an effort of will to remind herself that she was Freya Wetherby and the Jack Hunter she had met at the party was as much an imperson-ation as her fanciful re-incarnation of the girl they all called Emily Meadowcroft.

CHAPTER 5

A sliver of light streaming through a gap in the curtains roused Freya the next morning. For a moment she barely knew where she was. Her head pounded with a dull throb and her mouth felt dry as dust. Drinking champagne – even a large quantity – wouldn't usually affect her so badly. Why had the alcohol hit her so hard?

She lay with her eyes closed, her mind buzzing. Jangling images in hyper-real colours flooded her mind: Ralph looking fat and prosperous in his plum-coloured smoking jacket. May Morris, confident and assured in grey-blue velvet. Burne-Jones, fixing her with his piercingly intense gaze and asking permission to paint her. Irresistible Jack Hunter, with his sly cat's eyes and teasing smile, mocking the salon's dress-code in a blue artist's smock.

How had she got home? Oh yes, a night-bus. What time did she reach her flat? Around 1am. Go back to sleep, she told herself. But it was useless. She was wide-awake and desperately thirsty. Then she remembered her dream.

There – wearing the same dress with the ivory bodice,

walking with Jack Hunter in a country field on a bright, golden day. She feels happy and elated. There's a river. He leans down to the water and catches something floating past. It's a meringue. He breaks it in half and pulls out a strip of paper. In a flat voice he reads: *Justice for Emily*. He drops the paper as if it has scorched his hands. Caught by a breeze, it flutters up into the sky. Higher and higher. She bends her head right back and watches it rise above the trees. When she looks round Jack has vanished. A wave of disappointment engulfs her.

Freya's memory screeched to a halt. How peculiar, she thought. That wasn't the wording on the motto Jack read out at the party. She could remember it clearly. *Cherchez la femme*: *look for the woman.* Feeling bewildered and hung-over, she slid out of bed, wrapped herself in a dressing-gown and padded into the kitchen. Taking a mug of tea back to bed she propped herself against her pillows, sipping slowly while mentally replaying the dream. Its sharp, filmic quality felt just as real as anything she'd experienced at the party.

The puzzling dream-motto nagged at her though. What was her unconscious mind trying to tell her? The motto's meaning seemed just as obscure as the message extracted from her meringue the previous night. If anything, the meringue-motto was easier to grasp. *Look for the woman* … it was one of those French phrases with a hidden implication. How did it go? The source of a man's problem was likely to be traced to a woman. Wasn't it also a cliché in detective fiction? A mystery could be solved if you found the woman involved. As Freya reflected on this her fingers trembled and tea spilled on the pillow.

Mopping it up with a tissue, Freya's thoughts wandered into Ralph's bedroom. How grand and comfortable it seemed compared with her own small room. How lavishly he had furnished his home. Yet why was a painting of the Victorian girl in her portrait miniature hanging above his bed? Ralph hadn't said he recognised the girl when shown the miniature at the V&A, but he must have known it was the same person. Another thought struck like a punch in the gut. Had Ralph got someone to paint a copy of the photograph he took of the miniature? Was that possible? But why? None of it made any sense.

Feeling baffled, she cast her mind back to the phone conversation with her client, Rowena Vere. She had hinted that Ralph was somewhat eccentric, but presumably she'd never been invited to one of his extraordinary salons or she would surely have mentioned it.

Eccentric was hardly an exact description. Larger than life, yes. Obsessive, yes. Possibly even on the spectrum. And what about the friends who flocked to his salon last night? It certainly wasn't the same as attending a fancy-dress party. It had felt way more extreme than that. Not only had the guests dressed as eminent Victorians but wholeheartedly adopted their personae too. Were they all complicit in Ralph's fantasy re-enactments just for the sake of a good night out? Or was there more to it than that?

With her headache subsiding, Freya pulled on a pair of jeans and a baggy green sweater and went into the kitchen. Popping a slice of bread in the toaster, she switched on her phone and sent a text to Brooke. She couldn't wait to discuss the salon with her in person.

The toast popped up and Freya swathed it generously with honey. Receiving Brooke's prompt reply brought her sharply back to the here-and-now. It was reassuring to know there was someone she could talk to about the party. Someone she could trust.

Taking a bite of toast, she felt an unexpected twinge of

wistfulness. Posing as the girl in the portrait had made her feel clever, popular, talented – qualities she believed she possessed before she was thrown completely off-kilter by the debacle with Oliver and her mother's death. Now she was back inside Freya Wetherby's skin – but which did she really prefer?

One thing was for sure. She wanted to see Jack Hunter again. Badly. Her stomach fluttered as she brought his face to mind. Then she thought about the striking portrait in Ralph's bedroom. Even though she'd only studied it for a few moments, the girl's powerful hold over Jack – or at least his Victorian counterpart – sang out from the painting. An undeniable magnetism between artist and subject was evident – and, oh, how she envied her for that.

Recalling the soft press of Jack's mouth on her neck provoked a frisson of desire. She wanted more.

She popped a teabag into her mug. What was the key to unlocking his affections? Would it intrigue him if she morphed into the portrait girl as persuasively as Ralph's guests had absorbed the characteristics of other Victorians? Once she'd captured his interest it would be easy to tempt him further. But it would take more than simply wearing a similar silk dress and red flowers in her hair. She needed to inhabit the girl's identity completely.

A splatter of rain on the window startled her and she glanced out to see grey thunder clouds blotting the sky as her thoughts ran on. It was duplicitous, of course, but even if love was coaxed by sleight of hand, what harm was there in that? Ralph would be delighted if their romance blossomed at his salons, wouldn't he? He was, after all, responsible for bringing them together.

Yes, that was it. She would find out everything she could about the girl they called Emily Meadowcroft and slip – oh so subtly – under her skin.

Freya carried the mug of tea into the living room, opened her laptop and typed 'Emily Meadowcroft' into the search engine. Results popped up instantly. Jane Emily Meadowcroft topped the list but the links to Facebook, Pinterest and Instagram indicated she was most certainly alive. Well, that was no good. The portrait girl would have died about 150 years ago.

Scrolling further down the page, Freya halted abruptly at a link to an ancestry website. Ah! Could this be it? *Emily Meadowcroft, born February 1863.* She clicked through to the site itself then exhaled with disappointment as she read the two-line entry:

Emily Meadowcroft, born Chippenham, Wiltshire, to William Meadowcroft and Lillian Archer, February 1863. Died unmarried.

Was that all? Oh, how frustrating. Could these few lines just be a teaser to encourage users to pay for full membership of the site?

Frowning, she read the entry again. *Died unmarried.* Really? Surely the portrait miniature had been painted as a wedding gift.

How much more would she discover if she signed up to the website's genealogy community? She read through the joining information but there was no way of knowing if anything else would be revealed by paying the monthly subscription. In any case, she was under so much financial pressure right now that she was hesitant to commit to any further regular expense.

She would look for Jack Hunter on a free search engine instead. Typing in his name brought up several sites linked to an American movie series. Scrolling past the advertisements for boxsets and videos, she discovered that Jack Hunter was also a footballer, a medical practitioner and a television producer. And these were just the ones listed on the first page. Imagine how many Jack Hunters she would find on an ancestry website. It would take hours of research to track him down.

Impatiently, she moved on to the next page of Jack Hunters. Right at the top was a link to the Fife Gallery in Mayfair. Clicking through to the gallery's own website brought up an exhibition of Victorian art held two years earlier.

'*Wild Women* is a remarkable celebration of society portraits by lesser-known Victorian artists,' read the banner quote from the gallery's owner, Alasdair Fife. She scrolled down the page and – oh joy! – half-way along was a portrait sub-titled 'Lady Christabel Manners by Jack Hunter'. It had been on sale in the exhibition for £15,500.

Freya examined the portrait closely. The laptop's back-lit screen gave the painting a glowing depth. Lady Christabel was wearing a flaming orange gown with a garland of white flowers in her hair. She was sitting on a stone bench with a book in her hand looking coyly up at the artist from beneath heavy-lidded eyes. She was hardly a great beauty, Freya thought, but just as striking as the girl in her miniature. Perhaps the magic created by Jack's sensitive brushwork had brought commissions for this kind of work to the door of his studio.

Freya leaned back in her chair, temporarily satisfied. He really was a Victorian artist, even if a very minor one. Well, she would carry on with her research into Jack Hunter and his career another time. Right now, she was still on the hunt for Emily. And Lawrence. Why not try him as well?

She quickly typed 'Lawrence and Emily Meadowcroft' into the search engine. To her amazement up popped an auctioneer's website. She clicked on the link. A magnificent, gabled house with grey stone walls covered in Virginia creeper filled her screen. A banner headline read: 'Marchbank Slater to offer Meadowcroft Family House and Contents.'

Freya gaped at the image. Then she scrolled slowly down to the introductory text. 'This splendid six-bedroom mansion goes under the hammer at our Chippenham sale-room next Tuesday. The early Victorian house, set in four acres of gardens, has remained in the same family for more than 180 years. Most of its contents, including paintings, silver, furniture and objets d'art, will be included in the auction with viewing taking place the previous day.'

'The auction of property comprises objects which illustrate the family's passion for collecting. Highlights include: Two George II carved mahogany armchairs, circa 1755; *Love's Messenger* oil on panel by Lawrence Alma-Tadema (1836-1912); four carved cork 'Grand Tour' souvenirs, Naples, second quarter 19th century; a gold-mounted tortoiseshell snuff box from the Great Exhibition of 1851; ceramic lustreware sunflower vase by William de Morgan, circa 1880; an Edwardian silver cocktail shaker in the form of a penguin from Asprey. Two silver brooches, circa 1880, made by the owner's cousin are also included in the sale.'

'For more details and images of the property and contents please download the full particulars here.'

Freya sat back in her chair and ran a hand through her hair. The sale had taken place two years ago. Did that mean some of Emily's descendants were still alive? If she contacted the auction-house handling the sale perhaps they would put her in touch with the seller. Or not. Frowning, she recalled one of clients saying how unhelpful auctioneers could be about such matters. A trill from her phone interrupted her thoughts.

ICY SPITS PRICKED Freya's face as she made her way along Albemarle Street while yellowy-grey clouds threatened more sleet to come.. As if in tune with the weather, barbs of guilt and anxiety pecked away at her conscience too. She ought to be in her lock-up starting work on the necklace Ralph commissioned but Liz Russell's call had intervened. The opportunity to discover more about the portrait girl was too tempting to postpone and she set off for Mayfair within the hour. She'd sensed an unmistakable fizz of excitement in Liz's voice that couldn't be ignored. Why, though, had Liz insisted she came in person to the gallery rather than just talking on the phone?

Bracing herself for another chilly encounter with Boyd & Hart's receptionist, Freya pushed open the gallery's weighty, glass door. Today the blonde ice-maiden was wearing a flimsy scarlet top revealing upper arms that had clearly been put through their paces at the gym. Weather-inappropriate, Freya thought sourly.

'I've got an appointment with Liz Russell,' she said, glancing down at the receptionist's fingernails. There was something perverse about painting them mauve. It made her fingers look as if they belonged to a corpse.

'I'll see if she's free,' replied the blonde unsmilingly as she clamped a mobile phone to her ear. No trace of recognition crossed her features. Perhaps she's an avatar, thought Freya. A figment of some computer's imagination.

'You can go up to her office now – use those stairs.' The receptionist's eyes flicked towards the white staircase then dipped to a laptop where they remained fixed.

Freya hesitated when she reached Liz Russell's office. The door was ajar and she could see Liz sitting at her desk wearing a navy trouser suit, a pale blue top and a necklace of whimsically oversized pearls. With her glossy bob of coppery hair she appeared more glamorous than Freya remembered from their last encounter. It made her feel dishevelled and shabby in her jeans and boots. She knocked gently on the door and Liz looked up and smiled. Despite the surrounding clutter of books and files there was a crisp efficiency about her appearance and manner than Freya found reassuring.

'I've got some good news for you.' Liz gestured to a chair by her desk and Freya sat down without taking her eyes off her face.

'I now have a very good idea who painted your young lady,' she continued then paused as an actor would for dramatic effect. 'Does the name Annie Dixon mean anything to you?'

Freya shook her head. 'I've never heard of her.'

'She was a very talented artist who forged a highly successful career painting royal portrait miniatures for Queen Victoria,' said Liz authoritatively.

Freya leaned forward. 'Really? A royal portrait-painter? Are you sure?'

Liz sat back in her chair and put the tips of her fingers together. Her nails, cut short and square, were polished but unpainted. 'Yes, she received her first royal commission from Queen Victoria in 1859 and went on to paint at least a dozen portraits of royal children – the Queen's own and other branches of the royal family.'

'How on earth did she get that gig?' asked Freya.

'A stroke of luck,' replied Liz. 'I don't think she studied art in any formal way, but she did receive instruction from Magdalena Dalton – the sister of the renowned Victorian artist, Sir William Ross.'

Freya frowned. None of these names meant anything to her. 'Where does he fit into the picture?' she asked.

'Ross was employed by Queen Victoria to paint each of her many children when they reached the age of about four or five,' replied Liz. 'He began work on a series of circular portrait miniatures around 1845 but soon after painting Prince Leopold in 1857 he was struck down by a paralytic stroke from which he never recovered sufficiently to carry on with the commission. It was his sister, Magdalena, who suggested Annie Dixon might continue the work successfully because she recognized her remarkable talent for painting children.'

'Goodness,' said Freya. 'She must have been thrilled with that recommendation. It would throw the door wide-open to work for royalty.'

'There was another thing in her favour,' continued Liz. 'At that time Dixon wasn't particularly well-known in artistic circles, so her fees were very low.'

'Ha!' exclaimed Freya. 'Was Queen Victoria a bit of a cheapskate then?'

Liz grinned. 'Let's say she recognized good value when she saw it. Anyway, she had enough confidence in Dixon's abilities to ask her to complete the set of royal children after giving her an initial commission to paint a portrait miniature of Princess Blanche d'Orleans at Claremont House in 1859. After that Annie was the Queen's go-to girl for miniatures of the royal children and a number of other commissions including young royal cousins and the children of aristocratic friends.'

'But the girl in my portrait isn't a child,' said Freya.

'Dixon also painted girls in their late teens and early twenties, especially if marriage was on the horizon.'

'I still don't understand what makes you think she painted mine,' said Freya. 'My ancestors certainly don't have any royal connections.'

'That's where a good eye comes in,' replied Liz breezily. 'It's also the reason why I asked you to come into the gallery today.' She got up to heave an enormous book onto her desk from a stack on the floor. 'I've been sent an early review copy of this new survey of historical English portraiture and thought you'd like to see some of the miniatures Dixon painted.'

She opened the hefty tome at a page marked by yellow post-it notes. Freya stood up and leaned over it, eagerly scouring the photographs and glancing briefly at the descriptions.

'Once I started my research I remembered the warm flesh tones in your portrait and particularly the fine colouring on the forehead,' said Liz. 'Dixon was an arch-mistress of that kind of work. Of course, your portrait doesn't have the gilded background you can see in several of these illustrations, but the colouring and clarity of approach all indicate to me that she is the artist.'

Freya poured over the pages Liz had marked, lapping up the portraits of men, women and children. Most were solo representations but occasionally two children or babies featured together. Liz was right. In terms of colouring and style there were distinct echoes of the portrait in her possession.

Eventually she sat down, screwing up her eyes as the sun emerged from behind a cloud and a sudden burst of bright sunshine flooded through the window behind Liz's desk. 'Can you tell me a bit about Annie Dixon?' she asked. 'How did she start off?'

'In life?'

Freya nodded.

'I made some notes somewhere. Let's see if I can find them.' Liz opened a desk drawer and pulled out a small pad. Flicking through the pages, she eventually found the place and read out loud: 'Dixon was born in 1817. She was the eldest daughter of seven children – two sons and five daughters – and her father was a Lincolnshire corn chandler. The family lived in Horncastle, although Dixon's work took her all around the country. She died in 1901, having lived to the ripe old age of 83, and is buried in Horncastle cemetery.'

She snapped the notebook shut and balanced it on top of a pile of folders on her desk. 'Not a lot to go on, I know, but her early life isn't well-documented. I did find out that she was certainly painting with watercolours by the middle of the century and completed several portraits of local gentry in Horncastle.'

'Horncastle? That's Lincolnshire,' mused Freya. 'I don't know if we ever had any relations living there.'

'She seems to have travelled around a fair bit,' said Liz. 'She worked in Hull and on the Isle of Wight, of course, at Osborne House. She also visited Sandringham to paint the royal portraits. And London. She seems to have spent a lot of time here.'

'Painting the aristocracy?' suggested Freya.

'Indeed. Countesses. Duchesses. Earls. That sort of thing.'

Freya giggled. 'Perhaps I've got blue-blooded ancestry I never knew about...' She tailed off as she saw Liz checking her watch.

'I'm sorry – I've got another meeting in five minutes,' she said, pulling a face. 'With our financial department.'

Freya stood up hesitantly, feeling reluctant to leave Liz Russell's primrose office. It felt like a cocooning sanctuary despite the clutter.

Liz rose too. 'Well, that gives you a bit of a steer, hopefully,' she said with a bright, professional smile. 'And if you do decide to sell your portrait miniature we would, of course, be delighted to help.'

MID-AFTERNOON, Freya made her way to Chelsea. Heading through the automatic barriers at the underground station, she saw a bunch of uniformed police officers milling around the entrance.

'What's going on?' she murmured to a lanky man in a yellow hi-vis waistcoat who she took to be one of the station staff.

'Oh, they've been responding to an earlier incident,' he replied with a shrug.

'Mugging?'

'Yeah. They got the little buggers though and no one was hurt.'

'Thank goodness for that.'

The man shrugged again. 'Happens all the time now.'

Freya walked out of the station and turned down a side-street, all the while aware of the stark contrast between the extravagance of Ralph Merrick's party and the pitiful desperation that drove the capital's muggings. Scratch its busy, commercial surface and contemporary London really wasn't so far removed from its Victorian equivalent, she thought.

Despite everything that had happened – her mother's death, losing her business, Oliver's betrayal – Freya counted herself lucky. There were plenty of others living in the capital who were far less fortunate than herself – tenants living in ill-maintained accommodation, immigrants facing prejudice, single mothers struggling to make ends meet. Begging, crime and rough sleeping persisted as they had in Victorian times. True, there were more state and charitable safety-nets for those experiencing poverty than in the past but was life really so different today for some people than in the 19th century?

Entering a tiny Italian café, she found the lunch-hour rush was long gone. Two elderly ladies occupying a window-table were the only customers apart from Brooke, who was sitting alone at the back of the narrow space studying messages on her phone. She raised her head when Freya sat down, although it took a moment to finish her mouthful.

'Mmm. Best macaroons in town,' she murmured, appreciatively, licking her lips.

Freya smiled. After her unsettling experience the previous evening at Ralph's salon, seeing Brooke felt like a refreshing dip in a pool.

'You have to get what you want from the counter,' said Brooke with a nod towards the trays of cakes and biscuits glistening in a glass cabinet opposite their table.

Freya got up to inspect an oozing chocolate cake, tiny lemon biscuits and slices of panettone but returned to the table with only a cup of tea. Her stomach still felt slightly queasy.

'Well—?' queried Brooke, raising her eyebrows.

'It was extraordinary,' said Freya. 'Everyone was behaving as if they were someone else. I met Edward Burne-Jones, Robert Louis Stevenson and George Bernard Shaw. Oh, and William's Morris's daughter, May. John Ruskin was also there talking to Christina Rossetti. Most of the guests were artists or writers.'

'Blimey – how bizarre!' said Brooke, her hand halting halfway to her mouth. 'A whole history book of eminent Victorians. You must have felt as if you were in some parallel universe. What about Ralph? Who was he impersonating?'

Freya sipped some tea. 'He was himself. I mean, he didn't behave as if he had just stepped out of the history books. He acted like the perfect host.'

'Hmm.' Brooke continued chewing.

'He was like a sociable Master of Ceremonies, whirling me around and introducing me to everyone.' Freya paused as scenes from the evening rolled through her mind like a slideshow. 'It was very odd, though. He kept introducing me as Emily Meadowcroft and when I asked why he just ignored my question. I didn't want to spoil things because he was being so charming and as everyone was pretending to be someone else, I just played along with it.'

'The other strange thing is that he seems to think I'm related to the girl in my portrait miniature. He referred to her as my ancestor and since he seems to be so knowledgeable about the Victorian era I'm wondering if he's right.'

'Is that her name – your portrait girl?' asked Brooke, swallowing the remainder of her mouthful.

'Maybe – I don't know for sure,' replied Freya. 'I've started doing some online research but haven't got very far. Anyway, given that all the other guests assumed the names of Victorian characters, it might have just been a pseudonym that Ralph assigned to me for the evening.'

'When are you going to let me set eyes on her?'

'Tomorrow? After you've finished work?'

Brooke nodded, licking a macaroon crumb off her finger. 'Any riffraff or low-life at the party? Or just the Victorian crème de crème?'

'A couple of art students, one of whom turns out to be Emily Meadowcroft's brother, Lawrence.'

'Ah! Does he look like his sister?'

'No,' replied Freya. 'But he was stylishly dressed and rather charming. We chatted for a bit and then he introduced me to his friend, Jack Hunter. They're both studying at the National Art Training School. Except Jack never does any work apparently.'

Freya blushed, feeling Brooke's eyes searching her face for unspoken information.

'Good-looking? Jack, I mean,' asked Brooke slyly.

Freya felt her colour deepen. 'Very,' she admitted. 'But he's trouble, I suspect.'

'Oh, yes?' It wasn't so much a question as an instruction to continue speaking.

'I think he's a bit wild,' said Freya. 'And fond of a drink or two. At least, that's the impression I got last night. Lawrence told me he's in danger of being expelled from school.'

Brooke started laughing. 'You're talking as if these people really exist.'

Freya was silent for a moment, frowning. 'I know they don't – at least not as the characters they were impersonating last night. But when I was talking to them at the salon they seemed as real as you or me sitting here right now.' She shrugged. 'Maybe the atmosphere in Ralph's house had something to do with it, I don't know.'

'Or the free-flowing booze?' suggested Brooke. 'You sound a bit dazed by what was going on. Are you sure no one slipped something into your drink?'

Freya ignored her jibe. 'You know, just before I left the oddest thing happened. After I said goodbye to Ralph I wanted to go for a pee. There was a queue for the hall cloakroom, so I nipped upstairs to look for a bathroom. I went to the *en suite* in Ralph's bedroom and as I was about to leave, I noticed a painting hanging above his bed.' Freya paused, an anxious expression pinching her face. 'It was a larger version of the girl in my portrait miniature.'

'What?' Brooke looked as shocked as she sounded. 'Are you sure?'

Freya nodded. 'What's even more mystifying is that it was signed by Jack Hunter – Lawrence Meadowcroft's friend. The chap I'd just met downstairs.'

Brooke narrowed her eyes. 'That's interesting,' she said quietly.

'I was wondering if Ralph got the painting copied from the photograph he took of my miniature – but it didn't look quite the same and, in any case, it was miles bigger.'

'Would you recognise it again?' asked Brooke.

'I only saw it in dim light but I'd know that face anywhere now,' replied Freya.

'I wonder if there's more to this guy, Ralph, than meets the eye,' said Brooke with a cool edge to her voice.

They stared at each other across the table without speaking. Then Freya broke the silence. 'Oh Brooke, I don't know.' She shivered. 'I enjoyed the party at the time but now I can't help feeling it was – well – weird, really. I mean who goes around dressing up in a Victorian outfit, pretending to be some fancy figure from the past?'

An amused look crossed Brooke's face. 'Well, you did, for a start,' she said. 'Are you having regrets about masquerading as Emily Meadowcroft? It sounds as if you rather enjoyed the experience.'

'I did,' admitted Freya, smiling. 'It really took me out of myself and in some strange way made me feel closer to the girl in my portrait. I felt as if I was talking to the sort of people she mixed with – artists, writers, students. I know it sounds strange but I'm sure there's some sort of connection between us. I want to find out if we really are related.'

'Have you been able to remember anything your mother said about the miniature?' asked Brooke.

Freya shook her head. 'No, I'm pretty sure she never mentioned it to me.'

Brooke frowned. 'Could it have something to do with your father's side of the family?'

'Probably not,' replied Freya, pausing as she recalled the shock of her father's death when she was nine. 'Both his parents were teachers. I can't imagine they had any artistic or aristocratic connections.'

Brooke was silent for a moment, frowning as she fiddled with a silver ring on her index finger. Then she asked abruptly: 'Will you contact Ralph again?'

Freya's hand flew to her neck. 'Oh goodness, I haven't told you the best bit about last night,' she spluttered. 'Ralph asked me to make a necklace as a birthday gift for one of his friends. He wants a replica of an amazing design he spotted in an auction catalogue and he's going to pay serious money for it. Enough for me to get my business up and running again.'

'Wow – that's fantastic!' said Brooke. 'That should set you back on your feet.'

'With any luck,' agreed Freya. 'It's going to be quite a challenge though. He wants me to have it ready in time for his next salon.' She pulled a face. 'I should be working on it right now.'

Brooke raised an eyebrow. 'So, I assume Emily will be taking centre-stage at another soiree then?'

'Don't tease,' replied Freya tartly. 'You'd feel just as fascinated by the whole scene if you'd been there. All those eminent people, their clothes, the conversations. It was wonderful – like stepping into the Great Exhibition and meeting all the movers and shakers of the day.'

'I can see exactly why you're getting drawn in,' said Brooke. Then, lowering her voice, she added in a solicitous manner, 'Just be careful.'

Freya stared at her, alarmed. 'What do you mean?'

'Ralph's an unknown quantity, isn't he?' replied Brooke. 'Okay, he's rich and erudite and, no doubt, well-connected socially. but you don't know much about him yet, do you? Just be on your guard.'

Freya fell silent as an image of Ralph in his velvet smoking jacket played in her mind. He seemed every inch the benign art collector – wealthy, knowledgeable and steeped in his chosen era. He certainly had his idiosyncrasies, but Freya could hardly think he was dangerous. She couldn't imagine him being anything other than deeply eccentric yet affable and generous too.

'You might also bear in mind that you are, in fact, Freya – not Emily,' continued Brooke, grinning at her friend. Leaning across the table, her curtain of dark hair falling across her cheek, she added softly, 'It's best to live in the present, rather than the past, you know.'

CHAPTER 6

Waking at 6am, Freya resolved to spend the morning at her makeshift studio in the storage lockup, determined to start work on Ralph's commission. It would be the first piece of jewellery she had tackled for months and even though it would be a copy – not one of her own original designs – she relished the challenge.

Locating her hand-tools in a box at the back of the lock-up felt like meeting up with old friends. Dusting them off with a rag and laying them out on a small table boosted her sense of purpose. She would need to get a butane gas canister from a builder's merchant for her hand-torch but as soon as the jeweller's workbench she'd ordered online arrived she could really get going.

Two weeks. That was all she had to pull this off. If she failed to complete the commission on time – or worse, if Ralph considered the result unsuccessful – then what? The fear that he might refuse to pay the promised fee filled her with dread. It would mean she'd never have a chance to re-start her business. The bank had refused to extend her personal overdraft and every time she used her credit card, even to buy groceries, she felt physically sick.

Taking a deep breath, Freya braced herself to put in calls to trade suppliers in Hatton Garden. It had been months since she'd spoken to them. Would they remember who she was? Even if they did, would they trust her sufficiently to do business with her again?

With a knot of anxiety tightening in her stomach, her first call was to a bullion dealer she'd dealt with for many years. Yes, he remembered her. Yes, he had heard her company ran into trouble. No, he wasn't going to abandon her when she most needed him.

Tears of relief pricked Freya's eyes when he agreed to let her buy the sheets of gold and jump rings she needed on a month's credit. As soon as she ended the call, she emailed Ralph and asked him to settle the invoice immediately.

Next, she booked an appointment to visit a well-established stone dealer with an in-house lapidary where high-quality gems could be cut to her specifications. She'd often bought gems there in the past and knew from experience they would be both ethically sourced and the finest available. She was determined to make this necklace look even more stunning than the original Victorian one.

As her spirits rose, Freya thought about the future. It would take time to re-establish her business. She knew all too well that clients had short memories, but she could think of at least two who might be interested in buying a decorative piece in silver. Its malleable qualities and seductive shimmer had always entranced her, and the cost of purchasing sheet silver, jump links and silver wire would be relatively low, unlike Ralph's high-cost commission. Once she'd received his fee she could start buying materials and get her business going again.

Picking up a pencil, Freya began sketching shapes on a

small pad. Taking the beaten gold leaves of the Victorian necklace as a starting point, she elongated the lines and distorted them into curls and spirals. Then she re-drew the curlicues separately, filling in the empty space at their centres with sunflowers and the eyes of peacock feathers.

As she worked up the details, the shapes grew more engaging, taking on a free-flowing, art nouveau quality. Underneath the peacock's eye she idly wrote 'Choker for a Lady' then sat back, slightly surprised, as she realised that it did indeed resemble the kind of fancy pendant a young Victorian girl might have worn on a ribbon around her neck. Then she thought: why not? Why not create a small collection of Victorian-inspired jewellery intricately worked in silver? She would show it to a couple of former clients and see if they liked it. Who knows? It could be just the antidote needed to challenge the modern obsession with starkly minimal jewellery.

While she refined the embryonic designs, Freya found her thoughts returning once more to the miniature. Time and again she'd asked herself why she was so fascinated by the portrait. Perhaps the root of her obsession lay in what she imagined the girl's personality to be like – her qualities and attributes. She looked such a strong character. There was a clear streak of independence shining through those piercing eyes, and yet she also seemed to possess an innate charm and resilience.

Courage, Freya decided. That was the touchstone. The portrait girl appeared to have the capacity to push her life forward and take the consequences – unlike herself. How different they seemed in that respect.

Setting down her pencil, she stared unseeingly into the mews through a gap left between the doors to let in some air. The comparison was shaming. She'd been devastated by the collapse of her business – it was such a public humiliation, especially when Oliver had then gone cap in hand to his father. And she'd felt painfully crushed by her mother's death even though it was expected. It was as if a candle had been snuffed out, leaving behind a slurry of wax and a wisp of smoke.

Grief visited at unexpected moments. She would walk past window-boxes outside a house and find herself blinking back tears as she remembered her mother standing, trowel in hand, in her cottage garden. Or she'd spot a dress in a shop identical to the shade of fuchsia her mother loved and feel a hollow cavern of emptiness opening up inside her. Whoever talked of death's sting had described it accurately. It was like a raw, open wound that no amount of balm seemed to heal.

Coming hard on the heels of these two crises, Oliver's personal treachery had been the last straw. She hated him intensely for managing to profit from her own failure. To find such a paper-thin divide between love and loathing had come as a shocking revelation. It made her fear for her mental well-being. There had been times when she could barely get out of bed in the morning after dreaming about him and even mundane tasks like going to the supermarket induced panic attacks.

If only she had the portrait girl's resilience, her courage. Perhaps that was why the miniature meant so much to her. It was a kind of lucky talisman that might ward off further misfortune and disaster.

While her thoughts dipped and circled like birds in flight, Freya's persistence paid off. By late morning she had completed detailed drawings for three new jewellery designs and sat back, examining them forensically. An intricate, peacock's eye motif gave the compact little earring a delicate complexity. The sunflower embellishment on the ring looked a bit droopy but would, perhaps, spring to life when the piece was made in silver.

The pendant – well, that was the design that most delighted her. It would be tricky to make but she had managed to create the impression of a second pendant hanging within a larger one. This displayed a tiny head with flowing hair that looked both alluring and mysterious. Freya decided its sex should be ambivalent. She would let the wearer decide which way it went.

Pleased with her efforts, she checked her phone for missed calls and found one from the solicitor handling the probate on her mother's estate. A stack of paperwork had arrived in the post which she hadn't looked at yet and he was no doubt chasing her about that. Before she rang him, though, she wanted to speak to the estate agent about her mother's cottage.

Once the grant of probate came through and she could register the property in her name, she was planning to sell it. Was that the right thing to do though? The solicitor had explained there would be a capital gains tax liability so perhaps she should keep the cottage and let it out instead. That would cover the rent on her flat and allow her to stay in London indefinitely. She dialled the estate agent's number.

'Mr Roberts? It's Freya Wetherby. I was wondering if anyone has been to look at the cottage yet?'

There was a pause at the other end of the line. 'We've had no viewings since you gave me your instructions to test the market.'

Freya felt disappointed, more on her mother's behalf than her own. 'And what about later this week?' she asked.

The estate agent cleared his throat. 'No viewings booked in for this week or next, Miss Wetherby.'

'Oh.' Freya could feel her throat tightening with anxiety.

'I'm wondering if it might be better to take it off the market and rent it out?'

'You'd need to upgrade it first,' replied Mr Roberts bluntly. 'Tenants expect very high standards these days.'

'A lick of paint?' suggested Freya hopefully.

'More than that. I'd advise a complete refurbishment,' intoned the smooth, professional voice at the other end of the line.

Freya felt stung by his words, as if he had insulted her mother to her face.

'It needs, erm, significant modernisation,' Mr Roberts continued. 'The bathroom and kitchen particularly.'

'I can't afford that!' Freya heard her voice wobble as she spoke.

'Well, in that case the rent would need to be – realistic, shall we say?'

Freya took a deep breath. 'You mean it's not even worth considering trying to rent it out?'

Another pause. 'We could try,' said Mr Roberts, sounding dubious. 'Look, why don't you think it over and call me again in a few days' time?'

Freya ended the call feeling frustrated and indignant. I could go and live there myself, she thought wildly. But she knew it was unlikely she would make the break from London. The crowded, capital city had been a reassuringly constant thread in her life since completing her training in Birmingham. Unpicking it now, after all she'd been through, would completely unravel her.

Locking up the storage unit, Freya found herself picturing her mother standing in the cottage kitchen and her head buzzed with unshed tears. The thought of returning to a solitary sandwich at her flat was suddenly unbearable. She needed a distraction. Casting around for an idea, something Liz

Russell said came to mind and instead of going home she set off towards the underground.

THE NATIONAL PORTRAIT Gallery's revolving glass door churned incessantly as a stream of visitors flooded into its grand interior. Students clutching sketchbooks, a snaking group of Japanese tourists and several elderly couples with walking-sticks all made their way inside as Freya hovered outside the entrance waiting for a gap in the crowds.

Nerves fluttered in her stomach like pigeons flapping around the fountains in nearby Trafalgar Square. She felt edgy and uncertain without knowing why. Glancing down at the mosaic threshold, she could make out the pink initials NPG wrought in its small grey tesserae. That seemed quaint. A throwback to a previous, more confident era. As she raised her eyes, the lion and unicorn sculpted above the entrance seemed to confirm this thought.

A blast of chilled air hit Freya as she slipped through the revolving door, walked past a couple of uniformed gallery attendants and up a shallow flight of stone steps. Pausing by a lift, she studied a wall-guide to the collections then set off up another flight of steps to find the Victorians. On a landing at the top of the stairs she spotted an information table with an open laptop. Surely this would tell her where to look. She sat down and typed 'Annie Dixon' into the search box. Ah-ha, she thought, as the result popped up. Her hunch was paying off.

Freya rose to her feet and turned right then left into a long, narrow space with a lofty ceiling. Huge, gilt-framed portraits – mainly male – hung all the way along the left-hand wall opposite a run of glass-topped cabinets containing small, numbered portraits. About half-way along the gallery space, she stopped abruptly in front of one of these display-cases.

Scanning the little portraits of bearded gentlemen beneath the glass cover, her eye was drawn to the lower right-hand corner where a tiny watercolour, no more than three inches wide, was displayed. A label next to it read 'Annie Dixon by Louisa Anne Beresford, Marchioness of Waterford'. It also gave a date: '12 October 1887'. Here she is, Freya thought triumphantly – the artist who had painted her portrait miniature all those years ago.

A tingle of excitement ran down her spine. Despite the chilly air-conditioning, her hands felt sticky, and she wiped them on her jeans. Bending closer, her nose almost touched the glass cover. The sitter – who looked at least in her sixties – wore small, round spectacles and had her hair tied in a bun. She was wearing a black dress with a white frill at the collar and appeared to be sitting at a table, studying a large book with blank pages.

Freya swallowed, stood up straight for a moment, then leant down to peer at the portrait again. A background wash of brown, green and pink looked unfinished, or had perhaps been painted in a hurry. She could make out a suggestion of leaves in an area tinged green and guessed the artist had initially pencilled the sketch then added watercolours later.

A blast from the air-conditioning lifted the hairs on the back of her neck. Freya shivered and glanced over her shoulder, feeling as if someone was standing behind her. But no, the gallery was empty. The crowds had teemed into the temporary exhibitions on the ground floor.

Then her gaze returned to the woman's face. Downcast eyes created a pensive look but there was no mistaking the inherent resolve indicated by her jutting chin. The woman looked tenacious, even driven. Much like the girl in her miniature. What – or who - had brought them together? Well, now she had set eyes on the artist she was determined to find out.

'I'M sure there's some mystery about her,' said Freya, topping up her friend's glass before filling her own.

It had been Brooke's suggestion to meet near the contemporary design gallery where she worked in Shepherd Market. Now they were drinking inexpensive red wine in the cramped basement of a French café. The ground floor was full of early diners but down here only one other table was occupied. The couple sitting there were deep in conversation, hands clasped across the table, seemingly oblivious to anything beyond their own little bubble.

The décor was certainly not a big draw. Rustic baskets and hand-painted plates did little to camouflage the basement's distressed walls. Nor was its gaunt, cave-like appearance softened by bentwood chairs and bare, wooden tables lit by candles stuck into old-fashioned, brass holders. Still, the place had its own quirky charm, Freya decided, as a tempting whiff of grilled sausages wafted downstairs.

Three instantly recognisable posters by French Impressionist artists were pinned on the wall behind Brooke's chair and Freya found herself gazing directly into the soulful eyes of the barmaid at the Folies Bergère. It was too far away to be sure but wasn't that a small portrait miniature hanging from a black, velvet choker around the girl's neck? Freya flexed her shoulders impatiently. She was seeing portrait miniatures in the most unexpected places now. It was beginning to feel unnerving.

'I think this obsession of yours is getting a bit out of hand,' said Brooke, intuitively picking up on Freya's thoughts. 'But I can see you won't drop it until you've found out who she is. Any clues, my dear Sherlock?'

Freya grinned. 'I'm still researching. Liz Russell said most of Annie Dixon's later commissions came from the aristocracy or royalty, so she could certainly have been a high-society girl.'

'Ah, so many known unknowns,' sighed Brooke, fingering the long, gold chain she was wearing. 'Did you remember to bring it with you?'

Freya nodded and unzipped her handbag. She took out the miniature, unwrapping the tissue paper as she laid it on the table. Brooke picked it up, holding it close to the candle to catch the light.

'Be careful,' snapped Freya.

'It won't melt,' said Brooke sardonically. 'My, you're a little corker, aren't you? Go on – don't you want to tell us who you are?'

Freya remained silent while Brooke took her time studying the front, back and sides of the miniature, turning it over repeatedly and running her long, slim fingers over the case. 'Well, if I was you, I would certainly want to know if she was my ancestor,' she said approvingly. 'It might turn out that you're related to some errant aristo via the wrong side of the bed.'

Brooke placed the miniature gently in its nest of tissue paper then looked at Freya. 'What was the date of Dixon's first regal commission?' she asked.

'I think Liz said 1859,' replied Freya.

'And she thinks your portrait dates from 1860?' asked Brooke.

'Between 1860 and 1880.'

'Well, that would fit the timeframe for copycat commissions then,' said Brooke. 'The world and his wife probably piled in with orders after 1860.'

'I don't think Annie Dixon's popularity was only down to the royal halo effect,' said Freya.

'No? What else?' Brooke leaned forward to catch what she was saying as a noisy burst of chair-scraping broke out on the floor overhead.

'Liz said she was renowned for capturing a very good likeness at a time when portrait-painters were facing stiff competition from early explorations with photography.'

'Then it's almost like having a photograph of a missing person, as far as you're concerned,' said Brooke. Taking a swig of wine, she glanced sideways at the couple at the other table. 'Love is in the air,' she murmured, inclining her head.

Freya followed the direction of her gaze and saw that the couple, now sitting side by side, were kissing as if the world was about to end. A memory of behaving in much the same way with Oliver flashed into her mind. To expunge it she averted her eyes and directed them at Brooke's gold chain. Curious oblong lozenges, interspersed at intervals, gave it a quaintly Egyptian appearance. Freya wondered if she would spot any hieroglyphics if she magnified the lozenges under her jeweller's loop.

Brooke tuned into her banished thoughts like a mind-reader. 'Have you been in touch with Oliver since you got back to London?' she asked.

Freya flinched. 'We haven't spoken since he wound up the company and we cleared out the studio,' she replied.

'Aren't you going to have it out with him?' asked Brooke.

Freya shuddered as a wave of nausea swept over her. 'You mean about the sketches he stole?'

'And flogged to a celebrity jeweller who, no doubt, made a small fortune for them both since launching the design with such fanfare.' Brooke sounded outraged.

Freya swallowed, attempting to keep her voice level. 'I was

very grateful to you for spotting the advert and telling me what he'd done. But, no, I wasn't planning to discuss it with him.'

'Surely you're not going to treat his behaviour as collateral damage in the fall-out from your business, are you?' demanded Brooke. 'You could well have a case for theft of intellectual property here.'

Freya shrugged but said nothing.

'Aren't you mad at him?' continued Brooke, her dark eyes burning with indignation.

'Mad? I'm bloody furious,' said Freya.

'Then you should challenge him about it,' insisted Brooke. 'He messed you around big-time and now you need to set the record straight about that design.'

'I'd rather let it go,' said Freya wearily. 'It's not as if we're together anymore so what's the point?'

'Because he broke your heart and stole your work,' snapped Brooke. 'Really, he's no better than a thief. And, worse, he's undermined your confidence in your own creative abilities. I mean, how long is it since you designed and made a new piece? A year?'

Freya gasped, shocked by Brooke's criticism. She took a deep breath before speaking. 'Don't needle me,' she said coolly. 'Let's get the bill.'

CHAPTER 7

Bruised by Brooke's remarks, Freya slept fitfully, joined uneasily by Oliver in her dreams. She woke exhausted and made her way wearily to Hatton Garden, emerging from the underground in a downpour.

Choosing the stones, however, sent her spirits soaring. Oh yes, she was back in business alright, Freya thought, as she carefully selected four rubies, ethically sourced in Myanmar, whose dark-crimson intensity matched the colour of blood. No wonder people in ancient times used to think these gems held the power of life itself and would guard the wearer against misfortune. For the solo diamond she insisted on a virtually flawless and colour-less D-grade stone that would, when cut, sparkle fiercely from its setting.

Having arranged for the invoice covering the cost of the gems to be sent directly to Ralph, she decided to embrace the challenge of making the settings and fitting the stones herself. It would be a test of her abilities. Brooke's comment had put her on her mettle. She would find out if her dormant skills could be reignited. If the outcome proved successful it would be a big boost to her confidence.

Arriving back at her lock-up, Freya unearthed a dusty box where she'd packed away a collet block. Alongside it lay a metal punch which she would use to strike the annealed gold gently into the oval shapes of the collet block's hollowed-out cavities. Donning protective goggles, she fired the hand-torch and set to work at her bench.

As the flame hissed and spurted, she felt an unexpected surge of pleasure in her belly. By the time she was coaxing the initial setting into shape on a cement stick, then forcing the claws over the stone with a pusher it was as if she had emerged from a long winter hibernation and woken to spring sunshine. Moments like this made all the hours spent patiently cutting, soldering, hammering, filing, buffing and polishing her materials worthwhile.

As she worked, she pictured Eleanor's delight on opening Ralph's gift. She imagined her pleasure in fastening the heart-shaped clasp then turning to admire the necklace in a mirror as its essence – the evolution over millennia of the gems and gold – became part of her own identity and emotions.

An invitation to Ralph's next salon had arrived in the post and was now propped up on her workbench. This time the thick, gilt-edged card specifically requested the pleasure of the company of 'Miss Emily Meadowcroft' to 'a cultural Victorian salon'.

No beating about the bush. Ralph clearly wanted Emily – not Freya – at his salon.

Brooke's cautionary warning echoed in Freya's ears. *An unknown quantity* was how she'd described him. Yes, but that was part of Ralph's allure. If she probed a little, she would learn so much from him – about art, history, culture – as well as meeting all kinds of fascinating people within his social circle. Besides, he made her feel valued in a way that Oliver rarely had.

If pleasing him meant adopting Emily Meadowcroft's persona during his Victorian salons then she was willing to play along. Anyway, it was soothing to forget about her own problems for a while. Disconnecting from her own life and temporarily becoming someone else – especially someone inhabiting a more romantic, seemingly less complicated time than her own – had considerable appeal.

In a burst of bravado, Freya tossed her friend's advice aside. Lots of guests would be present, so what was the worst that could happen? Ralph might come on strong, try to kiss her. Freya shrugged – she'd tell him to get real. He wasn't dealing with an unworldly Victorian girl, even if he did think he could wheedle her into parting with her portrait miniature. She was a creative businesswoman, lauded as one of *Jewellery Now* magazine's rising stars. A top jeweller with an international clientele. Or used to be.

A voice in her head intervened, telling her it might be less of a struggle to get back on her feet if she got proper recognition for the design Oliver had stolen and launched so ostentatiously worldwide.

Should she confront him? Did she have the courage? The memory of their incendiary phone conversations about her failure to complete the company's last orders forced itself into her mind. Did she really want to repeat all that unpleasantness?

Freya brushed aside that unwanted thought by turning her attention for a few minutes to the initial designs for her Victorian jewellery collection.

The sunflower capping the ring looked limp and she would need to re-work the shape. Having invested in a small rolling mill meant she could flatten the metal and start again.

Fingering the unsatisfactory petals, she wondered whether to create a setting for a stone in the centre of the sunflower. That might give it the dynamism it deserved but was a cost she could ill-afford given that the collection was speculative.

Then she studied the pendant. This was the piece that pleased her most. The tiny head in the inner pendant was well-delineated. Every strand of flowing hair was visible to the naked eye. Freya picked up a scorper from the brown leather catch-all below her workbench and scraped between the silver strands, making them even crisper. She felt satisfied with its quirky appeal, but would these three designs be sufficient to convince clients that she was back in business? Perhaps she should add a brooch to the collection too.

Gazing around the cramped, windowless space, Freya regretted the loss of the spacious, light-filled studio from which she and Oliver had run their business. The contrast was bleak. Well, that had gone and now she must move on. But even if one of her former clients bought the finished pieces how would she set about developing her fledgling company?

Oliver had handled all that side of the business. He'd organised photography, booked advertisements, arranged launch parties, secured loans from the bank – over-ambitiously as it turned out – leaving her free to create a steady flow of new designs. She'd helped the photographer's assistant at shoots for glossy magazines, but Oliver had been the one who wooed the editors and persuaded buyers at luxury retailers to place orders. Now she would have to get to grips with all those aspects herself.

Catching sight of Ralph's invitation propped on her workbench, Freya felt an anxious stab of alarm. Given her current financial circumstances, his commission was far more important than her own embryonic collection. Thrusting the pendant aside, she resumed work on the replica Victorian necklace. Time was not on her side.

FREYA SPENT the rain-drenched days leading up to the salon in the lock-up. She finished working on the necklace with just a day to spare. It looked magnificent, even by her own professionally critical standards. Really there was so little difference between the original necklace photographed for the auction house catalogue and her creation that it would be hard for an untrained eye to tell them apart. Now all it needed was a suitably smart presentation box. Burlington Arcade would be a good place to find one. Which was convenient, as there was a place nearby, she was keen to visit.

For an institution as old as the Royal Academy of Arts, the building's clear-glass tubular lift seemed very contemporary as it sailed up to the second floor. Moments later, however, Freya felt as if she was stepping right back to 1768 – the Academy's founding year – as she entered its stately research library.

Huge, leather-bound volumes and dusty-looking rare editions packed full-height wooden shelves covering every inch of space around the walls of a long, narrow room. A large black rectangular table provided an ample surface for researchers at one end of the space, with wood-framed chairs – the kind you might find in an old-fashioned dining room – placed around it.

Half-way along the room stood an elevated marble statue of Victorian sculptor John Gibson's '*Wounded Warrior*', gazing down on a small formation of black desks where two archivists sat glued to their computer screens. The atmosphere was hushed, almost reverential. You would hardly know that Piccadilly's rush and roar was so close at hand.

Freya raised her eyes to a mezzanine floor whose walls were similarly covered by book-filled shelves, then glanced at the floor. Its covering of diamond-shaped tiles in faded colours gave the room a homely feel, as did tall French windows overlooking a big, paved courtyard at the front of the building. She felt like she'd walked into some Georgian gentleman's private residence.

Freya approached the archivist's desk. 'Hello, I rang yesterday to make an appointment,' she said quietly, not wishing to cut through the soothing silence. 'My name's Freya Wetherby.'

'Ah yes, you wanted to look at our bound copies of the Summer Exhibition catalogues,' said a grey-haired man, rising to his feet. 'If you sit here' – he gestured at the black table – 'I'll get them for you.' Scrutinising Freya more closely, he lowered his voice. 'This is a pencil-only library,' he said solemnly.

'Oh, goodness,' said Freya. 'I've only got a Biro in my bag.'

The archivist picked up a pencil from his desk and handed it to her. 'Now which years are you interested in seeing?'

'Around 1860 to 1880,' replied Freya, taking a seat at the table. While waiting for the archivist to return she studied the clock near the door. Its hands seemed permanently stuck at 11.35.

A few minutes later the archivist placed a fat volume in front of her. It had a pale tan spine with a magenta and cream-coloured marbled cover. Gold letters on the spine declared that it spanned the years 1876 to 1884.

'Please start with this and let me know if you need to see any earlier editions,' said the archivist.

Freya carefully opened the cover and leafed through the

thick, cream pages, randomly alighting on the frontispiece for the 1880 exhibition. 'Art is silent poetry' read the quotation at the centre of the page. She turned it over and scanned a list of honorary Academy members at the top of the next page. The Archbishop of York (chaplain), Rt. Hon. W.E. Gladstone MP (professor of ancient history) and The Duke of Westminster (professor of ancient literature) were among the names.

A list of Academicians followed in alphabetical order – Alma-Tadema, Lawrence Esq., Frith, William Powell Esq., Leighton, Sir Frederic, President and Trustee; Millais, John Everett Esq., Poynter, Edward J. Esq., Watts, George Frederick Esq., and so on until it concluded with Yeames, William Frederick Esq.

Freya turned another page. A plan of the rooms at the Academy showed where various artistic disciplines had been exhibited that year. Sculpture occupied the vestibule, central hall and sculpture gallery. Oil paintings were displayed in galleries one to seven while gallery eight was devoted to watercolours. Gallery nine was marked 'Architectural drawings, engravings etc and miniatures.' Ah, that was where to find them.

A burst of bright sunlight at the far end of the room momentarily distracted her. Glancing over at the French windows, Freya's hand shifted and she lost her place in the book as the pages fluttered over each other.

A more rigorous approach was clearly required. Freya started leafing through the pages from the back until she found an exhibition plan for the last catalogue bound into the book. That year – 1884 – the miniatures were displayed in gallery ten.

She turned to the page headed 'Gallery X' where the exhibits were listed. On the left-hand side was the title of each work and on the right was the artist's name. Running her eye quickly down the list, Freya froze as it alighted on Miss A. Dixon. Blinking, she looked at the name again. Yes, it really was Annie Dixon, the artist who had painted her portrait miniature.

She glanced sideways to see if the archivist had heard her gasp. No, his grey head was still bent over his computer screen. Looking back at the page, Freya felt her blood quickening. Her hunch had been correct. Annie Dixon had indeed shown her work at the Royal Academy's Summer Exhibition. Here, in Gallery X, not just one but four of her portraits were on display. No. 1480 – Francis, son of Colonel Waller. No. 1487 – Audrey, daughter of Charles Boyle. No. 1488 – Daughters of the Rev. William Hutchinson of Howden. No. 1513 – Miss Ellen Stableforth.

Well! Freya's mind raced. Were any of these young ladies the one she wanted to pin down? Was it Ellen? Audrey? Or the unnamed daughters of the vicar? How frustrating that the catalogue had no illustrations. How would she ever put a face to these names?

Refusing to be discouraged Freya carried on with her search, slowly turning the pages over until she reached the beginning of the previous catalogue. The miniatures, again displayed in gallery ten, contained a bumper crop of seven from Miss A. Dixon in 1883. Among the women listed were No. 1256 – Mrs Charles Cochrane, No.1271 – Miss Cecily Booker and No. 1284 – Lily, daughter of Wilson Noble Esq. The title of No. 1321 was simply given as 'Portrait of a Lady'.

Freya sat back in her chair frowning. Who was this portrait of a lady? Why wasn't her name listed in the same way as the other sitters? It would make her task of identifying the sitter in her portrait miniature even harder. She felt her throat tightening with disappointment.

Resuming her search, Freya turned the pages back to the

previous catalogue. 1882 had been another productive year for Annie Dixon. Eight miniatures were displayed in gallery ten. Six were named and two were described only as 'Portrait'. Swallowing her frustration, Freya ploughed on.

In 1881 the exhibition must have been smaller overall as the miniatures had retreated to gallery nine, but Annie Dixon still had a good showing of eight works with all the sitters named. Four were male and four female. Was her quarry Kathleen, daughter of Colonel C.C.H. Stewart, Gertrude Norman, Muriel Leslie Hanbury or even Lady Doreen Long? Freya wrote the names down in her notebook, as she had done with the other entries, wondering if the sitter in her portrait miniature was hiding among them.

Turning the pages back to the previous catalogue she reached the list of Academicians she had scoured earlier. Annie Dixon wasn't listed as an Academician, nor was she an associate academician, so she must have exhibited as a member of the public, Freya concluded. She leafed through the 1880 exhibition catalogue, found the pages for gallery nine and picked out the entries for Miss A. Dixon. No. 1377 – The Hon. Mabel Campbell, daughter of Viscount Emlyn. No. 1378 – Captain Windsor Cary Elwes. No. 1394 – Mrs Arthur Beale. No. 1409 – Lawrence, son of William Meadowcroft Esq. No. 1410 – Emily, daughter of William Meadowcroft Esq.

Freya froze, blinked and read the last two entries again. Emily Meadowcroft – the name she'd been called at Ralph's salon. So, Emily and her brother, Lawrence, had sat for Annie Dixon and had their portraits painted in 1880, perhaps commissioned by their father, William. Her heart gave a jerk. Here were their names in print – but what did they look like?

Glancing across at the archivist, Freya wondered how willing he might be to help. She got up and walked over to his desk.

'Excuse me,' she said quietly. 'Are there any versions of the summer exhibition catalogue with illustrations?'

The grey head looked up and regarded her with a patient expression. 'Yes, indeed, illustrated catalogues were produced from 1888 onwards, in addition to the full listings for the exhibition but only about ten per cent of the work in each exhibition was reproduced in them.' He paused. 'Would you like to see a set of later catalogues?'

Freya hesitated, remembering that 1888 was outside the period Liz Russell had suggested for her miniature. 'No thanks,' she replied. Raising her eyes to the mezzanine floor, she gazed at the hundreds of books on the shelves and an idea occurred to her. 'But I'd like to read some reviews of the summer exhibition published at the same time as the catalogues I've been looking through, please.'

'*The Art Journal* would be the best place to start,' said the archivist. 'And I'll get you *The Magazine of Art* as well since it launched in 1878. That one certainly contains engravings and reproductions of artworks.'

Freya returned to her seat and waited while they were extracted from the shelves. *The Art Journal* was an impressively large, heavy tome. The archivist had selected volume X1X for her to start with and Freya opened the cover and quickly scanned the list of articles. As promised, the Summer Exhibition was mentioned under 'Reviews'. She turned to the relevant page and began reading.

"Among the several pictures which give emphasis to the year 1880 none will make it so memorable as Val Prinsep's great historic work setting forth the manner of the assumption at Delhi by her Majesty the Queen of the title of Empress of India…"

Freya skipped a few paragraphs. "…we have more pictures in the present exhibition than have been seen on the walls of the Academy for many years. The number of exhibits on the present occasion is 1,658 and it is made up in this way – oil paintings 923, watercolour drawings 264, architectural drawings 139, engravings, etchings etc. 135, miniatures 51, sculpture 146. Of these the Academicians have produced 173, the remaining 1,485 being exhibited by 'outsiders'."

Ah, an outsider like Annie Dixon perhaps. Freya skimmed the text which took readers on a tour of the exhibition, picking out work in each of the galleries displaying oil paintings and watercolours. Frustratingly, it stopped short of describing the room containing engravings, etchings and miniatures.

Freya closed the heavy cover with a sigh and turned her attention to *The Magazine of Art* - a chunky book with a grey-green cloth cover. Again, the archivist had given her a volume published in 1880. Freya's spirits rose as she turned the pages. This looked much more promising. The articles – some quite lengthy – were illustrated with reproductions of artworks and specially-commissioned drawings and engravings. It must have seemed a fashionably cutting-edge periodical in its day.

Freya was surprised by its broad range of topics. An article about Art Needlework was counter-balanced by one on English Secular Architecture. Art in the Netherlands jostled for space with Favourite Sketching Grounds – Surrey Commons. Pictures of the Year competed with a discursive piece on 'Is Photography an Art?' And here – oh joy! – was a substantial article on Portrait Miniatures.

The article ran for six pages with two highly worked engravings centred on each page between closely printed chunks of text. Freya quickly scanned the portraits and captions. Reaching the fifth page, a shiver as cold as a gust of north wind ran down her spine. Staring up at her were two oval engravings – one male, one female – and the portrait on the right was one she knew intimately. Whoever had engraved it for the magazine had reproduced the face as crisply as if it was a monochrome photograph. It gazed out from the printed page, beckoning and challenging the reader.

Freya found herself trembling as she read the caption. 'Fine portrait miniatures of Lawrence and Emily Meadowcroft by Miss Annie Dixon were greatly admired at this year's Academy exhibition.'

Without a scintilla of doubt this was her portrait girl.

'Emily,' she whispered, feeling drained and tearful as a wave of emotion coursed through her, overwhelming in its intensity.

The engravings of sister and brother brought the siblings forcefully to life. They had lived their lives, for better or worse, and now lived on for ever in Annie Dixon's portrait and these engravings.

Then a new realisation struck with the force of a blow to the head. What she was looking at was an engraving of her own portrait miniature – the very same one she'd found in her mother's jewellery box – depicted in the year it was painted.

Freya closed her eyes as the thought settled in her mind. It was as if time itself had contracted and 'then' had morphed into 'now'.

A quiet warning from the archivist that the research library would soon be closing made her start. Deeply preoccupied with her thoughts, she made her way to the ground floor where the foyer was busy with visitors milling around as the main gallery was still open. In a dream, she wove her way through the crowd and out into the courtyard where a cool breeze struck her face.

Lowering her head momentarily to engage the zip on her parka, she gasped out loud as she raised her eyes and caught sight of the arched entrance opening into Piccadilly.

There. There. Just for a second, she glimpsed a young woman hurrying past, swathed in a long, green cape with a bonnet perched on an abundance of thick fair hair. Her chin tilted upwards in a display of optimism and determination while a secretive smile spoke of hidden knowledge and joy. Then she vanished from Freya's sight as if she'd never been there at all.

CHAPTER 8

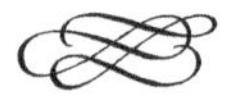

A sense of déjà vu hit Freya as she removed her cape and gave it to the maid. From where she was standing in the hall, she could see the portly outline of Ralph talking to a group of tail-coated men in the octagonal space ahead. Had time stood still since she left the last salon? As if preserved in ice, perhaps the freeze-framed scene could only thaw into motion now she had arrived.

Freya remained in the hall for a moment, smoothing the ivory silk dress over her hips and preparing herself for an enjoyable evening of play-acting. What a relief it was to forget about her own life for a while and pretend to be someone else. She could bury the grief over her mother, her rage at Oliver and all the anxieties about re-launching her business without a second thought.

Freya patted the flowers in her hair to make sure they were still in place. Using remnants of red silk left over from some long-forgotten project, she'd created the flowers on her kitchen table and tied them with a scrap of white lace to mirror the portrait miniature as closely as possible. Jack, she'd felt, was looking over her shoulder all the while.

Instead of Emily's fine diamond pendant, however, the intricate silver pendant she was planning to include in her Victorian jewellery collection hung around her neck. Fastening the clasp for the first time that evening seemed to bridge the historic distance between herself and Emily, bringing them closer in spirit. The thought emboldened her. It was as heady as drinking a glass of champagne.

With a mix of excitement and nerves fluttering in her stomach, Freya took a deep breath and glided down the short corridor towards Ralph. As she moved towards the circle of penguin suits, she heard a collective intake of breath as six pairs of eyes swivelled in her direction. Ralph broke off from the conversation and stepped forward, greedily grasping both her arms.

'My dear Emily… what a vision,' he murmured softly. 'You grow more beautiful by the day. I shall have to keep you close to my side this evening or my friends will tempt you away and that will never do.'

'Good evening, Ralph.' Freya's cool tone conveyed the hauteur with which she imagined Emily might have greeted him. Handing him an oblong, red leather box, she added triumphantly, 'I've brought the piece you requested.'

Seeing beads of sweat break out on his forehead, Freya silently revelled in her new power. She might not be nearly as learned and well-connected as her host but re-discovering her creative abilities was giving a massive boost to her confidence.

Ralph took the box from her and tucked it discreetly under one arm. 'Thank you, my dear, I'm extremely grateful,' he said quietly, his dark eyes glistening with appreciation. Then he pulled a voluminous, mustard-coloured handkerchief from the top pocket of his velvet smoking jacket and dabbed his brow.

'The postal service seems to be in some disarray so I'll send my invoice by email, if that's not too modern a method of communication,' said Freya, smiling.

'You do that, my dear, and I'll have the fee transferred to your account on receipt,' promised Ralph in a deep, reassuring voice. Then he enveloped her right forearm with one enormous hand and pulled her gently into the penguin circle.

'Allow me to introduce Arthur Balfour, who looks after his Hertford constituents so splendidly and is destined, we feel, to achieve great things for our country,' he said in a deferential manner. 'Arthur, this is a dear friend of mine, Miss Emily Meadowcroft – a great beauty, as you can see, with an intellect and artistic ability to match.'

Shaking Balfour's warm, dry hand, Freya looked up to see an attractively strong face with a thick moustache and dark hair neatly centre-parted. A humorous gleam lit intelligent eyes as he smiled down at her. 'A pleasure to meet a woman so clearly admired by Ralph,' said Balfour languidly.

'Good evening,' said Freya, feeling out of her depth.

'Arthur is not only an astute politician but an academic genius too,' said Ralph. 'His *Defence of Philosophic Doubt* has had us spurning frivolous pursuits in favour of reading, learning and debating.'

'You're too kind,' murmured Balfour, seemingly paying more attention to Freya's pendant than Ralph's ingratiating remarks.

Ralph turned to Freya. 'My dear, I'm sure you will remember meeting Edward Burne-Jones at my last salon. Did he mention the monumental task he is undertaking for Balfour's London residence? Perseus and his mythic encounters with Medusa and Andromeda will eventually hang all around the drawing-room at Carlton Gardens. Isn't that so, Balfour?'

'That's correct,' replied Balfour laconically. 'I left the choice of subject up to BJ. He tells me he plans to complete ten panels – their scale and impact sound remarkable. Having a free rein seems to have stirred him to a such a fever-pitch of creativity that he is busy designing relief panels on oak to hang between the painted scenes as well as special lighting for the room.' Giving a dry chuckle, he added, 'It will truly be a *Gesamtkunstwerk* – a total work of art – when it's finished.'

'Be sure to keep him to a tight schedule or you may find the scheme will take years to complete,' warned Ralph. Then his tone softened. 'Now, tell me: I believe you have a fine collection of Ned's drawings too, unless I'm mistaken.'

'I do indeed, and adding to it whenever I can,' drawled Balfour.

'I hope you will have them framed and put on display around your home so that we can all admire them,' said Ralph in a voice tinged with covetousness.

'Probably,' replied Balfour, sounding bored.

Freya frowned. Ralph seemed so envious of the artworks his friends owned. It wasn't a trait she admired. Still, perhaps collectors couldn't help but enjoy the thrill of the chase.

With Balfour losing interest in the conversation, Ralph propelled Freya towards a pair of younger, dapper-looking men. 'My dear, let me introduce you to Hugo Charteris and George Wyndham,' he said. 'Hugo is engaged to George's sister, Mary, who will be joining us later.'

Both men extended their hands simultaneously. Freya instantly decided to defy conventional etiquette and took hold of each hand in one of her own. 'As you will soon be related, I can see I must treat you equally,' she said with a gleeful smile.

Everyone laughed at the joke, sending a wave of euphoria

crashing over Freya. She was becoming a social success in the same way she was sure Emily had been all those years ago.

'Allow me to escort you to the inner sanctum,' said Ralph, taking Freya's arm and guiding her towards a drawing room off the central hall. Passing one of the tall vitrines on the way, Freya caught sight of a vase gaily painted with sunflowers on the top shelf. It took a moment to remember where she'd seen a similar one. In the Meadowcroft house sale particulars.

'We're a more intimate group this evening so I expect the Wyndhams will want to play a few games,' Ralph was saying.

'Games?' echoed Freya, alarmed.

Ralph chuckled. 'Nothing to worry yourself about. They love witty word-games – inventing epigrams or playing Character Sketches.'

'Whatever are Character Sketches?' asked Freya, wondering if this had anything to do with the Victorian alias adopted by each guest.

'We take it in turns to describe someone in the room in terms of something else,' replied Ralph.

'Like what?' asked Freya blankly.

'Oh, it could be anything. A vegetable, for example, or an animal. Even a colour perhaps. Would you care for a glass of champagne?' Ralph took a flute from a maid standing with a tray at the entrance to the drawing-room and handed it to Freya.

As she took it, he slipped an arm around her waist and she froze with anxiety. Ralph was a charming host, but this felt a bit too intimate for her liking.

Just at that moment a portly man with a bushy beard and moustache surged towards them from the middle of the room. He was incongruously dressed in a dishevelled, plaid jacket and waistcoat with a red fez on his head.

'Is Balfour out there?' he demanded. 'I want words with him.'

'Some of your more poetic ones, I hope,' said Ralph in an oily manner.

The man snorted. 'Choice ones, of course. And ask that maid of yours to bring me a whisky, would you?'

Ralph drew Freya to one side to allow his guest through the doorway and, in doing so, squeezed her waist more tightly. Bending towards her ear he whispered. 'That's Wilfrid Blunt. Try and avoid him please. He's a good writer but a frightful womaniser.'

'What does he write about?' asked Freya, wriggling sideways. It was all very well warning her about an errant guest, but she was getting the distinct impression that Ralph's protectiveness was more than just avuncular.

'Poetry. Political stuff. He's big on the Middle East and will bore you to death about the fun and games he and his wife have had in Egypt and the Syrian desert.'

'Does his wife travel with him to those places?' asked Freya enviously.

'She loves Egypt, by all accounts. Perhaps that's not surprising given her grandfather's romantic inclinations,' replied Ralph.

'And who was he?' asked Freya, sufficiently intrigued to admit her ignorance.

Ralph chuckled. 'Lady Anne Blunt is Lord Byron's granddaughter by way of Ada Lovelace.'

'Goodness!' exclaimed Freya, taking a sip of champagne quickly followed by another.

'His other pet subjects are Irish Home Rule and Imperialism,' continued Ralph. 'He supports the former and is against the latter. Misguided in both views I believe. Anyway, Balfour will make mincemeat of him so don't worry your pretty head about him anymore.' Ralph removed his arm from Freya's waist and gently took her hand. 'Shall we sit?'

Comfortably ensconced in a cherry-red velvet sofa, Freya took in her surroundings, caressed by what she saw. The room was papered in William Morris's exuberant *Honeysuckle* design while a Morris carpet – swirls of russet, yellow, bluey-green – enlivened the floor. A wood fire crackled noisily in the grate and above the carved stone fireplace hung a large oil painting reminiscent of the *Nocturne* series by James McNeill Whistler.

On each side of the fireplace stood matching, black-lacquer cabinets decorated with gilded blossom. At the far end of the room a black-and-gold japonaiserie screen partly concealed tall French windows, elaborately curtained in midnight-blue velvet.

Big armchairs – cherry-red, mustard-yellow, leaf-green - embraced guests talking animatedly in small groups throughout the long room. A mix of wood-smoke, cigars and beeswax filled the air. Breathing deeply as she absorbed the scene, Freya relaxed further with each sip of champagne. Before she had even finished her drink, a maid approached with a tray and replaced her glass with a full one.

Glancing sideways at Ralph, she was conscious of the close eye he kept on his guests. It reminded her of a broad-winged kite, lazily circling the skies while looking for prey below. Was his interest aroused by their allegiances or their peccadillos? It was hard to tell. His face remained passively genial.

Discreetly eyeing those closest to her, Freya could see no one she had met at the previous salon. She was hoping Jack Hunter had been invited but didn't dare ask Ralph. And she could hardly enquire whether Lawrence – purportedly her own brother – would be coming.

Judging by the men she'd met so far, tonight's salon seemed to embrace the political classes and aristocratic families like the Wyndhams, as well as artists and writers. She'd better stop her mind drifting and keep abreast of the conversation if she was to avoid a social gaffe. As it was, her host must surely think her very gauche compared to his distinguished friends.

Ralph gave her a nudge as Hugo Charteris wandered into the room holding a glass of champagne in one hand and a cigarette in the other. Perching on the arm of the sofa next to Ralph, he immediately struck up conversation with his host. 'Dizzy's out then – what d'you think of that?' he said excitedly.

'Good riddance,' replied Ralph. 'Now we might get a bit of sense drummed into our foreign policies.'

'He'll have to pull out all the stops to set things right here though,' countered Hugo, lazily dragging on his cigarette.

'You're telling me,' Ralph agreed. 'What with the worst harvest in a century last year, depressed wages and falling employment – he'll have his hands full sorting out the mess. And between you and me, Charteris, I wouldn't risk investing in rail stocks right now.'

Hugo chuckled. 'You think they've hit the buffers, so to speak?'

'It's no joke for anyone who has already invested their life savings,' chided Ralph. 'Fortunately, I never did trust the stock market. Artworks have always seemed a far safer asset to me.'

Hugo wasn't listening. His attention was snared by a tall woman swathed in a flowing, mustard gown standing in the central hall. A sash emphasised the extreme slenderness of her waist while her hair was pinned back in such a way that it added to her height. She was talking animatedly to Arthur Balfour in a clearly flirtatious manner. 'Oh, there's Mary – excuse me,' said Hugo, rising from his perch and sauntering towards the doorway.

Freya watched a slow smile creep across Ralph's face as he eyed Hugo trying to prise Mary away from Balfour. It was almost as if he was enjoying their discomfiture. She was also aware of his arm moving along the back of the sofa as he turned to speak to her. 'I'm wondering if you've had time to give any further consideration to my offer?' he asked quietly. 'I'm still keen to acquire the portrait miniature you showed me. It would fit so perfectly with other little gems in my collection. I could even carry out some in-depth research into the identity of the sitter for you.'

Freya felt her body stiffen as she swallowed the urge to mention her discovery at the Royal Academy's archives. Did he really not know the sitter's name? Or was he playing some obscure mind-game with her? She just couldn't tell from his courteous demeanour. Nor could she edge away from him. They were sitting so close together, his arm brushing the back of her head, that it would appear rude if she tried to move.

'I'm sorry but my answer is still the same,' she replied. 'I'm not intending to sell it. Anyway, I have no idea what it's worth. I would have to get a proper valuation from an expert.'

'Are you familiar with Boyd & Hart's gallery in Albemarle Street?' asked Ralph. 'I've found them to be quite helpful in the past. Talking of which, you seemed very interested in seeing my collections when you came to my last salon. Would you like to take a good look now? Most of the important pieces are upstairs but we can take our drinks with us.'

A tingle of uneasiness prickled the back of Freya's neck. She glanced around the room, prevaricating. Spotting Lawrence greeting Hugo and Mary in the central hall, she said gratefully, 'I see my brother has arrived at last – I must go and speak with him. Excuse me.'

Rising from the sofa without looking at Ralph, Freya made her way circuitously around groups of armchairs and out into the octagonal hall. Hugo and Mary had moved away from Lawrence and were now talking to George Wyndham.

Approaching Lawrence from the rear, Freya touched his arm lightly, smiling with anticipation.

'Oh,' he said abruptly, jerking round to face her. 'It's you.'

It was not the kind of response Freya had expected. 'Didn't you think Ralph would invite me?' she asked in surprise.

Lawrence scowled at her. 'I've got a bone to pick with you.'

'Have you?' asked Freya faintly, wondering what could have caused such a change in his manner since the last time they met.

Lawrence's eyes flicked around the groups of guests chatting in the hall. 'Not here,' he murmured. Gripping her arm tightly, he steered her into a room Freya recognised. It was where she had admired Ralph's collections of porcelain and silver. Where Jack had kissed her on the neck.

Lawrence closed the door firmly behind them. 'You can stop your meddling right now,' he said, glaring at her and spitting out the words as if they tasted bitter.

Freya's head swam with confusion. Was he addressing her in the guise of Emily Meadowcroft's brother or as a real-life friend of Ralph's? She couldn't be sure.

'What is it you think I've done?' she asked cautiously.

Lawrence exploded with fury. '*Think*? I *know* what you've done, you witch. And so will everyone else soon enough.'

Freya felt the colour drain from her face. Her heart was beating painfully fast, and blood roared in her ears, drowning out her thoughts. 'I'm sure I can explain if you just tell me…'

Before she could finish speaking Lawrence grabbed her wrist, twisting it in his hand. She tried to pull her arm away. 'You're hurting me!' she cried, clenching her other hand into a ball and beating his chest as hard as she could. 'Let me go!'

Lawrence dropped his hold and took a step back, looking shocked at her violent response.

Freya rubbed her sore wrist. 'Tell me what I've done to

deserve this,' she said as the pain subsided to a burning sensation like the sting of salt-water as it dries on damaged skin.

Briefly putting a hand over his eyes, Lawrence sighed. 'It was clear the last time we spoke that you were planning to help Jack,' he said. 'I didn't think you'd be so devious as to cheat on everyone else in the process.'

'Go on,' said Freya coldly, playing for time while she slipped back mentally into her adopted role.

'The designs he presented for his diploma show. There's no way Jack could have created anything half as intelligent or beautiful. They were your designs, weren't they?'

Freya remained silent.

Lawrence took a step towards her, bellowing in her face: '*Weren't they*??'

To her horror, Freya found herself nodding.

'I thought so,' said Lawrence, moving away from her. He strode over to the vitrine containing Ralph's porcelain and ran a finger down the front of the glass case. Then he turned to address her again.

'I'm going to tell the school's principal that Jack is a lying cheat who deserves to be expelled in disgrace – thanks to a wilful deception by my own sister. You know what that means? No employer will ever take a second look at Jack. He'll end up like so many impoverished artists, starving to death or worse, catching some horrible disease and having no money to pay for a doctor.'

Freya blinked and waited in silence. It was clear he hadn't finished his tirade.

Lawrence gave an unpleasant chuckle. 'You can save him though. If you wish.'

'How?' The question sounded like a breath of air rather than a spoken word.

Lawrence began to pace agitatedly in front of the vitrine,

staring at his feet as he moved from one side of the cabinet to the other. 'Let's have a little pact, shall we? Let's say I don't expose Jack for the lazy, good-for-nothing drunkard that he is. And let's say you do me a little favour in return.'

He stopped pacing the floor and turned to look at Freya directly. 'There's a commission I want you to complete on my behalf. Something May has suggested for Morris & Co. It's way beyond my capabilities but I didn't want to disappoint her father nor lose her friendship by turning it down.' He gave a short laugh then added, 'Her disapproval can be rather icy.'

Pausing to take a deep breath, Lawrence ran a hand through his hair. 'If you can complete the work on time then you have my word that I won't betray your underhand little ploy to help Jack,' he said.

'What is the nature of this work?' Freya felt the words spill from her mouth as if spoken by someone else.

'Jewellery,' replied Lawrence brusquely. 'A fine collection of medieval-inspired jewellery for a private client. A brooch, a pair of sleeve clasps and a necklace.'

'The work will carry your name?' asked Freya, guessing the answer before she even finished speaking.

'Exactly so, if Morris & Co wish to credit me – although they may, of course, simply produce the work under the firm's own name.' Lawrence paused, scowling at Freya. 'You would, of course, never mention to anyone – ever – that you created the pieces.'

Freya swallowed an acidic bubble of nausea. Her stomach felt queasy and glittery darts – silver, jade, black – flashed at the corner of her eyes. She had the sensation that the room was moving, taking her with it. She took a deep breath, fighting to hold on. Then the swirling motion receded and her vision cleared.

'You offer me no choice,' she said.

Lawrence's eyes gleamed. 'Then you accept my offer with all its conditions?'

'I do,' said Freya, wishing the conversation would end so she could leave the room.

'Excellent,' said Lawrence with a harsh note of triumph in his voice. 'Then there is no more to be said. I will give you the brief for the commission before we leave here tonight.'

He strode towards the door, opened it and gave a half-bow. As Freya hurried out towards the hall, desperate to get away from him, her toe caught the hem of her dress. Stumbling and throwing her arms forward to save herself from falling, she cannoned straight into Jack Hunter.

CHAPTER 9

Jack thrust his hands below Freya's forearms, supporting her while she regained her balance. Taking a deep breath to steady herself, she was conscious of his hands lingering on her bare arms a little longer than necessary, bringing their bodies deliciously close. Catching a whiff of musky sweetness on his skin, Freya felt her stomach kick with pleasure.

She noticed he had taken much more trouble over his appearance than the last time they met. Exchanging his artist's smock for a close-fitting, dark jacket made him look less like a student and more of a man-about town, especially with the embellishment of a white carnation in the buttonhole.

'Are you alright?' he asked with genuine concern in his voice.

'Oh Jack, I need to talk to you,' whispered Freya, peering over his shoulder to check if Ralph was in the vicinity. She was still feeling dazed from her encounter with Lawrence.

'It would be my pleasure,' said Jack gallantly. 'Take my arm and we'll find somewhere quiet to sit.'

Freya followed his instruction and they moved along the corridor leading to the dining room. Its magnificent double doors were closed but their mahogany surfaces gleamed under the subdued light from the passageway as fiercely as flames in a furnace. Freya remembered Ralph saying a light supper would be served in the study that evening. The dining room would be a good place to talk without being disturbed.

Grasping the massive bronze handle on the right-hand door, Jack gave it a yank and they slipped inside. No lights were lit nor were the curtains drawn. Jack pointed at the French windows. Although the room was in darkness, a silvery stream of moonlight allowed them to navigate the huge dining table and the monumental porcelain jardinieres as they approached the windows. A metal bar-handle grated loudly as Jack lowered it, pushed open the glass door and moved outside.

'Be careful of the steps,' he warned in a low voice. Freya hitched her dress up a few inches and crossed the threshold. Standing at the top of six stone steps, she gazed out at a garden as dramatically lit by moonlight as an Atkinson Grimshaw painting.

'There's a bench here,' whispered Jack from the shadows below her.

Freya made her way slowly down the steps and joined him on a rustic wooden bench set against the rear wall of the house. As she sat down Jack took her hand, leaning so close that his hair brushed against her cheek. A stab of desire shot through her as she inhaled again the intoxicating fragrance of his skin.

'What is it, my darling?' he asked quietly. 'What did you want to tell me?'

Freya took a deep breath. 'Lawrence is trying to blackmail me,' she bleated.

Still holding her hand, Jack put his free arm around her shoulders and pulled her close. Freya buried her face in his shoulder, enveloped by a fog of champagne and a pleasurable sense of unreality. The soothing repetition of Jack's hand stroking her hair felt as soporific as the suck and surge of waves on a shingle beach. She wanted the sensation to last forever; never to stop being Emily.

'Tell me, my darling,' he whispered.

'He knows I carried out the work for your diploma show and is threatening to expose us both as cheats and liars,' said Freya. 'Now he's forcing me to do something far more wicked and deceitful.' She paused, succumbing to Jack's caresses.

'Go on, sweetheart,' he said, close to her ear.

'He foolishly accepted a commission to make a jewellery collection for one of Morris & Co's private clients even though he knew he couldn't fulfil it. Now he's pressing me to make it on his behalf. He said if I can complete it on time then he won't betray us.'

'Did you agree to do that?' Jack sounded surprised.

'Yes,' said Freya miserably. 'He gave me no choice.'

'It's a prestigious commission,' said Jack, pushing a lock of hair gently away from her cheek. 'Morris & Co. have an extremely good reputation and are renowned worldwide for their work. It could set you on a golden path to the future if the client is pleased with the results.'

'Except that he swore me to silence,' said Freya in a small voice. 'No one will ever know that the designs are mine.'

Jack stopped stroking her hair and remained silent for a moment. Freya was startled by the caustic venom in his voice when he eventually spoke. 'Everyone will think Lawrence is a genius,' he said.

A faint tinkle of recognition sounded in a corner of Freya's befuddled mind. Yet the recollection slid away like dripping paint, fluid and messy, when she tried to grasp hold of the memory. It was much less effort to rest her head on Jack's shoulder, close her eyes and sink into his caresses which resumed a few moments later.

She felt the whisper of his breath on her cheek and then his lips lightly brushing hers. Another kiss followed, this time more searching, and she responded, abandoning any attempt to think or question. Now his hand was gently stroking her thigh through the silken folds of her dress, and she could feel her heart pounding. Despite the chill night air, she felt warm and glowing, excited and soothed in equal measure.

THEY LAY TOGETHER, caressing and kissing, for what seemed like an hour although Freya later reflected it was probably much less. Eventually Jack pulled away from her and sat upright. Freya watched him straightening his jacket and taking a deep breath, then another, as if bracing himself to deliver bad news. Unable to tear her eyes from his face, Freya tensed as she waited to hear what he would say.

Giving a barely perceptible sigh, Jack flexed his shoulders then turned towards her. When he spoke his voice was dispassionate, strangely unemotional, as if the intimate moment they'd just shared had been a chimera.

'My darling, we must do it like this until you have the baby.'

'The baby,' she echoed in a panicky whisper. Her baby. She was pregnant. No, *Emily* was pregnant. And Jack... he had been caressing *Emily*, not Freya. The realisation sank inside her like a stone. For a few honeyed moments, golden and precious, he'd made her feel desirable for the first time since Oliver's betrayal. Now she knew he'd just been toying with her, playing his part in a script written by an unknown hand for reasons Freya couldn't understand.

Jack shifted his position on the bench and then stood up. 'I suppose we should go back inside before Ralph notices we're missing,' he said, sounding reluctant.

Anxious about the state of her dress and hair, Freya shot up off the bench, smoothed her silk gown as best she could and ran her hands over her hair. The silk flowers were still there, as was the silver pendant dangling from her neck.

'Do I look as if I've been romancing the most handsome man in the world?' she asked with an uncertain little smile.

Jack gave a soft laugh. 'My darling, it will be obvious to no one but me,' he said in a reassuring tone.

Back inside the house they agreed to leave the dining room separately for the sake of discretion. Freya slipped out first and made her way down the corridor towards the crowd of guests in the octagonal hall. The salon was clearly still in full swing. Freya walked further along the passage to the entrance hall and was relieved to find the ladies' powder room empty.

Checking her face in the mirror she saw a glow in her cheeks and a bright sparkle in her eyes that had not been evident earlier in evening. Being Emily suits me, she thought with amusement. Secretly exulting in her al fresco encounter with Jack, she knew with a fiery certainty that she'd take it further if the opportunity arose. Then the door opened, and a tall woman dressed in an expensive-looking ochre gown entered the cloakroom.

'Good evening,' said Eleanor in a friendly voice as soon as she saw Freya. 'I think we met at Ralph's last salon, didn't we?'

'We did indeed,' replied Freya. 'Are you enjoying the party tonight?'

'I've always loved parties, even from a very young age,'

admitted Eleanor, smiling. 'And Ralph throws some of the best. He's such a wonderful host, don't you agree?'

'Oh yes,' replied Freya eagerly, still floating on a wave of euphoria from her liaison with Jack. 'He's a very generous friend too,' she added, thinking how thrilled Eleanor would be when she opened the red leather box she'd given Ralph earlier and, for the first time, setting eyes on its dazzling contents.

Opening her evening bag to look for a comb, Freya saw the folded sheet she'd torn from the auction house catalogue. What a nuisance. She'd intended to give it back to Ralph, along with the necklace, so he could compare her work with the original piece. As she extracted it from her bag, the page fluttered from her fingers onto the floor. Bending to pick it up, she heard Eleanor exclaim 'Oh!' and then, 'May I have a look at that?'

'Of course – it's just something I saw in an auction catalogue,' replied Freya, trying to downplay its significance. She had no wish to spoil Ralph's surprise by telling her more.

'How extraordinary,' said Eleanor, staring at the photograph on the page. 'My son gave me this very same necklace for my birthday last year. He told me the bidding was remarkably intense at the auction, especially from overseas collectors, but he triumphed in the end. You see, rubies are my birthstone – I was a July baby – and he was determined to acquire it for me.' She studied the photograph for a few more moments then handed the page back to Freya.

'Are you quite sure….?' Freya's voice trailed off as she folded the sheet and slipped it back inside her evening bag. Eleanor must be mistaken. Perhaps she'd had too much champagne. She was, after all, quite an old lady.

Leaving the cloakroom and walking back along the passage, Freya encountered a maid carrying a silver salver full of drinks. She seized a small glass containing amber liquid and took a gulp. Brandy. The fire reached her belly within seconds.

'Ah, there you are,' said Ralph as she reached a knot of guests in the octagonal hall. 'I've been looking for you.'

Freya paused, reluctant to engage with him. Eleanor's story had sown seeds of doubt in her mind that were hard to dismiss. Looking for an excuse to move away, she exchanged her empty glass for another brandy as the maid passed by.

Ralph caught her arm. 'This way,' he said, pulling her firmly to the foot of the stairs. 'The best things are on the first floor.'

A voice inside Freya's head told her to play along. He owed her a great deal of money for her work on the necklace, so it would be foolish to rebuff him.

Arriving at the minstrel's gallery running around the first floor, Ralph took a set of keys from the pocket of his smoking jacket and poked one into the elaborate brass escutcheon of the third door they reached. As it swung open, he put his hand in the small of Freya's back and pushed her gently inside.

Unlike the ostentatiously furnished rooms downstairs this space was clinically designed for a collector of precious objects. All around the walls stood tall, glass cases symmetrically housed in cherrywood frames. The only freestanding pieces of furniture were a standard lamp with a pink beaded silk shade and a circular ottoman, upholstered in dark green velvet, crouching in the centre of the space.

Freya shivered as she walked into the room. Although the chilly air-conditioning felt pleasantly cool on her hot skin, the multitude of objects in the cases made the atmosphere oppressively claustrophobic. Turning her head to look around, she had the sensation that the whole room was spinning.

Ralph closed the door then stood with his back to it, beaming as he looked around his lair. 'Welcome to my

Wanderkammer – my cabinet of curiosities,' he said expansively. 'Let me show you my most recent acquisition,' he added, donning a pair of white gloves hanging from a hook by the door.

Moving to the stack of display-cases on his left, he gently pulled a tiny, bronze knob at the top of a rectangular glass cover and lowered it to a horizontal position. Reaching inside, he brought out a gleaming, oval object. Holding it in the palm of his gloved hand, he showed it to Freya. A gold brooch engraved with Egyptian hieroglyphics winked up at her.

'Pharaonic, no less,' he said conspiratorially.

Freya gulped. 'How on earth did you get hold of that?' she asked.

'I have my ways and means,' replied Ralph, holding the brooch up towards the lamp and languidly twisting the oval form from side to side. It glinted and flashed as it caught the rosy glow of light.

Ralph pressed the brooch to his lips then replaced it carefully inside the case, raising the glass cover to secure it. Then he strolled over to a vitrine on the other side of the room. This time he brought out a small, mud-coloured, pottery bowl and showed it to Freya.

'Can you believe this was made around 2000 BC? It's four thousand years old.' He spoke in a low, hushed voice as if entering a place of worship.

Holding the bowl by its base, he turned it round slowly as he studied the weathered colours on its surface. 'Objects like this bring us directly in line with our ancient forebears,' he said reverently. 'They're stronger and more powerful than any family tree. A genealogical document only shows a line of descent on paper. It never brings people to life in the same way that objects do.'

Raising the bowl to his nose, Ralph closed his eyes and

inhaled deeply. 'I can smell the hand of the person who made this,' he said dreamily.

Exhaling, he opened his eyes and addressed the bowl rather than Freya. 'I can see his head bent over the material as he fashioned its form. I can watch the path of his thoughts as he struggled to create a perfectly round shape. I can feel the pleasure he felt in the finished object. It's the same pleasure I feel at this very moment holding it in my hand and in that way a direct link is made between myself and someone who lived four thousand years ago.'

Still holding the bowl, Ralph turned his gaze to Freya. 'Do you think about your ancestors? The people who trod a path so that you could exist?' He paused then regarded the bowl again. 'I think about mine all the time. How they coped with the great struggle of life, what choices they made, the people they loved, the children they created. Some say I spend a great deal of my life with ghosts, but they are wrong. I brush shoulders with the living people who produced these beautiful objects and feel their breath on my skin as I touch what they made.'

Freya remained silent, absorbed by what he was saying. Despite her better instincts, she was magnetised by his infectious fascination with the objects around them and his passionate response to their stories.

Then a mote of dust caught the back of her throat. Ralph flinched when she began to cough, as if roused from sleep. Gently replacing the bowl inside its glass case, he bent down to open a vitrine directly below. 'And I must show you this,' he said, drawing out a large, leather-bound book. 'Come and sit down,' he said, lowering himself onto the ottoman and balancing the book on his knee.

Freya sat next to him, curiosity overcoming her wariness. Ralph opened the cover and revealed a page dense with thick, black script in the centre of which danced an exquisitely painted illumination of two angels with feathery, golden wings taking flight.

'The Titchfield psalter,' he announced. 'It belonged to the Meadowcroft family.'

Startled, Freya's eyes flicked up from the page to Ralph's face. He was staring at her with an expression she couldn't fathom. The room temperature seemed to plunge, and she was conscious of dark shadows pulsing at the edge of her vision.

'Oh yes,' he said quietly. 'I thought this might interest you.' He began turning the thick pages slowly, almost lovingly. The book was filled with gilded, jewel-like illustrations whose rich colours glowed in the half-light of the room. The only sound was the crackle of stiff parchment spreading through the air like ripples in a pond.

'It's beautiful – the most beautiful thing I've ever seen,' said Freya passionately.

'It would have been yours, of course, had things not turned out differently,' said Ralph, slowly shaking his head while continuing to turn the pages.

'What do you mean?' Freya felt her hands turn clammy as she smoothed the creases in her dress at the top of her thighs.

Ralph closed the book without replying, got up and replaced it in its display-case. Then he sank down heavily on the ottoman.

'You don't remember?' he asked coldly, turning to face her.

'Remember what?' Freya felt an unpleasant tang of fear in her mouth.

'How you broke your promise to me?' Ralph's voice sounded gruff, almost surly.

Freya remained silent, nervously smoothing her dress. Her shoulders prickled with tension, and she was aware of an angry throb in her temples.

'Oh, let me remind you then as you seem to be so forgetful these days,' said Ralph sarcastically. Breathing heavily, he inched the white gloves off his hands, placed them neatly next to him on the ottoman and splayed his fingers over his knees. Freya followed his line of vision, thinking how large and strong his hands looked. They could easily encircle her neck, she thought with a shiver.

Ralph misinterpreted her response. 'Are you cold?' he asked, taking her hand. 'Yes, your hand feels very cold. Frigid. Like your heart.'

Freya's brain reeled. Had he seen her with Jack and taken offence? Or was he referring to Emily Meadowcroft?

'How useful to have a forgetful mind,' he continued with an edge to his voice. 'Because you'll tell me that I never did kneel down and propose to you on Saint Valentine's Day. And you'll say we were never engaged to be married after your parents gave me their blessing. You won't have any recollection of the magnificent betrothal party your family threw at their house in the countryside. Nor will you remember how you made me promise to save my passion for our wedding night.'

He paused as if to give her time to let his words sink in. Freya's pulse sped into a crescendo. He was behaving as if she really was Emily – not just playing a role for the evening. Horrified and confused, she struggled to grasp if he was acting out some historic psychodrama or truly believed what he was saying. Was it possible that his vanity and eccentricity were slipping into madness?

Before she could speak, he raised his left hand and touched her cheekbone. 'Such a pretty face,' he murmured. Then he spread his fingers wider, slipping his thumb under her chin and titling it upwards. Shifting his bulk closer, he awkwardly placed a wet kiss on her lips.

Freya squirmed and jerked her head sideways as a ball of

phlegm rose in her throat. All her instincts screamed at her to shake him off, get up and leave the room. Yet she couldn't move. Her heart was banging unpleasantly hard, and her legs had turned to jelly.

Ralph's hand fell from her face. 'That's the way of it now, is it?' he said icily. 'Once upon a time you were only too eager for a kiss and – almost more.' He gave a grating laugh. 'Until you jilted me.'

The words hung in the air like the smell of bad eggs.

Freya felt a claw of fear grip her stomach. They were alone together in this tomb of a room and no one in the world knew she was here with a man whose mania was becoming increasingly evident. She was trapped and afraid. Cornered like a mouse with a cat. He was so big and powerful there was no way she could fight him off if he attacked her. She swallowed, her mind racing. Perhaps she had no choice but to play along in her role as Emily Meadowcroft – at least until she could get away from him.

She cleared her throat. 'You behaved like a gentleman,' she said in as sweet a tone as she could muster. 'With dignity and kindness. And now I can't tell you how sorry I am. I was foolish and headstrong. Please forgive me.'

Ralph looked slightly mollified and made a sound halfway between a grunt and a sigh. He shifted his position on the ottoman and Freya felt his bulk relax. Her play-acting seemed to have broken the spell, so she took the opportunity to edge away from him, eyeing the distance between the ottoman and the door.

Ralph picked up the gloves, laying them on his knee and smoothing out each finger consecutively. 'I only discovered a few years ago just how entwined our ancestors were,' he said in a manner much closer to his normal demeanour. 'When the contents of the Meadowcroft house came up for sale I attended the auction and couldn't resist buying some of the best pieces. Annoyingly, I was outbid on a couple of the objects I had my eye on – a tiny bronze sculpture of a naked female figure and a charming watercolour of the house itself. They would have made perfect additions to my collection.'

Glancing at Freya, he gave a soft sigh. 'I'm sure you know that Emily's parents went to live in Italy latterly and left the house mothballed with just a housekeeper and gardener living there. When they died the house was inherited by her father's youngest brother and then, in turn, it passed to his son, Tom.'

'Tom is very old and in poor health now,' he continued. 'He seemed only too glad to be selling off the family heirlooms to collectors like me who would treasure them on his behalf. We got into conversation after the auction ended and I discovered this extraordinary connection between my esteemed great-grandfather and the Meadowcroft family.'

Ralph paused, looking down at his gloves reflectively. 'It's tragic he was treated so badly by Emily,' he said. 'It was very cruel to break off the engagement when he loved her so much. It destroyed him really. And it did Emily no good. Tom said none of the family had anything more to do with her after that.' Turning to Freya, his tone sharpened. 'But, of course, you know all this.'

Freya remained silent, avoiding direct eye contact as her thoughts took flight. Was this true? Could she trust what he was saying? Surely Emily wouldn't have behaved in such a careless and wilful manner...but if she really did break off the engagement, she must have had a very good reason if it meant estrangement from her family.

Ralph's story and his clear affection for his ancestor were touching. Yet instead of experiencing any sense of a rapport with him she felt deeply uncomfortable. His awkward attempt to kiss her had been unpleasant but it wouldn't be the first time she'd had to deal with that kind of thing. No, it was this puzzling conflation between herself and Emily that was so disturbing. She took a deep breath and waited tensely to see if his volatile mood would change again.

'The portrait miniature you inherited has far more meaning for me, you see, than it does for you,' said Ralph. 'That is why I'm prepared to offer you a great deal more than it would be worth on the open market.'

'The money isn't an issue,' said Freya. 'It has sentimental value for me and I don't want to part with it.'

'Perhaps not yet,' said Ralph, carefully picking up the gloves from his knee and slowly drawing them over each large hand in turn. 'But I'm prepared to wait, as you will see, for as long as it takes you to concede.'

Unsettled by his manner, Freya resisted the impulse to pull away from him too quickly and, instead, instinctively reverted to play-acting. Feeling her legs trembling beneath her gown, she spilled out a torrent of ameliorating words.

'Let's be friends,' she heard her voice pipe shrilly. 'It's too late to recapture what could have been but at least let's make the most of what we still have. Our friendship, our mutual interests, our friends and acquaintances.'

There was a silence in the chilly room so intense that Freya imagined she could hear her heartbeat ringing out.

Ralph cleared his throat. 'You're right,' he said eventually. 'It does no one any good to dwell on past mistakes. But promise me one thing.' He looked at Freya intently. 'Never speak to Jack Hunter again.'

Freya rose slowly from the ottoman, frowning as she pretended to consider his request. She took a small step towards the door, holding his gaze while she moved. Then another step.

'Well?' he demanded brusquely, suddenly standing up.

'I – I can't agree to that,' said Freya quietly, the truthful words tumbling out against her better judgment.

As Ralph's face flushed with anger, Freya took one more step then yanked the door open and dashed into the minstrel's gallery. Without slackening her pace, she raced down the stairs, barged through a surprised group of guests and headed for the entrance hall. Trembling, she waited a few tense moments while the maid retrieved her cape and phone. Then, bolting out of the front-door as soon as it opened, she ran down the steps and pelted as fast as she could along the street towards the night bus-stop.

CHAPTER 10

Not until 4am did Freya drop off to sleep. Reaching her flat, she stumbled into the bathroom and was violently sick. Too much champagne, too much brandy, too much of everything she thought feebly as she washed her face and cleaned her teeth.

Curled up in bed, clutching a pillow to her stomach, her brain fizzed and reeled. Jack, lovely Jack, had seemingly vanished when she'd needed him most. She hadn't spotted him among the other guests when she'd dashed through the central hall. Had he left the salon while she was upstairs with Ralph? Or was he chatting up another woman in the drawing room as she made her escape? And why was Lawrence so furious with her? Did his anger really stem from this story about Emily's efforts to help Jack with his diploma show or was there some other reason?

Another thought made her sit bolt upright in bed. 'Oh no,' she groaned aloud. She'd completely forgotten to take his brief for the Morris & Co commission before she left the party.

Something inside her tipped for a moment. Then her anxiety drained away as she lay back against the pillows, queasily remembering that the salon was just an elaborate charade. Lawrence wasn't really her brother and the brief – if it ever existed – was commissioned nearly 150 years ago.

And Jack? Had he been acting too? If only he was with her now. Lying with him on the garden bench had felt so delicious. She closed her eyes and slipped back into the moment, feeling the weight of his body and inhaling the sweet muskiness of his skin. When she opened her eyes again the memory slid away beyond her mental grasp. In its place came the cold acknowledgment that he was a stranger – a friend of Ralph's – and she didn't even know his real name.

Freya tossed and turned, trying to sleep, but a swirl of recollections blazed in her head, colours hyper-real, images spinning like a fairground carousel, faces looming impossibly large and then retreating into the distance. Just as insistently came the tumbling questions. Did Emily have Jack Hunter's baby? Was a warped kind of family pride behind Ralph's desire to own the portrait miniature? And why was he so certain that she was related to Emily?

Freya sat up again, only to find her head whirling and her stomach raw. Too many unanswered questions spun around her mind. She lay back, feeling dazed and shaky, no longer sure what was real and what was imaginary at the salons.

She must do more online research and find out for certain if she was related to Emily Meadowcroft. Ralph clearly thought so. Surely his assumption was only based on her inheritance of the portrait miniature from her mother though. Or did he know more than he had revealed in his collector's room?

A new kind of fear tugged at her. Ralph had seemed so

charming, so benign, when she first met him. Then he had become her patron with his irresistible jewellery commission. Her saviour, in fact. The means by which she would get her business up and running again. After last night's encounter, however, the thought of him left her feeling anxious and confused. Nor was it just his bizarre behaviour that was so unsettling. That odd conversation with Eleanor in the cloakroom had cast a shadow of uncertainty over why Ralph had commissioned the necklace at all.

Am I going mad? she thought. Eventually, drained by exhaustion, she fell asleep. Even then she wandered through fragmented, unsettling dreams, lost and in despair.

FREYA MADE no attempt to get out of bed until late morning. Feeling fragile and hungover, she made some tea and forced herself to eat a scrambled egg on toast. Wincing at the memory of Ralph's attempt to kiss her, Freya tried to block the image from her mind and stay strong.

Right now, she was aching for some emotional and mental support. Scrolling through the messages on her phone, she hoped to find a text from Brooke, Nothing. Of course not, she thought bleakly, she's busy at the gallery.

Get a grip, she told herself firmly, dialling Brooke's number. What are friends for if you can't call on them for a bit of support occasionally?

'It's Freya – can you talk?' she asked, trying to keep the anxiety out of her voice.

'Just for a moment,' came the hurried reply.

'I was at Ralph's house last night—'. Freya got no further before her friend interrupted.

'Another salon!' exclaimed Brooke. Her tone made it sound like the confirmation of a hunch, not a question. 'You don't surprise me. Somehow, I knew you wouldn't be able to resist returning to that fancy Victorian cockpit.'

'Yes – and it was even weirder than the last time,' said Freya.

'I can imagine,' sighed Brooke. 'Okay, just give me the key facts.'

'It's hard to separate facts from fiction,' said Freya in a hollow voice. 'I'm not really sure what's going on. The salons seem to be an opportunity for Ralph to live out a kind of fantasy life. A chance to immerse himself in the Victorian world he loves so much. I suspect they are also a way of feeding his ego. He gets to control everyone's mindset by persuading his friends and colleagues to dance to his tune. Somehow, he makes it surprisingly easy to slip into character. When I'm there I just get swept along by it all and take the things people say at face value. It's only afterwards that hundreds of questions start to nag.'

'Go on,' urged Brooke in a low voice.

'I think Emily Meadowcroft fell out with her brother big-time," said Freya. 'It sounds as if she secretly did all the work for Jack Hunter's diploma show and when Lawrence guessed what she'd done he threatened to expose the pair of them to the school's principal.' Freya paused, bracing herself to continue. 'It seems he was just as deceitful as Jack though – worse in some respects. Do you remember me saying I met William Morris's daughter, May, at the previous salon? Well, she wasn't there last night but Lawrence told me she'd invited him to create a bespoke jewellery collection for a private client and he accepted the commission even though he knew he wasn't up to tackling the job. Realising what Emily had done for Jack, he offered her a *quid pro quo*. If she designed and made the jewellery for Morris & Co., then he would keep quiet about the work in Jack's diploma show.'

'And take the credit and fee for the commission, I suppose,' said Brooke. 'Remind you of anyone?' she asked sharply.

Freya felt herself blushing. 'That's different,' she said defensively.

'In what way?' asked Brooke.

Freya swallowed. 'Alright, I admit it does sound horribly like Oliver's behaviour and I have to say I'm bloody furious on Emily's behalf.'

'And your own, I hope,' said Brooke.

'I've been giving the matter some thought,' Freya conceded, narrowing her eyes as an unpleasant memory of the previous shouting-matches with her ex-boyfriend came to mind.

'Go on — this is getting interesting. Was Jack Hunter there?'

'Surprisingly, yes,' replied Freya, straining to keep her voice sounding neutral. 'The other guests were mainly writers, politicians and their spouses – or pretending to be.'

'Do you think he gate-crashed?' asked Brooke.

'Jack? Possibly,' replied Freya.

'Or perhaps he heard you were coming,' suggested Brooke slyly.

'I think Ralph would have kept that to himself,' said Freya. 'There's no love lost between those two, believe me.'

'A fine piece of acting no doubt,' scoffed Brooke. 'What else did you discover?'

'That Emily was pregnant,' said Freya.

'By Jack?'

'Yup,' replied Freya succinctly. It was too embarrassing to say she'd thought for a split second that she was the one expecting a baby. Brooke would never get that.

'Did Ralph know?' asked Brooke.

'I'm not sure,' replied Freya.

'What about his painting of Emily?' asked Brooke. 'Did you talk to him about that?'

'How could I?' replied Freya. 'I wasn't meant to have been prowling around his bedroom at the previous salon, was I?'

'Were you able to sneak another look at it?' persisted Brooke.

'I didn't get the chance,' replied Freya. 'Ralph insisted on taking me to the room on the first floor where he keeps his important collections. He took huge pleasure in showing me some of the most valuable pieces then came out with all this stuff about Emily. How she was engaged to his great-grandfather – apparently with her parents' approval – and then broke it off. Jilted him, as he put it, although I don't think they got as far as a wedding.'

'Ooh,' said Brooke. 'That's juicy. Anything more?'

Freya took a deep breath. 'It was extremely weird,' she said in a puzzled voice. 'He behaved as if I really was Emily while he was telling me all this. And oh, Brooke, he tried to kiss me. Then I ran out of the house without speaking to anyone else and got the night-bus home.'

'Bloody hell!' exclaimed Brooke. 'That's sexual harassment. You could sue him for that.'

Freya sighed. 'I don't think so,' she said as her head started to throb again. 'But I do need to get to the bottom of this, if only for my own peace of mind.'

'Hold on a tick,' said Brooke.

Freya heard a muffled conversation going on in the background. Then, 'I've got to go, Freya. Let me know if I can do anything to help. And for God's sake, be careful.'

Freya clicked her phone off and laid it on the kitchen table. Then she boiled the kettle for another mug of tea. She felt better for speaking to Brooke, saner somehow. Sitting quietly, sipping tea, she reflected on everything she'd just told her friend. What screamed out – and made her deeply uneasy – was Ralph's eccentric play-acting. His peculiar desire to inhabit his ancestor's persona and treat Freya as his fiancée seemed to go way beyond the character impersonation he encouraged his guests to pursue at his Victorian salons. What the hell was he up to?

Taking the mug of tea into the living room, she sat at the table and flipped up the screen of her laptop. Typing 'Household Census' into the search engine brought up numerous websites. After a fair bit of trawling she began to look in detail at the censuses from 1851 onwards.

An hour ticked past. There was a wealth of information, but it took time to scan through it for any relevant nuggets. Freya carried on doggedly for another hour, then another as she combed the census for 1861 and 1871. Nothing came to light. She was beginning to despair when – oh eureka! – the 1881 household census brought up a listing for Lawrence Meadowcroft.

Freya felt her pulse speed up, sending yellow darts across her vision, as she scoured the hand-written entry. The cramped lines of spidery writing blurred and shifted as she tried to read them. She closed her eyes for a moment then blinked and the words settled into a steady shape.

Lawrence was living in London at an address in Kensington. As head of the household, he came top of the entry. Under his name was Emily's. A separate column gave her relationship to him as sister. Below her name was another female called Edith Gray.

Reading and re-reading the listing, Freya felt her heart racing and took a deep breath to calm herself. It seemed as if at least part of the story Ralph had told her was true. Emily really did leave home and go to live with her brother in London.

She peered at the screen more closely, eagerly searching for further information. The entry listed their ages – 21, 18, and 16 – and marital statuses. All three were unmarried. Under the heading 'Occupation' she found Lawrence was listed as 'scholar' and Edith Gray as 'servant'. Against Emily's name there was nothing. The space was blank.

Freya leaned back in her chair, her mind fizzing. Surely this listing must relate to the time when Lawrence was studying at the National Art Training School. So, what were the siblings doing at the time of the next census a decade later?

Another hour passed as Freya repeatedly trawled the 1891 census. Eventually she had to concede defeat. She could find nothing. Lawrence and Emily Meadowcroft appeared to have vanished into thin air.

Then she was struck by another idea. Still searching the 1891 census, Freya typed in Ralph Merrick's name without really expecting to see a result. To her astonishment an entry popped up. He was living in London with his wife, Agnes, and four children – two sons and two daughters. His household also included a housekeeper, cook and two maids.

Oh my God, Freya thought. Then he didn't marry Emily… so the story about being jilted could well be true.

She re-read the listing. Ha! He was clearly living in quite some style with all those servants. How could he afford that? Freya peered at the 'Occupation' column and deciphered the letters 'Ind'. Scrolling down to the end of the page, she found a sidenote explaining the abbreviation. It translated as having independent means.

Freya sat back and contemplated what that meant. Living on income from investments and property like most of the upper classes at that time. A wheeler-dealer, no doubt. A bit like his slippery descendant.

Then her heart started banging painfully as a new realisation crystallised in her mind. Ralph Merrick not only used the same name as his ancestor but was living at the same address.

CHAPTER 11

Hoxton Square had changed radically since Freya last visited Shoreditch. Once an unpromising area with run-down premises, its gritty ambience and cheap rents had attracted young British artists, design ateliers and small recording studios. Then youthful tech entrepreneurs and enterprising start-ups had moved in and turned it into a hip location. Gentrification was now in full swing, and it seemed the square had become a fashionable destination where only thriving businesses, restaurants and offices could now afford the rates and rent.

Freya screwed up her eyes, looking for numbers on the buildings she was passing. No clues were evident. She paused at a refurbished pub whose façade was decorated with hanging baskets full of bright flowers. It was warm enough to sit outside and all the early evening drinkers at the wooden tables spilling across the pavement seemed to be wearing an identical uniform: sunglasses, black tee-shirts, denim jeans. Everyone was glued to a phone. No one was talking directly to another person and the thought of trying to engage with anyone seemed impossibly daunting.

Just as Freya was about to go into the pub and ask for directions, a shaft of sunlight caught the silvery sheen of a railing guarding a corner building ahead of her. It was the smartest façade on the square. I bet that's it, she thought.

Approaching the tall white building, she could see the ground floor rooms had been turned into a large gallery space. The offices would be upstairs, she guessed. A discreet name on the lowest part of the window told her she had arrived at Gallery Greaves.

Freya stood outside, looking through the large picture window. White walls and blond floorboards offered a neutral backdrop for a collection of self-consciously placed designs. A row of metal stools, shaped like egg-timers, caught her eye. A tall lamp in the form of a giant sunflower stood at the rear of the space next to a gleaming, aluminium chair with a soaring, slatted back. Along the far wall hung a series of enormous platters with swirly, candy-coloured patterns while a low table with a bluey-green, stained glass top was positioned close to the window. It brought to mind the stained-glass panel Jack had shown her in the vitrine at Ralph's house although it lacked the delicate enchantment of that piece.

Freya collected her scattered thoughts and moved towards the building's freshly painted, black door. Choosing from a row of three, unmarked bells on the intercom, she rang the top one.

'I've got an appointment to see Oliver Greaves,' she lied.

'Third floor,' instructed a female voice with an Essex accent.

The door automatically clicked open, and Freya stepped into a white hallway. At the far end of the passage, she was faced with the choice of a lift with transparent glass sides or white-painted stairs. She decided to walk, hoping the physical exercise would calm her nerves.

Vivid abstracts on the walls accompanied her progress up the stairs as did a string of oval lights cascading through the stairwell like an oversized pearl necklace. The stairs culminated at the third floor, merging into an open-plan office flooded with natural light. Freya blinked as she stepped into the bright, airy space, dazzled by the early evening sunshine.

A young, pale-faced girl with spiky, dyed-red hair and kohl-rimmed eyes sat at a smoked-glass desk. She looked enquiringly at Freya who strode past, her eyes fixed on a bent head at the far side of the room. The thatch of golden hair jerked up as she approached.

'Freya!' Oliver shot up from his chair, knocking a folder onto the floor. 'My God, what are you doing here?'

'I've come for a chat,' Freya said in a friendly voice. 'For old times' sake,' she added sardonically.

Oliver subsided into a black leather chair behind the glass desk as if his legs would no longer support him. He gaped at her, open-mouthed, then swallowed and made an obvious effort to regain control. He gestured towards an uncomfortable-looking, smoked-glass chair next to his desk. 'Do sit down,' he said. 'Would you like a coffee?'

Freya smiled. 'You've forgotten I prefer tea,' she said.

A strange expression crossed Oliver's face. Was it regret or relief or perhaps a mixture of both?

'Gemma, would you make a cup of tea for Miss Wetherby and bring me another cappuccino please,' he called across the room authoritatively.

'Herbal or Indian?' piped Gemma who hadn't taken her eyes off Freya since she entered the room.

'Builder's, please,' replied Freya cheerfully.

Gemma remained at her desk as if frozen. 'That's Indian to

you and me,' explained Oliver patiently. Then his young assistant got up and disappeared behind a partition along one side of the room.

'You've got a nice space here,' said Freya, glancing around approvingly. 'Business must be going well.'

Oliver sat back in his chair looking wary. 'It's not so bad. I was lucky to sign up Sebastian Hayward and Giorgio Rondorelli to design some of the initial pieces of furniture for the gallery. People responded well and then I was able to persuade some other high-profile names to come on board. It was a good idea to branch out into designer furniture as well as home accessories and jewellery.'

'And we know exactly how you got off to such a brilliant start with the jewellery,' said Freya with an edge to her voice.

Oliver fiddled with a pen on his desk then raised his eyes to her. 'Tell me what you've been doing with yourself since we – parted company,' he said, sounding less sure of himself.

Freya took a deep breath. 'You know my mother died?'

'No, I hadn't heard. I'm sorry,' replied Oliver, his voice gratingly solicitous.

'She wasn't in hospital for long, thank heavens, and she wasn't in pain. It was all quite peaceful at the end.'

'I'm glad to hear that,' said Oliver. 'Even so, it must have been a shock for you.'

'What's been really difficult is having to deal with everything on my own,' admitted Freya, trying to ignore the ache in her throat. 'But her death has also made me realise how important it is not to waste time and to get on with the things you really want to do while you can.'

Oliver lounged back in his chair, twiddling the pen in his fingers. 'Like what?' he asked vaguely.

'Creating jewellery for my new company,' said Freya bluntly.

Oliver sat up straight and stared at her. 'Is that why you've come here?' he asked.

Freya smiled. 'Partly,' she replied, feeling pleased that Oliver seemed rattled.

At that moment Gemma appeared with two large stoneware cups on a tray. She put the tray on Oliver's desk between the stacks of folders then scuttled off to her own perch.

'Thanks, Gemma,' said Oliver. 'Hey, why don't you knock off early tonight?' he suggested, looking at his watch.

Despite her uncomfortable seat, Freya relaxed a little. It would be easier to talk to Oliver if his assistant left the office. She reached over and picked up the cup of tea. Sipping, she stole surreptitious glances at Oliver. He looked tired but he was still the same attractive man she once thought she would live with forever.

'Well?' he asked, licking a faint smudge of froth from his upper lip. 'Have you started designing again then?'

'Very much so,' replied Freya emphatically. 'I'm working on a Victorian-inspired collection which, I think, has the potential to be just as successful as my silver filigree cuff.'

Oliver did his best to mask a shudder. 'I hope you haven't come here to drag up past history,' he said. 'Look, I'm sorry. I shouldn't have done it. I know it wasn't entirely your fault that our company collapsed but I felt you owed me one. If you'd only managed to fulfil that last batch of orders, we might have been alright.'

Freya remained silent, watching him run a hand distractedly through his hair.

'It was just so demoralising having to go, cap in hand, to my father to pay off our creditors,' he said. 'Dealing with the bank and winding up the business was a horrible experience. Just horrible. After that I was on my uppers – no job, no income, no prospects. I was at my wit's end and desperate for a break. I showed the design to Stefan, and he was all over it like a rash. Insisted on putting it into production and paid zillions for all those ads. And when the sales took off, as he so rightly predicted, I persuaded him to back me with enough funding to set up Gallery Greaves.'

'Bloody hell, Oliver – how could you? That was my design, not yours.' Freya could feel her face blazing as she spoke. 'You're a cheat, Oliver – a complete scumbag,' she continued. 'You behaved like a common thief, selling the design and taking all the credit for my work. A street rat has more integrity than that.'

Oliver grimaced. 'I know – it wasn't my finest hour,' he admitted. 'I'm sorry. To tell you the truth I began to feel guilty when Stefan went bananas over the design but by then it was too late to try and rectify things.'

'Well, I'm offering you the chance to do that right now,' said Freya icily as molten anger turned to steely determination. 'And I'm not leaving here until you tell me what you're going to do about it.'

Hunching his shoulders, Oliver's golden thatch dipped as he stared down at the desk. He was silent for a moment, frowning. Then he picked up his cup, drained it and replaced it on the tray with a clumsy thud.

'Okay, okay,' he said tersely. 'I certainly don't want to carry on feeling guilty about it for the rest of my life so here's what I'll do. I'll transfer a design fee into your bank account at the usual percentage on sales. I'll also credit you retrospectively in a press release and say that, due to a silly mix-up, you were never properly acknowledged at the time. If the media choose to pick up on that and make a meal of it, too bad. I think my business is sufficiently robust to take a bit of flack if necessary.'

'Oliver, that would be—' Freya stopped mid-sentence as she felt a lump rise in her throat. She swallowed and tried again. 'That would certainly set the record straight,' she said. Then she added, more tartly, 'But how do I know you'll keep your word?'

'Oh, Freya, don't be like that,' replied Oliver in a tired voice. Picking up his mobile phone he pressed a key and dictated in a monotone, 'Usual press release letter-heading. Headline: Greaves Gallery makes surprise announcement. Indent paragraph. Greaves Gallery today revealed that London – hyphen – based jeweller – comma – Freya Wetherby – comma – was the design genius behind the enchanting Filigree Cuff produced by Stefan Zanutti in collaboration with Oliver Greaves – full stop.'

Oliver paused briefly to rub his eye then continued dictating. 'Indent second paragraph. The Filigree Cuff – open bracket – which recently featured in the *Financial Times*'s *How to Spend It* magazine, *Vogue* and *Harper's Bazaar* – close bracket – has become an international best-seller and the revelation that it was designed by one of the jewellery world's rising stars has delighted fans – full stop.'

'Indent third paragraph. Open quotation marks. Due to an administrative error Freya Wetherby was not credited properly at the launch and I'm happy to set the record straight – comma – close quotation marks – said Oliver Greaves – comma – founder of Greaves Gallery – full stop.'

Oliver clicked off the phone and glanced at Freya. 'Happy with that?'

'Will you email me a copy of the release when you send it out to the press, please?' asked Freya.

'God, you're so suspicious of me, aren't you?' snorted Oliver. 'Yes, I'll get Gemma to send it to you in the morning,' he said with exaggerated weariness. 'Now, if you'll excuse me,

I've got rather a lot to do. The wedding's on Saturday and there's a hell of a lot to sort out before we go off on honeymoon.'

Freya gulped. 'You're – getting married?' she asked in a faint voice.

'Oh, didn't you know?' Oliver scratched his nose, looking embarrassed. 'Robyn's an Aussie and she'll run into visa problems if we don't tie the knot.'

'I – I hadn't heard,' stammered Freya. Taking a deep breath, she added, 'I hope you'll be – very happy.'

'Thanks,' said Oliver in an offhand way, shuffling some papers on his desk.

Sliding off the glass chair, Freya got to her feet. 'Goodbye Oliver,' she said quietly, feeling drained.

'BASTARD,' snarled Freya as she strode past the pub in Hoxton Square. Turning into Old Street she could feel tears stinging her eyes and blinked them away as she hurried towards the underground station.

The tube carriage was unpleasantly full and Freya found herself squashed between a short, obese woman and a tall man with bad breath. The thought of going back to her silent flat was distinctly unappealing. At a loss what to do next, she squeezed her way out of the carriage at King's Cross and stood on the platform in a daze as people surged impatiently around her.

Get a grip, she told herself. Still undecided, she headed towards the Victoria line escalator and made her way down to the platform. Waiting for the tube to arrive, she thought bitterly about Oliver. How typical he should fall straight into arms of another woman after they split up.

He wasn't the kind of man who would cope well living alone.

The train whooshed into the station sending her hair flying into her eyes. The doors slid open and she stepped into the crowded carriage. Leaning against the glass partition next to the doors, Freya closed her eyes and pictured Oliver exchanging wedding rings with his bride. She sighed and wondered where he'd bought the engagement ring. At least he hadn't tried to commission it from her.

The tube rushed into Oxford Circus station. Without giving her destination much thought, Freya got out of the carriage and headed for the escalator leading to the exit. All the shops here would be open late and perhaps she could distract herself by looking for a summer dress.

Crossing Oxford Street at the traffic lights she strolled north into Regent Street, passing a string of fashion shops with music blaring through their open doors. The pavements were teeming with after-work shoppers. Dodging through the knots of people, any desire to hunt for summery clothes drained away. It all seemed too much effort.

Exhausted and upset, Freya turned into Margaret Street to avoid the crowds. She would look for a café and sit quietly, having a snack, before heading home.

Slowing her pace, Freya became aware of three smart-looking girls chatting as they strolled along the pavement in front of her. They all had blonde hair, wore black trousers and were talking animatedly. Then she saw another well-groomed woman cross the road and enter an office building on the same side of the street shortly after them.

Still hoping to find a café that didn't belong to a faceless coffee chain, she glanced down a passageway on her right and spotted a yellow awning. Situated at the end of a cul-de-sac, it seemed the perfect place for a quiet cup of tea.

Freya pushed the door open and went inside. Coming in from the strong evening sunshine, the interior seemed remarkably dark. She walked to the rear and sat down at a table furthest from the door. A young, smiley waitress took her order for a pot of tea and a warm panini.

'Have you been for an interview?' she asked Freya when she returned from the counter with a tray.

'No, why?' asked Freya.

'Oh, it's central casting around here,' replied the waitress, jerking her head in the direction of Margaret Street. 'You never know who'll pop in. It's brilliant for star-spotting,' she added with a giggle.

'Goodness,' said Freya.

'I'm hoping for a break myself,' confided the waitress with an eye on the door. 'I'm doing classes part-time.'

'Well, good luck with those,' said Freya, hoping to bring an end to the conversation.

Two tall, blonde girls wearing identical pink jackets entered the café and sat down at a table near the door. The waitress went over to take their order then disappeared behind the counter to operate a noisy espresso machine.

Freya idly watched the girls as she sipped her tea. They radiated a glossy confidence, a kind of golden aura. Was Oliver's fiancée like that? God! What a rat. Brooke had been so right about him.

Her thoughts ran on in a muddled chatter. He'd probably send out the press release tomorrow morning. It was no skin off his nose really. No doubt he would see it as a publicity opportunity for his gallery. If she'd heard nothing from Gemma by the afternoon, she'd call her to ask if it had been mailed out. She would also check her bank account to make sure the promised design fee had arrived.

Revived by the tea and panini, Freya was scrabbling in her

purse, looking for some change to pay the bill when the door opened. She glanced up as a young man came in and sat down with his back to her at a table next to the girls. Her throat tightened with alarm. It was Jack.

Sitting motionless, her purse lying open on the table, Freya tried to think calmly. Should she go and speak to him? Would he welcome that? Or was their intimacy at Ralph's salon just a one-off moment of madness for him?

Jack leant over towards the girls, and they all started chatting. Freya watched intently, straining to hear their conversation. Impossible. They were sitting too far away. Clearly, they had something in common though. Then the smiley waitress came over to take his order and joined in, giggling.

Acting. That was it. That was what they all did or wanted to do. Freya exhaled, feeling slightly dizzy from holding her breath for too long. Well, she couldn't leave now. Jack would see her walking past his table. Anyway, she would be too embarrassed to speak to him with those glossy girls sitting there. She would wait until he left the café and approach him outside when he was on his own.

Right now, as she studied the back of his head, a deep chasm was opening up inside her. Freya felt raw with disappointment and wounded by a painful sense of betrayal. She had dared to hope Jack cared for her but now it seemed as if their encounter on the garden bench had just been part of an elaborate act. He'd kissed and fondled her because Ralph had paid him to play a role. The duplicity – and her own foolishness – made her feel soiled and worthless.

Sitting silently at the table, Freya tried to gather her thoughts. If Jack really was an actor – or an aspiring actor – that probably meant Lawrence was as well. And what about the other guests at Ralph's salon? Were they genuine friends enjoying a bit of a lark or were they all actors too? Was the salon, in fact, some sort of elaborate stage set giving Ralph the opportunity to indulge his Victorian fantasies while directing his own personal cast and crew? That would certainly chime with her niggling suspicion that he enjoyed pulling the strings and watching everyone dance to his tune.

She must pull herself together and stay strong. If she could speak to Jack when he left the café then maybe she could get some answers. Just getting confirmation that he was a professional actor would give her a clue as to what was going on at the salons.

So much depended on how she handled the conversation. If it went well and she won his trust then he might even become an ally of sorts.

Seeing the waitress heading towards her table to collect the coins she'd put in the saucer, Freya dipped her head and pretended to look for something in her handbag to avoid a conversation. Then, to her dismay, she saw Jack getting up at the same time as the two girls. He went over to the counter to pay his bill and they all left the café together.

Freya waited a few moments before leaving the cafe. Outside, she could see all three of them half-way up the passage, still chatting. She began to follow slowly, watching them part with numerous air-kisses when they reached Margaret Street. They went in opposite directions. Jack turned to the right and Freya increased her pace. She was curious to see where he was going.

Again, Jack turned right, this time into Wells Street. Freya carried on following, leaving a short distance between them. She halted in the street while he waited on the pavement for a break in the traffic along Oxford Street. Then she ran across the road after him, narrowly avoiding being hit by a taxi.

Dodging around the late-night shoppers on Oxford Street, she nearly missed spotting him head into Berwick Street. He carried on walking for several minutes then turned left. Freya halted at the corner and peered along a short, badly lit street. Glimpsing him turn left again, she started to walk down the street. Then she stopped and bit her lip. Should she really be stalking him like this? It felt as if hours had passed since she left home. The light was fading, and it was getting chilly.

An image of Oliver floated into her mind. Angrily pushing it aside, Freya carried on walking and turned into a narrow alley. There were no streetlights here and Jack seemed to have vanished. She could just make out some movement at the end of the passage where there was a faint light above a door. Keeping close to the wall, she inched along the alley towards it.

Creeping nearer, she could make out Jack's silhouette and the glow of a cigarette. What on earth was he doing here? She got as close as she dared then stood motionless, leaning against the wall, peering into the gloom ahead. Rough mortar scraped the back of her hand as she brushed it against the wall. She could feel a pulse thud in her neck as fear tugged at her throat. Like a trickle of rain sliding down a window, what little trust she had left in Jack began to ebb away.

A conversation began. Jack was talking to two men, both shorter and slighter than himself. She couldn't see their faces, but their words bounced back to her off the alley's high, narrow walls.

'What a lush,' said the man holding a cigarette. 'Splashing out on Soho's top tailor.'

'Premium service,' replied Jack. 'Measured me this morning and ready to pick up now from his workshop upstairs.'

'Trust you to land on your feet with a cushy job like that,' said the other man with a chuckle.

'Just a lucky break,' said Jack cheerfully.

'Can you get us on board as extras?' asked the first speaker, drawing on his cigarette.

'Yeah, a bit of character acting would be right up our boulevard,' added his friend.

'Sorry guys, that's not an option,' replied Jack.

'That's a shame,' said the second speaker. 'Fancy slumming it tonight at the King's Arms?'

'No time – I've just come to collect my rig and now I must scoot,' replied Jack.

'Well, have fun at the party, breaking hearts and causing mayhem,' said the smoker.

Freya backed away, her heart pounding. Terrified of being seen, she turned and inched slowly towards the alley's entrance with one hand following the wall, keeping as close to its dark shadow as possible. Reaching the street, she began to run.

CHAPTER 12

Waking with a throbbing head, Freya regretted knocking back a full tumbler of whisky when she got home. Her throat felt as scratchy as sandpaper and her brain as tiny as a pea.

'No!' she bleated out loud as memories of the previous evening flooded her mind. What an idiot she'd been to fall for Jack and believe – so stupidly – he cared for her. How naive! She'd been duped into thinking the attraction was mutual. That he fancied her as much as she did him. And it was all a mirage!

Jack – that probably wasn't even his real name, damn it. Now she'd discovered he was an actor – just a hired hand plying his trade – she felt cheated and angry. Furious with herself as much as him.

'No!' she cried again as her phone rang. Fumbling for it on the bedside table, she answered blearily, failing to recognise the caller's number.

'Miss Wetherby? It's Alan Roberts. I've got some good news for you.'

It took Freya a moment to remember that Alan Roberts was the estate agent involved in selling her mother's cottage.

'Oh, yes?' she asked.

'I've had some interest from a client looking for a bolthole in the countryside. I showed him round the cottage yesterday and he's put in an offer. It's significantly below the asking price we discussed but I think it's fair, bearing in mind the work he'll need to do on both the interior and exterior.'

A stab of regret made Freya wince. This reluctance to part with her mother's cottage was about holding onto the past – she acknowledged that – and yet she knew Brooke had a point when she'd said it was best to live in the present rather than the past.

'Do you think you could persuade him to increase it?' she asked, choosing to prevaricate.

'Possibly,' replied the estate agent in a doubtful tone. 'Look, all I can do is ask. I'll get back to you once I've spoken to him again.'

Freya switched off the phone and sank back on the pillows groaning. This was the last thing she needed right now. She closed her eyes. As if it hadn't been horrible enough hearing about Oliver's marriage. Then to see Jack.... Doing what? Her head swam unpleasantly. What exactly had she seen and heard? Sighing, she heaved herself out of bed and began to get dressed.

An hour later Freya left the flat with the intention of spending the morning in her workshop. Pausing in the communal hallway, she checked her pigeon-hole for correspondence. Usually, it was empty except for bills and letters from utility companies or unsolicited leaflets shoved through the letterbox by local shops and businesses. Today a large, plum-coloured envelope was sitting there. Freya guessed in a flash what it contained. She scooped it up and walked round to her lock-up before ripping it open there.

A RESTLESS, fidgety morning followed. Unnerved by the events of the previous evening, Freya felt increasingly edgy and ill-tempered. The invitation lay on her workbench, unsettling her each time she glanced at it. It was impossible to focus properly on any work.

Freya picked up the invitation and scanned the elaborate, Gothic script for the tenth time. 'Ralph Merrick requests the pleasure of Miss Emily Meadowcroft's company for A Dark Circle'. A date and time followed along with his address. As with previous invitations the dress-code was 'Victorian'.

Shuddering, she pictured Ralph kissing her in his collector's den. If that wasn't disgusting enough, what about his warped obsession with her miniature? Was he psychologically damaged – unbalanced even? All that talk about communing with his ancestors sounded so weird. It was as if he relished inhabiting their skins.

Freya froze, sitting motionless at her workbench with a needle file in one hand and a buff stick in the other. A chilling thought had struck her. Wasn't she guilty of behaving exactly like Ralph by adopting Emily Meadowcroft's persona at the salons? Hadn't she thoroughly enjoyed slipping under her peachy skin and adopting her mind-set? Even when Lawrence challenged her so forcefully about Emily's wilful behaviour, she hadn't denied the pretence. In fact, she'd gone along with it even to the extent of worrying about the Morris & Co. commission when she got to bed.

Blood sang in her ears as a guilty flush heated her face. In some ways she was even worse than Ralph. She had hoped to win Jack's affection by maintaining the charade and staying in character even when they were so intimate on the garden bench. If she was truly honest, she had to admit it was deceitful. She should feel ashamed of herself for behaving in that way.

Anyway, it had done her no good. Jack – damn him, whoever he was – had been playing a role too. Even if his actions had been directed by Ralph he was still responsible for carrying out the deception and duping her into thinking he was emotionally involved.

A wave of despair engulfed her. First Oliver then Jack – why did things never work out romantically? There must be some flaw in her character that led her to fall for men who betrayed or cheated her.

Perhaps it had something to do with the absence of her father – or even a father-figure – when she was growing up. His exit from her life when she was just nine had been painfully sudden. Maybe the loss had affected her in more ways than she'd realised, causing her to get involved with men who would deceive or fail her.

Blinking back tears, Freya stared at the invitation again. Would she feel more inclined to attend another salon if it wasn't billed as 'A Dark Circle'? The phrase brought back buried memories. A craze for holding dark circles – seances – had been a welcome diversion from exam preparations in her last year at school. Belle, ever the experimenter, had kicked them off with table-turning sessions in a disused garage where they congregated after school-hours.

Freya had remained a silent sceptic from the outset. The notion of communicating with the dead seemed unbelievably far-fetched to her. Rightly or wrongly, she suspected Belle of foul-play – of pushing the upturned glass across a makeshift table towards the letters encircling it and spelling out whatever took her fancy instead of allowing it to move of its own accord.

Freya recalled her friends shrieking in fright – or mock-fright – at the messages that emerged from these sessions. It had been a bit of a lark then. Attending a séance in all seriousness at Ralph's house was a different matter entirely.

Laying down her tools, Freya wiped clammy hands on her jeans and wondered how Ralph would treat her this time if she attended the salon. He had behaved so courteously towards her initially, exuding charm and bonhomie. She'd been flattered by his encouragement to join his social circle and indebted to him for his generosity over the necklace commission.

Would he realise he'd overstepped the mark last time? It was impossible to predict his behaviour – his moods seemed so volatile – and the thought of a similarly intimate encounter with him made her stomach churn. Yet she had to accept his invitation if she was ever to find out why he would seemingly do anything to acquire Emily's portrait miniature.

Tension tugged between her shoulder-blades and she flexed her back to ease it. Picking up the needle file, Freya ran a finger over its sharp point until she could feel it tingling. Ralph was clearly one of those people who were never satisfied with simply admiring a beautiful object until they owned it themselves. Perhaps he pressured his other friends until they reluctantly allowed him to buy their artworks too. He had certainly quizzed some of his guests closely enough about their cherished possessions for her to notice his acquisitiveness.

Should she accept his invitation? Freya considered her options. Declining meant it was unlikely she would find out much more about Emily Meadowcroft than her internet searches had already thrown up. She would have a better chance if she went to the salon. Ralph appeared to have insider knowledge, both from his own family and from the conversation he'd had with Tom Meadowcroft at the house sale. But was she putting herself at risk if she attended the event? Ralph could be mercurial – she knew that now – and she would have to tread carefully not to antagonise him.

What about Lawrence? If push came to shove, would he – as Emily's sibling – take her side against Ralph? If they both stayed in character, he could be an ally, but first she would need to appease his fury over Emily's behaviour. How could she gain his support?

Racking her brains, the germ of an idea emerged. If she did decide to go to the salon she could make and wear a medieval-style brooch that might pass muster as one of Emily's creations for Morris & Co. That would surely seal an allegiance with Lawrence.

And then there was Jack – would he be invited to the Dark Circle given Ralph's evident hostility towards him?

Freya sighed at the memory of lying entwined with him on the garden bench As the delicious recollection flooded back, a wistful query fingered its way into her mind. Surely his emotional warmth – tenderness, even – couldn't have been entirely fabricated. Was it possible that the actor she knew as Jack had not been completely acting a part?

Despite the anguish over her discovery, she couldn't help wondering if the magnetic attraction between Jack and Emily could endure 'out of character' away from the salons.

Tossing her head to dismiss a tiny spark of hope ignited by the thought, Freya picked up her tools again.

ALL THROUGH THE morning questions jostled in Freya's mind as fiercely as birds fighting for scraps in the mews outside her workshop. Should she attend the salon or not? Did something sinister lie behind Ralph's motives for holding a Dark Circle? Something that could put her in real jeopardy?

She remembered Belle telling her that people often fainted, and some had even died of fright at seances in the past. Participating in Ralph's Dark Circle could be dangerous. She'd be putting herself in his hands and letting him call the shots with no one else around her she could trust. Was she brave enough to risk it?

Reflecting on her experiences at the previous salons, Freya had the uncomfortable feeling that Ralph was reeling her into his fantasy world inch by inch. She was being played for a reason she couldn't quite grasp, however hard she reached for answers. Even though she now knew Jack was a hired actor, it wasn't at all clear why she'd been steered into playing a role in Ralph's grand charade. After all, he seemed to have plenty of friends prepared to do just that.

Sweating with anxiety, she tried to make up her mind. One minute she decided it would be better not to go. It was just too risky after the way Ralph had behaved in his collector's room. The next she felt desperate for another chance to see Jack and uncover the full story about Emily Meadowcroft. What should she do?

Feeling urgently in need of a change of scene, Freya locked up the workshop at lunchtime and headed towards the underground, hoping to spot Brooke at the Ryder gallery. Arriving at Green Park, Freya made a circular tour of Shepherd Market's narrow streets then cut through a passageway and ambled past the gallery. Brooke's dark head was clearly visible even though she had her back to the window. She appeared to be deep in conversation with a red-haired woman wearing a chic black suit.

By the time Freya passed the window again the woman had disappeared. A client? A lover? Freya shrugged and told herself it was none of her business. At that moment Brooke looked up and strode towards the door waving wildly, leaving Freya in no doubt she was glad to see her.

'Good, a welcome distraction,' said Brooke, yanking open the glass door. 'Come in. Richard's just gone off for lunch with one of our more demanding clients. I'm holding the fort.'

'Oh Brooke, I've had another invitation from Ralph,' blurted Freya, stepping across the threshold. 'To a séance.'

'How very Victorian.' Brooke rolled her eyes as she closed the door. 'At his house in Chelsea?'

Freya nodded.

'Will you go?' asked Brooke, moving towards the rear of the gallery.

Freya followed. 'I'm in two minds,' she replied. 'The thought of seeing Ralph terrifies me but it's the only way I'm going to find out more about Emily.'

Brooke paused and turned to face her, resting her hands on the back of a chair constructed from multi-coloured planks. 'Ah-ha,' she said. 'I meant to call you about Emily, but I was so busy this morning I forgot.'

'What about her?' asked Freya.

'That portrait you saw at Ralph's house – the one Jack Hunter painted – has turned up on an art-tracing register.' Brooke moved over to a desk at the back of the gallery, picked up a computer print-out and handed it to Freya.

Alongside a few lines of description was a colour reproduction of a painting. Freya felt as if the floor beneath her feet was shifting. She blinked and looked at the image again. 'That's it,' she breathed. 'It's identical to the one in Ralph's bedroom.' Her eyes widened as she stared at Brooke. 'So – it was stolen?'

Brooke nodded. 'Possibly. Read what it says.'

Freya read the short description out loud: 'Portrait of Emily Meadowcroft painted circa 1882 by Jack Hunter at his studio in Bow. Family heirloom stolen from a private residence in London on Christmas Day while the owner was out at lunch.' She raised her eyes and scowled at Brooke. 'What a mean thing to do.'

'Of course, it doesn't necessarily mean the painting you saw at Ralph's house is the one listed as missing,' said Brooke. 'It could be part of a series or even a copy. Interesting coincidence though, isn't it?'

Freya glanced down at the sheet of paper in her hand and silently re-read the description. 'It doesn't say who the owner is.'

'These databases of lost and stolen items rarely do,' replied Brooke airily. 'But the editor of the website is an old friend of mine. I phoned him and he gave me the owner's name in confidence – Alice Clarendon. Do you know who she is?'

'No, I've never heard of her,' replied Freya. "Hmm...1882 was the year after the household census. Emily would have been nineteen.'

'Maybe we should try and get in touch with Alice Clarendon, whoever she is,' suggested Brooke.

'No!' exclaimed Freya. 'Not before I go to Ralph's next salon. We could try and see her after that, but even then I'd feel hesitant about telling her where I think her painting is hanging. Like you said, how can we be sure it's the same one?'

'Maybe you're right,' said Brooke. 'Look, are you sure about going to this séance? It sounds pretty dodgy to me.'

'I want to find out more about Emily Meadowcroft and figure out why Ralph behaves as if I'm her,' said Freya. 'And if that means standing up to him and holding my ground then I'll do it.'

'Is this the only way you can suss it out?' asked Brooke, narrowing her eyes.

'What do you mean?' asked Freya.

'Well, your host might – or might not – be mixed up in receiving stolen goods,' replied Brooke bluntly. 'There's no way of knowing if that's the case or not right now. If I were you, I'd err of the side of caution and give Ralph and his blasted salons an extremely wide berth.'

'Well, you're not me, are you?' said Freya. 'As for owning a painting of Emily – well, why shouldn't he? There's a family connection – he told me she was briefly engaged to his great-grandfather - and, after all, he is an art historian and a collector.'

Brooke's dark eyes flashed with irritation. 'I really don't think you should go,' she said. 'Your track record with men isn't exactly great. You're just too trusting – a soft target for unscrupulous shits. Look at what happened with Oliver.'

'There's no need to bring that up.' Freya felt her body stiffen. 'I'm quite capable of looking after myself, whatever you may think.'

They glared at each other for a moment then Brooke turned away with a shrug. 'Well, since you're here, do you want to look at our new stuff downstairs? I'll have to stay rooted to the spot in case anyone comes in.'

A flight of stairs led to the basement showroom. It was clear to Freya that the bespoke pieces on display were a cut above those in Oliver's gallery. While the designs at Gallery Greaves might appeal to any homeowner with a sense of contemporary style, the Ryder Gallery specialised in one-off pieces exquisitely made with luxurious materials like alabaster marble, shagreen and rare wood. It was the kind of work the design critics would call 'museum-quality'.

Running her fingers over the shimmering surface of a sunrise-pink dining-table intricately inlaid with straw-marquetry, Freya edged round its oval form and moved towards an elegant cocktail cabinet in the corner. A marquetry snake in various exotic timbers – yellow, green, russet – writhed across the cabinet's façade. Freya spotted a tiny, red apple at the top of the door. Placing the tip of her finger on the apple, she pressed it gently. The door sprang open to reveal a pale-green suede interior backed by an illuminated mirror with glass shelves for bottles and glasses. Eat your heart out, Ralph, Freya thought, this is true craftsmanship.

Negotiating a low, circular table created from a stack of up-ended logs, Freya strolled over to inspect a row of brightly coloured beetles displayed on the far wall. These turned out to be made from painted wood. As she stroked the surface of one design, each of the two main wings slid apart to reveal a small storage space inside. Then a glittery, opaquely white console table caught her eye. Bending down to read the label attached to its metal leg, she discovered the surface was made from a mineral called mica. On its twinkling surface sat a fat, black, ceramic buddha with a knowing smile.

At that moment, the gallery door opened overhead; she heard a man's voice speaking and Brooke's muffled reply. It was time to beat a retreat. When she emerged at the top of the stairs the pair were still in conversation at the rear of the space. Brooke glanced briefly in her direction as Freya gave her a wave and let herself out of the gallery.

Making her way back to the underground station, Freya wished she could have spent longer discussing Ralph's invitation and persuading Brooke to see things from her own perspective. Brooke was a tough cookie – she'd always admired that aspect of her personality – but perhaps a bit blinkered about men. They were all beyond redemption, in her opinion. Where Ralph was concerned, however, she could well be right.

Would it be foolish to join Ralph's Dark Circle without any idea of what she was letting herself in for? She was in two minds again. Brooke had put her on her mettle and it was becoming a matter of pride to show she could be just as resilient as her friend.

Making her way along a narrow, dim street towards Piccadilly, she tripped and nearly fell. Glancing back to see what had caught her ankle-boot, she gave an involuntary start as she realised that someone – a woman – was huddled in the doorway of an unlit building. A dark headscarf covered most of her face although some wisps of straggling, fair hair had escaped. Her bowed head and sagging shoulders suggested she was in the grip of drugs or despair. Beyond hope. Beyond caring.

For a moment Freya wondered if she had been tripped up deliberately but the woman made no move to beg for money or speak to her so she carried on walking towards Piccadilly feeling as light-headed as if she'd seen a ghost.

Pausing to pick up an *Evening Standard* from a pile at the entrance to Green Park underground station, Freya tried hard to stop her spirits sinking as she plodded down the escalator, too fidgety to stand still while it slowly descended to the platform. For if she was to face her fears and attend the Dark Circle then she felt – superstitiously – it would be better to go with Brooke's blessing. As it was, their quarrel had left her feeling raw, painfully friendless and alone.

WITH NO DESIRE TO return to her lock-up and confront the invitation on her workbench, Freya took the Piccadilly line to South Kensington. Outside the underground station, near a takeaway coffee shop, sat an unshaven, hollow-cheeked man with a skinny, brown dog.

'Spare any change?' he pleaded as Freya passed him. Hardening her heart, she carried on walking up to the Cromwell Road, past a row of cafes where intrepid diners were eating at small tables outdoors despite the cool breeze.

Poverty – could it ever be eradicated? There were perhaps wider safety-nets than in the Victorian era, yet it still prevailed as did the vast social chasm between rich and poor. A stray nugget from a school history lesson came to mind. The 1824 Vagrancy Act made it a criminal offence to beg or be homeless on the streets of England. Its draconian unfairness irked her as strongly as it had at school. Not only that – the law had yet to be repealed, which was why it had stuck in her memory.

Would Emily Meadowcroft have personally encountered beggars on the streets of London, Freya wondered. She would surely have seen them when she was living with her brother, even if she'd been accompanied by him or Jack when she was moving around the capital. If Ralph's story about Emily's estrangement from her well-to-do family was true, she would have been all too aware of the dangers of poverty and the desperate plight of impecunious women forced into prostitution to make a living.

Breaking off her engagement to a wealthy suitor and pinning her hopes of happiness on a charming but lazy art student must have filled Emily with fear and trepidation about the future.

Freya grimaced. Her own precarious financial situation offered some insight into what she might have felt. Scared. Watchful. Lonely.

Was Emily brave or foolhardy, Freya wondered as she crossed the road and made her way towards the V&A museum.

By-passing a knot of visitors swarming around the information desk inside the V&A, Freya walked briskly through the museum shop then strolled along the sculpture court and made her way up the imposing stone staircase with its decorative ironwork balustrades. Pausing at the entrance to the jewellery gallery, she found the glittering space much less crowded than on her last visit. It became even emptier as she stood aside to let a group of young Japanese visitors skitter pass. Now she could take her time without dodging around other people.

Rising to the ceiling, a run of glass vitrines flanked both sides of the long, narrow space. Each dazzling piece of jewellery pinned to the black background was individually spot-lit by a tiny, directional light, turning these functional museum cabinets into seductively alluring treasure-chests. Below the displays, at hip height, were detailed descriptions relating to the numbered jewels above.

Winding sinuously through the centre of the space were freestanding, semi-circular vitrines and a snaking seat with black cushions. Computer terminals offering information about the collection were positioned at each end of the seat. Freya had often used them on previous visits when she'd come in search of inspiration for her own designs.

Running her eyes over the glittering jewels in the wall-cabinets, Freya strolled along until she reached a spiral staircase punctuating the centre of the gallery. Vivid blue up-lighting illuminated wedge-shaped, glass steps, giving the whole structure a ghostly appearance. The staircase led to an upper gallery where more treasures were displayed but Freya moved on slowly, blinking at the sharp points of light in the display-cases, until she reached a section devoted to the Arts & Crafts period.

Beautifully crafted in gold, silver and painted enamel, many pieces looked as if they had been expressly designed for damsels gracing the pages of illustrated stories about the knights of the Round Table: elaborate waist girdles, brooches in the form of flowers or butterflies, pendants embellished with painted figures, earrings with complicated drops.

Freya unzipped her handbag, extracted a small notebook and started making rough sketches. She had forgotten how remarkable these designs were. Yet none employed the flashy, overly extravagant jewels used in the earlier Victorian work on show. To her eyes these Arts & Crafts pieces seemed deliberately restrained, relying on the integrity of design and craftmanship for their appeal rather than the high value of precious gems. Ostentatiously flaunting one's wealth clearly wasn't the goal for the original wearers of these pieces. Instead, they whispered their worth in far more subtle ways.

A stunning silver girdle caught her eye. Triple chains were linked at intervals by silver discs embossed with a flower motif and domed, jade-like gems. Echoing these sea-green pebbles were four, heart-shaped stones set on a larger disc at the girdle's centre. Here they were placed in a geometric pattern with four, circular garnets and four freshwater pearls. The design looked splendidly medieval. Freya imagined The Lady of Shallot wearing the girdle over a flowing silk gown as she gazed at Camelot's reflection in her mirror.

Sketching the girdle's lines and patterns in her notebook, Freya pondered about tackling a similar piece. Silver was malleable, responsive and alluring. It was one of her favourite materials. Bending closer to peer at the information label below the girdle, she banged her forehead on the glass case and her notebook fell from her hand onto the floor. After retrieving it she inspected the label again. Yes, she had read it correctly. The design was credited to May Morris. 'Perfect', she murmured under her breath.

Pinned to the black background, close to the girdle, she spotted another piece by May Morris. It was even more magical than the waist girdle. The silver, heart-shaped pendant was etched with graceful, floral motifs and embellished with greenish amazonite and williamsite stones, tiny seed-pearl circles and a chunky drop of blue-white lapis lazuli. How clever of May to create such an endearing piece. Freya moved on to the next vitrine, notebook in hand, in a dreamy reverie. And then she saw them.

If she hadn't already known what a sleeve clasp looked like it would have been easy to mistake the designs for a fantastical pair of chandelier earrings. Time spent studying the paintings of Elizabethan women at Tate Britain had taught her what they were: a jewel used at a point on the sleeve where a chemise worn underneath the dress could be pulled through slashes in the material.

The sleeve clasps winking at her in the vitrine were magnificent examples of these historic ornaments. Six domed garnets glowed like a bowl of black grapes at the top of each clasp. From these dropped a trio of large, ocean-blue, lapis lazuli stones. Directly below these hung three, oval-shaped agates and off to the side of each lapis lazuli gem hung a small, intensely dark, red ruby.

Freya was transfixed. This was a truly remarkable design. The visual equivalent of a virtuoso operatic performance. Standing there, admiring the powerful combination of colour, form and material felt like drinking the finest wine from the world's best vineyard.

Displayed alongside the sleeve clasps was a heart-shaped, silver brooch of such exquisite delicacy that Freya could feel her heart racing. The flourishes and curlicues within the heart were clearly designed to speak the Victorian language of flowers. What did they signify – devotion? Fidelity?

The red flowers worn in Emily Meadowcroft's hair in the portrait miniature popped into Freya's mind. Not for the first time she wondered whether they had been intended as a means of communication rather than just an aesthetic accessory.

Next to the brooch hung a long necklace made from small glass beads in at least three shades of blue. These were interspersed in a regular pattern with gleaming blobs of mother-of-pearl. Baton-shaped jade beads appeared at varying intervals and at the foot of the necklace glowed a huge lump of amber.

Standing in front of the vitrine, Freya recalled the book illustrations she loved as a child. It was the kind of necklace that Lancelot might have presented to Queen Guinevere. Frowning with concentration as she sketched the design in her notebook, she wondered who had worn it in the past.

Flicking up her eyes to read the information label, Freya gasped so loudly that a man standing on the opposite side of the gallery turned and stared at her. All three designs were credited to Lawrence Meadowcroft. The words seemed to quiver before her eyes as she read and re-read the label. 'Made circa 1881-2 for a private client of Morris & Co. Given by Anna Playford.'

Freya's head swam. So, it was true! The outcome of the story she'd heard at the salon was here, right in front of her eyes. Without doubt these had to be the pieces Emily created in exchange for her brother's silence. The heart-shaped brooch looked remarkably like the two designs she'd seen in the Meadowcroft house sale particulars and the one on display here had clearly been made by the same hand.

In fulfilling the commission on her brother's behalf, Emily had produced pieces unrivalled in their remarkable ingenuity and beauty. They were magnificent – a tour de force – yet Lawrence had taken all the credit for these extraordinary designs. And anyone seeing these pieces in the gallery today would never know the truth.

Freya could feel a tight knot of indignation and hatred gathering in the pit of her stomach. Jewellery, she knew, was one of the first areas of Arts & Crafts design in which women received real acknowledgement for their work. That was denied to Emily, thanks to her blackmailing brother. Standing there, glaring at the vitrine, Freya could feel a scorching fury burn through her whole body.

She remained motionless, consumed by anger, until eventually the air-conditioning cooled her rage. All the while her brain was whirring frantically.

These were the same designs that the man posing as Lawrence at Ralph's salons had tried to blackmail her – in her role as Emily – into making. Sucked into the strange atmosphere of Ralph's salon, she'd had the sense that he had genuinely been challenging her to create real pieces of jewellery. But he had left the salon before giving her the full brief.

Did he – or Ralph – know that Emily's original work was here at the V&A? If so, why would they want Freya to create similar designs in real life? Could it just have been a devious way to test her capabilities as a jewellery designer? Or was it yet another aspect of Ralph's bizarre mania?

Damn them, she thought. They want to humiliate and undermine me. I'll bloody well show them I'm up to the mark.

The work would certainly be demanding. Emily's elaborate sleeve-clasps wouldn't suit the style of her own silk dress. Nor would the necklace work. The brooch was a different matter.

While it would undoubtedly be tricky to create anything as distinctive as Emily's piece she could certainly try.

Seized by a resolute desire to restore Emily's reputation as a highly talented designer and prove herself to Ralph – and everyone else – Freya snapped her notebook shut, marched out of the gallery and returned to her lock-up simmering with a cold, steely sense of determination.

CHAPTER 13

The next few days were bright and sunny, but Freya resisted their lure and spent all her time at her workbench. The space felt less claustrophobic with the lock-up doors thrown open, letting in sunlight and fresh air.

The challenge of creating a medieval-style brooch like the one credited to Lawrence Meadowcroft in the V&A's jewellery gallery sparked an intense burst of emotional, physical and mental activity. How absorbing it was to engage in making another new design. As if guided by some unseen hand, Freya instinctively knew how to work the silver, bringing a fresh approach to the piece she was proud to call her own.

Instead of replicating the graceful flourishes and curlicues of the original design she made the flower shapes within the heart sharper and more angular. It gave the piece a crisply geometric look, closer to Art Deco than a free-flowing Arts & Crafts style. Deco, she knew, held great appeal for contemporary audiences and a plan emerged in Freya's mind as she worked on the piece. She would contact some former clients in New York and Paris as well as London, and show them the new pieces, including this one. If her timing was right and she caught the mood of the moment she could start building up her clientele internationally again.

Along with the three pieces from her Victorian collection - the silver pendant, sunflower ring and peacock's eye earrings – this brooch could prove just the catalyst she needed to set her new business off on a successful trajectory. Which jogged her memory - she must check her bank account again to see if Ralph's fee had arrived yet. Unlike Oliver's surprisingly prompt payment, the transfer seemed to be taking some time. Surely there wouldn't be a problem as the commission was confirmed in writing and yet a sneaking worry kept niggling her like toothache.

At lunchtime Freya locked up her makeshift workshop and walked back to her flat to make a sandwich and run through her emails. Reaching the last one, she was about to flick the kettle switch when her phone rang unexpectedly. Much to her surprise Liz Russell's number popped up.

'Hello,' she said, moving into a shaft of buttery sunshine pouring through the window.

'Freya? Something rather odd has happened,' said Liz. 'You couldn't spare me a few moments this afternoon, could you? In my office?'

'Yes, of course,' replied Freya, suddenly on high alert. 'Would two-thirty be okay?'

'That's fine,' replied Liz. 'And would it be possible to bring your portrait miniature with you please?'

Freya switched the phone off, staring at her empty mug. Why on earth did Liz Russell want to see the miniature again? Had she discovered something else?

Pushing open Boyd & Hart's heavy glass door, Freya found the reception area had been refurbished. The icy seascape had vanished. In its place hung a framed glass case containing three rows of portrait miniatures. Either side of the case were two large-scale portraits – an austere-looking, grey-haired man with side-whiskers and a young woman whose sombre black dress contrasted dramatically with her extremely pale face.

Judging by the sitters' costumes and uniforms the portrait miniatures appeared to have been painted much earlier than her own. Freya ran her eye over the labels giving the artists' names – John Smart, George Engleheart, Richard Cosway, George Hargreaves – but she barely had time to study the sitters before the receptionist told her to go upstairs.

Reaching the threshold of Liz Russell's office, an uneasy premonition brought her to a nervous halt. Torn between uncertainty and curiosity, she hovered for a moment by the open door. Curling her fingers to knock, she felt a trickle of sweat run down her back.

Liz looked up and greeted her with a smile. 'Hello Freya – how are you?' she asked. 'Did you see our wonderful display downstairs? We like to give our reception a bit of a re-vamp every few weeks and I felt it was high time we had some portrait miniatures on show.' She paused, still smiling, but Freya was conscious of an underlying tension in her manner. 'You did bring yours with you, I hope?'

'Yes, I've got it here.' Freya unzipped her handbag and put the tissue-wrapped miniature on Liz's desk before moving a book from a chair and sitting down. 'Amazingly, I now know her name – Emily Meadowcroft,' she said, lingering affectionately over the last two words.

Liz's eyes gleamed. 'I thought so,' she said, peeling back the tissue paper and gazing at the portrait. 'This was exhibited as part of a pair at the Royal Academy's Summer Exhibition in 1880.'

'Did your research lead you to the Royal Academy's archives?' asked Freya, recalling her own moment of triumph.

Liz looked at her sharply. 'No. Someone told me yesterday when they brought in the matching portrait miniature of Emily's brother, Lawrence Meadowcroft.'

Freya felt the colour drain from her face. She clutched the side of Liz's desk with a shaky hand as the blood roared in her ears.

'Are you okay?' asked Liz.

Freya forced a smile. 'Sorry. I suddenly felt a bit faint but I'm fine now,' she said. 'I've been working to a deadline and probably shouldn't have been skipping meals.'

Liz smiled. 'Well, we've all been there in our time,' she said kindly. Picking up the miniature, she studied it under a jewellery loop for a few moments then replaced it in the tissue paper.

'Can you tell me who's got the miniature of Lawrence?' asked Freya, removing her hand from the desk and giving her stomach a gentle rub.

'I'm afraid I can't,' replied Liz. 'I'm sure you appreciate we have to respect client confidentiality. However, I can tell you it's someone we've done business with before.'

Clasping her hands together on the desk, she continued, 'I've run into a bit of a problem though and was hoping you might be able to help.' Liz paused, weighing her words before she spoke. 'The person who brought in the miniature of Lawrence Meadowcroft isn't looking to sell. In fact, they wanted to have a quiet word with us because of our reputation.'

Freya looked at her blankly.

'Our reputation for handling portrait miniatures,' clarified

Liz. 'He—' she halted, correcting herself, 'this person asked us if we could track down the matching portrait of Emily. No, don't worry – of course I didn't mention that I'd seen it or knew where it was.'

Freya blinked. 'But it's not for sale—' she began but stopped abruptly when she saw Liz grimacing.

'I'm afraid it's more complicated than that,' Liz said, sounding troubled. 'This person tells me both miniatures were bought from a private dealer last year and the one of Emily was recently stolen from his house.' She took a deep breath. 'I'm sorry to ask this, Freya, but do you have anything that proves you actually own the miniature?'

Freya swallowed. Her mouth was dry and her chest felt tight, as if squeezed by an iron cage. 'It was in my mother's jewellery box,' she said. 'I only found it after she died.'

'Did you come across a receipt while you were dealing with your mother's affairs or anything to show where it was bought?' asked Liz briskly.

'I think she inherited it,' replied Freya.

'A will, then?' suggested Liz. "Either your mother's or one of her parents'?'

'It's not mentioned in my mother's will,' said Freya. 'I don't think I've got the other ones. I'll have to go through the paper-work again.'

'What about an insurance document – or a valuation as part of the process for probate?' suggested Liz. 'Or even a photograph showing your mother wearing it?'

'I know she didn't have any insurance,' said Freya. 'She didn't think her jewellery was valuable enough and it wasn't—' she hesitated, '—assessed for probate.'

Liz was silent for a moment, inspecting the polished fingernails on her clasped hands. 'This puts me in rather an awkward position,' she said eventually. 'I asked if the police were informed about the theft and was told it wasn't reported at the time. *Entre nous,* the owner is an art dealer and didn't want to draw attention to the loss. Business would be on the line if clients thought their premises weren't sufficiently secure to withstand a break-in. I was asked to let this person know if anyone approached us with the portrait miniature of Emily Meadowcroft. Well, when I heard all this yesterday it occurred to me that perhaps yours was a copy – either made at the time of the original or a more recent copy. That's why I asked you to bring it in. Now I've looked at it again I realise it can't be a copy. No artist would deliberately replicate the blemish – that tiny white mark – below Emily's collarbone.'

She paused, giving Freya a steely look. 'The person who came in yesterday said they took a photograph of the miniature for insurance purposes. When I saw the image on their phone, I spotted an identical mark on the portrait.'

Freya felt her stomach knot into a tight ball. Shadows pulsed, black and glittering, at the corner of her vision. As she tried to blink them away, the acid taste of nausea rose in her throat. Then she heard her voice coming from a long distance away. 'What makes you think this person is the real owner?'

'I asked to see the paperwork relating to the acquisition of both miniatures and was told it would be emailed to me,' replied Liz. 'It hasn't arrived yet but when it does – and if it's all in order – then I'm very sorry, Freya, but I'll have to report this matter to the police. Now the gallery has been made aware of the situation I feel duty-bound to do that even if the owner would prefer to hush things up.'

STUMBLING OUT OF BOYD & Hart's glass door into Albemarle street, Freya's mind chattered frantically. It was Ralph, wasn't it? Or could it be another collector, even one of his guests at the salons?

It had to be Ralph. She'd let him take a photograph of the miniature on his phone when they first met at the V&A. Clearly, he would stop at nothing to possess it. Who else would want the miniature of Emily so badly? It wasn't as if it was particularly valuable – a few thousand pounds Liz had said – which made it unlikely to be some other collector. The only people for whom it had any meaning were herself and Ralph. But if it was Ralph then why had he never mentioned that he owned the matching portrait miniature of Lawrence?

Her thoughts ran on in a nervous, jerky fashion. Would Liz Russell really stick to her guns and inform the police?

She had nothing at all to prove that Emily's miniature belonged to her. What a fool she'd been. She could have shown it to the valuer for probate or taken out some form of insurance. Then there would be a record of it.

As Freya descended the steps into Green Park underground station she felt as if her legs might give way beneath her. Fumbling for her pass, she dropped it on the floor before retrieving it and passing through the ticket barrier. Normally she would walk briskly down the escalator. Today she remained rooted to a moving stair, her trembling fingers glued to the rubber handrail.

What on earth was she going to do? Liz seemed utterly serious about reporting her to the police. How long did she have before Ralph sent through some fake paperwork showing he had purchased the miniatures from a dealer? A day? Two days? It probably wouldn't be more than that.

Arriving back home Freya found her neighbour Caroline, who lived below her in a ground floor flat, standing on the doorstep of the building with a workman. He was rummaging in a kitbag and appeared to be mending the lock to the communal front door.

'What's up?' she asked.

'Oh Freya, it's good you didn't come home any earlier or you wouldn't have been able to get in,' said Caroline,. 'I came back early from the office and couldn't get my key to work. I called Vauxhall Security and they sent Rob over. He says the deadlock's been triggered so he's re-setting it.'

'Do you know what happened?' asked Freya.

'I'm not sure,' replied Caroline. 'Rob thinks it could have been tampered with. Fortunately, the fail-safe mechanism kicked in.'

'No one got inside?' asked Freya anxiously.

'No, everything's okay,' replied Caroline. 'Rob says the lock did what it's meant to do. I think we need to be careful though. People are leaving their windows open now it's getting warmer. I'll stick a note in the hallway to warn everyone about the door.'

'Thanks for sorting it out,' said Freya, stepping into the hallway as Rob stood aside to let her pass.

Slamming the door of her flat, Freya ran into the living room. The boxes she'd brought back from the cottage were still sitting, unpacked, in a corner. Now she began rummaging furiously, looking for something – anything at all – that would prove to the police that the portrait miniature truly belonged to her.

CHAPTER 14

Scrabbling around frantically in the boxes in her living room, Freya could feel her heart pounding unnaturally fast.

Folders stuffed with papers were strewn over the carpet around her. Most contained bank and building society statements, utility bills and council tax demands for the cottage – everything she'd kept for the purpose of probate – but she knew her mother had hung onto some old letters from her father. If she could lay her hands on them maybe they would mention the portrait miniature.

There they were – tucked into small, faded envelopes with ancient postage stamps underneath one of the folders at the bottom of the box. Freya seized the envelopes and extracted the handwritten letters. Silently reading through them, she began to feel increasingly uncomfortable – as if intruding into her mother's private life. Anyway, it was a wasted effort. There was no reference to the portrait miniature in any of them.

Disappointed, she turned instead to a folder filled with old receipts and warranties. Now why had her mother kept these?

Only for the sake of contacting manufacturers in case of need, it seemed.

Freya read through her mother's will again, even though she knew its contents off by heart. Starting to despair, she pulled out a large brown envelope tucked inside one of the folders and shook out a batch of old photographs. Sifting through them made her smile. The black and white shots of her parents at their wedding reception and on honeymoon looked so dated.

Then there were numerous glossy colour photographs of herself at various stages – in a pram, playing in a sandpit, sitting in a garden clutching a teddy-bear. The shots of herself as a teenager made her wince. Had she really looked so goofy then? Shoving them all back into the envelope, Freya sat back on her heels and gazed around at the mess on the floor.

Turning her attention to another box, she picked up a bunch of postcards secured with a rubber band. She recognised the handwriting instantly: Aunt Jenny's. Holiday postcards scribbled by her mother's older sister in large, looping, generous strokes. Torquay, Bournemouth, Margate. Nowhere exotic. At the back of the stash was a blue envelope in the same handwriting. Freya pulled out a folded sheet of writing paper and quickly scanned the letter from Aunt Jenny to her mother.

My dearest Helen, she read,

Thanks for your lovely card. I'm glad you had good weather for your trip to Scarborough and managed to see Jane. It hasn't stopped raining here all week. In answer to your question about the pendant I'll tell you what I know, which isn't much. It belonged to Granny, but I don't know who is in the picture. It might be one of her cousins. You remember Mum giving me Granny's pearl necklace for my 21st birthday? Well, just before my birthday, she showed me both the necklace and the pendant and said Granny wanted you to have the pendant when you turned 21 because you enjoy painting and you're more artistic than me. Too right!

When I asked Mum, who was in the picture, she told me she wasn't part of our family and didn't know who she was. I remember thinking she was being a bit cagey about it – as if she didn't approve of the girl – and got the impression there was a whiff of scandal in the air. It was too late by then to ask Granny and now we can't ask Mum either.

You say she gave you the impression it was a picture of Granny as a young girl, but I don't think that's right because I've still got that ancient photograph of Granny on her wedding day, and she looks completely different. I wish I'd asked more about it, but at least you know it's a family heirloom so keep it safe, even if you don't want to wear it again after what I've told you. Enough of the past. I'm so looking forward to seeing you in August and meeting James at last. From what you say I'm sure he is The One. With all my love, Jenny.

FREYA ROCKED BACK on her heels, her mind spinning. *Granny wanted you to have the pendant.* Was Aunt Jenny talking about the portrait miniature? It certainly sounded like that. Yet it wasn't crystal clear. It could have been some other keepsake. *It belonged to Granny, but I don't know who is in the picture.* Was she describing a photograph or a painting? That wasn't explicit either.

The letter was dated 15th July 1985 – the year before Freya's parents got married. Would that have had anything to do with her mother's query?

Frowning, Freya tried to work out a succession of dates in her head. The Granny mentioned in the letter – Jenny and Helen's grandmother – died in 1967. That was one of the discoveries she'd made on the ancestry website she'd now reluctantly paid to join. That meant Helen's mother must have kept this locket safely for her until 1976 when she turned 21.

Freya had never known her own maternal grandmother – Jenny and Helen's mother – as she'd died unexpectedly of an aneurism in 1984. That was two years before her parents got married. She remembered her mother saying how sad she'd felt that her own mother wasn't among the wedding guests. In fact she'd never met Freya's father, James, at all.

Tears welled in Freya's eyes at the recollection of this conversation which had gone on to reveal that her mother suffered two miscarriages in the years before Freya was born. She would have welcomed a sibling or two instead of feeling so utterly alone right now.

Blinking back her tears, Freya tried to re-focus on the task at hand. It seemed quite possible that her mother's question to Aunt Jenny could have been prompted by getting engaged to her father. Perhaps it was sparked by wearing the diamond ring he'd given her. Or, if they talked about having children, maybe she was thinking about the generations that preceded her as well as the ones to come.

If the pendant mentioned in Aunt Jenny's letter really was the portrait miniature, then it might explain why it had lain unworn in her mother's jewellery box for so long. *It's a family heirloom so keep it safe, even if you don't want to wear it again after what I've told you.* Perhaps the hint of family scandal convinced her mother it would be unlucky to carry on wearing it.

Freya read the letter again with mounting frustration. The sisters had always been close and if Aunt Jenny hadn't been able tell her mother much about this pendant, then there was little hope of finding out more since her aunt had died three years ago.

Freya sighed, feeling utterly thwarted. The letter simply

didn't provide the definitive proof she needed for Liz Russell. She must keep looking for rock-solid evidence even though her hope of finding anything among this stash of old paper-work was fading fast.

Picking out the last folder at the bottom the box, she remembered it contained the deeds to the cottage and put it aside. Underneath that was a stiff, cream envelope. Freya lifted the flap and pulled out some studio photographs of her mother looking like a Hollywood film starlet. Goodness, who had she been trying to impress by having these taken?

Freya had no recollection of ever seeing her mother wearing the Chinese dress with a stand-up collar. She looked young – possibly in her early twenties – and had clearly been told to wear her smartest outfit and bring some props. In one photograph she was glancing up coyly from behind an open fan. In another she was wearing a pill-box hat.

The focal point of another appeared to be an elaborate hair-slide. The pose in that one seemed very awkward. Her mother was leaning back against a cushion, looking up at the camera from beneath long eyelashes. Freya's eyes skimmed the image, taking in the swept-up hair, the cupid's bow lips, the stand-up collar's delicate embroidery and – the portrait of Emily dangling from a long chain around the neck of the Chinese dress.

A sound halfway between a hiss and a gasp escaped from her open mouth. Still kneeling on the floor, Freya held the photograph up to the light so she could see the details better. The miniature was hanging at a slight angle, but it was definitely the portrait of Emily Meadowcroft. She closed her eyes momentarily as a flood of relief washed over her. The release was so visceral it felt like venturing into a garden refreshed by a thunderstorm. A renewal. An absolution.

Jumping to her feet, Freya extracted the phone from her

handbag on the desk. Within minutes she'd made the call and left the flat, heading back to Albemarle Street.

'I'M VERY glad you found this,' said Liz Russell, beaming at Freya from behind her cluttered desk. 'I think we can let the matter drop now. I've received no paperwork about the acquisition of the miniatures yet, but if there are any further developments I will, of course, let you know.'

'Thank you for staying late to see me,' said Freya, feeling light-headed. 'I can't tell you how relieved I am. I wish I could ask my mother how she came to be wearing the miniature. But even though that's not possible, I do feel Emily Meadowcroft is part of the family now.'

Liz smiled. 'Are you any closer to discovering how you are related?' she asked, handing the photograph back to Freya.

'I've tried Googling but keep hitting a dead end,' replied Freya. 'I get a glimpse and then she vanishes. I signed up to one of those ancestry websites and traced my direct family line back three generations to my great-grandmother but haven't found Emily yet, so I don't know where she fits in.'

Sliding the photograph of her mother back into its envelope, she remembered a thought that had occurred on the way over.

'I've been wanting ask you something,' she said. 'I think you said you've done business in the past with the person who claimed to own the Meadowcroft miniatures. I'm wondering – did he offer you anything for sale when he came into the gallery?'

'I shouldn't really discuss this as client confidentiality reigns supreme,' replied Liz carefully. 'But, *entre nous*, you've got me out of a very tricky situation over the miniature.' She paused for a moment as if weighing the odds on a bet. 'Yes, I was offered something,' she said eventually. 'A charming little painting. I've only been shown a photograph at this stage but was told it would be available for viewing within the next few weeks.'

'Is it by a well-known artist?' asked Freya, shifting uneasily on her seat.

Liz pursed her lips, unwilling to disclose any further information. Then, seeing Freya's tired face grow more anxious, she gave a small shrug and relented. 'It's an early, undocumented work by Dante Gabriel Rossetti. A remarkable find. I can't wait to see it in the flesh, so to speak.'

Freya stared at her, silently digesting this information as a shiver of suspicion ran down her spine.

'Why do you ask?' said Liz, giving Freya a searching look.

'Oh, I – oh, I just wondered if there might be another connection with Emily Meadowcroft,' lied Freya.

'I'm afraid not,' said Liz, relaxing into a smile. 'You'll have to carry on with your own research into that interesting young lady.'

TURNING into Piccadilly Freya strode blindly through the crowds, unaware of passers-by, shop windows and even The Ritz. She felt as desperate for open space and fresh air as a prisoner on remand.

Crossing the street at the traffic lights, Freya took the sloping path into Green Park, grabbing an *Evening Standard* as she passed a newspaper stand at its entrance. The warmer, lighter evenings had brought people into the park after work and deckchairs dotted around the grass gave it a relaxed, seaside insouciance.

Freya slumped into a vacated chair, rested her head against the green and white striped plastic canvas and closed her eyes. A saxophone was playing faintly in the distance. The notes were long and lazy, sensual and soothing. A whiff of cigarette smoke carried her back to other times, other places. The evening sunshine warmed her face. Summer was on its way.

Revived by this welcome moment of relaxation, Freya sat up and rubbed her eyes then flicked open the *Evening Standard* on her lap. She read the main news story then skimmed through the celebrity gossip. Reaching The Londoner's diary pages, she chuckled at a couple of ironic, political titbits then glanced at a story in the lower part of the spread. Next to it was a photograph of a party taking place at a Mayfair art gallery. As she surveyed the guests her stomach gave an unpleasant lurch. Staring out to the left of the photograph was the man she knew only as Arthur Balfour.

For a moment her mind went completely blank. She felt stunned, as if reeling from a blow to the head, and screwed her eyes tight as a wave of dizziness passed over her. Taking a deep breath, she quickly scanned the story again. The event had been held the previous evening to mark the opening of a selling exhibition of Pre-Raphaelite drawings. Attending the party, the report said, were 'a number of prominent collectors including David Freeman (left) pictured with gallery owner, Alasdair Fife'.

Freya peered at the photograph intently. There could be no mistake. David Freeman was indeed the same person as the man who had attended Ralph's salon in the guise of Arthur Balfour. Deeply shocked, she forced herself to think things through.

Not all the guests at Ralph's salons were actors then. Some, like Jack and Lawrence, were clearly thespians but others, like David Freeman, must be wealthy collectors who enjoyed a bit of fun impersonating the Victorian characters they admired while relishing conversations about the artworks they owned. Yes, that must be it. Hadn't Ralph made a point of asking Balfour about some Edward Burne-Jones drawings he collected? And chatted to the youthful George Bernard Shaw about his William Morris tapestries?

Those Victorian doppelgangers at the salons clearly had real, modern-day selves who were as passionate about art and design as their historic counterparts. Just as Arthur Balfour collected Edward Burne-Jones drawings more than a century ago so did David Freeman today. She wondered idly who Edward Burne-Jones was in real life and whether he really did own Rossetti's *Guinevere* painting.

A chill shot up Freya's spine leaving an unpleasant, crawling sensation at its base. Liz Russell said the person who claimed to own the Meadowcroft miniatures – Ralph, she suspected – had offered her an early, undocumented painting by Rossetti. Could it be the little *Guinevere*? If so, why was Ralph trying to sell it to Boyd & Hart? On behalf of his friend? Or—

A shocking realisation clicked sharply into focus. These wealthy collectors weren't just their host's friends and social acquaintances. They were also Ralph's 'marks'.

Christ! Now she understood what he was up to at his wretched salons. Casing the joint. Quizzing guests about their artworks and those owned by their friends. Then going thieving, either for his own gratification or for profit.

Freya bit her lip as her thoughts went into overdrive. Alice Clarendon's stolen painting – or a copy of it – was hanging in Ralph's bedroom. Hadn't he also asked Burne-Jones – or whoever was posing as Burne-Jones – whether he still had 'Gabriel's painting'? The reply had been affirmative. No wonder Ralph only had a photograph on his phone to show

Liz Russell when he went to see her. Within weeks, though, he had promised to bring the painting into the gallery. Would he steal it himself or get an associate to do his dirty work?

Freya could feel the blood pounding in her ears. Could this really be true? How on earth would he get away with nicking such an important work as a Rossetti? Liz had said the painting was undocumented. Perhaps that would make it easier to sell. Anything seemed possible where Ralph was involved. After all, he was on the point of conning Liz Russell about the miniatures had she not found a photograph of her mother wearing Emily's portrait.

And yet it was all quite feasible. The Rossetti painting – 'my little *Guinevere*' as Burne-Jones called it – sounded sufficiently small to be spirited away under a heavy coat. Would anyone notice if a clever copy took its place on the wall?

A clever copy. A replica. A lookalike that he could substitute for the original piece.

Nausea rose in Freya's throat as she grasped the significance of this realisation. An identical design. A replica like the necklace Ralph had commissioned her to make. The original of which belonged to Eleanor. Whose son had bid for it at auction last year. Whose birthday party Ralph would soon be attending.

'Oh God,' Freya groaned out loud as her thoughts slid uncontrollably from dismay into horrified agitation. Starting to feel hot and panicky, she mentally ran through the implications of her own involvement. What was on her laptop? A confirmation of her acceptance of the commission that she'd initially sent to Ralph. A note about the cost of the stones and gold with the bank accounts and addresses of the suppliers he should pay. Photographs of the finished necklace. A copy of her own invoice to Ralph with all the details about the piece. Then there was the auction catalogue page sitting on her desk at home. And there would shortly be £20,000 transferred from Ralph's bank account into her own because – oh God! – she had unwittingly become his accomplice in a meticulously planned theft.

Bile soured her mouth and for a moment Freya thought she would vomit. Lying in the deckchair, eyes closed, she waited wretchedly for the feeling to subside. Then another alarming thought snapped at her mind. The jewellery Lawrence had tried to blackmail her into making – Emily's mis-credited work for Morris & Co – was displayed at the V&A. Could Ralph actually be considering mounting an audacious heist to steal the Victorian pieces and substitute replicas? That would be completely outrageous, and yet she wouldn't put it past him.

She gave an involuntary shudder. Thank God she'd left the salon without the brief which would, no doubt, have been a precise description of the jewellery on display in the museum. Her own Art Deco interpretation of Emily's brooch was too dissimilar in style ever to be considered a copy of the original piece. Unlike the necklace for Eleanor.

Think, she told herself. For God's sake, think. Work out what to do.

There was only one course of action. She had to retrieve the necklace from Ralph's house before he could make the swap at Eleanor's party. And her only opportunity would be during his next salon. Now she knew what he was up to there was no alternative but to attend his ominous Dark Circle séance. There was no longer any doubt in her mind about it. She had to go.

It was a while before Freya heaved herself out of the deckchair and walked back to Piccadilly. Crossing the street, she made her way past the underground station and took the turn into White Horse Street. It was quieter here and she slackened her pace, trying to keep her anxieties in check until she could share them with Brooke. The Ryder Gallery always stayed open late into the evening and she was hopeful of finding her friend still there.

Unlike her last visit to the gallery its picture-window display featured one single object. It appeared to be a huge screen consisting of dozens of separate boxes arranged in three long rows. A single neon letter flashed in a rapidly changing sequence within each box. Freya glanced at the design without pausing and pushed open the gallery door.

She could see no sign of Brooke. Instead, a slim, dark-haired man languidly detached himself from the rear of the space and approached her. He had the kind of good looks Freya associated with films set in the 1940s and the cut of his double-breasted, dark-blue suit seemed to match that impression perfectly.

'Can I help you?' he asked in a smooth, cultured voice.

'I was wondering if Brooke Swift might be here,' said Freya, pushing her hair back from her face.

The man frowned slightly. 'No, I'm sorry. You've just missed her. She's gone to see a client. Is there anything I can do?'

Disappointment doused Freya like a cold shower. 'Oh, no – thank you. I'm a friend of Brooke's. It's really her I came to see.'

The man smiled faintly. 'I don't think we've met before, have we? I'm Richard Ryder,' he said, extending his hand.

'Freya Wetherby,' she said solemnly as they shook hands. 'I'm sorry – I haven't really come to look at the work in your lovely gallery, although I did admire some of the designs the last time I was here.'

'Well, at least allow me to show you our very latest conceptual artwork,' said Richard in a friendly manner. 'It's a first for the Ryder Gallery so I'm rather proud of it.' He walked towards the door and held it open, adding, 'It's best if you look at it from outside.'

Freya preceded him and then they stood, side by side, in front of the gallery window gazing at a giant box of red neon letters tumbling into place like pictures of fruit on a gaming machine.

'It's based on Nixie tubes – you know, those cold-cathode, gas-discharge tubes used for neon signs,' explained Richard. 'You used to see a lot of them in Soho and they've started to become fashionable again for residential environments as well as commercial ones like bars and restaurants.'

'How does it work?' asked Freya, her curiosity piqued despite her frustration at missing Brooke.

'It runs on customised electronics in a pre-programmed, timed sequence that alters the letters every five seconds,' replied Richard. 'Each tube contains layers of letters made from bespoke filaments. When scrambled, the letters can create thousands of words and phrases. What's particularly clever though is the way the designer exploits the phenomenon known as typoglycemia – the ability of the human brain to understand words even when the letters between the first and last one are shown in an unusual order.'

'What does it spell out?' asked Freya with her eyes glued to the rapidly changing letters.

'*Simultaneously*,' replied Richard. 'But the programme isn't designed to let you read the whole word at once. Because the letters keep changing so quickly, your eye picks out what your brain wants to see. Every viewer perceives a different word combination even when they're looking at it simultaneously, so to speak.'

Gazing at the lights, he began to laugh. 'I keep seeing *sensuous* for some strange reason,' he said. 'Even though an 's' is missing, my brain seems to ignore the gap between the letters displayed and the text it understands.' He paused and glanced at Freya. 'What is it saying to you?'

Freya didn't reply for a moment, focusing on the flashing neon lights. Then her words hissed out in a hoarse whisper. '*Emily*. I keep seeing the name *Emily*.'

Standing there as if mesmerised, they carried on watching the tumbling display. Dazed by the rapid succession of letters, Freya wondered if the words had any significance at all or whether they were totally random.

'What else do you see?' asked Richard, enjoying the artwork's novelty. 'I'm getting *luminous* and – ooh, I like that – *money*.'

Freya blinked twice. '*Stolen*,' she replied, feeling baffled. 'And *atone*.'

CHAPTER 15

Barely a light was visible from the street. Nervously approaching Ralph's house, Freya wondered why it looked so forbiddingly dark. On previous visits oil lamps had illuminated every window. With no curtains drawn, it had been easy to glimpse the grand interiors of some of the downstairs rooms. Now all she could see was the faintest glow coming from the ground floor. The upper levels seemed to be in complete darkness.

Shivering in the ivory silk dress she'd hand-washed and ironed so carefully after the last salon, Freya wondered how Victorian women had ever kept warm. Pulling her cape more closely around her body, she fingered the heart-shaped brooch through its woollen folds.

Re-creating Emily's design had been challenging enough. Now she was questioning whether the contemporary twist she'd given it really worked after all. By making the entwining flowers within the heart much sharper and more angular she had ended up with a piece that was altogether less delicate than the original. No matter. It would serve as her lucky amulet tonight. She certainly needed the scales of good fortune to tilt in her favour. Retrieving the replica necklace she'd made for Ralph was her sole reason for returning here tonight. The consequences of failing to find it didn't bear thinking about.

Bracing herself mentally, she rang the bell and summoned her courage as she waited. It was a different maid who opened the door yet seemingly no friendlier than the previous one. Freya peeled off her cape as she stepped inside and handed it over with a forced smile.

'Wait here please,' said the maid as she folded it over her arm and moved towards the coatroom.

Freya felt some relief that she hadn't been asked to hand over her phone as at previous salons. Perhaps Ralph felt it wasn't necessary when only a small group of intimate friends were in the house. Or maybe this new maid had just forgotten. She glanced around the dimly lit hall. It felt strangely altered from her last visit. A pale gleam shone from a couple of burners high on the wall. Heavens, was that gaslight?

The passage leading to the octagonal hall was full of shadows. Freya could barely see the way ahead as she followed the maid, edgy with anticipation. Would Ralph have put her replica necklace in one of the ground floor vitrines until he visited Eleanor? It was too dark to see inside them. Perhaps it was in a cabinet inside that extraordinary room where Jack had first kissed her. She'd need to find a good excuse to slip inside as all the doors leading off the central space were closed except for the one opening into the study. Glancing up at their pointed Gothic arches, she had the fleeting impression of standing at the threshold of a chapel.

'Miss Emily Meadowcroft,' announced the maid.

Freya gave the artificial smile she'd practised while dressing that evening. Hoping it would mask her nervy anxiety, she had repeated the exercise until her face ached.

Ralph strode over to greet her. It was impossible not to be bowled over by his compelling appearance. Tonight, he was wearing a green velvet smoking jacket with a plum-coloured handkerchief billowing from the top pocket. With his dark, curly hair and exuberant beard, he looked prosperous and commanding. Very much the master of ceremonies.

'You're looking as lovely as ever, my dear,' he said, taking her hand and kissing it. Freya felt a wave of revulsion as his beard touched her skin.

'Good evening Ralph,' she said cautiously, praying he would make no mention of their previous visit to his collector's room.

'You're here to enter into the spirit of the evening, I trust?' he asked cordially, placing an emphasis on the word *spirit*. 'It promises to be a night to remember.'

Hopefully not for the same reason as the last one, Freya thought, running a damp palm down the side of her dress. 'Of course,' she said sweetly, adding, 'isn't it dark in here tonight?'

'Let me guide you to a comfortable seat,' offered Ralph, taking her arm and propelling her forward into the gloom, then leaving her marooned on her own for a moment.

Pools of light cast by shaded table-lamps illuminated individual areas of the room as if it was a spot-lit stage. Freya realised the study had been re-arranged since her previous visit and the furniture was not as she remembered. Two elongated, yellow sofas faced each other in front of the huge fireplace with a low, red-lacquered table in between. However, as far as she could see, there were no new cabinets or vitrines in the room and no obvious place where Ralph could have put her necklace.

Two figures sat in shadow at the far end of each sofa. They were talking quietly but the room was so dark that Freya couldn't make out if she had met either of them previously. She was reluctant to interrupt their conversation, so she continued standing hesitantly where she was, gazing at the fireplace ahead.

A fire crackled in the grate while an oil lamp at each end of the mantelpiece highlighted the adjacent medieval figures painted on the wall, leaving the ones in the centre of the frieze in shadow. As Freya gazed at them, recalling her conversation with Edward Burne-Jones, a gust of wind sent the fire roaring up the chimney and the figures seemed to leap and dance in its sudden flare.

Unnerved by their animated movement, Freya flicked her eyes away from the frieze and peered around the room. The wood-panelled walls and towering bookcases seemed to be closing in on her, incarcerating and suffocating her.

Blinking hard, she tried to focus on a specific object as if she was a seasick sailor staring at the horizon. Her gaze alighted on the octagonal marble table in the centre of the study. She remembered it from a previous visit although the vulgar gilded cherub had vanished and a ring of high-back chairs, upholstered in red velvet, now encircled it. She assumed the séance would take place here in the middle of this shadowy room and her stomach kicked with nerves at the thought.

'A glass of champagne, my dear?' Ralph was moving towards her clutching an over-sized flute fizzing with amber liquid. 'I do admire your brooch,' he said in an ingratiating manner as she took the glass from him. 'Is this one of your own creations? It's spectacular.'

'You're very kind,' said Freya, taking a sip of champagne. 'Yes, I did design and make it myself,' she added pointedly, all the while wondering where Ralph would have put her necklace.

'Am I correct in thinking it converses in the language of flowers?' asked Ralph in a sly tone. A waft of mandarin swept over Freya as he bent closer to her breast to inspect it.

'Indeed,' she replied, holding herself very still.

Ralph straightened up. 'Should I be thinking of Millais' *Ophelia*? Or is it more along the lines of John Singer Sargent's *Carnation, Lily, Lily, Rose*? He gave a crafty smile and Freya caught sight of his sharply pointed canine teeth.

'Neither,' replied Freya. 'The flower that looks a bit like a daisy is coltsfoot – your gardener will know it as *Tussilago farfara* – and the other is columbine.'

'What a romantic nosegay,' said Ralph in an oily voice. 'A tussie-mussie, as we Victorians call them. And what exactly does this charming, sweet-talking bouquet wish to say to us?'

Freya felt her body tense. Priming herself for this conversation while she was getting dressed, she had practised her reply repeatedly. Now the moment had arrived it felt as if a hidden spring had been triggered in some antique desk and a secret compartment would pop out.

'Coltsfoot for "justice",' she said emphatically. 'Columbine for "resolved to win". The ivy entwining the two flower-heads stands for "fidelity and friendship".'

'Or "marriage", perhaps?' suggested Ralph in a smooth, neutral tone. He smiled again, stroking his beard, looking down at Freya's lacy décolletage with a smug expression.

Freya felt a stab of disappointment. Her revelation about the secret meaning of the flowers had failed to produce the intended effect. Practising the moment at home, she had pictured his face registering dismay and consternation – alarm, even. Yet he had remained impassive, undaunted by her words, not because he hadn't understood their implications but because he was wily enough to deflect them back at her. She told herself to be grateful he hadn't tried to kiss her. Then she thought grimly that she would even endure that if it led to finding the necklace.

'I was inspired by a design I came across in the V&A's jewellery gallery,' she said brightly, determined not to drop the subject.

'Ah, a great source of inspiration no doubt,' purred Ralph, gazing down at the brooch as if he couldn't drag his eyes away.

Undeterred by his nonchalant remark, Freya pushed on regardless. 'On a recent visit I saw three wonderful pieces by the same designer: a brooch, a necklace and a pair of sleeve-clasps. All three are magnificent example of Arts & Crafts work but I have a feeling they may have been misattributed. Surprisingly, the museum seems unaware of the error.'

'Surely not.' Ralph's voice was ice-cool but Freya caught a glimpse of irritation in his eyes.

'I suspect Anna Playford – the woman who donated the brooch to the museum – may not have known who really designed and made the piece,' said Freya. 'It seems to me that if she received it as a present, rather than inheriting a family heirloom, then that could well be the case.'

Before Ralph had time to reply his maid appeared at the study door. 'Mr Arthur Balfour,' she announced.

'Excuse me,' said Ralph hurriedly. 'Balfour was keen to attend tonight's séance. I must go and welcome him.'

Feeling increasingly agitated about finding the necklace, Freya considered slipping past them into the hall and running upstairs. But within moments Ralph re-joined her with Balfour at his side. 'I believe you met Miss Meadowcroft at my last salon?' he said deferentially.

Yes, and I know who you really are, Mr Freeman, thought Freya as she flashed her practised smile. Balfour bowed in acknowledgment and murmured a polite 'Good evening'.

'Balfour is President of the Society for Psychical Research,' said Ralph. 'He's a keen spiritualist like his brother-in-law, the philosopher Henry Sidgwick.'

'I'm not yet acquainted with the Society,' said Freya, cautiously adopting a formal tone. 'Perhaps you would be kind enough to tell me a little about it.'

'Certainly,' replied Balfour with the conviction of a proselyte. 'Our main aim is to prove the existence of a spirit world using scientific analysis.'

'The SPR was founded by a group of Cambridge scientists,' added Ralph. 'They work with evidence-based material – not the kind of nonsense you read about in the newspapers.' He turned to Balfour, puffing out his barrel chest. 'We modern men are great innovators. Let's see if we can't match our great engineers for technical ingenuity tonight.'

'Will the usual gang be here?' asked Balfour in a laconic voice.

'Yes, I thought it best to keep it in the family, so to speak, as it will be such a special séance,' replied Ralph. 'In any case I prefer to introduce only one new guest at each sitting in case it disturbs the spirit guide. Tonight, I invited Emily.'

Balfour nodded gravely. 'Very wise.' He screwed up his eyes, peering through the gloom at the figures on the sofas. 'I see Madeline is here already. Talking to Watts, of course. Glad he's got that Ellen Terry business behind him now.'

'Do join them while we wait for the other guests to arrive,' urged Ralph. Turning to Freya as Balfour moved away, he said quietly, 'Watch out for Watts.'

'Watts?' echoed Freya blankly.

'George Frederic Watts – the artist who painted that gorgeous portrait of Ellen Terry. What did he call it now? Ah yes, *Choosing*. Daft to marry the girl though. She hadn't even turned seventeen. He told me his divorce papers have just arrived so he's in an exceptionally good mood tonight.'

The firelight made silhouettes of the two guests sitting at the end of the sofas. Freya studied their profiles. The one lolling on the left-hand sofa had a long nose and a straggly, unkempt beard. 'Was he a lot older than Ellen when they married?' she asked.

Ralph snorted. 'She was thirty years younger. I ask you! That's why I said you should be careful.' He glanced round as a maid appeared at his elbow with a tray of glasses. Waving her towards his guests, Ralph carried on gossiping quietly with Freya as if she was his closest confidante. 'Watts painted that magnificent portrait of Madeline Wyndham. Did you see it at the Grosvenor Gallery? Apparently, it took ages to complete. Her husband – who commissioned it – said the pair of them spent far more time chatting than they ever did posing and painting. They've all been firm friends ever since.'

Freya inclined her head towards the fireplace. 'That's Madeline, over there?'

Ralph nodded. 'Unlike her daughter, Mary, she's very keen on this spirit business. She frequently invites a medium to her house in the country and she's a regular at my séances here.'

He consulted his pocket watch. 'Now we're just waiting for Leighton, Ruskin and Miss Little to arrive, and then we can get started.'

Freya was on the point of excusing herself on the pretext of visiting the cloakroom. If she could just slip upstairs quickly before the séance began, she might have time to look for her necklace in Ralph's bedroom while everyone was still in the study. Within moments, though, the maid appeared at the doorway and announced: 'Miss Margaret Little.'

Ralph strode towards the newcomer. She was slender and

slightly built with red-golden hair, carefully combed around her head to tumble in waves down the right-hand side of her emerald silk dress. Freya watched him greet her with the same courtesy that he had shown her earlier. The Ringmaster, she thought cynically as Ralph bent to kiss Miss Little's hand. He pulls the strings as if we are puppets dancing to his tune.

'Emily, may I introduce you to Miss Margaret Little? Minnie, this is Emily Meadowcroft.' He cleared his throat then added: 'You may find you have much in common.'

Leaving them together, Ralph moved towards the sofas where his other guests remained sitting. Freya and Margaret inspected each other with as much curiosity as a pair of stray dogs in a garden square.

Freya spoke first. 'Margaret—'

The girl interrupted before she could finish her remark. 'Do call me Minnie. Everyone does. It's a play on my name.'

Freya frowned, trying to puzzle it out.

'Minnie as in little – or miniature. I have Ralph to thank for that.' Margaret smiled, smoothing her abundant hair with a thin, pale hand.

'Have you known him long?' asked Freya.

'I virtually grew up with him,' replied Minnie, taking a glass of champagne from the maid's tray. 'He's a family friend. And may I ask how you know Ralph?'

'It's a long story,' replied Freya, sounding vague. Deliberately changing the subject, she asked, 'Have you ever attended a séance before tonight?'

'Oh yes, indeed,' replied Minnie. 'I find great comfort in reaching the other side.' Her gaze dropped from Freya's face. 'My fiancé died last year.'

'I'm very sorry,' murmured Freya.

'He was out in India, working in the civil service, and was due to return to England when he caught typhoid.'

'That's terrible,' said Freya.

'We all have difficulties to face in life,' said Minnie with a soft sigh. 'I have been very unhappy this past year but when I receive a message from him it does give me the strength to carry on.' She paused, giving Freya a searching look. 'I feel you are very unhappy too.'

'Me?' asked Freya, widening her eyes in surprise. 'Why should you think that?'

'Because of the way Jack Hunter is behaving.' Minnie's hand shot to her pale cheek. 'Oh, I shouldn't have said that.'

'Please continue,' said Freya, mentally bracing herself.

'I don't know if I should. Ralph told me not to say anything.'

'I would rather hear it from you than Ralph,' said Freya.

Minnie swallowed. 'His models. The girls – and boys — he meets on the street and takes back to his studio to paint.'

A vivid picture of Jack with two men in a dark alleyway in Soho flashed into Freya's mind. She winced. 'Go on, tell me more.'

Minnie remained silent, nervously fingering her mane of red hair.

'He commits improprieties?' suggested Freya.

Minnie nodded, glancing over to the other guests, then lowered her voice to a whisper. 'Worse than that, I'm afraid.' She swallowed then continued. 'I know you've set up home with Jack, but I feel I should warn you about the reputation he's acquiring. No one will want him to paint portraits of their sons and daughters if he carries on as he has been doing.'

'I feared as much,' said Freya with an edge to her voice.

'I feel badly about telling you,' said Minnie. 'Especially so soon after you lost poor Lawrence.'

The over-sized champagne flute slipped from Freya's

fingers and shattered as it crashed onto the wooden floor. In the silence that followed every head turned to stare at her.

Ralph stood up, summoning the maid who hurried over to gather up pieces of broken glass and lay them on her tray. Minnie stepped out of her way. As she moved off into the gloom to join the other guests, Freya saw her glance back over her shoulder with a smug expression on her pale face.

CHAPTER 16

The next thing Freya heard was a maid's voice announcing the arrival of Sir Frederic Leighton. Oh, my word – a Greek god, she thought, catching sight of the imposing figure entering the room.

Curly hair, heavy eyebrows and a white-flecked beard and moustache conveyed a patrician air, though his stern features were softened by the gentle lines of a loose-fitting, brown velvet jacket topped by a billowing, fawn-coloured cravat.

'My dear fellow, you managed to get here in time,' said Ralph, greeting his guest with a vigorous handshake. 'We feared you were detained indefinitely, wrestling with a python.'

Leighton burst out laughing. 'I would need to be more of an athlete than I truly am for that to be the case,' he replied.

Ralph winked at Freya. 'You're familiar with Leighton's remarkable sculpture, I expect. Such a wonderfully dramatic example of motion frozen in time. Let me introduce you formally though. Sir Frederic Leighton is our devoted President of the Royal Academy and the finest artist of our age.

And this is Miss Emily Meadowcroft, whose own artistic skills merit great esteem.'

Turning back to Leighton, he added obsequiously, 'Your python will surely herald a fine renaissance in British sculpture.'

'You're too kind,' said Leighton, eyeing Freya's brooch with interest.

'I think we should start proceedings,' said Ralph, checking his pocket watch. 'We can't wait all evening for Ruskin. I'll give orders not to be disturbed if he does show up but he's probably nose-to-page on some lengthy, erudite tract and has simply forgotten the engagement altogether.'

He strode towards the door, spoke quietly to the maid, then raising his voice he addressed his guests with the commanding air of a master-of-ceremonies. 'Let us move into the dining room where our state-of-the-art séance will take place tonight. Please follow me.'

Freya was last to leave the study, hoping to snatch the opportunity to ask Minnie what she knew about Lawrence. She didn't get a chance. Minnie glued herself firmly to Watts's side and they left the room together. Freya trailed behind them, lingering by the vitrines they passed in the central hall in the hope of spotting her necklace. As far as she could tell it wasn't there.

The grand double doors of the dining room were thrown wide open. Recalling the first time she had admired its dazzling interior, Freya was disappointed to find the room in darkness. Just enough light was spilling in from the corridor for Ralph to direct his guests to their seats around the massive, oval table. Even so, it took Freya a few moments to realise that someone – a woman – was already sitting at the far end.

Fumbling her way towards her allocated chair, Freya heard Minnie whisper from the opposite side of the table. 'It's lucky we won't be holding hands tonight as I don't think I could reach yours.'

'Are the seances always held in here?' asked Freya quietly, peering at Minnie in the gloom. 'It's so dark – I can hardly see a thing.'

'Yes, usually in here, although the last one I attended was in the study,' replied Minnie. 'I think he'll get the candles going in a minute or so.'

With all his guests seated, Ralph closed each of the double doors in turn. Then a thicket of flickering light jerked brilliantly to life at one end of the room. Easing himself into a stately, gilded chair, he sat at the foot of the table with Freya on his right and Minnie to his left. Neither spoke as their host settled into his seat. Sitting with his back to the animated, incandescent candlelight made Ralph's bulk seem even more colossal to Freya's eyes. A sheen of light on his dark curly hair gave her the impression of a halo hovering around his head.

'Candlelight is so benign; it gives everyone a healthy glow,' said Ralph cordially. Leaning towards Freya he added, 'especially my candles.'

'Are they very special ones?' asked Freya, thinking how foolish her query sounded.

Ralph beamed. 'Indeed. Invention and innovation are not the sole preserve of our forebears. I feel we have a duty to carry on the good work of the generations that preceded us.' He paused, then added in a self-congratulatory manner, 'I like to think my candles have the same flow and flicker as the wax candles that lit up our ancestors' lives. In fact, each one is powered by 250 light-emitting diodes and paired with a circuit-board and micro-processer.'

'What? Are they activated by a computer?' asked Freya with amazement. 'They look so real.'

'Exactly so,' replied Ralph in a proud voice. 'Computer-operated with customised software. I'm sure Ada Lovelace would have applauded the results. A smart, random algorithm prevents the sequence of movements ever repeating itself. That's why they look so natural. Indistinguishable from the real thing, in my opinion.'

Narcissist, thought Freya sourly. You could have lit the room with ordinary candles or the oil lamps from the drawing room. But you just couldn't resist showing off your technical brilliance to your guests, could you? Nor relinquish total control over the mood in this room right now.

Raising his voice, Ralph addressed the whole table. 'Let us commence,' he said grandly. 'Tonight, we are honoured to welcome the celebrated trance-medium, Miss Augusta Bird. You will all have heard of her extraordinary powers, no doubt. She has kindly agreed to communicate personal messages, through her spirit-guide, from those who dwell upon another shore.' He hesitated then added with a dramatic flourish, 'please prepare yourselves to expect the unexpected.'

Freya shifted uneasily in her seat, recalling her school-girl scepticism about séances. This felt very different. Serious and more believable.

All the candles extinguished simultaneously, plunging the room into a darkness so thick that Freya could see none of the other guests. Within seconds a burst of dazzling light metamorphosed into a bright, white forest of trees on each wall. Remaining static for a few minutes, the trees gradually became more animated. Slender tree-trunks clambered vertically up the walls with boughs swaying gently, as if blown by a breeze. Freya watched, mesmerised, as the boughs grew and lengthened. Buds appeared, followed by leaves that gradually unfurled into their full shapes. Slowly detaching themselves from the boughs they glided to the floor, tumbling into heaps.

'Light,' thought Freya, recalling the Ryder Gallery's

conceptual artwork. 'It's a clever light-projection.' Totally absorbed, she spotted loose seeds leaping across the space to pollinate and grow on other walls. The buds swelled, leaves gracefully appeared and then, in slow-motion, drifted to the floor and wafted along the skirting-board, seemingly blown by an unfelt gust of wind.

A moan from the far end of the table startled Freya out of her reverie.

'Is the spirit here with us?' asked Ralph in a low, conspiratorial voice.

No reply came from Augusta Bird, just another moan and a rushing sound like a running tap as the forest faded and disappeared from the walls. Out of the total darkness a pale light appeared. A tiny square at first, it grew into a large rectangle then mutated into a different shape. A man's shirt. Trembling, it moved higher and began to float in the air before returning to rest on the table in front of Augusta Bird. Then it vanished as unexpectedly as it arrived.

Freya peered into the black space, trying to make out how other guests were reacting to this phenomenon. It was no good. She couldn't see a thing. Then, out of the corner of her eye, she saw a white flash. She spun round towards Ralph. He was waving his hands in the air. Hands encased in white gloves like the ones he wore in his collecting room.

On the far wall behind Augusta Bird, a painting appeared. Freya recognised it immediately: *The Death of Chatterton*. She had seen it many times at Tate Britain. Only this time Chatterton wasn't dead. He was in the process of dying.

Agonised groans filled the room. Someone – Freya thought it was Minnie – gave a shriek. A trickle of blood ran from Chatterton's mouth as he lay on the bed in his garret clutching his stomach. His pale face feebly moved to one side and Freya tried not to look at the vomit on the floor. Then gradually she became aware of a change in his features. His high forehead and cheekbones were slowly morphing into another face. Could it be – yes, it belonged to someone Freya had last seen at Ralph's house a few weeks ago. Lawrence Meadowcroft.

Freya's brain whirled. She had read about Chatterton at the Tate. He died of arsenic poisoning. Was this a coded message? Had Lawrence died in the same awful way?

Wiping clammy hands on her dress, she reminded herself that this was a technical trick – a video projection conjured, she guessed, by Ralph's glove-waving. Even so, its subliminal message concerning Lawrence seemed specifically directed at her rather than any of the other guests. Could that really be so?

Mentally scrambling through Chatterton's story, Freya recalled how he had created verses in the manner of a medieval monk, even copying them onto parchment as if they were historical manuscripts. Censured by critics as a forger, he failed to earn a living as a poet and, starving, committed suicide in a London garret at the age of 17. To many he became a tragic hero and Freya remembered reading that Henry Wallis' painting of Chatterton had been much admired in Victorian days, especially by John Ruskin.

What, she thought rapidly, did any of this have to do with Lawrence Meadowcroft? His age? Lawrence was listed as twenty-one in the 1881 census – older than Chatterton when he died – so age had nothing to do with it. Had Lawrence committed suicide? Was that the point of this video charade? Some sort of warning that she would likewise meet a gruesome end if she didn't dance to Ralph's tune?

Freya shivered, queasiness spreading in her belly. Whatever message was being conveyed, Ralph was clearly the conduit, not Augusta Bird and her spirit guide. Intuitively, she knew how much he was enjoying watching his guests' uncomfortable reactions to this gruesome scenario.

"'Cut is the branch that might have grown full straight and burned is Apollo's laurel bough,'" intoned Ralph as the image faded away. Minnie gave a sob and Freya heard someone – Madeline she thought – sigh deeply. One of the men cleared his throat, then there was silence.

Silence and darkness. Freya found she was holding her breath and gripping the edge of her chair, tense as a taut spring.

The silence was broken by the sound of buzzing. Growing louder and more insistent, it filled the room as a swarm of insects swept over their heads, darting from one end of the room to the other. Freya automatically ducked. Minnie cried out in alarm and even Madeline gasped. Raising her head tentatively, Freya tried to make out the species. As the creatures swarmed overhead, all she could see were tiny points of light. Were they eyes? Or illuminated tails?

Think, Freya told herself, think clearly.

Could this swarm of creatures really be made from tiny pinpoints of light? Was their collective flocking movement driven by computer algorithms, like the candles, making their behaviour replicate a multitude of insects? Yes – that was it! Another technical trick deliberately designed to discomfort and confuse the assembled guests.

Freya could hear Ralph chuckling softly to himself. He's an arch-manipulator, she thought savagely. He's enjoying scaring the hell out of us all.

Despite her antipathy, a grudging admiration seeped through her. With minimal equipment – computer software, customised circuit boards and sensors – he had tricked everyone into believing they were seeing a physical object, a swarm, when in fact there were only tiny lights flashing on and off. It was a clever manipulation of his guests' visual and sensory responses. A cunning sleight of hand.

Freya relaxed. If this séance was just a showcase for Ralph's technical expertise and fancy gadgetry, then she had nothing to fear.

A piercing moan from Augusta Bird caught her unawares. She sat up straight, alert to what might happen next. Again, she heard the strange rushing sound then Augusta began to speak in a low monotone.

'A young lady wishes to join us. She is close at hand.'

A vivid light exploded into the centre of the room. To Freya's eyes it looked like a bright green obelisk surrounded by a cage of red lines. It hovered above the table and then, to Freya's horror, moved towards her. There it remained, quivering slightly, at head height.

'Hold the cage and she will say what she wishes to be known,' intoned Augusta.

Freya took a deep breath and held her hands out on either side of the cage, making sure she didn't touch the lights. She could feel her heart racing. Everything in the room was still. And silent. A bead of sweat ran off her forehead. Not daring to move her hands, she let it roll down her cheek unchecked.

Still nothing happened. The seconds lengthened into minutes. Freya could hear her breath coming in short, anxious bursts. Her heart pounded uncomfortably, sounding so loud to her that surely everyone else could hear it too. The lights altered in colour. Green turned to blue and red to silver. The quivering grew stronger and then more violent still as the cage rocked wildly from side to side.

'For pity's sake give me justice,' pleaded a young woman's voice.

The voice was completely at odds with Augusta Bird's drab monotone. It had a distinct timbre – a melodious quality despite its anguish. Freya could feel the hairs on her neck bristle. 'Emily,' she thought wildly.

'Tell everyone the truth.' The words hung in the thick, black air like a snatch of music over water.

Freya's hands began to tremble. The obelisk and cage turned gold, burned brighter still then vanished, leaving the room even darker than before.

She sank back in her chair as a wave of nausea engulfed her. Was this another of Ralph's tricks? Or had Emily spoken to her through the medium's spirit-guide? No answers came to mind. Her brain felt fogged and cloudy, but she must keep alert as there might be more madness to come.

CHAPTER 17

A movement to her left caught Freya's eye. Turning to see Ralph's white-gloved hand delve into his jacket pocket, she watched closely as he brought out what looked like a large coin. Placing it on the table in front of him, he gazed at it for a moment and then picked it up and raised it to eye-level. Holding it upright between finger and thumb, he swung round in his chair to face the curtained windows.

Hearing Minnie gasp, Freya twisted round to see what she was staring at. Something was happening behind her back. Had Minnie seen some ghastly apparition emerging from behind the curtains? Strangely, it seemed to be one of the monumental jardinieres standing beside the curtain that had startled her. Freya stared at it hard. Now spot-lit, the blue-and-white ceramic urn was morphing into a cradle. And in the cradle lay a tiny baby, just a few days old.

The cradle, superimposed onto the planter, began to rock slowly from side to side. Had Ralph's coin somehow created this effect? Freya recalled the way her phone interacted with signs on posters or in shop windows, conjuring up images and data from graphic symbols. Was that what was happening here? Could this be a similarly clever system of digital layering in which images, unseen by the naked eye, are revealed via technology as an augmented version of reality?

Freya watched as a pair of hands delved into the cradle and picked up the baby. Giving one loud cry, it was handed over to another pair of hands. Indistinct murmurs – women's voices – could be heard, then a softly-spoken conversation gradually became audible.

'My dear, she's beautiful – how can you bear to part with her?' said one voice.

'I have no choice,' came the distressed reply.

Was that the same voice they'd heard a few minutes ago? Its light musicality sounded similar. Freya tensed, straining to listen more intently.

'What name have you given her?' said the first voice.

'Grace,' came the soft reply.

'God give me the grace to nurture her well. I will treat her as one of my own daughters, I promise.'

'Oh, Violet – God bless you for your loyalty and friendship. I will try and send what little money I can.'

'Please don't be anxious on my account. Henry's inheritance will look after all of us well enough.'

'I'm so very grateful to you both.' A rustle and a faint chink as something enclosed in one hand was passed to another. 'Please take this and keep it safe for her.'

Silence. A snuffle. Then the first voice spoke again. 'Is Jack working?'

'Barely. He is rarely in his studio these days. He tells me he paints portraits of young ladies in their homes, but I never see the results. He hasn't exhibited all year.'

'Will you stay with him?'

'Where can I go? My parents turned their back on me when I went to live with him. I haven't spoken to them since.'

'And Lawrence left you nothing?'

'Only debts which my father paid off.'

A pause. Then, 'Do you still love Jack?'

A sigh. Then a crackle like poor reception on the radio. Freya strained to hear the reply. It came as a vicious hiss.

'I despise him.'

The cradle vanished, plunging the room into darkness.

Shaking with emotion, Freya swivelled round in her seat and clutched the edge of the table to steady herself. The after-image of the cradle had imprinted itself on her vision, swaying and rocking violently. She felt as if the room was spinning, sucking her into its slipstream. Taking several deep breaths, she willed her heart to stop pounding while trying to process what she had seen and heard.

A harsh cough broke the silence in the room. Startled, Freya wondered if it was Leighton or Watts but the direction it came from was the far end of the table where Augusta Bird was sitting.

Now the voice of a young man could be heard. 'You must be very brave, my darling Minnie.' Another racking cough. 'Next month will mark the anniversary of our engagement but I forbid you to be sad because I am here with you always, my darling. I will never leave you.'

Freya could hear Minnie sobbing quietly on the opposite side of table. It was the only sound in the room. The atmosphere felt tense and expectant as if everyone was holding their breath, waiting for more.

Nothing came. Augusta coughed again but this time in a higher, lighter register. Minnie stopped crying and blew her nose. Then the room fell completely silent.

Minutes ticked by as they sat there in darkness. Was the

séance over? Freya wondered whether Ralph would ignite the candles to mark its conclusion. Nothing happened. The room felt hot and airless. She longed to get up and leave but felt obliged to remain while everyone else continued sitting there. She fidgeted in her seat. The wait was becoming unendurable.

A tremendous blast of vivid green light jolted her back to vigilance. Rapidly flashing on and off, patterns formed within the pulsating lines – webs, nets, weaves, criss-cross shapes. Dazzled, she blinked and looked again. Now a shape emerged between the jarring, flashing lines. A person – a woman with thick, golden hair – was standing in an empty room. An easel in the centre of the pulsing space held a large canvas. And between the shimmering beams Freya thought she glimpsed a face within its dancing rectangle.

The coruscating light was blurring her vision. Freya closed her eyelids and pressed her fingers hard into the corners by her nose. Still the colours seared her retina. Opening her eyes, she gazed in horror as the woman picked up a paint-caked knife from the easel's lip and slashed repeatedly at her wrist. Blood spurted from the wounds. Amid the flaring, flashing lights Freya saw her sink to the floor and lie quite still with a red tide slowly seeping across her pale dress. Then the vibrating green lights gave one last convulsion and exploded like a firework, fragmenting and rupturing the scene.

Back in the study, guests discussed the séance as the maid handed round glasses of madeira and slices of cake. Ralph had left the room to bid Augusta Bird farewell in the hall and a more relaxed mood prevailed in his absence, encouraging a lively exchange of opinions.

'What a disappointment,' said Madeline. 'I'd heard so much

about her powers. I was expecting many more messages to come through.'

'True,' said Watts, helping himself to a second slice of cake. 'But you must agree she conjured up some spectacular effects. I found those colours most inspiring.'

'I really couldn't grasp what was happening in that last sequence,' said Balfour. 'I thought those flashing lights might well trigger a fit, so I stared at the table then closed my eyes.'

'Just as well,' said Madeline. 'It wasn't at all pleasant. I wonder who the poor girl was?'

'I'm sure she wasn't connected to anyone present,' said Freya quickly. 'Perhaps the messages get muddled up sometimes and Miss Bird delivers ones that should really be received by other people – a bit like the postal service on a bad day.'

'Well, I heard the message that was meant for me,' said Minnie. 'And how glad I am to receive it.'

'Such a comfort for you, dear,' murmured Madeline, sipping her glass of madeira.

'Hmm. Ruskin didn't miss anything, that's for sure,' said Leighton gruffly.

'Did any of it have a special meaning for you, Miss Meadowcroft?' asked Watts.

Before Freya could reply Ralph returned and sat down heavily next to her on the sofa. 'Miss Bird has another sitting elsewhere tonight,' he said apologetically. 'I think she may have been saving her greater powers for that one.'

'She gave us the matinée performance,' suggested Balfour.

Everyone laughed uneasily. Now Ralph was back in the room the conversation faltered and eventually petered out. Watts got up from the sofa. 'I think I'll call it a night,' he said. Turning to Madeline, he added, 'May I give you a lift home?'

'Thank you, I'd be very glad of that,' said Madeline, rising to her feet along with Balfour and Leighton. 'Minnie? Shall we drop you off on our way?'

'Yes, please.' Minnie glanced at Freya as she left the room. Her face seemed impassive. Unlike earlier that evening it was devoid of any expression.

As Ralph followed his guests out to the central hall to bid them goodnight, Leighton remained standing then turned to Freya. 'I must say I'm rather intrigued to meet you,' he said loftily. 'You see, I became acquainted with the Meadowcroft family a few years ago when—'. He broke off, glancing at Ralph returning to the room.

'I was just about to tell Emily—' he began saying but was cut off mid-flow by his host.

'I'm delighted you made each other's acquaintance tonight,' said Ralph in a smoothly assertive manner. 'I particularly wanted you both to meet because you do realise you own two things that, of course, belong to Emily.'

'I do?' Leighton looked startled.

'Yes – a sumptuously beautiful, bronze figure of a naked female form and a charming watercolour of the Meadowcroft residence,' continued Ralph in a honeyed tone.

'What?' exclaimed Leighton, sounding surprised. 'Are you referring to the acquisitions I made at the Meadowcroft house sale?'

'Correct,' said Ralph. 'Or rather, incorrect. Because those pieces are precious family heirlooms and should naturally be returned to their true owner.'

Leighton's jaw dropped. 'But I bought them in good faith at auction,' he said. 'There was never any doubt about their provenance.'

'My dear fellow, I wasn't suggesting for a minute that there was,' said Ralph. Moving closer to Leighton, he clapped him on the shoulder in a jovial manner. 'Come on, old chap. Do the right thing and say you'll let me buy those pieces from you so I can give them to Emily. After all, they would be the only things she has to remind her of her family since they cut her off without a penny to her name.'

Leighton bristled. 'Come now,' he protested. 'I bid for them fairly and squarely – and paid over the odds for them.'

Freya felt the floor dip beneath her feet as two different eras – Victorian and contemporary – now collided in a baffling display of greed and possessiveness.

'Ah, that may well be the case, but I'm appealing to your better self – your personal integrity,' wheedled Ralph. 'Surely, you're aware that the charming little watercolour of the Meadowcroft house was painted by Emily herself? Now you wouldn't want to deprive the artist of her own work, would you?'

Leighton was silent, weighing up the situation as he glanced uneasily from Ralph to Freya then back again to Ralph.

Freya could see he was clearly struggling with the dichotomy of his situation. Should he step out of character and behave towards Ralph as any contemporary colleague would do and risk upsetting him by refusing to comply? Or should he play along in his Victorian guise and agree to his host's apparently magnanimous suggestion?

Freya's stomach tensed with fury. How scheming – how outrageously underhand – of Ralph to conflate past and present so inextricably to get what he wanted.

No one spoke for a moment. Then Ralph added in a sly voice, 'You wouldn't want people to think you are—' he paused for a moment, '—a looter?'

Leighton swallowed audibly. 'That's a bit rich,' he said indignantly. 'You make it sound as if I plundered the Meadowcroft estate and walked away with ill-gotten gains.'

Ralph narrowed his eyes. 'Maybe not,' he said quietly. 'But you've certainly robbed Emily of her rightful inheritance. I wish only to see the artworks returned to her.'

The silence that followed felt uncomfortably painful to Freya's ears, but her thoughts were sharply lucid. Now she understood why Ralph was so keen for Miss Emily Meadowcroft to attend his Dark Circle. As a hostage to fortune. A means of leverage to acquire those pieces he missed out on at the auction.

After a few minutes Leighton exhaled heavily. 'Alright,' he said brusquely. 'I concede on the understanding that you remunerate me in full. I want precisely the same amount that I paid for them at the auction. Including the buyer's commission.'

'Good chap – I knew you'd do the right thing,' said Ralph cordially. 'Now, would you be kind enough to bring them to my next salon please?'

Leighton stared at him, speechless, then turned on his heel. As he left the room, Freya stood up and moved away from the sofa. 'Emily, please wait a moment,' said Ralph. 'I have something to discuss with you.'

Freya's heart sank as she watched him follow Leighton to the central hall, clap him on the shoulder and bid him goodnight. Could she take advantage of his temporary absence and dash upstairs to look for the necklace? It would take too long. Tensely fingering the silk fringe of her evening-purse, she avoided looking directly at Ralph when he returned to the room.

'Leighton's a fine fellow,' he said expansively 'Invariably generous, although I've noticed he avoids any kind of intimacy. Married to his art, he says, but I rather think that little statue of a boy in the Narcissus Hall of his house – a replica of one found at a villa in Pompeii, I believe – tells us more.'

He gave a snort of laughter then moved over to the table where the maid had left a decanter of madeira. 'A night-cap?' he suggested, pouring the amber liquid into one of the unused glasses.

Freya shook her head. She was torn between a burning desire to leave and the fear of relinquishing her only opportunity to retrieve the replica necklace.

'The interior of Leighton's house in Holland Park is really something to behold,' said Ralph, replacing the glass stopper on the decanter with a clink. 'You, of all people, would appreciate the craftsmanship. That fern-coloured fabric covering the walls of the Silk Room, next to his studio, is exquisite – all greenery-yallery/Grosvenor Gallery, as Gilbert & Sullivan would have it. As for the Arab Hall, well, what a glorious showcase. He tells me some of the tiles were sourced in Persia by his explorer friend, Richard Burton. All lapis, gold leaf and peacock blue. I admit they inspired me to commission my own fireplace tiles here.'

Ralph sipped the madeira then continued, smiling broadly. 'He's a splendid host, of course, but you do need to avoid imbibing too vigorously at his supper-parties. One poor chap suffered the indignity of falling into the impluvium at the centre of the Arab Hall, joining the Japanese tench swimming there. Ned was amongst those having dinner there that night and witnessed his misfortune. You can imagine how colourfully he related that amusing anecdote afterwards. Well, next time Leighton invites me to dinner I shall certainly suggest you accompany me but, right now, I have a more immediate proposal for you.'

Freya's whole body froze as her eyes flicked fearfully up to his face.

'I've come to the conclusion we should join forces,' he said with a treacly sweetness. 'Your work on the necklace for

Eleanor was outstanding. You really are remarkably talented, and I can envisage many projects of a similar nature we could do together. So, I'm proposing a partnership in which I will secure a number of jewellery commissions and you will carry out the work. All very high-scale, of course.' He paused, eyeing her thoughtfully. 'Your share of the profits would, of course, be – substantial.'

Freya's mind reeled. 'You want us to become – partners?' she stuttered.

'Yes, my dear,' he replied. 'It makes perfect sense.'

An instinctive, emphatic refusal never left Freya's lips. Just as she was about to respond, her thoughts took a handbrake turn. The offer, she realised, could be used as a bargaining chip. It was as if she'd been handed the Ace of Spades. She would keep it in reserve until needed.

'It's an interesting proposal,' she said with feigned enthusiasm. 'Let me give it some thought.'

'Well, don't wait too long,' said Ralph. 'I have something in mind already.' Draining his glass, he set it down on the table next to the decanter. 'Come with me,' he added softly. 'There's something I'd like to show you.'

A chill shot down Freya's spine. 'It's late Ralph,' she said. 'Couldn't we leave this for another time?'

'No, it's too important,' he replied, moving towards her and standing closer than she would have liked. Sweat had broken out on his forehead and she could smell the mandarin oil on his skin. Thrusting a hand under her upper arm, he propelled her from the room and into the central hall.

Fear tugged at Freya's chest. It felt so tight she could barely breath.

Up the stairs they went. As they reached the first-floor landing Freya tried to halt their progress by craning her neck to look up at the illuminated stained glass in the octagonal tower above them. Gripping her arm more tightly, Ralph manœuvred her away and up the second flight of stairs. Once they reached this landing she knew exactly where they were heading. She hoped the door was locked. If he had to use a key it might give her time to run back down the stairs.

Turning the knob with his free hand, he pushed her inside then kicked the door shut behind him with his foot.

The room hadn't changed since the last time she was here. A pair of red-shaded oil lamps gave the room a spectral glow. The vast bed, piled with cushions and covered in a golden, velvet throw, sprawled between the nightstands. Above the elaborate headboard with its gilded cherubs and praying angels hung Jack Hunter's searing painting of Emily Meadowcroft. It still sang as powerfully as the night she had inadvertently discovered it on her first visit to Ralph's house.

Freya stood at the foot of the bed gazing at Emily. She could feel Ralph's breath on the back of her neck and flinched. Out of nowhere a fragment of advice from a news report about hostage-taking leapt into her mind.

Always talk to your captor.

Feeling sweaty and panicky, she started babbling about the painting. What a remarkable face. How well it was painted. How closely the subject resembled the girl depicted in her portrait miniature. Anything to hold Ralph at bay.

It worked for a few moments. He remained standing motionless behind her, breathing hard. She thought he was looking at the painting. Then he lent over her and began to kiss her neck. She tried tilting her head to one side only to expose more of her neck and feel his wet lips creeping along her skin. She jerked her body backwards to no effect. He caught her round the waist and tightened his grip.

'Let me go, Ralph, let me go.' She could hear her voice rising to a terrified shriek.

'You chose to step into her shoes and now you have the opportunity to make amends for what she did,' he said in a low voice close to her ear.

'What do you mean?' Freya could feel sweat dripping off her forehead as she tried to swivel out of his embrace.

'Surely you remember?' he teased unpleasantly. 'I told you the last time you were here.'

'She jilted you,' said Freya in a shaky voice.

'Ralph Merrick – my esteemed great-grandfather – was jilted by Emily Meadowcroft, the little witch. She led him to believe she loved him while all the while giving herself to another man. Romancing him to the point of madness, she never gave him the satisfaction of fulfilling his desires. Now, as her direct descendant, you have the chance to redress that injustice.'

'What makes you think I'm related to her?' blurted Freya, trying desperately to pull away from him.

'You showed me your portrait miniature. As soon as I saw her face, I felt history repeating itself. Except this time, I knew we would succeed where our ancestors failed.'

'But I'm not related —'

'You inherited it from your mother,' interrupted Ralph. 'You told me that. It came down your family's blood-line.'

Then, as if a switch had been flicked, his mood abruptly changed. Loosening his grip on her waist, Ralph turned Freya round to face him as gently as if she were another valuable piece of porcelain in his collection. With one hand he tilted up her chin so he could look directly into her eyes. A waft of mandarin oil accompanied the soft caress of his velvet cuff where it brushed Freya's skin.

'You've already agreed to consider becoming my business partner,' he said in a soft mesmeric voice, creamy with the anticipation of possession. 'Now let us become partners in life as well. We have the chance to join forces in a way that was denied to our ancestors. Let us right that wrong and re-write history by uniting our lives.'

Freya blinked. For one mad moment everything he could offer her – the house, his wealth, his social and artistic contacts – spun before her eyes. She took a deep breath, but before any words could leave her mouth the door burst open. Ralph whirled round, dropping his hold on her waist.

'What the hell – who are you?' he shouted furiously at the intruder. 'Get out of my house.'

Freya dived for the door, whimpering. 'Thank God,' she gasped, as she saw who it was. 'Thank God.'

CHAPTER 18

'Wait,' yelped Freya, hitching up her dress so she could run along the pavement more easily.

'Come on,' urged Brooke, turning to watch her catch up. 'We need to leg it.' Then she carried on pounding up the street towards her shiny black Mini. 'Tell me where to go,' she ordered, firing the engine as soon as Freya slammed the passenger door.

'West,' panted Freya. 'We need to get on the M4.'

They drove in silence as the rows of brightly lit shops grew sparser and the streets became increasingly residential. It wasn't until they were on the motorway that the tight coil in Freya's stomach began to unwind. She couldn't stop shivering though. In their mad dash from the house there had been no time to look for her cape.

'My jacket is on the back seat if you're cold,' said Brooke, glancing in her side mirror as a van sped past the car.

Freya unclipped her seatbelt, reached over to grab the jacket and wriggled into the red suede cocoon. 'I must look a sight,' she said, pulling the collar up to her nose and huddling down in the seat.

'I've seen worse,' said Brooke.

'How on earth did you know where I was?' asked Freya, her voice wobbling as she fought back tears.

'You told me about the Dark Circle when you came to the gallery,' replied Brooke.

'But what made you turn up like that?' asked Freya, trying to keep a plaintive whine out of her voice.

Brooke gave a snort of laughter. 'I had this ludicrous idea about gate-crashing the party.'

'Seriously?' asked Freya, astonished.

'I was intrigued,' replied Brooke. 'You described the salons in such lurid detail that I was curious to see for myself how it all worked. Anyway, Ralph's clearly a psychopath and I was worried about you.' Glancing in the rear-view mirror, she put her foot down hard on the accelerator and the car shot forward. 'I wanted to see the ringmaster cracking the whip,' she added sardonically. 'The arch-manipulator at work and play.'

'Go on,' Freya kept her eyes on the road, unnerved by the car's sudden burst of speed.

Brooke wriggled back in her seat and slid her hands further up the steering-wheel. 'From what you told me it sounds as if he had you all in the palm of his hand. Telling you what to wear, how to behave, briefing some of the guests, making leading remarks about the social, artistic and political concerns of the day. I was curious to see him resurrect all those eminent Victorians from their graves.'

Freya was silent for a moment as a wave of exhaustion rolled over her. She slumped against the headrest, limp as a ragdoll, with every ounce of energy sapped by the stress and drama of the evening. Her failure to retrieve the replica necklace nagged at her.like a throbbing migraine. After what had just happened how would she ever get hold of it now?

'You didn't bother to come in character,' she remarked in a weak attempt at humour.

'On the contrary,' said Brooke. 'I'm wearing a tuxedo.'

Freya glanced at her, wearily realising that she hadn't actually noticed what her friend was wearing. From what she could see in the headlights of a passing car, the tuxedo suited Brooke, giving her a more androgynous appearance. Letting her thoughts drift, Freya was imagining Brooke mingling with the guests in Ralph's study when the Mini shot out from the middle lane to overtake a white van and Freya gripped the edge of her seat in alarm.

'How did you get into the house?' she asked, after they sailed past the vehicle.

'I saw someone leaving – a big chap with curly grey hair and a beard – so I skipped up the steps and he charmingly held the front door open for me. Told me the séance was over and said Ralph was still in the study talking to you if I wanted to join you both for a glass of madeira. He called you Emily, of course, but I knew it was you.'

Brooke glanced in the mirror and put her foot flat on the floor. The car sped forward again with pent-up energy as if grateful for the exercise. 'The ground floor was deserted so I assumed you were both upstairs,' she continued. 'I remembered what you said about your previous visit to his bedroom and pelted up to the top floor.'

'With no thought for your own safety,' said Freya. 'You can't imagine how relieved I was to see you. Really, I can't thank you enough.'

'He needed a good kick in the balls and that's exactly what he got,' said Brooke proudly. 'Anyway, you haven't told me what happened at the séance.'

'We need to branch off the motorway fairly soon,' said Freya, watching the road signs flashing past.

'Well?' asked Brooke impatiently. 'Spill the beans.'

Freya sighed. 'I'm exhausted. Can we leave this till the morning? All I want to do is sleep. Oh God, neither of the beds are made up in the cottage. In fact, there's not much there. I've taken all the bits I want to keep back to London.'

'It doesn't matter,' said Brooke. 'There isn't much of the night left anyway. We can just go commando and forage for anything we need in the morning.'

A FEW HOURS later Freya was in the kitchen boiling a kettle. Glancing at Brooke, it struck her what a curious pair they made. She had discarded her crumpled silk dress and was wearing her mother's ancient gardening sweater and muddy trousers, left behind in the wardrobe after her clear-out. Brooke was dressed in her chic black tuxedo with satin lapels.

After three hours asleep, Freya had abandoned any attempt to drop off again and had got up, only to find Brooke downstairs already. Offering to buy provisions for breakfast, Brooke returned from the shop with bacon, eggs, bread, teabags, coffee and milk. 'You're cooking,' she announced, dumping the bag of groceries on the kitchen table. 'I don't do cooking, as you know.'

Freya smiled. It was a long-standing joke dating from their time at college.

She took a pair of scissors from the drawer and cut open the packet of bacon. Pouring a little oil from a bottle and swishing it around the frying pan, she felt a rush of gratitude. Brooke was brave, resilient and loyal. It was a friendship worth cherishing and nurturing. She felt lucky it had endured for so long.

Freya flipped the spitting rashers with a spatula as her thoughts ran on. Didn't their friendship mean more, in fact, than her relationship with Oliver ever had? Okay, it wasn't sexual, but there were significant compensations. Like trust and honesty and – for heaven's sake – fun.

After they finished eating breakfast, Freya washed the plates in the sink, made another cup of tea for herself and a coffee for Brooke, then sank into a kitchen chair exhausted. Her anxiety about the necklace still nagged at the back of her weary mind like a sore tooth.

'Run this by me again,' said Brooke, cupping her hands around a mug. 'Emily – the real one, I mean – is engaged to Ralph Merrick. Her parents consider it a good match as he is a thrusting, young MP with a solid majority in his constituency at the general election in 1880. Even though she is only seventeen, they give their blessing to the betrothal and begin to plan the wedding. Then Emily breaks off the engagement without any proper explanation and takes herself off to London to live with her brother, Lawrence. We know that because of your research with the 1881 census. So far, so clear.'

Brooke took a swig of coffee then continued. 'What Ralph doesn't know, of course, is that she's having an affair with Jack Hunter. Then – either before Emily gets pregnant or after – she moves out of Lawrence's place and sets up home with Jack. She's brought enormous shame on her family, so they cut her off and won't speak to her again. The baby is born and she names her Grace. Within days of the birth, she gives the baby to her friend, Violet, who says she will bring the child up as if it's her own. That's right, isn't it?'

'Yes,' replied Freya with a sigh. 'That's what the séance revealed.'

'Are you sure it wasn't a set-up?' asked Brooke. 'Ralph could have fed Augusta Bird a line.'

' 'Maybe that's right but the conversation between Emily and Violet felt horribly real,' said Freya with an involuntary shudder. 'Even if Ralph was manipulating all the special effects – which he probably was – I'm pretty sure that what I heard and saw must be close to the truth because he's so obsessed with Emily. The first time he took me to his collector's room he said that old Tom Meadowcroft had told him all about the family, so he knows what took place or, at least, some version of it.'

'When I heard Emily's plea for justice, I realised it related to her unacknowledged work as a jewellery designer but Ralph, of course, twisted it into a pretext for propositioning me.' She gave a half-hearted laugh. 'I think the whole charade was Ralph's warped way of showing me what could happen if I didn't go along with his plans to make me his business partner and – oh God – his girlfriend.'

'History repeating itself?' asked Brooke.

'Something like that,' replied Freya. 'Poor Emily.'

'She did the best thing for her baby by the sound of it,' said Brooke. 'If Jack wasn't earning any money, Grace would have starved. There weren't any social security safety-nets in those days.'

'Maybe that's why Emily slashed her wrist,' said Freya pensively. 'They say suicides are more often caused by money worries than failed love-affairs.'

'I wonder if it could have been some sort of copy-cat reaction to Lawrence's death,' said Brooke. 'Your séance seems to indicate that he took his own life.' She frowned. 'Or maybe there was a different reason altogether for Emily's actions that we don't know about.'

They eyed each other across the table for a moment,

neither speaking. Brooke scratched her head. 'And you say there's no-one in your family called Grace?'

'No – which means I'm not descended from Emily even though Ralph Merrick thinks I am,' said Freya. The aching disappointment caused by this realisation, which came when she finally lay down on her mother's bed in the early hours, struck her again like a punch in the stomach. She took a deep breath. 'Emily is not related to me at all,' she said.

With the night's dramas receding, it was becoming clear to Freya how closely she had identified with Emily Meadowcroft. Dressing in the kind of gown Emily wore, creating and wearing a replica of the brooch she designed, having the sort of conversations with artists and writers that Emily had enjoyed, flirting with Jack Hunter's avatar had all helped to restore her confidence.

It was more than that though. Inhabiting Emily's skin had added a new dimension to her life, making her feel stronger and more resilient. while inspiring her to fresh heights of creativity.

'What are you thinking?' Brooke's question dragged Freya out of her reverie.

'Oh, nothing really,' she replied, finishing her tea. 'I was thinking about my great-grandmother's name. My mother used to make a joke about the family cocktail having a pair of olives.'

'Eh?' Brooke wrinkled her nose uncomprehendingly.

'Both my grandmother and great-grandmother were called Olive.'

'Hmm.' Brooke frowned. Looking out of the window as a burst of sunshine brightened the room, she surveyed the tangled garden with its weed-filled borders. 'Are you still planning to sell the cottage?' she asked.

'Probably,' replied Freya. 'That reminds me, I must ask

Alan Roberts if his client came back with an increased offer.' She looked around the kitchen. It felt warm in the sunshine with an appetising smell of bacon lingering in the air. After the horrors of the night, the familiar room felt comforting and safe.

Freya pulled a face. 'I don't really want to sell,' she admitted. 'It holds too many memories for me.'

'Well, do you have to?' asked Brooke. 'From a financial point of view, I mean?'

'I could invest the money in my new business as well as paying off my overdraft,' replied Freya, remembering with a jolt that she needed to check her bank account again. Thank heavens Oliver had done the decent thing and paid her a fee for the design he stole. It would keep her afloat for the time being. That was vital as she'd already decided to return Ralph's remittance as soon as it arrived. There would be a paper-trail, of course, but at least she wouldn't be in possession of his payment even if she never managed to retrieve the necklace.

'Keep the cottage,' urged Brooke. 'Then you've got the option of renting it out or using it yourself.'

Freya looked at her thoughtfully. 'Would you come and visit if I kept it as a bolthole?' she asked.

'Of course,' replied Brooke. 'London gets a bit much even for me at times.'

Freya smiled. 'Maybe you're right,' she said warmly. 'I must try and do something about the garden though – and I don't suppose you'd fancy helping me paint a few walls, would you?'

Brooke's dark eyes gleamed. 'Couldn't think of anything more creative than wielding a big, fat paintbrush,' she said in a mocking voice.

'Now that I've got rid of so much stuff it would be a good moment to do a bit of redecorating,' said Freya, glancing at an area of peeling paint on the wall above the window.

'Were you able to sell any of your mother's things or did you give it all to charity?' asked Brooke.

'I gave quite a lot away and took some of it back to my flat to sort through – china and glasses, pictures, various bits and pieces like photos and books,' replied Freya.

'Books?' echoed Brooke. 'Old ones or paperbacks?'

'A mixture.'

'Are any of them still here?'

'I couldn't cram them all into the boxes, so I left some of them upstairs in my mother's bedroom,' replied Freya. 'They're in terrible condition. The covers are falling off and I was going to give them to one of the charity shops in the village.'

'Let's have a look,' said Brooke, narrowing her eyes.

'Why?' asked Freya, puzzled.

'Just a hunch,' replied Brooke. 'We put on a show at the gallery last year of amazing art books with really wild, hand-crafted covers and endpapers. Some of the artists involved signed them, which Richard said would add to their value."

They went upstairs to the dusty bedroom. Freya opened the wardrobe and scooped the books off the top shelf. Plonking them down on the bed where Brooke was sitting, she tried to grab one of the soft leather covers as it fell off and flopped onto the floor.

Brooke picked up one of the books and inspected the battered spine. 'Ha! Jane Austen,' she said. Looking at two more books, she added, 'All Jane Austen. Someone must have wanted a set.'

Fingering the faded cover on one of them, Brooke peeled it back, gazed at the marbled endpaper then turned over to the next page. Her expression changed as she stared at a neat, hand-written inscription on the flyleaf. With mounting excitement in her voice, she read the words out loud: 'To my darling daughter, Olive, from her loving mother Violet. Christmas 1904.'

'Let me see,' Freya demanded, holding out her hand.

Brooke passed the book to her, grabbed another and went straight to the flyleaf. 'To my darling daughter, Olive, from her loving mother Violet. 10th October 1905,' she read aloud. 'Must have been a birthday present. And look —' she pointed to the inscription on the fly-leaf of the book whose cover had fallen on the floor, '— Christmas 1905. Lucky girl, she got two Jane Austen's that year.'

'Oh, my goodness,' said Freya. 'I had no idea they belonged to my grandmother. They—'

'I think the dates are too early,' interrupted Brooke. 'It's got to be the previous generation. Your great-grandmother Olive.'

Freya stared at her, open-mouthed, as the realisation sank in. 'So, Olive's mother was Violet.... Emily's friend, Violet. The one she entrusted with her baby.' The words left her mouth as if weighted with stones.

Grasping the implication of what she'd just said, her eyes opened wider. 'That means – oh goodness – it looks like my great-grandmother, Olive, must have grown up with Grace.'

'And treated her like an older or younger sister,' suggested Brooke.

'Which could explain how Emily Meadowcroft's portrait miniature ended up in my mother's jewellery box,' said Freya, flopping down on the bed next to her friend. 'Well!'

Neither spoke for a moment as they inspected the inscriptions again. The truth, thought Freya, had been hiding here all these years in plain view. She'd never looked at the books properly, dismissing them as old-fashioned when she was young. They had no illustrations, and the type was small and dense. The modern editions of Jane Austen she'd borrowed from the local library had been much easier to skim through.

'I don't think my mother had any idea about this or she would have told me,' she said eventually.

'Or didn't want to tell you,' said Brooke. 'Not everyone likes finding a skeleton in the cupboard.'

Freya frowned as Aunt Jenny's letter came to mind. Perhaps Brooke was right about skeletons. What had Aunt Jenny been told about the portrait miniature? *She wasn't part of our family.* Well, no, strictly speaking, that was correct. Emily wasn't part of the family – but her baby, Grace, was brought up as if she was.

Aunt Jenny clearly wasn't told the full story. Yet she'd gleaned enough from her mother to make a good guess.

I remember thinking she was being a bit cagey about it – as if she didn't approve of the girl – and got the impression there was a whiff of scandal in the air.

Freya's thoughts ran on uncomfortably. As sisters, Aunt Jenny and her own mother had always been very close. Did that mean her mother had known about Emily's connection with their family too? If so, it must have been a deliberate decision not to discuss it – or even give Freya any hint about the portrait miniature's origins.

She remained silent, digesting this possibility, then her conjectures returned to Emily. 'After she broke off her engagement to Ralph, I imagine they would have returned each other's letters and love-tokens as it was considered the honourable way to behave in those days,' she said. 'That would explain why the miniature remained with Emily, even though it was meant to be a present for her fiancé. I wonder if she gave it to Violet so Grace would have some idea of what she looked like as she was growing up.'

'Well, that makes sense,' said Brooke. 'Then I guess your great-grandmother, Olive, must have inherited the miniature and eventually it came down the family to your own mother.'

Freya frowned. 'I don't understand how it ended up with Olive though. If Violet gave it to Grace, as Emily presumably intended, then why did Grace give it to Olive?'

Brooke shrugged. 'Any number of reasons. Maybe Grace died young, like many Victorian children, and it was given to her so-called sister. Or perhaps she never married and wanted Olive to pass it on to her brood.'

'Which, in fact, Olive did,' said Freya, thinking again of Aunt Jenny's letter.

Granny wanted you to have the pendant when you turned 21.

Freya's thoughts switched to her own mother. Well, she had indeed been given the miniature for her twenty-first birthday and worn it in those photographs in which she looked like a Hollywood starlet. Then, the year before she got married, she'd asked her sister about its provenance and received Aunt Jenny's cryptic reply. After that she put it away in her jewellery box and never wore it again.

Her mother would have known that Freya – her only child – would, of course, inherit it eventually. By not telling her about its origins, however, she must have felt she was protecting her daughter from any ill-fortune she believed might be linked to the portrait.

Even if her mother had withheld the truth, she'd done it with the best of intentions. Freya could not, in all conscience, blame her for that.

Her thoughts were interrupted by Brooke. 'It must have given Ralph a real shock when you first showed it to him, given his obsession with Emily.'

'Yes, no wonder he was so intrigued... Even though he knew exactly what Emily looked like because he already had Jack Hunter's painting. Except he wasn't telling me that at the time.'

Freya got up off the bed and walked over to the window.

Speaking about Ralph had made her feel very tense. She flexed her shoulders as she looked out at the garden, thinking about the painting of Emily hanging above his bed. The nightmare of last night would take a long time to erase from her memory but now the salon was over perhaps it was time to tell Alice Clarendon where she might find her stolen painting.

'I wonder if there's a way of getting in touch with Alice Clarendon,' she said. 'It would be interesting to know how she came to own Jack Hunter's painting. She might also be able to tell us a bit more about Emily and why she took her own life.'

'Well, the guys who run the art-tracing website would probably be able to help,' said Brooke. 'I could contact them on a professional basis and say I've got some information that might be of interest to the painting's owner. Shall I do that?'

'That would be fantastic – thanks,' said Freya. 'If we were able to meet up with Alice, I could show her the portrait miniature too.' She fell silent for a moment as she placed the loose, leather cover over the top of the flyleaf, lining it up precisely with the edges of the book. Then she gave a chuckle. 'I'm glad I didn't dump these off at the charity shop. I'll take them back to London.'

'Talking of which,' said Brooke, 'I ought to be thinking about heading into work. Are you coming back with me?'

Freya hesitated, fretting about Eleanor's necklace again. Now she was certain about Ralph's motives for holding the salons it was imperative to recover her replica before he could take the scam any further.

She was reluctant to admit to Brooke what a fool she'd been to accept the commission at face value. Nor how desperate she was to retrieve the necklace. It was more than just hurt pride. It would be best if Brooke was kept in the dark. Not only about the necklace but Ralph's whole, unscrupulous operation. At least for now. That way, there could be no shred of complicity.

'Are you still worried Ralph will beat a path to your door like you said last night?' asked Brooke, sensing her tension.

Freya nodded. 'Yes, I put my address on the thank you card I sent him after the first salon and his subsequent invitations came by post,' she said in a hollow voice. 'Ralph knows exactly where I live.'

CHAPTER 19

A few days after their midnight dash to the cottage, a promise of summer was floating in the warm, dusty air as they hovered on the wide, stone steps of a red-brick Victorian mansion block near Baker Street.

Freya gave Brooke a conspiratorial smile, cupping a hand above her eyes to shield them from the glare of dazzling afternoon sunshine. The piercing blue sky heralded better months to come yet her mouth felt dry, and her stomach was fluttering with nerves.

Brooke rang the bell and announced their arrival. A soft response drifted through the intercom. Then the lock on the sturdy, wooden door gave a click as it automatically released. Once inside the cool hallway, the screech of traffic diminished to a faint hum and the street aromas of exhaust fumes, cigarettes and fast-food vanished without trace.

'Nervous?' teased Brooke, slamming the lift's heavy metal grille.

'Only of heights,' retorted Freya.

Groaning and clanking, the lift clambered to the sixth

floor. In transit, Freya made a mental note of an engaging pattern of entwined lilies decorating the grille. Inspiration for her Victorian jewellery collection was popping up at the most unexpected moments these days.

Stepping out of the lift, they hesitated for a moment in a narrow hallway where a vase of pale pink peonies billowed over a wooden console table. On either side of the hall was a grey-blue door. Number 12 was on the left. Freya pressed the bell and after a few moments they heard the rattle of a security chain as the door was unlocked. A bone-thin, white-haired woman with china-blue eyes greeted them. 'Do come in,' she said, moving stiffly aside to let them pass into a tiny hall.

They followed her into a living room flooded with late afternoon sunshine and smelling faintly of lavender. Facing the windows was a faded orange sofa with a rattan coffee-table in front of it. An old wicker armchair to the right of the sofa was piled with cushions while a high-back, wing chair to its left faced a television squatting on a low wooden table in the corner of the room. Silver photograph frames sparkled on a small, circular table close to the wing chair. Freya caught sight of a black-and-white wedding photograph and numerous colour prints of children.

'Please sit down,' said Alice Clarendon, pulling a red, woollen cardigan more closely around her gaunt body. 'Would you like some tea?'

'Oh, yes please,' said Freya as she settled down on the sofa. 'What a lovely, bright room.'

Alice smiled. 'It always gets the afternoon sunshine,' she said, standing behind the wing chair with both hands on its back.

'And the view is fantastic,' said Brooke, striding over to the window. 'You can see right across to Hyde Park.'

'How long have you lived here?' asked Freya.

'About thirty years,' replied Alice. 'I moved here after my husband died. It was the marvellous view that attracted me. Now I don't get out so much it's wonderful to see everything going on in the city from my little eerie.' She paused, eyeing Brooke's black cotton shirt and ripped white jeans with a doubtful expression. 'I'll go and put the kettle on.'

After she left the room, Brooke flopped into the wicker chair. 'Game old bird, isn't she?' she said. 'She must be well over ninety.'

'Ssh.' Freya frowned at Brooke then glanced around the room. A bookcase-cum-writing desk backed onto the wall opposite the television. Inside the glass doors of the upper section were several rows of leather-covered volumes. They brought to mind the books she had so nearly given to the charity shop and she wondered idly what secrets their flyleaves might divulge.

Framed paintings decorated the room – moody landscapes and several portraits of children. A dark rectangle on the wall where Jack Hunter's painting had hung next to the writing desk was so obvious it seemed to Freya like a missing tooth.

The minutes ticked by, softly marked by a carriage clock on the bureau. Freya got up and called from the doorway, 'Would you like a hand with anything?'

'If you could please carry the tray that would be very helpful,' came the reply.

Freya walked down the passage into the tiny kitchen where Alice was filling a silver teapot. Carrying the tray back to the living room, she placed it on the rattan table and waited for Alice to sit down and pour the tea into three bone china cups. Then she handed a cup and saucer decorated with swags of pink roses to Brooke.

'Do pass your friend the shortbread biscuits,' said Alice. 'I made them this morning.'

'It's very kind of you to welcome us like this,' said Freya.

Alice Clarendon's e eyes brightened. 'But you are part of the family it seems,' she said.

Freya blinked and sipped some tea to hide her surprise. Why on earth did Alice think that?

'Your friend said on the telephone that you had something to tell me about Jack Hunter's painting of Emily Meadowcroft,' said Alice, smiling.

Freya placed her cup and saucer carefully on the tray and put a hand on her stomach to quell a fluttering sensation. 'I was so sorry to hear your painting had been stolen,' she said, still weighing up whether to say where she thought it was now hanging.

When Brooke offered to get hold of Alice's address from the art tracing website's editor it had seemed like a good idea – a kindness, even – to tell her. Now she was changing her mind. It was too risky. Alice might inform the police and she needed to retrieve the replica necklace from Ralph's house first.

'Unfortunately, I can't throw any light on that,' she continued. 'But I thought you would be interested to see the portrait miniature I found among my mother's belongings after she died.' Unzipping her handbag, Freya took out the miniature and discarded the tissue paper wrapping on the sofa. Then she got up and moved over to Alice's chair.

'Look,' she said, gently placing the miniature in the palm of Alice's papery hand. 'Do you recognise her?'

'Emily!' exclaimed Alice. 'Oh, my word, how remarkable she looks.' She held the portrait at arm's length, gazing at the likeness then glanced up at Freya hovering at her shoulder. 'Do you know who painted this?'

'I think it's Annie Dixon,' replied Freya. 'Have you heard of her?'

'Oh yes, indeed,' replied Alice, tracing the outline of Emily's face with her forefinger. 'She painted all those miniatures of Queen Victoria's children, didn't she? May I ask how your mother came to have this portrait?'

Freya exchanged glances with Brooke. 'I think it was given to Emily's friend, Violet. I only discovered recently that Violet was my mother's great-grandmother.'

'Ah, Violet,' said Alice dreamily, dangling the miniature like a pendulum from her veined hand. The gilt case flashed in the sunshine as it danced on the end of its chain. 'Yes, she was a fine woman by all accounts. Matriarch of a large family and very involved with the early suffrage movement and prison reform. Like her husband, Henry, she held strong opinions on all sorts of subjects and brought her children up to be as forthright and candid as she was herself.'

Brooke leant forward, clattering her cup and saucer as she put them down on the tray. Still leaning towards Alice, she said loudly, 'We'd love to hear about the Meadowcroft siblings if you can tell us anything about them.'

Alice sighed and coiled the chain in her hand. Handing the miniature back to Freya, she said, 'You must wear this for her sake.'

'I will,' promised Freya, unfastening the clasp and putting the chain around her neck. She sat down on the sofa and no one spoke for a moment as they fixed their eyes on the small portrait resting on Freya's pale green tee-shirt.

'You want to know about Emily? Well, she was a woman before her time,' said Alice. 'If she were alive today, she would be an artist. Perhaps even a famous one.' Clearing her throat, she dabbed at her mouth with a lacy, cotton handkerchief then replaced it in the pocket of her cardigan. Neither Freya nor Brooke spoke as they waited for her to continue.

'Emily was intensely creative and could turn her hand to all manner of artistic work - painting, drawing, print-making,' said Alice. 'She made some wonderful jewellery and even designed ceramic tiles for a restaurant at the South Kensington Museum – it's now the V&A, of course, as I'm sure you must know. She really was very talented but what's so surprising is that she achieved all this without any formal training, as far as I understand.'

'What about her personality?' asked Brooke.

'Well, she was very lively and extremely popular by all accounts,' replied Alice. 'She loved parties and could charm the birds off the trees.' A dry cough interrupted her flow. Pulling the handkerchief from her pocket, Alice patted her lips then continued holding it in a ball in her hands. Freya and Brooke remained motionless, their eyes glued to Alice's lined face.

'Did you know she got engaged at a very young age?' asked Alice with a smile. 'Ralph Merrick was the Member of Parliament for Yorkshire South Riding – a young man with excellent prospects. He came from a wealthy family and all seemed to be set fair for a good marriage. Both families approved the match and even though Emily was just seventeen her parents gave it their blessing. Unfortunately, it seems no one had quite grasped that Emily was a rebel at heart and disliked conforming to the expectations of the day.'

As Alice paused for a sip of tea Freya could feel her heart starting to pound. Even though she knew what was coming it felt unnerving to hear the story directly from someone else, particularly a stranger.

Alice replaced her teacup in its saucer and resumed her tale. 'Emily was visiting her brother in London when he introduced her to Jack Hunter. Lawrence and Jack were both studying at the National Art Training School and by the sound of if it they had a lot of high jinks together, mixing with a very bohemian, artistic crowd. Emily fell in love with Jack and when she returned home she broke off her engagement to Ralph Merrick.'

'Both families were mortified,' continued Alice. 'Emily's parents cut her off completely – they wouldn't speak to her or continue to provide her with an allowance – so she went to live with Lawrence and shortly after that she moved in with Jack. Of course, you couldn't do something like that in those days if you came from a good family – it was considered highly immoral.' Alice gave a wry laugh. 'Life is very different today,' she added. 'No one would bat an eyelid.'

'Well,' she continued, 'the inevitable happened and Emily became pregnant. Even though Jack gained qualifications from the National Art Training School, he was barely earning enough to put food on the table for two of them, let alone three. Emily had the baby – a little girl called Grace – but was so fearful for her future that within days of the birth she asked a friend to take her in and bring her up as one of her own daughters. Tragically, a few days later she committed suicide in Jack's studio. She was only twenty one.' Alice pursed her lips and looked down at the handkerchief balled in her hands, squeezing it tightly. 'I've never been able to understand why,' she added sadly.

Freya glanced at Brooke and gave her a warning look. She wanted to handle the situation herself, fearful that Alice might get upset. 'It's such a heart-breaking story,' she said gently. 'But it's odd, isn't it? You'd think she would use her artistic skills to earn some money and keep the relationship on track.'

'I've often thought that too, given her exceptional talents,' said Alice. 'You have to remember though that it wasn't so easy for women in those days. They were very much second-class citizens. A woman's whole existence was in the domestic sphere. Their role as a wife was to organise the home and look after children. Of course, there were notable exceptions, but it was very difficult to pursue a career without patronage or private wealth. And an unmarried mother living with a man would have been virtually unemployable.'

Alice paused, gazing at the miniature with a troubled expression. As she raised her eyes, Freya glimpsed a flicker of uncertainty. 'Lawrence was very jealous of Emily's talents,' she said with a note of bitterness creeping into her voice. 'He disliked being outshone by his younger sister and there was even a rumour that he wrote to his tutor saying Emily had done the work for Jack's diploma show.' She pursed her lips thoughtfully. 'I don't know whether she did or not, but I'm sure she could have done if she had put her mind to it.'

Brooke took a bite from a shortbread biscuit and carelessly brushed some crumbs from her knee. 'Do you think your painting by Jack Hunter dates from the time they set up home together or earlier when she was living with Lawrence?' she asked.

'Most likely when she was living with Lawrence,' replied Alice. 'I think he painted the portrait in the first flush of their romance. You can almost feel the raw emotion in his brush-strokes.' Twisting the handkerchief ball in her lap, she added, 'Poor Emily. She could not have known when they met that Jack was a hopeless philanderer. I'm sure he genuinely did love her, but he also seems to have loved most of the young women he met. His behaviour was quite scandalous – even by the standards of their artistic friends – and his appalling reputation would have tainted Emily dreadfully. Had she lived, she could never have mixed in the social circles she was born into. Any respectable family would have barred her from their door.'

'What happened to Jack after Emily died?' asked Freya.

'He carried on seducing the women he painted,' replied Alice. 'His reputation sank beyond repair, and he died impoverished after developing pneumonia a few years after Emily committed suicide.'

'Oh, that's just so sad,' said Freya. Although Alice had only confirmed her suspicions, it was still shocking to hear the truth.

Brooke flashed her a scornful look then addressed Alice in a crisply polite tone. 'Could you tell us, please, how the painting came to you?'

'Oh, didn't I say?' Alice looked surprised. 'Grace was my grandmother.'

Freya's hand shot to her cheek. It was as if someone had slapped her painfully in the face. 'Emily's daughter – was your grandmother?' she echoed faintly.

Alice nodded. 'Yes, that's right dear. That's how I know the whole story. Grace's illegitimacy was publicly hushed up when she became part of Violet and Henry Stapleton's big family, and she never suffered the kind of stigma so common in those days. She was very fortunate in that respect. But Violet and Henry were quite open about everything with their children. They felt it was right that they should all know the truth, including Grace.'

'Then my great-grandmother, Olive, would have known about Emily and Grace,' said Freya, as if confirming the fact to herself.

'Oh yes, and so did her brothers and sisters,' said Alice. 'Violet and Henry didn't believe in keeping secrets among family members, although they were both perfectly discreet outside the home, of course.'

Freya fingered the smooth case of the miniature as she reflected on what Alice was saying. Perhaps she could throw light on something else that nagged at her. 'Do you have any idea why Grace might have given this to Olive?' she asked. 'Surely it was the most precious thing she owned.'

Alice eyed the miniature thoughtfully before she spoke. 'I don't know, dear. All I can tell you is what my mother told me. Olive was the youngest of Violet's five children. Grace was four years older but was very fond of her, treating her like a baby sister. I wouldn't be surprised if Olive received it after Grace died. She volunteered as a nurse during the Great War and was killed in Belgium.'

'Oh!' Freya felt cheated. A moment earlier, she was picturing Grace playing with all the other children in their clumsy Victorian outfits in a large garden. She'd heard shouts and laughter. Now Grace had vanished from sight.

'Who did Grace marry?' asked Brooke.

'An army officer called Arthur Lyndon,' replied Alice. 'They married in 1902 and my mother, Florence, was born the following year. She married my father, George Hurst, in 1921 and my sister – Olive Penelope – was born later that year. They named her after Olive Stapleton, but she never liked her first name, so everyone called her Penny. I was born in 1926 – a bit of an afterthought really.' Her creased face crinkled into laughter lines. 'There now – you have my entire family history.'

Freya gazed at her, searching for any physical resemblance to Emily's portrait, but found none. Yet could there be certain traits – personal characteristics – that were carried down the generations? Alice was clearly a strong, independent woman, even now in old age. She would have grown up during the privations of the Second World War and went on to marry and survive her husband by thirty years. She wondered if her older sister was still alive and how to ask this tactfully.

'Does your sister, Penny, also live in London?' she ventured.

Alice sighed. 'No, dear. Sadly, she disappeared during the Blitz not long after marrying her boyfriend, David Williams. We thought they got caught in the dreadful Kennington Park raid but their bodies were never recovered from the shelter. It wasn't even possible for us to get a death certificate because no one knew exactly what had happened.'

'Oh, I'm so sorry.' Freya's words slipped out automatically as her mind turned cartwheels. Olive Williams – that was her grandmother's name. But now she'd just learned that it was also the married name of Alice's sister – even if she preferred to be called Penny.

Could this be the reason why Ralph thought Emily was Freya's ancestor? Had his obsession with Emily and her portrait miniature deluded him into thinking Freya was Penny's grandchild? He could have found records for her birth and marriage, but not her death.

Freya was on the point of asking Alice whether she had any children and grandchildren when her friend intervened.

'Did Jack ever get married after Emily died?' asked Brooke, frowning as if she was trying to solve a puzzle.

'No, he didn't,' replied Alice.

'Perhaps he was too traumatised by Emily's death,' suggested Freya.

'Oh no, dear – I don't think that would have stopped him,' said Alice. 'Reading between the lines of what my mother told me, I think he went downhill fast after Emily died. He was no prospect at all for a well-bred, young woman with any common sense.'

Brooke leant forward to attract Alice's attention. 'I'm guessing Jack's painting of Emily was given to Grace,' she said. 'Was it then passed on to you from your mother, Florence?'

'My mother told me that Jack sent the portrait to Violet Stapleton shortly before he died,' said Alice. 'I think he sensed he didn't have long to live and wanted to make sure his daughter received it, even though she was still a child. He had nothing else to leave her.'

No one spoke for a moment then Freya broke the silence. 'When I was trying to find out about Emily, I came across some details on the internet about an auction of the Meadowcroft family's house and contents. It took place about two years ago. Were you aware of that?'

Alice sighed. 'My grand-daughter, Tania, told me. She works at an estate agency and heard about it through work. Of course, she knows the story of our family connections. She attended the sale with her husband, Ian, and asked me if I wanted to go with them. I didn't. Sometimes I think it's best to leave the past where it is.'

'Did they buy anything at the sale?' asked Brooke.

Alice smiled. 'Just one thing. A framed sampler that Emily stitched as a present for her mother when she was ten. It has her name and a date on it. It's hanging in their living room now.'

'Do you have anything here that belonged to Emily?' asked Brooke bluntly.

Freya darted a warning frown in her direction. Alice, however, appeared to take no offence. She got up stiffly from her chair and went over to the bookcase. Opening the glass door, she took out an oblong shaped book with a grey cover and passed it to Freya. 'Only this,' she said.

Freya flicked open the soft, fabric cover, turned a few pages then gave a loud gasp. 'Oh, my God,' she exclaimed.

'What is it?' demanded Brooke, leaning forward in the wicker chair.

'Her sketchbook,' replied Freya, slowly turning the stiff,

cream pages. 'Beautiful studies of flowers and berries. Interior scenes – a bedroom, a kitchen, what looks like an artist's studio. Drawings of hands and faces. And – oh Brooke, look – jewellery.' She turned another page and then another in rapid succession. 'Oh, my goodness, I think these must be her preparatory drawings for Morris & Co. The jewellery looks almost identical to the pieces I saw in the V&A.'

'Have you found something of interest?' asked Alice mildly as she settled back into her chair.

'Oh yes,' replied Freya vehemently, closing the book and handing it to Brooke. 'The proof I need to set the record straight.'

CHAPTER 20

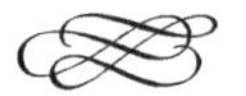

'That's a good bus route,' remarked Brooke, striding along the pavement. 'Not being a south-of-the-river girl, I'm unfamiliar with this neck of the woods.'

'But you've been to my flat before,' said Freya, indicating that they needed to cross the road at the traffic lights.

'Not for a long time,' said Brooke. 'And not by bus. I've always used the Tube.'

Suggesting they returned to her flat after meeting Alice Clarendon had seemed a good idea at the time. As they walked the short distance from the bus-stop to the street where she lived, Freya began to regret her offer to cook supper. What was in the fridge? More wine than food probably. Oh well, she would rustle up a risotto with whatever ingredients she could find.

Closing the door to her flat, Freya hoped she hadn't left the kitchen in too much of a mess. How shabby her home must seem to someone who spent her working days surrounded by top-quality art and design. Still, Brooke was never one to make unfair comparisons.

Freya opened the fridge door and pulled out a bottle of pinot grigio. 'Is this alright?' she asked, scrabbling in the drawer for a corkscrew.

'If you haven't got any champagne then I guess we can slum it,' replied Brooke.

'Oh, do shut up,' said Freya, laughing as she poured the wine into two, long-stemmed glasses. 'Here's to Alice Clarendon,' she said, clinking her glass against Brooke's.

'Here's to Alice,' echoed Brooke, taking a gulp. 'What a trooper. She pretty much confirmed everything you wanted to find out.'

'I feel a bit guilty, you know, about her painting,' said Freya, taking a sip then putting her glass down on a work-surface. Opening a cupboard, she took out a jar of arborio rice then plucked an onion from a straw basket on the counter. 'I could have told her I'd seen it in Ralph's house.'

'We can give the information to Gus at the art-tracing website whenever you want,' said Brooke. 'Anyway, you don't know for sure it's the same one,' she added, fixing her friend with a beady stare. 'And I hope to God you won't be going back to find out.'

Freya started to chop an onion, deliberately keeping her back turned on her friend. She was determined not to involve Brooke in her plans to retrieve the replica necklace.

'What a weirdo,' said Brooke, pulling out a chair from the kitchen table and sitting down. 'I still can't get my head around the way he behaved – treating you as if you were Emily's actual reincarnation. And yet he was the chief mover and shaker behind the salons – the set designer, producer and executive director as it were – so he was fully aware it was all a charade. Talk about coercive control. He must be right up there on the pathological narcissist scale.'

Freya tossed the chopped onions into a pan of heated oil

and agitated them briskly with a wooden spoon. Adding the rice, she carried on stirring for a moment. 'He certainly lives in a fantasy world of his own making,' she said.

'Do you think all his guests are actors?' asked Brooke. 'It sounds as if he treats his house like some kind of giant stage-set.'

'Only some,' replied Freya, pouring a little stock into the pan and stirring hard. 'I think most of them are Ralph's friends who enjoy being wined and dined and are happy to play along with his theatrics when he encourages them to behave in character. They probably think it's just a bit of a laugh.'

'Lawrence and Jack must be hired luvvies though, because it seems they were deliberately planted to provoke you,' said Brooke.

'I think you're right,' said Freya, pondering whether to tell her friend about spotting Jack in the café and deciding against it. Admitting that she'd stalked him through Soho was just too embarrassing. And a part of her was still longing to know if the emotional connection between them might have been genuine in different circumstances – a very personal conundrum.

'I'm guessing Minnie might also be an actor,' she added. 'Now I come to think of it, Ralph used me as an actor too by encouraging me to play my role as Emily Meadowcroft to perfection.'

'D'you mean with Jack and Lawrence?' asked Brooke.

'And others,' replied Freya, adding more stock to the rice. 'That tall chap with the curly hair you met at the front door on the night of the séance – the Frederic Leighton lookalike - outbid Ralph on a couple of pieces at the Meadowcroft house sale. Before he left Ralph forced him to agree to hand them over at his next salon by implying they belonged to Emily

Meadowcroft and had, more or less, been stolen from under my nose.'

'You're joking!' exclaimed Brooke. 'Just hand them over?'

'Not exactly,' replied Freya, stirring vigorously. 'Whoever was posing as Leighton demanded that Ralph gave him the same amount he'd paid for them at auction. But I expect some sleight of hand will be involved. As with everything Ralph does.'

Foraging in the fridge, Freya brought out a packet of ham, some mushrooms, a tiny chunk of parmesan cheese and the bottle of wine. Refilling Brooke's glass and then her own kept her moving around the kitchen, dodging her friend's perceptive gaze. Avoiding any mention of her plan to return to Ralph's house was essential. Turning her back again, she stood at the counter chopping the ham and mushrooms and grating some parmesan.

'Ralph clearly knew much more about Emily than he was letting on when you first met him,' remarked Brooke, playing with the stem of her glass.

Freya was silent for a moment, pouring in more stock and stirring the pan. 'Perhaps I do resemble her – not in appearance, of course, but in character and personality,' she said. 'What do you think?'

Brooke began to chuckle. 'A case of mistaken identity – that's what I think.'

'Oh, do be serious if you can,' chided Freya. 'What about artistic creativity? Don't I have that in common with Emily?'

'Soul sisters,' said Brooke with mock seriousness. 'Let's have another look at her, shall we?'

'Emily?' asked Freya, startled.

'Who else?' replied Brooke with a mischievous gleam in her eyes.

Freya poured in the last of the stock and gave the pan a stir. 'Okay,' she agreed reluctantly. 'Keep an eye on this for me.'

Returning from her bedroom, she put the miniature on the kitchen table in front of Brooke then resumed her position by the stove so she could carry on stirring the risotto.

'Hmm. She does look rebellious, doesn't she?' said Brooke. 'Clearly too much of a handful for a staid politician.' She turned the miniature over and studied the back of the case. 'I wonder…' she said softly, running her fingernail around the edge of the case.

'Liz Russell said that artists sometimes signed their paintings on the reverse,' said Freya. 'But I didn't want the case ruined by breaking it open.'

'That was before you started to inhabit Emily – body, mind and spirit,' said Brooke. 'Now put yourself in her position. She was blackmailed by Lawrence to carry out his commission for Morris & Co which she did – incognito – with no credit or any recognition of her skills. And she knew she had no hope of rectifying that situation.'

Brooke drained her glass then continued. 'Unlike you and Oliver. You managed to shame him into making amends for stealing your design by paying you a design fee and acknowledging your work publicly. Emily had no means of doing that. But we know how headstrong she was. Would she not have found a way to reveal the truth?'

'Well, in a way she did,' said Freya. 'It's all there in the sketchbooks. I can't wait to show them to someone at the V&A and get their opinion.' She stared at her friend for a moment and then back at the pan. Almost all the liquid had been absorbed by the rice. Picking up the chopping board, she scooped the ham and mushrooms into the pan then added the grated parmesan. 'This is ready,' she said. 'Let's eat.'

Forking up the risotto, Freya deliberately avoided

mentioning Ralph and his salons again. With no wish to bicker about her plans to sneak back to his house, she turned the conversation to Brooke's work for the Ryder gallery. 'Tell me the latest gossip about Richard Ryder,' she began, hoping this would elicit a torrent of anecdotes. Brooke could be a good raconteur when she was in the right mood which she clearly was tonight.

After clearing their plates Freya poured the remainder of the bottle into their glasses. The combination of risotto and wine had mellowed them both. She was glad she'd cooked supper for Brooke, however humble the meal. Her friend would never have made the effort for herself.

The portrait miniature still sat on the far side of the kitchen table where she'd pushed it before dishing up the risotto. Now she drew it towards them. The pendant light overhead brought the painted features vividly to life. Headstrong and wilful, Emily gazed out with her taunting look as if challenging Freya to a dare.

She wants me to do it. The thought moved through Freya's mind with the force of an avalanche slowly gathering speed. *Okay, I will.*

Seizing a vegetable knife from a wooden block on the kitchen counter, she held the miniature on its side and stabbed the knife into the place where the two sides met and prized them apart.

Brooke gasped. 'What are you *doing?*'

The clear glass oval protecting the painting sprang off, slid across the table and came to rest against a peppermill. Holding the painted ivory disc face down in her hand, Freya removed the back of the case and picked off the silk fabric with the knife's sharp point.

'Oh heavens – what's this?' Freya exclaimed, winkling out a sliver of paper with the tip of the knife. The scrap fluttered onto the table in front of her. Picking it up between finger and thumb, she unfolded it and gently smoothed it flat on the table.

Squinting at the tiny curls of cursive handwriting, Freya read the words out loud in a faltering voice:

My brother holds me to never-ending ransom. He died by my hand. God forgive me.

Freya's face turned pale as she glanced at Brooke then again at the yellowy fragment. 'It's a confession,' she said shakily. 'Oh – oh, my goodness – she must have poisoned him.'

'Blimey,' said Brooke, sounding rattled. 'I didn't expect that. I thought there might be something – a note for posterity about her work perhaps – but not anything like this. Can I see?' She picked up the scrap from the table and studied it closely. Then she looked at Freya and said quietly, 'She would have hung for this except she beat them to it.'

'I can't believe it,' said Freya blankly, clutching the edge of the table to stop her hands quivering. She felt dazed and ice-cold despite the kitchen's warmth.

'Do you think Ralph Merrick knew?' asked Brooke in a sombre tone.

'I doubt it.' Freya winced. 'He showed us Lawrence dying in the most horrible way at the séance. When the image of Thomas Chatterton morphed into Lawrence, I guessed he might have died from arsenic poisoning – but there was no indication Emily was involved.'

They sat silently for a moment, Brooke examining the tiny piece of paper and Freya watching her with anguished eyes.

Until she remembered.

Jumping up from her chair, she ran into the bedroom. Her mother's jewellery box was lying open on her bed. Inside was the black velvet pouch. Picking it up, she poked in her forefinger and carefully slid out the note she'd found previously.

Friday without fail.

The rusty, faded words were written in a copper-plate script, starkly different from Emily's rounded handwriting. Could it be Jack's or—

Freya sank onto her bed and buried her face in her hands as the realisation penetrated. The message had nothing to do a lover's tryst, as she'd fondly imagined. It was a blackmail note from Lawrence to Emily.

She had no way of identifying the handwriting, of course, but knew intuitively that it belonged to Lawrence. Unpleasant as it was, her conviction rang with the solid peal of truth.

After sitting on her bed for a while, Freya returned to the kitchen.

Brooke glanced up from fiddling with the portrait miniature case. 'Are you alright?'

Freya nodded and sat down at the table, feeling dazed.

'I can't get the two sides to fit together properly,' said Brooke.

'Leave it – I can fix it tomorrow,' said Freya wearily as a wave of exhaustion rolled over her. Deeply upset by Emily's tragic confession and Lawrence's threatening note, she wanted to think about these discoveries quietly on her own.

CHAPTER 21

Tossing and turning, Freya slept in short bursts of an hour or less throughout the night. Her thoughts reverted time and again to Emily's distressing confession.

Everything had turned out so badly for her. Was it simply a matter of ill-fortune or was some flaw in her character to blame? If the fault lay deep within her, then the comparison Freya had drawn between herself and Emily while chatting to Brooke did not bode well. Not least for the course of action she now needed to take.

Or did she? Couldn't she just leave matters alone and hope for the best? Perhaps Eleanor would fail to notice Ralph's sleight of hand. After all, the replica she had crafted so meticulously was virtually identical to the Victorian necklace bought at auction by Eleanor's son. How proud of her creative abilities she'd felt when she presented it to Ralph. How ironic that seemed now. What an idiot she'd been to get caught up in this racket.

If she just let things lie, perhaps nothing would happen. Ralph might sell the original Victorian necklace after exchanging it with her replica, if he wasn't intending to add it to his collection. Maybe the scam would never come to light. It was unlikely he would take the risk of selling it on the open market. He'd contact a private collector who would, no doubt, pay him some vast sum. The legitimate paper-trail would conclude with Eleanor's son buying it at auction. There would be nothing to link the Victorian necklace to Ralph. Nor, with any luck, might the substitute necklace ever be traced back to Freya.

She turned over in bed again. It was tempting to trust to luck but too dangerous to risk it. In any case it would mean living with the guilt of deceiving Eleanor – an elderly lady who never deserved to be treated so badly. She really couldn't do that. Morally, it was just plain wrong.

How was she going to get the replica back though? The only way would be to think of an excuse to return to Ralph's house – something she thought she'd never do again. And even if she did – then what?

Turning over, she lay on her back and stared at a chink of light between the curtains. She would have to employ every ounce of intelligence she possessed to outwit Ralph. And it wasn't only intelligence she would need. Resilience too. Like Lady Macbeth, she would need to screw her courage to the sticking-place to have any hope of calling time on Ralph's shameful and criminal activities.

WITH HER HAND TREMBLING UNCONTROLLABLY, it was only at the third attempt that Freya's forefinger successfully engaged with the bellpush. Standing at Ralph's Neo-Gothic front door felt as if she was acting out some surreal nightmare. When she escaped with Brooke after the séance, she never thought she would visit the house ever again. Yet here she was, alone and vulnerable. Was she completely mad?

Freya took a deep breath as the heavy, wooden door swung open, expecting to see the maid in her black and white uniform. To her horror she found Ralph standing there. He was wearing a tweed jacket and cavalry twill trousers. A cinnamon-coloured handkerchief billowed from his top pocket and his dark, curly hair glistened in the sunshine. He looked even more commanding than the last time she'd seen him. If she didn't know any better, it would be natural to think he was the kind of person who could be universally trusted and respected.

An oily smile crept across his face as soon as he set eyes on her. 'Do come in,' he said in his smooth, urbane way. 'My housekeeper is out for a few hours, so you are in my hands this morning.'

Freya attempted to say something in reply but only a squeak came out of her mouth. Clearing her throat, she tried again. 'What a lovely morning,' she murmured blandly, taking the opportunity to steady her nerves by swivelling away from Ralph and appearing to inspect the sunlit street. Swallowing hard, she turned back and forced herself to step past Ralph into the hallway. Her legs felt like jelly.

Ralph closed the door firmly behind her. 'Shall I take your jacket and bag?' he offered.

'No thanks,' replied Freya, pinning her shoulder-bag against her body with her elbow. She felt like a fly caught in a spider's web.

Ralph took a step towards her, looking down into her face. 'You seem unusually pale, my dear,' he said, putting his fore-finger under her chin and tipping it up towards him.

Nausea rose in Freya's throat but subsided when Ralph removed his hand. 'I'm so glad you've decided to see sense at last,' he said. 'You're such an intelligent woman that I felt it was only a matter of time. Shall we have some coffee in the study before we go up to my cabinet of curiosities?'

'Mmm,' replied Freya, barely trusting herself to speak. Following Ralph along the passage, she felt as breathless as if she was drowning. In the central hall the tall, glass vitrines sparkled in the sunlight coming through the stained glass in the octagonal tower above. Were they all full of stolen items? And to what lengths had he gone to acquire them?

Catching sight of the sunflower vase, Freya remembered he'd acquired it at the Meadowcroft house sale. Yet even that was unlikely to have been a straightforward purchase. No doubt it was paid for with money made from selling other stolen artworks, she thought cynically.

The door to the study was open and Ralph ushered her inside. The room had changed since Freya's last visit, and she quickly realised the furniture had been re-arranged again. The yellow sofas were now pushed back against the bookcases. Taking the place of one of them was a chaise longue, upholstered in blush-pink velvet, sprawling at right-angles to the fireplace. Facing this was a black, armless, wooden chair whose elongated back was decorated with carved flowers highlighted by pinpoints of mother-of-pearl. Seeing this incongruous layout made Freya feel even more uneasy. It put her in mind of a psychotherapist's consultation room.

No fire burned in the grate although it was piled with logs. Instead, the gilded cherub Freya remembered from the salon evenings stood on the marble slab in front of the fireplace. Between the chaise longue and the chair was a low, lacquered table on which rested a tray with a silver coffee-pot and two large, yellow, china cups with saucers.

Ralph gestured towards the chaise longue with its sweeping headrest. 'Do sit down. I'm sure you're very tired.'

Tired? Alarm bells rang in Freya's head. He'd already told her she looked pale. What was he driving at? Still, it was wiser to do as he suggested at this point in their meeting. She sat down nervously, next to the headrest, with her bag close by her side and crossed her legs.

Ralph bent over the tray to pour the coffee, adding milk at Freya's request and handing her a cup and saucer. Then he lowered his imposing bulk carefully onto the wooden chair directly opposite her.

'I'm worried about you,' he said. 'It looks like you've lost a lot of weight. You've clearly been working yourself to death since we last met.' He gave a sly chuckle. 'Esme – my house-keeper – should have left us some cake and biscuits. That would help to fatten you up.'

Freya said nothing, observing how tightly Ralph's jacket encased his sturdy shoulders and upper arms. He had left it casually unbuttoned and beneath it she could see a cream linen shirt straining across his powerful torso.

'It's not good to run yourself down,' he continued in a kindly voice. 'That's the way mental problems begin.' He took a sip of coffee without taking his dark eyes off Freya's face. 'Poor Emily. She was badly afflicted towards the end, I believe.'

The hairs on Freya's neck bristled. Where was this conver-sation heading? To hide her alarm, she took a gulp of coffee. It was far too bitter, burning her throat and making her head buzz with the sudden rush of caffeine. Leaning forward, she put the cup and saucer down on the tray then sat back with her elbow against the headrest.

'Please feel free to rest your legs on the couch,' said Ralph gently, as if to an invalid.

'I'm not tired, thank you,' replied Freya, fighting a wave of giddiness.

Ralph ignored her remark. 'Emily's brother, Lawrence, was

also affected in the same way,' he continued softly. 'Sadly, it led him to take his own life.'

'What makes you think that?' asked Freya casually, masking her own knowledge about his demise.

'Old Tom Meadowcroft gave me chapter and verse when we were chatting about his family after the Meadowcroft house sale,' replied Ralph. 'Emily was distraught, of course, and it wasn't long before her own mental weakness resulted in suicide too.' Closing his eyes for a moment, he let out a long sigh then opened them wide and continued speaking. 'It seems to me that a faulty gene running through the Meadowcroft line lies at the heart of all this pain and anguish.' Staring hard at Freya, he added, 'I wonder if this is something you've ever considered?'

'What?' Freya could barely get her mind around what he was implying. 'Certainly not,' she added firmly. 'In any case I'm not related to Emily and Lawrence Meadowcroft.'

Ralph gave a mirthless chuckle. 'Come, come, my dear. We both know about your ancestry and how your family was once so closely entwined with mine. There's no denying what's past. But perhaps it's the present that worries you more?'

With horrified fascination Freya watched the tip of his tongue flick out to wet the corner of his lips before he began speaking in a quiet, almost soporific, voice.

'Think of all the little indications that give the game away. At first, forgetfulness. The email you meant to send. The dress you never collected from the dry cleaners. Next come the moments when your mind goes blank. At first, just moments. Then they last for longer stretches. Eventually whole days. And, of course, there's the switchback turmoil of the emotional roller-coaster. The sudden outbursts of anger – with yourself, with other people. The rudeness that makes your friends avoid you. And then the final outrageous act that sees you sectioned...'

'No!' Freya shot up from the chaise longue, angry and frightened.

Ralph appeared mildly surprised. 'Sit down, my dear. There's no need to get upset. I'm sure you wouldn't want me to think you are starting to display signs of the condition I've just described?'

'I did *not* come here to be gaslit,' hissed Freya, remaining on her feet.

Ralph shrugged. 'I'm only trying to help,' he said calmly. 'You must admit your behaviour has been quite erratic the last few times we've met.'

Freya blinked, barely able to believe what she was hearing. Whatever she tried to say, he would twist it to fit his strange, warped way of thinking. He was like Robert Louis Stevenson's Jekyll and Hyde character – benign and friendly one moment, rapacious and predatory the next. And most sinister of all when he assumed his role as an eminent Victorian.

It was as if the past and the present were all rolled into one for him. Perhaps that's what she needed to do to survive this ordeal. Make a clear division between then and now. If she could call a halt to this festering, time-slip trap perhaps it would lead to a path out of the maze of his mind-games. It was worth taking a chance.

'That was Emily's bad behaviour – not mine,' she said. 'I expect she was over-stimulated by meeting so many interesting people at the salons.'

'Ah,' said Ralph dreamily, putting the tips of his fingers together in front of his waist. 'She always loved a party.'

'I'm not Emily, of course,' said Freya. 'She died a very long time ago so the portrait I've brought with me this morning is really just a little bit of history.... The portrait you very much desire to call your own,' she added, hoping to appeal to his innate acquisitiveness.

A waft of mandarin oil accompanied Ralph as he rose to his feet. He seemed surprisingly nimble for such a big man. 'Shall we go upstairs to my cabinet of curiosities and look at it there?' he suggested.

'Please lead on,' said Freya, quickly reckoning that Ralph was less of a threat if he was in front of her than behind.

As she moved away from the chaise longue she noticed a small crimson stain at the base of the headrest, just where she'd been sitting. Her stomach heaved. It looked like blood.

Following Ralph slowly up the stairs, Freya's fingers trembled on the handrail as her fears went into freefall. What had happened on the chaise longue before she sat there? Was he capable of killing to get what he wanted? Ralph unlocked the door to the collector's room and Freya followed him inside. The vitrines seemed even more crammed with objects than she remembered from her previous visit. How much thieving had taken place since she was last here? Who were the true owners of all these remarkable things?

Ralph closed the door and stood with his back against it. The room was extremely chilly, and Freya found herself shivering. How would she escape this time if he attacked her? At least he hadn't locked the door from the inside. Feeling sick with fear, she moved away from Ralph and pretended to inspect a gleaming gold crocodile in one of the glass display-cases. She took a few steps further, stared at a giant ammonite, then moved towards the cabinet furthest from the door and lingered there as if examining an exquisitely painted Chinese bowl.

Glancing across at the vitrines on the other side of the room, the floor-lamp's rosy glow caught the beaten-gold leaves of an object in the facing cabinet. Her heart gave a stabbing lurch and she froze, motionless, feeling as if she'd swallowed a hook that was jerking tight inside her. Without any doubt at all, she was staring at the replica necklace Ralph had commissioned her to make.

She quickly turned back to the cabinet containing the Chinese bowl, giving no outward sign of spotting the necklace. Out of the corner of her eye she saw Ralph flexing his fingers in a pair of white gloves.

'Please don't make me wait any longer,' he said, gesturing towards the green velvet ottoman. Pulling the cinnamon-coloured handkerchief from the top pocket of his tweed jacket, he laid it on the ottoman with a flourish.

With a pounding heart, Freya moved towards him and unzipped her handbag. Slowly unwrapping the miniature, she let the tissue paper flutter to the floor and placed the portrait in the centre of Ralph's handkerchief. Then she backed away again.

'Ah, Emily,' said Ralph with a long sigh. 'At last.' He stood, gazing down at the miniature for a moment before greedily picking it up and holding the portrait to his lips.

Freya's stomach heaved as she watched this sickening display of acquisitive lust, while all the time focusing her periphery vision on the necklace. The glass doors to the display cases had no locks. All she had to do was pull the bronze knob to lower the glass pane to a horizontal position, reach inside and grab it.

'What finally made you decide to sell?' asked Ralph, glancing briefly at Freya as he held the miniature in the palm of one large, gloved hand.

Freya cleared her throat. 'I thought it was time she came home,' she said, improvising with bravado.

Ralph gave her a brooding smile. 'You're right, my dear. Her home is with me. She can rest in peace at last.'

'That's what I thought,' murmured Freya, side-stepping slowly around the end of the ottoman. 'You can be together now,' she added, watching Ralph's movements intently. As his head dipped to study the portrait again, she grabbed the bronze knob, opened the glass door and scooped out the necklace.

Her quicksilver movements alerted Ralph. His head jerked up, a look of fury crossing his face. 'Hey!' he said, taking a step forward but the ottoman crouched between them now.

'I'd forgotten how beautifully the light plays on the stones,' Freya said in a dreamy manner, holding the necklace up to catch the floor-lamp's lambent glow. Then, in a flash, it was round her neck and she was fastening the clasp.

'Put that back right now,' ordered Ralph menacingly, moving towards her.

Freya slowly circled round the other side of the ottoman towards the door. 'That partnership you mentioned previously – is this the kind of work you might require?'

'Oh!' Ralph halted, looking nonplussed. 'Well, yes – I hadn't realised you'd come to a decision about my offer.'

'Didn't I say? Oh, I'm very keen,' lied Freya, taking a further step towards the door. Her breath was coming in unpleasantly short bursts, and she could feel her heart banging against her ribcage. Panicking, she realised she'd never get out of the house wearing the necklace. He would easily overpower her before she reached the front door.

Clutching her stomach, she gave a loud moan. 'Oh, Ralph – I need the bathroom,' she cried.

Alarm flashed in Ralph's dark eyes. 'Take it off first.'

'I'm – going to vomit.' Freya clapped a hand over her mouth.

'Alright, this way.' Grabbing her arm roughly, Ralph yanked the doorhandle with his free hand and propelled her from the room. Opening the second door on the left, he shoved her inside the cloakroom and closed the door with a thud.

Freya turned the key in the lock and held her breath. She could hear his noisy breathing on the other side of the door. He must be standing directly outside, guarding her from escaping while she was wearing the necklace.

She moved away from the door. So far, so good. His fastidiousness had given her the opportunity to put her plan into action. Vomiting was the last thing he wanted in his precious collector's room.

Freya dumped her shoulder-bag on the carpet, knelt down and rummaged inside. She'd come armed with some workshop tools and drew out a small pair of side-cutters. Then she unclasped the necklace and laid it on the floor.

Her heart jerked uncomfortably as Ralph banged on the door. 'Are you alright?' he called gruffly.

As if you care, she thought, wrestling with the heart-shaped clasp. 'I'm okay. I won't be long,' she called back.

It went against the grain to break the necklace deliberately after all the long hours she'd spent making it. The side-cutters had small, very sharp blades that would be strong enough to bend or even snap the clasp. Applying pressure, she gave it a hard twist and managed to wrench the clasp sufficiently so that the chain couldn't close. Then she sat on the lavatory and relieved herself.

Taking her time, Freya washed and dried her hands then shoved the side-cutters back in her shoulder-bag, leaving it unzipped. Picking up the necklace, she held it in her hand as she unlocked the door.

Ralph sprang aside then clamped his hand on her shoulder. 'Are you finished in there?' he asked without warmth.

'Yes, sorry, it must have been something I ate last night,' said Freya.

A look of disgust crossed Ralph's face as he pushed her towards the collector's room. Through the open door she could see the miniature still sitting in the middle of his handkerchief on the ottoman.

Pausing at the threshold, Freya made a show of holding up the two ends of the necklace with the twisted clasp dangling limply from the chain. 'I don't know how this happened, but the clasp has broken,' she said. 'The whole thing fell off me onto the bathroom floor.'

Looking startled, Ralph opened his mouth but before he could say anything Freya continued speaking. 'Don't worry. I can easily fix it. I just need to do a little repair in my workshop.' The words slid over her tongue as smoothly as ice-cream.

'How quickly?' Ralph looked agitated. 'Eleanor's party is tonight. I need it back by this evening.'

'Oh, it won't take me long,' replied Freya in an offhand manner. 'I could go and do it immediately if you like.'

Ralph hesitated. A wave of edgy vigilance transmitted itself to Freya. He was clearly torn between letting the replica necklace out of his sight and the realisation that he had no choice if the repair was to be made before the evening.

'As partners, I'll often be making repairs like this I expect,' said Freya.

It was as if her words tipped a stack of dominos into a rippling line.

He consulted his watch then spoke briskly with his usual authority. 'I'll be here until 3pm, then I need to go out to an appointment. Come back with it as quickly as you can and we'll talk about the price you want for the portrait miniature when you return. I expect you have something in mind.'

'Yes, of course, but now we've settled on the sale I'd like to present the portrait in the kind of box it deserves,' said Freya, moving towards the ottoman. 'There are several beautiful leather boxes in my workshop. I'll just take this with me for the moment so I can get the size right.' Leaning down, she scooped up the miniature and stuffed it into her handbag along with the necklace.

In a flash one of Ralph's large hands gripped the back of her neck. The other seized a handful of hair, pulling hard.

'You tricky little bitch,' he hissed as she wriggled and yelped. 'What the hell do you think you're doing?'

'Stop, please stop,' cried Freya, coughing and spluttering, trying to tear herself away from his crushing grip. It was useless. He was far too strong.

In a paroxysm of fear Freya gathered what little saliva she could muster, turned her head and spat it into his face.

Lurching backwards, Ralph momentarily loosened his grip and Freya sprang away from him and bolted into the minstrel's gallery. Without slackening her pace, she ran down the stairs and through the central hall.

Just as she reached the front door it opened from outside. Freya nearly knocked the housekeeper over in her dash from the house. Pounding up the street without looking back, it wasn't until she reached the junction with the main road that she slowed her pace and caught her breath.

Checking her watch, she saw it was already 1pm. Ralph would be at home for another two hours. She wanted to make the call as quickly as possible without being overheard.

She strode past an internet café. Not there. It was too public. Turning right, she walked briskly along a residential street of terraced houses leading towards the river. Crossing the Embankment at a set of traffic lights, she headed for a wooden bench and sat down, still feeling shaky.

It could all have gone so horribly wrong and very nearly did. She could still feel the pressure he'd applied to her neck.

She touched her throat gently and swallowed. She'd been lucky. So lucky. Her plan had succeeded thanks to a combination of luck and devious opportunism. Some force in the universe had lifted her up and carried her safely over the brink. A surge of relief ran through her body. It felt like a deliverance from evil.

Gradually Freya felt her pounding heart subside. There was something soothing about being close to the fast-moving, grey waters of the Thames. Glancing up at the sky, she saw a pair of seagulls dipping and circling, following a barge downriver. Taking a deep breath, she pulled her phone from her handbag. Then, for the first time in her life, she pressed nine three times. Whatever happened next would be up to the police.

CHAPTER 22

The café was much busier than on her previous visit. Casting her eyes over the occupants of each table, Freya walked slowly to the rear and sat at the table furthest from the door. It was the same table, the same chair, she'd used before. It was also the same young, smiley waitress who came to take her order.

'How are the classes going?' asked Freya, raising her voice above the café's clatter and chatter.

'Hard work,' replied the waitress, pouting. Lowering her voice, she confided, 'I don't get much time off so it's tricky getting there. So,' she added more loudly, 'What d'you fancy – a nice, toasted cheese panini?'

'Yes, please, and a pot of Earl Grey tea,' replied Freya cheerfully.

As the waitress headed back towards the counter, Freya checked her watch. It was the same day of the week and pretty much the same time she'd come here previously. Now, with any luck, all she had to do was wait patiently. She pulled a paperback out of her bag, propped it against the condiments holder and pretended to read. Each time the door opened she raised her eyes expectantly then dropped them again to her book.

The panini and pot of tea arrived. Freya ate and drank slowly, spinning out the minutes. Alert, yet calm, she reflected on the extraordinary events of the past few weeks. Every time she thought of Ralph Merrick facing a long jail sentence an immense surge of relief wafted her into a cloud of serenity so palpable it felt like wallowing in a warm, fragrant bath. And every time she thought about the possibility of seeing Jack – or whatever his real name was – she felt her stomach give a little kick. That, of course, was why she was here. It was a very long shot, but how else would she find him in a city of several million people?

Freya checked her watch. Nearly an hour had passed. She hailed the waitress and ordered another pot of tea. The stream of customers was diminishing but people were still coming in for a snack or a coffee. She had nothing to lose by waiting a bit longer.

In the meantime, her thoughts chattered on relentlessly. Tomorrow she would have a drink with Brooke at the Arts Club. Freya had called her as soon as she saw the *Evening Standard*'s report about Ralph's arrest and was looking forward to having a forensic chat with her friend about it all. After that, she was determined to put the whole bizarre affair behind her and focus on developing her fledgling business.

Finding a private client who might be interested in buying the replica Victorian necklace she'd made for Ralph would be a good start. She needed to cover the cost of its materials, at the very least. Ralph, of course, had failed to pay her suppliers. Thank goodness she had long-standing relationships with them. After some extremely difficult negotiations they'd agreed to let her meet their bills in instalments. Even so, she would need to sell a significant amount of work over the next few months. If the orders for her Victorian collection took off that would really help.

It was fortunate, too, that Ralph's promised fee never landed in her bank account. That proved a saving grace when the squad from the Serious Acquisitive Crime Unit came to interview her after their raid on Ralph's house. All she'd needed to mention was seeing Jack Hunter's painting of Emily Meadowcroft in Ralph's bedroom and recognising it as the one reported missing on the art-tracing website. It was exactly the same information she'd given them in her initial phone-call. All the other stolen artworks in his house were discovered by the police themselves.

As for her exchange of emails with Ralph about the necklace, well, if the police wanted to question her again after trawling through his laptop, she would just protest her innocence. No one could blame her for discussing a potential commission in good faith nor for failing to suspect Ralph's motives. It wasn't as if it was a legal prerequisite to carry out due diligence before accepting a bespoke order. If they wanted to see the necklace, she would show it to them and say the clasp had broken before she'd had a chance to deliver it to him.

Freya drained her cup then checked her watch again. Another half-hour had passed. She couldn't sit here all evening. It was time to abandon this idea as a non-starter. Sighing, she stuffed the paperback in her bag, got up and went over to the counter to pay her bill.

'Good luck with your classes,' she said to the waitress encouragingly as she handed her a small tip.

Reaching the door, Freya was surprised to find it held open for her by a tall young man coming in from the alley.

He looked searchingly at her face as she stepped over the

threshold. 'Don't I know you from somewhere?' he asked, breaking into a crooked smile.

'Jack!' exclaimed Freya as her heart gave a painful lurch. Even though she'd been hoping he would come it was still a shock to see him.

'It's Simon,' he replied, looking puzzled. 'Simon Chandler.' He smiled again. 'Just remind me where we met?'

A fog of qualm doused Freya's confidence. Had he forgotten all about their intimate moment on the garden bench at Ralph's house? She'd better tread warily. Taking a deep breath to compose herself, she replied, 'Ralph Merrick's house in Chelsea. At the Victorian salon.'

'Ah yes – Emily Meadowcroft,' he replied, giving her an amused look. 'Well, well. I was just thinking I hadn't heard from the old Master of Ceremonies for a while.'

'Excuse me,' said a voice behind Freya's shoulder. Realising that she was blocking the exit, Freya stood aside to let a slim, dark-haired woman leave the café.

'Hi Josie,' said Simon. 'Any good?'

The woman shook her head. 'Sadly not,' she replied without stopping to talk. Turning to watch her retreating figure walk up the alley, Simon called out, 'Better luck next time.' Josie showed no sign of hearing his remark and, giving a shrug, he turned back to Freya.

'Are you leaving or staying?' he asked in a friendly manner.

'I wouldn't mind another cup of tea,' replied Freya. Moving back into the cafe, she made her way to a table near the window. It was brighter here than where she'd sat earlier and felt more inviting.

'I'm not Emily, of course,' she said as she sat down. 'My name is Freya Wetherby.'

Simon's green cat's-eyes crinkled at the corners as he

pulled out a chair opposite her. 'Freya,' he repeated, placing an emphasis on the first syllable. 'That's an unusual name.'

The waitress came over to take their order, all smiles and dimples. 'Hi Simon,' she said as if they had known each other for years. For an anxious moment Freya thought the girl might comment on the length of time she'd already spent in the café but, no, this didn't seem to have registered. Glancing across the room, she realised that only two other tables were now occupied and those were half-way down the space. They would be able to talk freely here.

'It sounds as if you haven't heard about Ralph,' said Freya, eyeing Simon's dishevelled, fair hair and wondering whether he was working or 'resting'.

'No? What about him?' Simon looked surprised.

Without replying, Freya unzipped her handbag, pulled out the folded page from the *Evening Standard* and pushed it across the table.

Simon glanced at her with a raised eyebrow. Then he unfolded the page and read the piece aloud in a low, clear voice beginning with the headline: *'Art Scam Arrest'.*

'A wealthy London art collector was today arrested at his Chelsea home, charged with receiving stolen goods worth millions of pounds.

Ralph Merrick, 45, is allegedly involved in a steal-to-order scam plaguing the capital. Following a tip-off, he was arrested as part of an on-going investigation by the Metropolitan police into a spate of high-value art thefts.

Police raided his £16 million house in Chelsea this afternoon, seizing a quantity of valuable works reportedly stolen over the past few years. Paintings, silver, porcelain and rare books are said to be among the haul.

Merrick is believed to have passed information about artworks, owners and locations to a gang of high-class associates who stole to order from numerous addresses in and around the capital. It's thought many of the works were taken over the Christmas holiday last year and it is hoped they will eventually be reunited with their owners.'

Simon raised his eyes from the report and stared at Freya. 'Bloody hell! I had no idea,' he said, looking shaken. 'When did this happen?'

Freya pointed to the date at the top of the page. 'Last week,' she said.

'He always did seem a bit slippery to me but – to be involved in a racket like this! I can hardly believe…' Simon stopped abruptly as the waitress unloaded a pot of tea from her tray and placed a large mug of frothy cappuccino, sprinkled with chocolate shavings, in front of him.

Once she'd sauntered back towards the counter Simon lowered his voice and continued speaking. 'Did you have any idea what he was up to?' he asked.

Freya shook her head. 'Not until I saw Jack Hunter's painting of Emily Meadowcroft in his bedroom, and even then, it took some time to cotton on.'

'His *bed*room?' echoed Simon as if the word had two syllables.

Freya began to laugh. 'I didn't go there on purpose,' she protested. 'I was looking for a bathroom and ended up using his *en suite*. A few days after the salon a friend showed me an image of a stolen painting on an art-tracing website, and I realised it was probably the same one.'

'That was smart,' said Simon approvingly.

Freya felt herself blushing. 'Not really,' she said, flexing her shoulders. 'I should have figured out that he was up to no good when I first met him.'

'Which was where?' asked Simon, taking a gulp of coffee.

'I bumped into him – literally, because it was so dark – in a gallery at the V&A.' Freya paused, gazing at an endearing smudge of chocolate left on Simon's chin. She felt reluctant to admit she had deliberately arranged to meet Ralph there. It would make her appear so naïve.

'Anyway, we got chatting and he invited me to one of his Victorian salons which was where I met you.' Pouring tea into her cup, she added, 'And how did you get to know him?'

'Through Mark – we're old comrades-in-arms,' replied Simon. 'You'll know him from the salons as Lawrence Meadowcroft. We were in the same year at drama college. We've both done a fair amount of rep since then and now we're in rehearsals for a revival of Noel Coward's *Hay Fever* at the Garrick.'

'Who introduced Mark to Ralph?' asked Freya, intent on pinning him down.

'Our agent,' Simon jerked his head in the direction of Margaret Street. 'The office is just round the corner. Mark told me he'd met this charismatic, larger-than-life character in the agency one day and seemed very impressed by him.'

'Did Ralph book you both to come and – act – at his salons?' asked Freya, sounding incredulous.

Simon's face relaxed into an amused grin. 'There were no lines to learn as such, but it wasn't all off-the-cuff stuff,' he replied. 'He briefed us over the phone first and was pretty specific about what he wanted.'

Freya narrowed her eyes. 'What did he ask you to do?' She wasn't sure if she really wanted to hear the answer.

'Well, he sketched out the background story about Jack, Lawrence and Emily so we had a framework from which we could improvise. And he told us what to wear and how we should behave. But he also encouraged us to ad-lib creatively when we were at the salons. He said the whole idea was to entertain his guests by re-enacting a slice of living history and help to recreate a genuinely Victorian atmosphere.' Simon chuckled. 'Frankly, we just thought it was an easy gig – virtually no lines to learn, fantastic food and drink and a big, fat fee.'

'But weren't you a bit suspicious when he asked you to follow such a very specific storyline about the Meadowcrofts?' asked Freya. 'Didn't that make you question his intentions?'

Simon shrugged. 'Not really. You get used to weird and wonderful requests in the theatre. And Ralph didn't exactly welcome interrogation. He was the one paying our fees and it was very much a master-servant relationship as far as he was concerned.'

He frowned momentarily then changed the direction of conversation, as if veering away from an unpleasant memory. 'Anyway, tell me how you became acquainted with our dear friend Emily Meadowcroft,' he said lightly.

Smiling at the way he put it, Freya answered in the same jokey vein. 'The initial introduction took place when I opened my late mother's jewellery box and found a miniature painting inside. At the time I didn't know it was a portrait of Emily and only found that out after I'd done some research.' She halted, recalling the tingle of excitement she'd felt at her discovery in the Royal Academy archives.

'Is she related to you?' asked Simon.

'Emily's daughter, Grace—' Freya broke off, blushing, then pushed herself to continue, —the child conceived with Jack Hunter was brought up by my great-great grandmother as one of her own children.'

'Jeez!' Simon looked startled. 'You're turning the script into a real-life docu-drama.'

Freya looked down at her half-drunk cup of tea, feeling loathe to reveal the full story in case he mocked her for taking it all so seriously.

'There's more, isn't there?' prodded Simon, watching her face.

Freya nodded but remained silent, gazing unseeingly into the distance beyond his shoulder.

'Well, let's leave it for another day if you don't feel like talking about it right now,' said Simon. 'But tell me, what happened to Jack Hunter in the end?'

Freya looked surprised. 'Ralph didn't say?' she asked, sounding disconcerted.

Simon shook his head and started laughing. 'I fear he came to no good.'

His laughter felt jarring to Freya and the muscles in her face tensed. 'You're right,' she said tersely. 'He died penniless a few years after Emily committed suicide in his studio.'

The smile instantly disappeared from Simon's face. 'Ralph didn't mention any of that to me,' he said. 'I'm sorry – these people were just characters in some goddamn play for me, but they clearly mean more to you than that.'

An awkward silence ensued. Freya watched a couple from another table pay their bill at the counter and walk past their table to the exit.

Simon fidgeted with the cuff-button on his denim shirt. 'I've forgotten how Jack met Emily all those years ago,' he said, half-heartedly attempting to re-ignite the conversation.

'At a party when Emily was staying with her brother in London,' replied Freya in a lukewarm voice. 'No doubt Ralph told you that Jack was Lawrence's best friend when they were students at the National Art Training School in Kensington.'

'A bit like me and Mark,' suggested Simon in a brighter tone. 'Well, Ralph got the best mates bit right when he booked us for the job.' He paused, eyeing Freya thoughtfully. 'What about the chemistry between Jack and Emily? Did he get that right too?'

Freya met his gaze directly and smiled. 'I thought so at the time,' she said.

Simon smiled back at her. 'Did you enjoy being Emily for the night?' he asked in a playful manner.

Freya nodded. 'And you? Did you enjoy playing the role of Jack Hunter?'

Simon's clear green eyes crinkled at the corners. 'What do you think?' he teased.

Freya swallowed, unsure for a moment how best to reply. She looked at Simon's attractive face and decided to chance it. 'I think you felt very comfortable in Jack Hunter's skin,' she said.

Simon laughed. 'I certainly wasn't acting when we were in the garden, if that's what you mean,' he said with a grin. 'I knew from Ralph's brief that Jack fancied Emily, but the fact is I really did like you, and when we started kissing, I found I didn't want to stop. I'm sorry if things got a bit out of hand.' Then he looked at Freya more soberly. 'It was rather an odd way for us to meet though.'

'You mean both of us pretending to be someone else?' asked Freya, smiling. 'It was a novelty for me, but I guess it's just par for the course for you.'

'Yes, I do a lot of that in my line of business,' said Simon.

'And you find that – satisfactory?' asked Freya, enjoying their banter again.

'Hmm, it has its merits,' replied Simon. 'Like helping me pay the rent.'

'Well, that's fine so long as you don't forget who you really are,' said Freya. She was on the point of teasing him further when Simon's smile vanished and his face took on a serious expression.

'I also find it helps me avoid dwelling on the more painful things in my own life,' he said quietly.

Freya swallowed what she was about to say and reflected that the failure to deal with her own grief and disenchantment allowed her to get swept up in Ralph's fantasy world so perilously. Instead of coming to terms with adversity she'd willingly shed her own skin to become someone else. How foolish she thought, as she sat silent and tense, waiting for him to continue. Taking a tiny sip of tea, she found it was stone cold.

Simon cleared his throat. 'I went through a very unpleasant divorce last year,' he said in a flat voice.

'Oh goodness, I'm so sorry,' said Freya, feeling disconcerted and unsettled.

Simon grimaced. 'Yeah, it was all pretty raw. Not an experience I'd recommend.'

Freya's heart sank. Two minutes ago, everything had seemed so encouraging. Now that sunny moment was slipping away. If she reached out just far enough, perhaps she could grab it before it drifted from her grasp but surely the ghost of an ex-wife was always going to be there no matter what she said or did?

Out of nowhere an image of Emily floated into her mind so vividly it made her flinch. It wasn't a recollection of Jack Hunter's painting on Ralph's bedroom wall. Nor the miniature portrait in her pendant. It was Emily herself, alive and laughing with a school-friend as they battled in a breeze to set up artists' easels in the garden of the Meadowcroft house. Powerful and joyous, it sent a visceral surge of blood ringing though Freya's body.

'But you survived,' she said, feeling her composure return. 'Had you been married long?'

'Only two years,' said Simon. 'One year good, one year bad. It was the usual story – tragic yet horribly banal. She met someone through work and six months later walked out of our flat and moved into his place.'

'That must have been such a shock,' said Freya.

Simon gave a weak smile. 'It was at the time. I spent ages feeling sorry for myself until I realised I wasn't the only person in the world going through this kind of thing. It's fairly common among the acting fraternity, you know.'

'Is she an actor too?' asked Freya, hating the compulsion that drove her to probe further.

'Yes – and ten times more successful than me. She's over in Hollywood right now doing screen tests. Lauren Kyle. You may have seen her in that BBC crime drama, *Sidestream*.'

Freya shook her head. 'No, I don't really watch much television.'

'Or the Netflix thriller, *Light on the Water*?'

'Missed that one too.' Freya glanced out of the window as a ray of evening sunshine struck the paving stones, turning them pale gold. Despite Simon's candour, she could feel her curiosity evaporating. Right now, she just didn't want to hear anything more about his ex-wife or her successful career.

'Well, I'll come and see you and Mark in *Hay Fever* when it opens,' she said, deliberately creating an opportunity to meet again. 'I haven't been to the theatre for ages.'

'Good, that's one more ticket sold,' said Simon. 'Just several hundred more to go.'

They both fell silent for a moment then Freya coughed and made a show of looking at her watch. 'Goodness, is that the time? I'd better be off.'

She hesitated, making no attempt to move from her seat, hoping Simon would say something but he just gave her a rueful smile.

'I'll get this,' she said, getting up and walking over to the counter to pay the bill.

When she returned to their table, she saw a stack of small coins sitting on a paper napkin beside her teacup.

'I'm not a starving artist like Jack – or even a starving actor, surprising as it may seem,' said Simon.

'Oh, thanks,' said Freya, scooping up the coins and depositing them in her purse. Standing there, looking down at him she noticed how thin his shoulders seemed beneath his denim shirt and felt a rush of tenderness towards him. It was hard to tear herself away.

'Well, goodbye for now,' she said brightly. 'I hope our paths cross again soon.'

'Take that with you – it might come in handy,' said Simon, nodding towards her empty teacup.

Surprised by his remark, Freya glanced at the paper napkin beside her cup and realised he'd scrawled a phone number on it in ballpoint pen while she had her back turned, paying the bill. She picked it up, shoved it into the back pocket of her jeans and left the café with a smile on her face.

She was still smiling when she pulled it out her pocket on the way home and zipped it safely into her bag. They had a chance, didn't they?

CHAPTER 23

Slipping into a seat at a quiet corner table, Freya sat back and admired the imaginative decoration of the V&A's Morris Room.

Elizabethan-style wall-panelling in a dark, forest green created a womb-like cosiness. Stained glass windows featuring images of medieval women added an ecclesiastical touch. Leaning back against the wall behind her, she tilted her head to admire the geometric patterns and golden arabesques dancing across the frost-white ceiling then dropped her gaze to a colourful frieze of hounds energetically chasing hares around the walls.

Enjoying the rich, medieval ambience the room's designer had clearly sought to conjure, Freya emptied her mind of any concerns about meeting the jewellery gallery's curator and let the surroundings waft her to a different era. Fingering the portrait miniature hanging around her neck, she succumbed to a dreamy reverie, half absorbed in the present and half in the past.

It wasn't long before a slender figure with a short bob of

golden hair arrived. Smartly dressed in a red jacket, white shirt and black trousers, she didn't seem to Freya like a conventional museum employee. Her simple yet glamorous jet necklace hinted, however, at the nature of the department she curated.

'Hello, I'm Alex Nielsen,' she said, shaking hands with Freya across the table. 'I'm so glad you wanted to meet here – it's one of my favourite places in the museum.'

'It's the first time I've been in this restaurant,' said Freya. 'For some reason I thought it was reserved for private functions, but now I see anyone can eat in here.'

'You know the history behind this room, don't you?' asked Alex, pulling out a chair and sitting opposite Freya. 'Our founder, Henry Cole, had the bright idea of offering visitors some refreshments. So, we were the first museum in the world to have a public restaurant. It became so popular he added two more and they're all still going strong today.'

'When did this one open?' asked Freya, trying to picture the room filling with women wearing bonnets, shawls and long dresses in Victorian days.

'About 1868,' replied Alex. 'It was originally called the Green Dining Room and was William Morris's first public commission. He was only 31 at the time and his firm wasn't very well-known so he wanted to make a splash with the decoration.'

'He succeeded in that respect,' remarked Freya, smiling up at the frieze of animated animals.

'Yes, it was a bold move to give this room a medieval flavour since most of the museum's architecture is classical in style,' said Alex. 'Being Morris, of course he called in his mates to help him. Isn't the plasterwork splendid? Philip Webb designed that. And Edward Burne-Jones designed the figures for the stained-glass windows and painted the wall-panels.'

'It's amazing how brightly the gold paint still shines,' said Freya, gently fingering a painted scene on the wall-panel next to their table. 'It turns these cameos into little icons. The Victorians must have loved it.'

'Come back on a Friday afternoon and we'll even serve you a high Victorian afternoon tea in here,' said Alex with a chuckle. 'Mrs Beeton's cucumber sandwiches, Indian ham sandwiches, fruit scones – the lot. I'm afraid I can't offer you that today, but would you like a cup of tea or coffee?'

'Oh, tea please,' replied Freya distractedly as she glanced back to the hares and hounds leaping around the room below a plaster relief of olive boughs. Refreshment of any kind was the least of her priorities right now. It was one thing lingering over a cup of tea with Simon as it had enjoyably prolonged their encounter, but this was different. Too much was at stake. Still, she had no wish to seem impolite.

Alex waved at a young waitress hovering at the restaurant's entrance who came over to take her order. When she began speaking again her face looked more serious. 'Now I understand from your email that you've got some important information for me,' she said, sounding coolly professional.

Freya hesitated, unsure how her news would be received. 'Yes, that's right,' she said with a nervous smile. 'It concerns three pieces of jewellery on display in your gallery. The information labels say they were made for one of Morris & Co.'s private clients and credit Lawrence Meadowcroft as the designer.' She paused to clear her throat. 'That's not correct though. I believe they were created by his sister, Emily Meadowcroft.'

Alex frowned. 'What makes you think that?' she asked sharply.

'I've discovered that Lawrence – er – couldn't complete the commission so he asked his sister to design and make the jewellery on his behalf,' replied Freya, choosing her words carefully.

Alex gave a slight shrug. 'We've got a number of Morris & Co. daybooks in our archives,' she said. 'It's likely one of them would list the designer who was commissioned to make the pieces. We can double-check.'

'That's the problem,' said Freya, twisting her hands together below the table. 'If the name of the designer is listed it will be Lawrence Meadowcroft.'

'Why do you think that might not be correct?' asked Alex, sounding perplexed. 'After all, it's primary source material and if Emily Meadowcroft had received the commission, then she would be listed as the designer, not Lawrence.'

At that moment the waitress arrived with a tray and unloaded two large cups, a milk jug and china teapot. Alex poured tea into both cups and pushed the milk jug across the table. Watching her do this, Freya wondered how much of Emily's back-story to reveal. Mentioning her suicide to a professional museum curator – someone she had only just met – felt like a personal betrayal.

'I've been speaking to one of Emily's descendants,' said Freya cautiously, pouring some milk into her cup of tea. She felt on safe ground with that remark. Revealing how she had learned about Lawrence's blackmailing activities was a more delicate issue. She cleared her throat again. 'I understand that Lawrence cajoled Emily into making the pieces for him in return for his silence about – another matter.'

Alex's clear blue eyes widened. 'A devil's pact?' she asked with a grin.

Freya nodded but remained silent, fiddling with her silver earring and running a finger along the scalloped edge of its long, slender scroll. It was important, she felt, for Alex to hear how Emily came to design the jewellery before showing her the sketches, otherwise she might not believe they were genuine.

'I'm intrigued,' said Alex, still smiling. 'May I ask the nature of this other matter?'

'Lawrence was studying at the National Art Training School and Emily helped one of his friends by secretly carrying out the work for his diploma show,' replied Freya. 'She wanted to keep that quiet, for obvious reasons.'

'Studying here?' Alex started laughing. 'How extraordinary. You know the school was based on this site originally? Later, of course, it became the Royal College of Art and moved up the road.'

'Emily also designed a set of ceramic tiles for one of the restaurants here, according to her relative,' said Freya, glancing around the room and failing to spot any tiles among the green wall-panelling.

'Really?' Alex raised her eyebrows. 'Some of the tiles in the Poynter room were certainly painted by female students attending a special porcelain class for women at the school. Was she studying here at the same time as her brother?'

'No,' said Freya, feeling disappointed on Emily's behalf. 'I don't think her parents allowed her to attend the school, although she should have done as she was certainly very talented.'

She was just about to pull the sketchbook out of her rucksack when she remembered something else. Unclasping the chain at the nape of her neck, Freya placed the portrait miniature on the table facing Alex. 'I put this on today to show you what she looked like,' she said, watching the curator's face closely.

Surprise, admiration and pleasure registered in quick succession. 'Oh, she's sensational,' said Alex. 'What the Victorian artists would have called a "stunner". Really striking –

with a fiery temperament to match, no doubt.' Her eyes flashed up to meet Freya's. 'Where did you acquire this?'

'I found it in my late mother's belongings and after doing some – er – research I discovered Emily gave it to my mother's great-grandmother,' replied Freya. 'Then, when I was talking to Emily's relative, I learned she'd inherited a painting in which she looks very similar.'

'And may I ask the name of this relative?' asked Alex.

'I'd rather not say,' replied Freya. 'She's very old and I wouldn't want to upset her.'

Alex's smile faded. 'Well, we would need some hard evidence if we're going to consider re-attribution,' she said. 'We couldn't change the credit for those three pieces of jewellery in the gallery just because of hearsay – even if the story does come from a member of her family.'

'I do have proof,' said Freya doggedly, bending down and pulling the sketchbook out of her rucksack. Laying it on the table facing Alex, she leafed through the drawings until she reached the sketches of jewellery. 'This is Emily Meadowcroft's sketchbook – look, here's her name on the fly-leaf and the date,' she said, briefly flicking back to the front of the book. 'Now do you see how closely her jewellery designs match the pieces in your gallery?'

'My goodness, you're right,' said Alex, sounding startled. 'They look almost identical. How amazing! You know that's pretty unusual for a finished design to alter so little from an initial sketch.'

Freya smiled. 'I do know,' she said in a level tone. 'I'm a jewellery designer myself.'

Alex's face brightened, her eyes alert and interested. 'Ah, I did wonder about your lovely earrings. I've been admiring them. They're very stylish.'

'I made them some time ago,' said Freya. Then she

remained silent, sipping her tea, as Alex dropped her gaze to the sketchbook and slowly turned the pages back and forth, pausing to look more closely at some of the earlier drawings before inspecting the jewellery sketches again.

'I see she dated all her drawings quite meticulously,' said the curator, still leafing through the book. 'And do you see this?' She pointed to the initials below the sketches of jewellery.

'Yes, I think it's significant that she only initialled those sketches and none of the other drawings,' said Freya. 'It's as if she was distinguishing between professional work and personal practice.'

'No, that wasn't what I meant,' said Alex. 'See here – these five absolutely miniscule letters above her initials.' Taking a jeweller's loop from her jacket pocket, she peered closely at the page. 'I thought so,' she said quietly. 'Fecit – the Latin word for "he or she made it". Artists used to put that next to their signature to identify the creator.' She put the loop down on the table and looked directly at Freya. 'Well, I would say that's cast-iron evidence in her favour.'

'May I?' Freya picked up the loop and studied the combination of letters and initials. Alex was right. Emily had provided her own corroboration. She put the loop down on the table. 'What will happen now?' she asked, wiping clammy hands on the knees of her trousers.

'If the misattribution was particularly controversial I would refer it to the museum's director,' replied Alex. 'He would consult external authorities and then decide what to do. A case like this is so cut-and-dried, however, that I can take the decision myself.'

She looked across the table, beaming. 'I'm so glad you drew this to my attention, Freya. We must, of course, credit Emily

Meadowcroft for her designs. It would be a dereliction of duty to do otherwise.'

Freya leant back in her chair, feeling as if a stone had been lifted from her chest. She took a deep breath and gazed around the Morris Room where tables were filling up with visitors enjoying a coffee or having an early lunch. A buzz of chatter in several languages filled the air. The place felt vibrant, alive, despite its medieval trappings.

'That's wonderful,' she said jubilantly. 'I can't thank you enough.'

Alex smiled. 'We may be more than a hundred years late, but we do get there in the end,' she said. Then she narrowed her eyes, frowning slightly. 'I don't suppose it would be possible to retain the sketchbook for our archives, would it? Of course, it would need to be a donation. In these financially strapped times we don't really have the budget to acquire it.'

'I'd have to ask,' said Freya. 'This – relative – of Emily's was a bit reluctant to let the sketchbook out of her sight, but if she knew it would be kept here safely and looked after for posterity then I'm sure she would agree.'

'Then do please ask her and let me know the response,' said Alex warmly. 'You'd be doing me a great favour if you could secure it for us.' She paused, looking reflectively at Freya's earrings. 'And perhaps I can do something for you in return. I know our retail merchandise manager is looking for a jeweller to make good copies of some of the pieces in our collection to sell in the museum shop. If that might be of interest – and depending on your style of work, of course – I could put you in touch with her to see if there's any common ground.'

Freya's jaw dropped. 'I've already made one of the pieces,' she replied, barely able to keep the astonishment out of her voice. 'Emily's heart-shaped brooch – although I tried to give it a more contemporary flavour. I could certainly show that to your retail manager and see if there's any potential in collaborating on a project together.'

'Perfect,' said Alex, glancing at her watch. 'I'm sure she'd love to see it. Now if you'll excuse me, I need to go to another meeting.'

She stood up, hovering for a moment, looking thoughtfully at the portrait miniature lying next to the sketchbook on the table.

'I do think jewellery has a remarkable gift for revealing personal narratives and passions,' she said reflectively. Then she smiled at Freya with a gleam of amusement in her eyes and added breezily, 'I wonder what Emily Meadowcroft would have made of it all.'

'I wonder,' repeated Freya softly as the word *vindicated* came to mind.

BEFORE YOU GO

I hope you enjoyed reading *The Portrait Girl* as much as I enjoyed writing it. As you suspected, it takes weeks, months or years to write a book. It exists today through dedication, passion and love. Reviews help persuade readers to give this book a shot. You are helping the community discover and support new writing. It will take *less than a minute* and can be *just a line* to say what you liked or didn't. Please leave me a review wherever you bought this book from. A big thank you.

Nicole Swengley

AUTHOR'S NOTE

Annie Dixon (1817-1901) was a well-regarded portrait miniaturist. The tiny watercolour portrait of her by Louisa Anne Beresford, Marchioness of Waterford, is in the National Portrait Gallery's archive but not on public display.

The miniatures and watercolours exhibited by Annie Dixon at the Royal Academy's summer exhibition each year from 1882 to 1893 are listed in the Royal Academy's archival catalogues. The RA's Research Library and Archive is open to the public by appointment. Her portrait miniatures of Emily and Lawrence Meadowcroft are works of my imagination.

May Morris's jewellery is on display in The William & Judith Bollinger gallery at the V&A museum, Cromwell Road, London SW7.

I have taken the liberty of adding a small painting of *Guinevere* to Dante Gabriel Rossetti's canon of work and *Love's Messenger*, an oil painting, to Lawrence Alma-Tadema's œuvre. Both works are imaginary.

The parliamentary constituency of Yorkshire South Riding is also imaginary.

ABOUT THE AUTHOR

Nicole Swengley is a freelance journalist who has written about design-related topics for the *Financial Times*, the *Telegraph, The Times, Wall Street Journal* and *London Evening Standard* amongst many other publications. Her short stories have been featured in women's magazines, a crime anthology (Pavilion) and *Order & Chaos*, a themed anthology (Breakthrough Books). One of her stories was shortlisted in a national TV/magazine competition. She has also written a travel guide, *Welcome to Britain* (Collins) and compiled a collection of humorous celebrity sailing anecdotes, *Rogue Waves* (Adlard Coles). *The Portrait Girl* is her first novel.

ACKNOWLEDGMENTS

Writing a novel can be a long and winding road with inevitable bumps along the way. It is, however, made sweeter by supportive cheerleaders and I would like to thank the following for their advice and encouragement: Rowan Coleman (my tutor on a Faber Academy fiction course), Anne Perry, Celia Hayley, authors Nicola Doherty, N.J. Barker, Helen Chislett, Stephanie Bretherton and Patrick Kincaid, Cornerstones literary consultancy and everyone at Breakthrough Books. Huge thanks also to Ivy Ngeow for her wonderful cover design.

Thanks also to Vicky Broackes, former senior curator, Theatre & Performance at the V&A museum, portrait miniature specialist Claudia Hill and jeweller Kiki McDonough. Any errors about creating jewellery – or indeed anything else - are entirely my own.

I am indebted to the authors of the following books: *May Morris Arts & Crafts Designer* by Anna Mason, Jan Marsh, Jenny Lister, Rowan Bain and Hanne Faurby (Thames & Hudson in association with the V&A museum). *Those Wild Wyndhams* by Claudia Renton (William Collins). *Edward Burne-Jones: A Life* by Penelope Fitzgerald (Fourth Estate). *A Circle of Sisters* by Judith Flanders (Penguin Books).

I would also like to acknowledge the following contemporary designers whose work inspired some of the designs fictionalised here: Fredrikson Stallard, Gosling, Dominic

Harris, Simon Heijdens, Mischer'Traxler, Random International, the late Patrick Reyntiens, Moritz Waldemeyer, Zelouf & Bell.

Milton Keynes UK
Ingram Content Group UK Ltd.
UKHW042040041024
449101UK00004B/240

9 781739 379384